WOLF'S PROVIDENCE

EVE L. MITCHELL

WOLF'S PROVIDENCE

Book Description

Willow Harper's world has been shattered.

The man she trusted—the shifter bound to her by fate—has done the unthinkable. Caleb Foster's demons pushed him to the edge, and Willow paid the price.

Now Caleb has disappeared again, lost in guilt and shame. Haunted by the damage he's caused, he's left her alone. But Willow knows his absence won't stop the enemies who've been hunting her from the shadows, their motives still a mystery.

As dark forces close in, Willow faces an impossible choice—save herself or risk everything for the man whose past threatens to consume him.

With her heart and her life hanging in the balance, she must confront a harsh truth that some wounds may never heal and some bonds may never be broken.

In a world where trust is fragile and danger is everywhere, can Willow and Caleb survive the storm ahead...and will Caleb ever forgive himself for what he's done?

Prologue

My eyes opened.

The lights were so bright.

Why did the lights have to be so bright?

I needed to turn them down. Trying to sit up caused an intense pain to shoot through me. Looking down, I saw the thick white bandages wrapped around me.

"What the hell…"

The door opening caused me to look up. "Lily?"

My best friend burst into tears when she saw me. "Oh my God, Willow!" As she rushed to my bedside, I didn't have time to brace myself as she launched herself at me.

"Ow!"

"I'm sorry, I'm sorry!"

The door opened again and both of us looked up at the same time, bumping heads, causing both of us to curse.

Shaking my head to clear it, I looked at Doc.

And I remembered everything.

"Where is he?"

ONE

Willow

The room was quiet. Too quiet. It was the kind of silence that settled so deep into your bones you were sure that something bad was going to happen. That something had gone terribly, terribly wrong.

Hadn't it?

Lying, staring at the ceiling, I felt the weight of emotion threaten to overwhelm me once more. If it wasn't bad enough that my entire body ached, that the slow throbbing pain in my abdomen was in rhythm with the sluggish thudding of my heart, there was something else too. Something warm, humming under my skin, vibrating in my veins softly.

Irritating me.

I wanted to scratch my body, and I envisioned grizzlies rubbing up against a tree to satisfy that itch, but I didn't have the luxury of tree rubbing. I had chicken pox when I was six, and the itch was similar. This itch felt "off." I wasn't entirely sure it felt natural.

Trying to move made the bed creak beneath me. The bed was soft, not as comfy as mine at home, but I couldn't complain. The bunker walls were a pale yellow, and the window across from me let in sharp, clean air with the faint scent of pine and earth—so typically a smell I would always associate with packlands.

But not Caleb's.

My heart skipped a beat at the thought of him, but I shoved it down.

I wasn't ready for that.

Not yet.

Caleb would have to wait until I was allowed out of this bed, had left this room, and got off this mountain.

I didn't want to wait, though.

I wanted answers. My groan of frustration was low, but it was loaded with pent-up emotion. All I had wanted since I met that freaking man was answers. Another few days wouldn't hurt.

Slowly, I tried to push myself up into a sitting position. The wounds in my abdomen protested loudly, and the rest of my body echoed its agreement as my yelp of pain echoed in the empty room. Wincing when I heard the sound of feet approaching, I braced myself for the reprimand.

"Willow!" Lily entered the room, her face already frowning as her eyes met mine. "I told you to call for me if you needed help!"

"I should be able to sit up," I grumbled as she hooked her arms under mine and heaved. I tried not to take it personally that she sounded like she was trying to shift an elephant and barely moved me an inch.

"You can't sit up by yourself because of your accident, you *know* this."

Because even though she was here, on Blackridge Peak, she

was still absolutely clueless about shifters. So, instead of telling her that my friend-slash-lover-slash-headache, Caleb, had gouged four big holes in my stomach, she thought I had been in a car accident. Because she never knew about the *first* car accident, Doc thought it made sense to cover the lie with the truth.

Or something.

Either way, she was here, for which I was eternally grateful. She was just in the dark about some of the finer things of the town of Blackridge. She had whispered more than once that they were some weird cult, and I hadn't had a counterargument. So, while I was sure Lily was convinced the residents of Blackridge Peak were waiting for the spaceship to come and ascend them to a higher plane, I was just happy she was here.

I still remembered the look on her face when I woke up. I had never seen Lily scared before, not really, but I wouldn't ever forget the look she wore.

"You know you're supposed to be taking it easy," she scolded, her eyes wide with concern, her frown deepening. "And you haven't had enough sleep."

"I'm bedridden," I reminded her. "I literally cannot take it any easier."

"Don't be cranky."

"How long was I asleep this time?"

"Not long enough," Lily grumbled. She must have seen the look on my face, because her frown softened as she took hold of my hand. "You were hurt really badly, remember. You're so lucky you'll be okay." Lily took in the "private hospital" I was in. "Such a weird place to have a hospital," she murmured more to herself than me.

I was fuzzy on the details, but I *think* they had told her it was a local hospital for the town, and it was the nearest one to my "accident." Lily was fully expecting me to be transferred to a bigger hospital. I didn't know who was going to tell her that *that* wasn't happening, but I knew it wouldn't be me.

"I saw the doctor on my way in," she told me with a smile. "He's so refreshing."

"He is?"

"Most doctors are kind of superior, and I get it, they can be —they literally hold your life in their hands—but your doctor is so down to earth. It's so nice."

I needed to get Lily off this mountain. I knew it the day I woke up. I knew it every day she said something like this.

"Yeah, Doc's the best," I mumbled weakly.

"Glad to hear the cheerleading there, Willow," Doc said as he entered the room. His warm smile made Lily flush, while I scowled at him. "You're sleeping less," he told me matter-of-factly as he approached.

"Even I can't sleep forever," I grumbled. "Can you sit me up?"

Doc nodded, and with more care and strength than Lily, he lifted me further up the bed into a semi-sitting position. "I need to check them," he told me quietly. Turning to Lily, he gave her his charismatic smile once more. "Do you mind stepping out while I check Willow?"

Lily nodded, and we waited until the door was closed behind her.

"You don't worry she'll go wandering?" I asked for what felt like the millionth time.

"Nope, all the doors are closed, except hers, and she hasn't tried to go outside yet." He grinned at me. "Having a faithful friend who wants to be so near to you shouldn't have you glaring at me like that."

"The whole backstory is insane," I hissed at him. "You should have told her the truth."

"Not my call." Doc pulled my cover off me. "You ready for your inspection?"

The death glare I gave him only made him grin wider. While he unwrapped my bandages, and I pretended my abdomen didn't hurt like a bitch, I tried not to think of the night that put me here.

It was so hard to escape it, though. After I woke up the first time, it had come hurtling into my memory like floodwaters from a burst river. Every time I saw the horror on Caleb's face as he realized what he'd done, it felt like a punch to the gut, knocking the air from my lungs each and every time. I remembered my blood spilling over his hands, so much blood, and his feeble attempts to stop it from pouring out of me as he whispered his pleas for me not to die.

"I thought I was going to die," I whispered, more to myself than to Doc.

Doc looked up at me, nodding once, before he averted his gaze, his attention back on my wounds. "I thought you were, too."

Studying him, I took in his calm and steady presence. He was in his late thirties, and I appreciated the no-nonsense look in his eyes when he spoke. The fact that he was part shifter, who only had some of the benefits, must suck for him. Not human. Not a shifter. I wondered if he was a hybrid? Would that be a thing? Was it rude to ask? He had some speeded-up healing, slower to show signs of his age, but not like shifters who were his age but looked ten to fifteen years younger, but otherwise, he was pretty much like me.

Human.

"How are you going to transfer me to another hospital?" I asked him seriously. "She'll never understand if I stay here."

Doc was studying my wounds, only half listening. I kept my head averted. The first time I looked, I almost threw up, so I learned to stare at the window, which was too high for me to see much, and hope that the examination was quick.

"How are you feeling?"

"It hurts."

"Still?" His look was assessing.

"*Yes*, still," I snapped at him. "I had four claws sticking into me like I was meat on a kebab." Scratching my arm, I avoided looking at him. "And this itchy skin is making me insane! Are you sure I can't get an antihistamine or something?"

Doc was frowning at me as he watched me scratch. "I need to talk to Cannon." He didn't blink as he spoke. "I also need for Lily to leave this mountain. Suggestions?"

"You *just* said I was lucky to have her here."

"You are." His smile was tight. "But now I need her to leave."

Narrowing my eyes, I watched him suspiciously. "Why?"

"I need to speak to my alpha." Doc stepped back. I hadn't noticed him re-covering my wounds. "Try to rest, I won't be long. Oh, and think of a reason for her to leave, yeah?"

I had a very good reason for Lily to leave. It was one word, which started with *shift* and ended with *er*. But I couldn't tell her. *They* definitely weren't going to tell her, so instead, I had to lie.

And I was a shit liar.

Doc changing his mind about Lily being here was odd. He'd been pleased she was here, and now he sounded as if he wanted her off Blackridge Peak as soon as possible. I was more amazed she'd stayed in the bunker. Lily was adventurous and bold. It was so out of character for her to remain in the place where she was told.

Or maybe...she was faking it as much as I was? Maybe she knew there was something *more* here and was staying close because I was someone she trusted. I mean, the whole bunker hospital was insane. If that was the case, then getting Lily to go home may be easier than they thought.

While I loved that she was here when I woke up, the fact that she was *here* was also terrifying. My absence had been too long for Lily's liking, especially not hearing from me, so in true Nancy Drew style, she'd decided to track me down.

There was no cell service on Shadowridge Peak, but there was on Blackridge Peak, and when I'd been taken here, they'd taken my backpack. My cell was on, and that meant I was traceable.

Cannon had switched it off as soon as they found out a woman and a ranger were heading up their mountain.

Thankfully, I was still out cold when that encounter took place. I didn't think Doc was popular with his alpha for bringing that kind of attention to them. But, as Doc said, it was either that or I died.

I was hopeful that Cannon was team "keep Willow alive."

Weariness settled on me like a blanket. I might've been sleeping less, but I was still exhausted. I was just drifting off to sleep when the door creaked open.

Opening my eyes, I saw Cannon and Doc come in. Cannon's face was unreadable as always. Doc's smile was weaker.

Oh boy, here we go.

"Hi." Cannon was really nice, but he was so intimidating

sometimes that it made me wish for Caleb. Because while Caleb was a contrary son-of-a-swear word, he was still *Caleb*. I could read him, I *knew* him. Cannon was just...big. And intimidating.

Doc exchanged a glance with Cannon before they both focused on me. The look on their faces didn't change, and I just knew I was going to hate whatever they said next.

"How are you feeling?" Cannon asked, lifting the seat Lily used, turning it, and sitting on it back to front. His huge forearms rested on the back of the seat as he watched me.

"Sore," I answered him quickly. "Which I know is to be expected. My head hurts," I added, seeing Doc note it down. "I'm tired, but I know my body is trying to heal."

"Doc says you're itchy."

"I am, everywhere, it's really irritating."

I had managed to push it down to an irksome throb, but with him mentioning it, I felt it flare up again.

Doc moved forward. "Willow," he started, sitting down on the edge of the bed, "there's something we need to talk about."

"Tell her I'm infectious," I burst out. "I know, you need Lily gone, I get it. Thank you for letting her stay," I said with a look at Cannon. "Tell her I caught something and need to be, I dunno, quarantined. Encourage her to go back home. Then we can move me to another hospital, an *actual* hospital, and it'll be fine."

Doc sighed, rubbing his hand over his jaw. "The infection thing may work," he said to Cannon before his attention slipped back to me. "The transfer to another hospital won't though."

"Why?" I asked warily, looking between the two of them suspiciously. "What's happened now?"

Cannon cleared his throat. "You were dying. Caleb wounded you badly," he hesitated. "Fatally."

Letting out a little huff of displeasure, I looked at the too-high window and the white covering of cloud beyond. "Obviously not fatally," I mumbled grumpily. "I'm still here."

"Exactly." Cannon's snappy answer held too much coldness to his tone, causing me to turn my attention back to him. "You were dying," he said again. "And Caleb...well, Caleb made a choice."

My heart rate picked up, and I felt my hands turn clammy. "What kind of choice?"

"He gave you his blood," Doc spoke quietly, his eyes holding mine.

That made no sense. How was that possible? I'd been in that cabin for days; there was no blood transfusion equipment in it.

"His blood?" I asked them cautiously. "How? There were no needles or tubes or anything there."

Doc nodded slowly. "I know, but he forced his blood into your system."

"Forced it? How?"

"You were dying," Cannon spoke gruffly. "He bit his wrist." He looked to Doc, who nodded in confirmation. "And..." Cannon sat back. He looked as perplexed as I felt. "I don't know what the fuck he was thinking."

"Excuse me?"

Doc leaned forward. "I got there. I had turned back because I had a bad feeling about leaving you both on that mountain. I'm not a full shifter, as you know, so it took me longer than it would someone like Cannon or one of the others, but I wanted to try to talk to you, convince you to leave." Rubbing his forehead, he looked at me, and I saw how weary he was. "But I was too late. Caleb had already hurt you—"

"It was an accident." They both gave me the same look they'd given me the first time I said it. "It was an accident," I repeated firmly. "He didn't mean it. It wasn't him."

"We can argue about *that* another time," Cannon murmured.

"When I got there," Doc carried on as if neither of us had interrupted him, "his wrist was at your mouth. I told him to stop."

That made sense. I was human, he was not, he didn't have healing properties, and this wasn't make-believe. I held back my snort at my own musings. The fact that this *was* my reality, well...another day for that as well, I guessed.

"You told me shifters heal when they shift," I said quickly. "I'm human, I can't, so where is this going?"

"I know, and you're right," Doc spoke carefully. "And that's why this is so complicated. Shifter blood in a human's body—especially in the way Caleb was trying—it shouldn't work."

"Shouldn't?" I asked dubiously.

"But...I think it's what saved you," Doc added quietly.

TWO

Willow

MY HANDS WERE SHAKING AS I LIFTED THE COVER OFF my body, pushing it slowly down my body, revealing the thick white swathes of gauze that covered my wounds. "I saw my wounds," I told them both, my voice no more than a whisper. "It made me almost vomit." I looked up at Doc. "Remember?" When he nodded, I felt myself nod in response. Good, I hadn't imagined that. "So...what are you saying?"

Standing, he gently helped me peel back the layer, the look in his eye telling me to look at my stomach. Bracing myself, I looked down, expecting the worst. I looked up at them in shock from the sight of my almost healed skin.

"Doc!" Fear gripped me as I clutched his arm. "What the hell is happening? I'm still... Oh my God, am I still human?" Because there was no way on God's green earth that I should be looking at my life-threatening wounds of one week ago and now seeing they were almost healed completely. "Cannon?" I looked up at the alpha, who was also studying my wounds with a frown. "Did I become something else?"

"You're still human," he assured me with a quick smile.

Doc covered me gently. "Definitely still human," he confirmed. "Caleb's blood didn't change that. It's just... Well, it's just his blood did *something*, and I'm not quite sure what."

"He forced his blood into me, not knowing if it would heal me?" I asked as my mind reeled, struggling to process the enormity of what they were saying.

"An act of desperation," Cannon murmured, and I couldn't tell if he meant to say it out loud.

"He only wanted to save you," Doc confirmed with a sharp look at his alpha.

"Has this been done before?" I asked them both.

"Yes," Cannon spoke clearly. "And failed every time. We don't know why it would work on you when it's never worked before." He saw my look, and the corner of his mouth hooked up slyly. "You think our ancestors haven't experimented?" he asked me. "How do you think we know so much about ourselves? Only the Goddess gives us the magic to heal quicker and heal completely through the shift."

"Only two full-blooded shifters can make full shifters," Doc reminded me, and I heard the resigned bitterness in his voice.

"Is Caleb in danger?" They both looked confused by the question. "Is there some, I dunno, pack law that prohibits him from doing this?"

"There will be consequences," Cannon told me sagely. "But his actions and behavior were heading that way anyway."

"Where is he?" I'd really tried not to ask after the first time when I'd been met with such suffocating silence I hadn't asked again. "Do you have him? Is he here?"

"He's gone, Willow." Doc looked at me with sympathy. "He left after...after he thought you were dead."

I felt my eyes widen as I looked at him incredulously. "He thinks I'm *dead*?"

"He didn't stick around to find out," Cannon growled, his eyes flashing with anger.

"We need to find him!" I tried to sit up but flinched with pain. "Why am I so sore if I'm practically healed?" I demanded of Doc.

"Because your body is in conflict with itself," he told me, but I saw his hesitancy.

"You have no idea, do you?"

Doc shook his head. "I don't," he admitted. "Not fully. The fact you're alive at all, I can't even explain that. But I *saw* it. I witnessed it with my own eyes. Your body started to heal, the skin knitted together and then it just stopped as suddenly as it started."

"And now?" I heard the tremor in my voice, and I knew I was going to freak out.

"Now, I think your mind is trying to catch up." He shared a look with Cannon. "The damage that was done is almost healed, but it's like your brain never got the memo, so it's still processing the pain you would have felt, not realizing that you're healing has bypassed it."

My chest felt tight. The weight of it all, and Caleb thinking I was dead, was too much. "I don't think I can handle this," I told them both. "It's too much."

"It is a lot," Cannon agreed. "I've reached out to the shaman. Hopefully, he'll know more."

My attention was on Doc, whose head was down. "I'm a medical marvel?" I tried to joke—God knows why, none of it was funny.

He looked up and offered a weak smile. "You understand why Lily can't stay?"

Because my near-death experience had been fast-forwarded several months to almost being right as rain? Yeah, I got it.

"Tell her I got an infection," I repeated what I said earlier. "Tell her I must be quarantined. Open wounds and things, they freak her out. It's why she's so good at leaving when you check the bandages." Leaning my head back on the pillow, I closed my eyes. "Use lots of medical terms. She's not stupid, but it'll remind her you're the professional."

"The fact you protect our secret is appreciated by us all," Cannon told me as he stood, and I saw he meant it. "Don't underestimate the gratitude we have to you for that."

"There's no need," I murmured, embarrassed. "It's never been my secret to tell." My body itched. "The itching?" I asked Doc, eager to change the subject. "It's his blood, isn't it?"

He nodded slowly. "I think so. But...I don't really know."

There was a lot they didn't know. That *I* didn't know. Did the shaman? Did Caleb? He must have known something before he did such a thing as shove his blood down my throat. Shouldn't he have?

Or was it an act of a desperate man?

My hands curled into fists, and the ache in my body flared as I struggled to make any sense of it.

And once more, I was left with more questions than answers.

LILY WAS NOT HAPPY ABOUT GOING, BUT SHE DIDN'T protest too much. She understood the severity of the situation, and when they told her I would be transferred as soon as it was safe to do so, she quieted down.

Of course, I was "infected," so she couldn't come and see me to say goodbye, which sucked. Doc told me he gave her all the medical jargon to convince her to go, and Cannon had added that I was stressing out about my business. Which was only true when he mentioned it to me. I'd forgotten all about my store.

How? This was my livelihood; how had I been so quick to forget it for a guy? I mean, was I really that shallow? Or was Caleb really just that thought-consuming? I hated that it was probably the latter.

I watched the door more than I should have. With Lily gone, the days had gotten lonelier. Doc was in and out, but he was clearly uncomfortable when he sat down to "spend time with me." It didn't help that my brain still thought I was in excruciating pain when I wasn't. My blood and Caleb's blood were mixing, and from the feel of it, it wasn't blending well. The itch was still there and still getting on my very last nerve.

However, Doc's company was better than no company. Alone with my thoughts may be worse. The silence was becoming oppressive, thick, and suffocating. I knew I should be relieved. I knew that being alive and breathing and not hanging to life by a thread were all things to be grateful for, but...I couldn't lose the knot of anxiety that twisted tighter and tighter in my chest.

He was gone. Again.

The idea he was out there thinking I was dead? Fear filled me at the thought of how lost he would feel. My hands trembled as I pulled the covers up and around my shoulders, the cold of the room seeping into my bones. He always said that shifters ran hot. Why didn't I get that perk as his blood coursed through me?

His blood. I still couldn't fully wrap my head around it all.

He had to know something about giving humans blood before he tried it. It was such a desperate act for someone like him. He was so steadfast and stern. They were being tight-lipped about it, but I was pretty confident that blood sharing was not something the pack law allowed.

The whole thing was a nightmare. Something that couldn't possibly be real. But the ache in my body was very real, and so was the lingering itch beneath my skin, reminding me with every moment that I was no longer the same.

Not entirely.

Tentatively I ran my fingers over the bandages that still protected my wounds from the what? Air? Elements? I was in a place where there were no diseases, well, not infectious ones. Were the bandages for show? So my poor human brain didn't freak out completely?

I wanted Caleb. I wanted him here. I wanted to ask him what the hell he was thinking, and I wanted him to know I was okay.

I thought I knew him. I *did* know him. He was the man who'd stood beside me, protected me, and cared for me, even when his own demons threatened to tear him apart.

Swallowing hard, I blinked away the sting of tears. I hated this. The not knowing. The constant push and pull of my emotions warring inside me wasn't helping. It kept my head spinning. Caught between thankful and confused, I was close to losing it altogether.

Puffing out my cheeks, I exhaled slowly. I needed to stop dwelling. This was what it was, the actions were done, and I had to learn to live with the consequences, if there were any. I was still human, people got blood transfusions every day, and I was no different. Moving in the bed to get more comfortable, I couldn't ignore the slight hum under my skin. It was subtle, lying under the not-so-subtle itch, and when I concentrated on it, I felt...something familiar.

Something that felt a lot like a connection to Caleb.

It was familiar yet alien. Was I manifesting an awareness of Caleb, desperate for a connection to a man who was no longer here? Or was I *actually* connected to him? All I knew was I couldn't put it into words, but it was there.

And Caleb wasn't.

The ache in my chest wasn't just physical, it felt deeper. It felt *raw*. If I closed my eyes, I could still feel his arms around me that night. I could still hear him beg me to stay with him, his cry to Luna that she save me.

Had she listened?

I was here, wasn't I? But why would she listen?

I wanted to ask Caleb, but he had left. Doc said that he walked in on him, but why would Caleb flee? Was he scared of the consequences? Or had he thought I was gone and didn't want to stay where another person he cared for died?

That made more sense. Shadowridge Peak held so much heartache for him—was my "death" the last straw? I remember telling him that I didn't blame him. But Caleb would feel guilty. I knew he would. How many times had he pushed me away, believing he wasn't good enough, that he was too broken? For him to be the one who caused the hurt, he would be suffering more under his own hand than anyone else.

I needed someone to find him and tell him I was okay. I hadn't lied to him, I didn't blame him, I wasn't angry. But I *was* hurt that he left. Deeply. But he had saved me, and as I felt the hum under my skin, I was beginning to think he'd left more than his blood with me.

The fact he had left pissed me off, but I was content to scream at him when he stood in front of me once more. Plus, I wanted to ask him if he felt this weird connection too. It was more than when I drew him, this was constant.

Always present.

Unlike him.

"What have you done?" I whispered into the empty room. "Can you feel it, too?"

The link between us had been there from the start, but I knew now it was something more. Something I needed someone to explain to me. Would it always be there? Would it cause the connection to get stronger? Would it haunt me, always pulling me back to him? And him, me? Could he feel it? And if he could, did that mean he knew I was alive, and was staying away anyway?

Because that would *really* piss me off.

What annoyed me off even more was how much I missed him. I kept expecting him to walk through the door and tell me that it would be okay. But that would probably be just another of his lies.

"I'm exhausted," I told the empty room. "I close my eyes, and I see you. I hear your fear. I can't escape this pain, this phantom pain because I'm practically healed. What did you do? Do you even care?"

The sound of the door opening snapped me out of my misery. My breath caught as I waited to see who was coming into my room.

But it wasn't Caleb.

Ned grinned at me when he saw I was awake. He crossed the room in a few strides, taking a seat as if he belonged there. "I'm getting déjà vu. Me in a seat, and you in a hospital bed."

"I'm predictable, right?" I joked, pleased to see someone new.

"You being in a hospital bed shouldn't be so familiar," he admonished. "You good for me to sit awhile?"

"Definitely, I could use the company."

Ned settled into the chair, his manspread unencumbered. "You making yourself miserable?"

"You know me too well," I muttered and saw his wide grin. "Shut up."

"I want to tell you he ain't worth worrying about, but I won't waste my breath."

I knew I looked surprised because Ned laughed. "It's complicated," I argued.

"No, it isn't." Ned kicked his feet up onto my bed, ignoring the fact his boots were dirty and my legs were in the way. "He hurt you, freaked out, and disappeared. Leaving you dying. You're lucky Doc decided to turn back."

Which was all true, but he'd also healed me. Did Ned know that? I wasn't sure, and I wasn't going to be the one to tell him if Cannon hadn't.

"Have you been to Shadowridge Peak?" I asked instead. "Have you been one of the ones to look for him?"

"Nope." He met my look. "Let his ghosts have him, I say."

"Ned!"

"What? The guy's a mess. You have enough to worry about without worrying about a lost shifter."

"It's not that easy."

"Why?"

We were in a stare-off and although Ned was challenging me, he wasn't being aggressive about it. His eyebrow quirked the longer I stayed quiet, and I rolled my eyes at him.

"I don't know what to do," I confessed.

Ned studied me for a long moment and then sighed loudly. "Do you want me to go after him?"

"If he doesn't want to be found, it will make no difference." I couldn't meet his gaze. "Did they tell you what he did?"

"Fucked you up and then decided to give you a blood donation."

I winced at the bluntness. "Wasn't sure you knew the last bit."

"Cannon told me. He is *not* happy with your guy."

"I know." Plucking at a thread on my bedsheet, I avoided the harsh truth of Ned.

"Well, if you're worried he's affected you, don't." Ned stretched back in the chair. "You're still agonizing over every little detail; you're definitely still you."

I laughed, I couldn't help it. Ned grinned at me, and I felt better. "You're a bad friend," I scolded.

"Bullshit. I'm the friend you need to tell you, in no uncertain terms, you're wasting your time on him."

"Am I?"

Ned frowned but said nothing,

"If you went to look for him, you could punch him... for me."

Ned gave me a look of appraisal. "For real?"

"Totally, you could say I specifically requested it."

"You want me to punch him?"

I laughed again. "Punch him? I want you to kick his ass right off that mountain."

Ned stood in one fluid motion. "Now *there's* the girl I know." Leaning forward, he placed a hand on my arm, his touch gentle, as he looked into my eyes. "Willow, I will gladly go and find your man and beat the shit out of him. For you." His eyes danced with laughter, and I couldn't hold back my grin.

"You're going to enjoy it, aren't you?"

"I'm going to love it," he told me as he walked to the door. "He deserves it. You don't. And I am quite happy to be the one to tell him." At the door, he looked at me. "You're still you, nothing's changed." With a wink, he left me.

I wanted to believe that. I really did. But deep down, there was a part of me that wasn't so sure anymore.

THREE

Willow

THE DOOR OPENED AND I PUSHED MYSELF UP THE BED in preparation of Doc's visit. However, it wasn't Doc who came around the door.

"Hi?" I heard the uncertainty in my voice, and the shaman must have too, as he gave me a kind smile.

I watched in fascination as he deftly maneuvered around the chair in his path and sat down with confidence. I found it fascinating every time I saw him that someone whose vision was impaired was able to master so much.

"How do you feel?" the shaman asked me as he settled back in the chair.

"Weird." It was out before I could stop it. "Sorry," I hastily added.

He waved off my apology. His eyes were sharp as he watched me, which I knew was physically impossible, given the milky film over them, but still, I felt like he was staring at me with an intensity that made me squirm.

"Weird is probably an apt description," he told me amicably.

"And since it is what I want to talk to you about, then it is a good place to start."

"Did you have another name?" I asked him curiously, and for the first time, I saw him look uncertain. "Is that rude? To ask that?" I asked him, my cheeks flushing. "If it is, I didn't mean to offend."

"Then why ask?" he asked gently. "You are feeling uncomfortable, and your question is in the hopes of making me feel equally uncomfortable."

I was already shaking my head. "No! I'm genuinely sorry, I meant no offense. I just had the random thought that you couldn't always have been known as shaman, and I spoke without thinking."

He smiled, an air of smugness about him that had me narrowing my eyes. "I joke with you, young Willow," he told me with a chuckle. "Once we take the mantle of the shaman, we are known as shaman only. Possessions, desires, even attachments—they belong to the life we leave behind."

"Like priests?" I asked, engrossed even though I knew that this wasn't what he was here to talk about. "Or monks?"

"Both servants to their God, yes?" he asked, seeking clarification.

"Yeah." I was nodding. "I guess they are."

The shaman nodded. "Then I suppose we are similar." He tapped the corner of his eye. "Worldly possessions are not the only thing we give up."

"Why take your sight?" The question was soft, but I genuinely wanted to know.

"My sight has not been taken," he corrected me gently. "I see clearly what the Goddess wants me to see."

Perhaps it was the fact I'd been in this room for longer than

I wanted to be, but I held up three fingers. "Does she want you to see these?"

The shaman's lips twitched as he gave me his attention. "I see beyond the mortal realm, no matter how many fingers are gestured at me." There was no reprimand in his tone, but still, I felt childish and dropped my hand back to the bedcover. "Your three fingers were two more than I am used to," he winked.

"That's freaky," I mumbled.

"In answer to your question, the name I carried before is not the name that suits me now." He sat at ease and didn't fidget. I envied him for the ability to sit still and not fidget. "My duty is to the balance, to the natural order of things. To carry out the Goddess's Will."

"Is she fair?"

"She is Luna."

That was the answer? She was Luna? Maybe she took more than his eyes...maybe their Goddess robbed them of their common sense too.

"I came to talk to you, to tell you what I can."

I tilted my head as I felt unease settle in my belly. "Tell me what?"

"The situation, as I see it."

I had no idea if he was being funny or ironic with his choice of words.

"Ten years ago, Caleb's pack was massacred," the shaman spoke clearly and confidently. "The few that survived were not on Shadowridge Peak the day it happened."

"Few?"

"More than Caleb remains of the Shadowridge Peak Pack." He frowned. "Only one still calls himself of that pack; the others, the few who survived, were told to find new packs.

Caleb did not want to lead them. He chose to grieve in solitude, and he has traveled far from his duties in the years that have passed." The shaman produced a small wooden bowl and a leather pouch. I was already slipping my hands under my blanket. I recognized that bowl. I saw his lips curve into a faint smile and knew my stealthy move had been seen. "Your sickness... where were you when you caught it?"

"Where was I?" I blinked rapidly. "You mean what foster home was I in?"

"You said you caught a fever. The fever leaves you weak, and...illness can occur?"

For the first time, he sounded unsure, and I didn't think he knew how *human* that made him appear. Relatable. "Yes, I got glandular fever, or mono as it's more commonly known. I developed ME not long after." He nodded, but he looked at me expectantly. "I was in a place called Werben Hills, it's south of Colorado Springs. Small, but big enough."

"Your foster parents were already deceased?" he asked me.

"Yes, a month or two before, I don't remember." I looked away. "It's a bit fuzzy." Clearing my throat, I looked back at him. "I mourned them," I added quietly. "The following months were hazy."

The shaman listened, watching me, and then he opened his pouch, and I inhaled the pungent herbs as they hung heavy in the air. "I wish to make a potion for you. Will you drink it?"

"Do I have a choice?"

He laughed, his hand patting the bedside table that stood adjacent to my bed. "There is always a choice, child."

I wasn't sure there was, but I didn't say that. "Does it taste bad?"

"Probably."

"You're not selling the whole 'drink the funky potion, Willow' thing."

"I'm not selling it, as I don't expect you to buy it, but I would prefer you drink it. I feel It would aid us all." He had my tumbler, using the water I had left over from lunch to make his concoction. From one pocket, he produced a knife and from another, there was a brown cube of something unrecognizable to me. I watched him deftly cut thin slices off the cube and add them to my tumbler. He stirred the liquid vigorously but didn't spill a drop.

As he held it out to me, I peered into the cup at the thick sludge-like substance. "Do I want to know what's in it?"

"I would say it's not needed."

"Right." Taking the cup off him, I sniffed it and then wished I hadn't. "Jesus Lord, what the hell?"

"Drink."

I could already feel my stomach roiling as I put the tumbler to my lips, and then with my eyes fixed on the shaman's, I took a gulp, fighting the urge to spit it out.

"All of it," he encouraged. "Don't think about it, just swallow."

That's what he said. The joke made me grin, but I drank faster, and then with a triumphant gasp, I placed the empty cup on the table.

"Done."

"Excellent." He scooped the cup up and peered into it. "Nothing left, very good, Willow."

The praise made me blush, and then I realized I was being an idiot. "Now do you tell me why?"

"We have a situation, it's one you're familiar with. Your illness, your dreams, your tie to Caleb, they are all connected."

"I don't think I needed a foul-tasting concoction to know that," I muttered. "I know it's all connected, excluding my ME."

"You developed a sickness at the same time that a great evil was done on shifter land. A terrible wrong was done to Caleb and his pack. I don't think it's too much of a stretch to say it's connected."

"Werben Hills is nowhere near Shadowridge Peak." The potion aftertaste was almost as bad as the original taste, and it was distracting me from the conversation.

"It doesn't matter where it is located. What matters is when you first got sick." The shaman poured some water from the jug and handed me the tumbler. "It will remove the bitterness." After I took several gulps, he continued. "The act of the Cristone Pack that day leaves a scar on the land." His fingers tapped off his thigh, and I decided he fidgeted after all.

"You are weak—"

"Whoa, thanks."

He smiled tightly. "Your body is weak, your mind is strong. Now." The shaman stroked his chin as he watched me thoughtfully. "But as a child, after losing your parents, you would have been weak in body and mind."

"Foster parents," I corrected him. "They never adopted me."

The shaman waved that off too. "The lack of a piece of paper making something formal does not make their love for you any less real."

"True." Chewing the inside of the corner of my mouth, I was almost afraid to ask. "What does this have to do with Caleb?" Saying his name sent a pang through my chest.

"When you started drawing him, how did you feel?"

"I felt normal. I didn't know that I was drawing a real person at the time."

"Cannon tells me that you referred to it as an awareness of Caleb?"

"Yeah, I..." I blew out a breath. "I just needed to draw him," I added lamely.

"Landscapes, flowers, meadows, that's more your preferred scene?"

"I sketch my friends, my parents," I clarified.

"People known to you?" He didn't wait for me to confirm. "You didn't think it strange you started drawing a man you'd never seen?"

"I thought I'd maybe seen him before," I mumbled. "It's... it's what it is. What is this about?"

"The tie between you two was curious before," the shaman told me, leaning back in his chair once more. "But now, with his blood in your body, there is something deeper at work here, something unusual...hidden."

"Describe unusual," I asked, leaning forward.

He rested his elbows on the table, steepling his fingers. "Shifters' blood is potent, Willow. It carries our essence—strength, resilience, even pieces of our spirit. When Caleb's blood mingled with yours, it seems to have left an imprint."

I frowned, shaking my head. "He didn't mean to—he was trying to save me."

The shaman's expression softened. "I have no doubt. But intent matters little in these things. Blood is blood. And though it may not have taken hold yet, it's there, waiting. A seed, if you will, planted deep within you."

I swallowed hard, my throat dry. "A seed for what?"

"That's harder to say. What I do know is that it may be tied to your illness. Your body isn't used to holding something so foreign, so...primal. They tell me you are having dizziness, correct?"

"I thought it was part of my recovery," I told him bitterly.

"And the dreams? Are they still vivid?"

"The urge to draw him has lessened, but it's not gone."

The shaman puffed out his cheeks as he considered my words. "To me, they're signs of a struggle within you. You and Caleb are connected now, more than before, and possibly more than either of you realizes."

I sat back, my head spinning. The room felt smaller, the air heavier. "So...what? I'll turn into a shifter?"

The shaman let out a chuckle, but this wasn't funny. "No, nothing so dramatic. At least, I don't expect it. I expect Caleb's blood to leave its mark, one way or another. It's not just a bond of the heart, Willow. It's a bond of the body, and the spirit. And bonds like these can be...complicated."

I clenched my hands into fists, my nails digging into my palms. "Can it be undone?"

He hesitated, his silence louder than any answer he could have given.

"That's what I thought," I muttered, my voice as bitter as I felt inside.

"Caleb will not yet understand the full extent of what he's done," the shaman said gently. "But he'll feel it too, in time. You're tied to him now, Willow. And whether you choose to sever that tie or nurture it, you'll both have to face it eventually."

I didn't respond, my mind too tangled to form words.

The shaman tapped his thigh, his gaze never leaving mine. "For now, focus on healing. Your body is there, but your mind may need more time to process. Your own strength will determine how this plays out. And remember, the bond may feel like a weight now, but it could also become your greatest asset—if you let it."

I stared at him, my stomach twisting with equal parts fear and anger. Whatever Caleb had done, whatever this "seed" was, it was already changing my life in ways I couldn't control. And though I didn't want to admit it, I wasn't sure I could face it alone.

"This was a very depressing conversation," I griped as I shuffled up the bed, while the shaman stood.

"You're standing at a crossroads, Willow. One path leads you back to what you've always known—a life of stability, safety, maybe even happiness in time. The other?" He paused, letting the words linger in the cool air. "The other ties you to something greater, something primal and wild. Caleb may have started this connection unintentionally, but it won't be undone without consequences. You have to decide if you're willing to carry that weight."

I stared at him, the words sinking in like stones. "And what about Caleb? Doesn't he have a say in this?"

His lips curved into a faint, enigmatic smile. "Caleb is as bound as you are. Perhaps more so. His choices may feel like his own, but the bond shapes both of you, pulling you toward a shared fate."

My pulse quickened. "You're saying I have no choice but to accept this?"

"I'm saying that choices have consequences. And sometimes, the harder path is the one that leads to freedom."

I swallowed hard, the weight of his words pressing against

my chest. His role as a shaman might have stripped him of personal desires, but it gave him a clarity I couldn't ignore.

"Think carefully, Willow," he said, his voice softer now. "This isn't just about you. Or Caleb. It's about what this bond could mean—for both of you and for the balance you may be destined to protect."

"Protect? What are we protecting?"

"Possessions, desires, attachments—they mean nothing to a shaman. But to you, Willow? They may mean everything."

I didn't understand half of what he said. He left not long thereafter, but my thoughts were a storm, his final words lingering in my mind like the echo of a distant drumbeat.

And not for the first time, I wondered if Caleb's absence wasn't just painful—it was dangerous.

FOUR

Caleb

I looked out from the Peak, down to the forest below, the jagged tree line silhouetted against the fading light. The sky was streaked with purple and gray, reminding me of bruises, the kind of sky that always felt like something bad was coming. It was fitting.

The scent of crisp earth, snow on the air, and the unmistakable taste of pine filled the air, but I could still catch the faintest whiff of blood under it all.

Her blood.

The metallic tang of Willow was burned into my memory, following me everywhere I went, every second that I'd left her.

My eyes narrowed as I glared at the landscape below me. I wanted to rip it all up, destroy it, and never look back. The wolf inside me was restless, my rage simmering, clawing at the edge of my control. Closing my eyes, I forced myself to breathe and focus on the sounds of the mountain—the sound of the falling snow, the distant cry of a bird—anything to keep from reliving the night I hurt her.

It did no good. Every time I tried to shut it out, Willow's

face came rushing back—pale, twisted in pain, the life slipping out of her as I held her in my arms. I remembered the desperation, the fear that had driven me to do the unthinkable.

I hadn't hesitated. Feeding her my blood was reckless, a wild act borne of a grim warning from my childhood. But I'd done it anyway.

And it worked. She was alive.

And I'd left her.

I had to though. Didn't I? I couldn't stay there after what I'd done to her. After the pain I caused her.

The shame tore at my insides, sharp and restless, constant. Shoving a hand through my hair, my grip tightened, but it was a futile wish that I could pull the guilt right out of my body along with my roots. I was a danger to her, I always had been. I told her that from the beginning, hadn't I? Yet I hadn't stayed away. I kept going *back* to her—drawn to her, needing to be close to her.

And then I'd done what I knew I would. I'd hurt her. I'd lost control and I'd almost killed her.

And she told me she didn't blame me. *How could she not?* I did. Doc did.

To make it worse, I could still *feel* her. My blood was inside her, and the thread that connected us before was now constantly pulling at me from across the distance.

I would never be free of her.

I had thought the worst the night I left her with Doc, and I knew I had to get out of that cabin. I was on the ridge when I felt it, that undeniable tug that tethered me to the woman below. I'd wanted more than anything to run back to her, but I knew I couldn't.

How could I face her?

I'd already made things worse. Giving in to the demons that whispered in my ear, listening to the darkness that surrounded my soul and claimed it as its own. Every day, I'd been closer to the edge, closer to something wholly dark and utterly irreversible.

And then it happened. I hurt *her* and I would never be able to forgive myself.

It was better for us all if I stayed away.

"Hiding won't fix anything, you know."

Turning, I looked at the old man who had come up behind me. I hadn't felt his presence, a trick I would like to know.

Shifting into my human form, I regarded the shaman as I checked around me for more intruders.

"How did you get here?" I asked cautiously. Was he real?

"Same as you, boy, four paws and a strong will." Walking towards me, he looked down over Shadowridge Peak. "Beautiful...but deadly," he murmured. "Too old to be standing on the highest peak in my birthday suit, boy. Let's go down where my clothes are, and put some heat back in my bones."

"I didn't ask you to come."

He tilted his head as he considered me with his milky white eyes. "Good thing I don't answer to you." He pointed upwards, where the moon was just appearing. "Someone I *do* answer to asked me to come." He looked over his shoulder as he walked away. "Not freezing on this mountain for you, Caleb. You're not too far gone you'll disobey the wish of your Goddess."

He shifted into his wolf, and while his words irked me, I had no choice but to follow. He was right, Luna was my Goddess, and you didn't mess with the Goddess...or her shaman.

We descended the peak together. The shaman was sure-footed, and had I not known better, I would have said he was familiar with this peak, but I did know better, and despite myself, I kept looking up warily at the moon.

At the heart of my packlands, I kept to the trees, but he refused to shift until I made my way across to him. I didn't look at where her blood had spilled. The shaman shifted. Picking up a small pack, he pulled out some clothes, and with a gesture to the fire, he drilled me with a look.

"Won't light itself," he grumbled.

"Wasn't sure if it was your next trick," I snarked back at him as I looked around. My last pair of jeans were gone. When I turned back, the shaman was holding out a pair of sweatpants and a long-sleeved shirt.

"They should fit. They're crumpled but clean."

Taking them from him, I didn't ask where he got them, and when a pair of thick socks were tossed at my feet, I pulled them on also.

With the fire going, he stood close to it. "Been a while since I climbed this peak alone," he told me. "Ten years," he mused. "I was too late then. Am I too late again?"

"Depends on what you're hoping to be here for," I answered flatly. "If it was to stop me harming Willow, you're too late."

"Do you grow tired of running?" he asked as he held his hands over the fire.

"I'm not running," I bit back, hearing how hollow the words sounded to my own ears.

The shaman chortled. "Of course not." He smiled as he faced the fire, rubbing his hands together. "So...what do you call this? Hiding here in the middle of a graveyard, skulking in the forest, while the woman you love is healing in someone else's pack?"

I heard her words in my head. *"I would have loved you..."* *Would have* and *did* were two different things. *Love.* It was a word I hadn't thought of in a long time and did not deserve to think of it now.

"I have no choice," I said instead. "You know what I did. I could have killed her."

"But you didn't," the shaman shot back. "You saved her, that's what matters."

"She wouldn't have *needed* saving if I hadn't hurt her!" Anger laced my tone, making my words harsher.

"Semantics."

I gaped at him. "Are you serious?"

The shaman turned to look at me. "Are you?"

Clenching my jaw to stop my anger from pouring out, I averted my gaze and tried to focus on something else before I said something I shouldn't to a vessel of Luna.

"Look at you, biting back your words," he chuckled in amusement. "And you're trying to tell me you have no control," he mocked.

"You don't understand." My jaw was so tight my words hardly made it out. "You weren't there. I *felt* them. I felt them all around me, they're everywhere. If I hadn't pulled back when I did..."

"But you *did* pull back. And you know it was not *your* actions that dug your claws into Willow. It was *you* who withdrew your claws. It was *you* that saved her." The shaman sighed softly. "I know you are scared of becoming something you cannot control. But leaving her? It's not the answer. Especially now."

Watching him carefully, I mulled over his words. What was the plan here? "I thought you were concerned I was rogue?"

"I am." His answer was simple, no hidden weight. It made me wary. "The Goddess is too. The more you stay in your wolf form, the more the humanity inside you dies. Your darkness is unforgiving, Caleb. You need to come back into the light."

"There's no light left for me, old one."

The truth was harsh, but it was the truth nonetheless. I knew the danger of turning rogue. I'd seen it in others. I'd seen the madness in their eyes, the pure animalistic rage that consumed them when the beast within was untamed. I used to think it was a fate worse than death. But I knew, little by little, inching closer every day, it had been creeping up on me.

And I had let it.

I knew, the moment I stepped back on Shadowridge Peak, they were waiting for me.

My nightmares.

"I can still control it," I told him softly. "I thought I had it under control, but that night—" I felt the lump in my throat. "I hurt her. I almost killed her because I thought she was *them*. I will never risk that happening again."

"I understand." The shaman turned to look at the moon above us. "But you didn't lose yourself, you're still here." His gaze was steady. "You're still you, Caleb."

I was already shaking my head. "No. You don't understand, I'm broken. Something inside of me, it's broken. And around Willow...when I'm around her, the more I feel I'm losing myself." Pushing my hair back, I looked at him. "I feel her blood on my hands every moment. I know how close I was to losing her."

"Yet you left her."

"To *protect* her!"

"From you?"

"*Yes* from me! I'm the only one who's *hurt* her!"

"Mm-hmm. And the shifters hunting her, the ones who broke into her shop? Her home? The ones who ran her off the road and put her in the hospital? They haven't hurt her?"

"It's not the same."

The shaman snorted. "Tell that to Willow. Pain is pain."

Angrily, I stared at the flames of the fire. His words were tough, making my stomach twist at the other dangers she faced. Who would protect her? "I gave her my blood."

"You did." He sounded thoughtful. "Old magic that. Blood magic is dangerous for the untrained."

"I know." Wiping my hand over my eyes, I gave a mirthless laugh. "I *know* the danger, I *know* how unnatural it is, and *I did it anyway.*"

"Because you love her and you were scared," the shaman's sharp voice cut through the night. "And you're *still* scared, and you left not because you caused her wounds but because you *know* what a blood bond means." He turned slightly so he was facing me. "And you're afraid of facing her after what you've done."

"I can feel her," I whispered so quietly that I wasn't sure he heard me. "Every moment of the day, I feel her."

"And she can feel you. And it's pissing her off," he added with a small smile. "She's describing it as an insufferable itch." His smile widened. "I'd say that's pretty accurate."

"Does she know what it means?" I asked cautiously. I hadn't known she would feel it too, and I wasn't sure how I felt about that.

"No, none of them do." He turned back to rubbing his

hands. "Old magic, very few know of it. I thought it was only shamans."

"And grandmothers who liked to put the fear of Luna into their grandson's bedtime stories."

"Ahh. I see." The shaman nodded in satisfaction at knowing how I knew the ritual. "You can never share that knowledge."

"Why would I want anyone else to have this pain?"

"The pain dulls the closer you are to her." For the first time since he arrived, he looked at me with sympathy. "You may have caused the wounds, but you also saved her; that's what your blood did. There are consequences for such an act. Do you really think Willow should face them alone?"

"She has you."

"I'm an old man, ready for Luna to call me home. I am not what Willow needs. Or *wants*."

My hands curled into fists, nails digging into my palms. "And if I hurt her again? Blood magic only works once."

"You won't." The shaman shook his arms before placing them over the fire once more. "Now, more than ever, you're connected to her. The bond you shared is strengthened, it's ever-present. A reminder of what you're fighting for. You feel her now. You know she is alive because of you. Your blood is hers. *She* is yours."

I could feel my throat tightening at his words. He was right, I could feel her. Every heartbeat, every breath. Faint but constant, pulling at me to join her.

It was terrifying.

"If the bond breaks?" I didn't like how scared I sounded.

"She dies. You know that." The shaman puffed out his cheeks. "You're afraid to lose her?"

My silence was a good enough answer for him.

"She's stronger than you think."

"I know." I'd told her many times myself.

"And so are you, Caleb," he added. "But you are weaker apart, and you cannot protect her by staying away."

"And if she tells me to leave?" My heart was pounding, the weight of the truth settling around me.

"Try groveling."

I blinked. "Wh-what?"

"You put four claws into her innards and only just managed to stop yourself from spilling them over this ground. I think groveling is a given, no?"

"That's your advice?"

"Should that have to be advice?" he asked shrewdly. "Just go to her, Caleb. She needs you."

"I don't think I can face her."

"Try."

"And what do I tell the Pack Council when they come for me for breaking pack law?"

"A fluke of nature." The shaman shrugged. "Who cares? This is between you and Willow and the Goddess."

Staring out into the dark trees, I struggled with what to do. I wanted to go to her, but...I was scared.

Scared of her turning me away.

"Is she still human?" I asked him suddenly.

"Yes, werewolves are a human fantasy, not Luna's."

"Do you know who hunts her?" I asked, moving closer to the fire, suddenly feeling the chill in the air.

"I know many things, suspect a lot more."

Giving him a flat look, I waited. "What the fuck was that bullshit?"

"I thought it sounded good."

"I thought it sounded like mumbo jumbo BS," I countered.

He pulled his shirt off and dropped his pants, rolling them up into a ball and putting them back in the small pack. "Next time I stand here, I expect your demons to be purged. Now go back to your woman, fix your mistakes, *forgive* yourself, and move on."

"That easy, huh?" I mocked.

"Nothing worth winning should be easy. Fight, Caleb, remember who and what you're fighting for, and I think you'll surprise yourself."

He shifted into his wolf, picked up his pack, turned, and left the clearing. I watched him disappear into the tree line, and as his tail vanished out of sight, so did the light of the moon from the sky as the clouds covered it once more.

With a deep breath, I turned away from the trees and the darkness and looked south where Willow lay. Was she waiting for me?

I was about to find out.

FIVE

Willow

I WOKE TO THE SOUND OF THE WIND BASHING AND whistling as it rushed over the bunker. The snow falling heavily against my window let me know that the weather on the mountains in November was no fun. I was glad Lily had left, because I had no idea how these people on this mountain survived over winter. I feared it may involve a lot of them shifting to their wolf form to keep warm, and she didn't need to see that.

The fact that they weren't people should probably be the answer, but still, they weren't invincible.

Struggling to sit up, I rubbed my chest, trying to soothe my racing heart. Sweat clung to my skin. My body was cool in the room, but the fear of my dream still lingered.

With a shaky breath, I pushed my hair back with trembling fingers. Slowly, I pushed myself up further on the bed, wincing at the pain from my abdomen and then scowling when I remembered it wasn't real pain. Although, even though I looked healed on the outside, there was a lot to be said for internal injuries.

With great effort, pushing the covers off me, I swung my

legs over the side of the bed and tried to muster the courage to stand unaided. It may have looked like nothing happened, but my body was protesting loudly that I was not ready to stand.

"Stop being so weak," I grumbled to myself, and slowly, tentatively, I stretched my leg, my toe grazing the hard floor like I was a nervous swimmer, testing the waters before getting in.

If Caleb were here, he would be hiding his grin at how silly I looked, I just knew it. I winced again, this time at the memory of Caleb. Thinking of him was still painful. It conjured every detail of that night, which was burned into my mind. The pain, the blood, the way I had been ready to slip into the darkness, believing this was the end. Caleb holding me, begging me to hold on, his eyes wide with fear.

Telling him I loved him.

My cheeks burned in remembrance at *that* confession. And then...nothing.

Until I woke up, thinking I was severely damaged with life-threatening injuries. Only to learn I was healed.

Because of him.

My fingers pressed into my abdomen. Doc had removed the bandages, so there was no barrier between my fingers and the raised skin where the worst of the wounds had been.

Biting my lip, I tried to stop the thudding of my heart. I was supposed to die in his arms that night.

I knew it deep down. I wasn't being dramatic; I *knew* in my bones, that night on Shadowridge Peak was supposed to be my last.

And Caleb had done what Caleb does—he wrote his own script, and instead of letting me go, he saved me.

Squeezing my eyes shut, I tried to ignore the flood of emotions that came whenever I thought about Caleb. They were so overwhelming, too much and too fast, and I was constantly struggling to find my footing. One second, I was angry—furious at him for leaving, especially after everything that had just happened—and then...there was that something else. That something that dwelled deep within me, pulling at me, the need I had for him, the feelings I tried to ignore, but other memories, of us in the car, entwined with each other, made my chest tighten whenever I thought about him.

But truthfully, whether I felt one emotion or the other, I didn't understand any of it.

With a deep breath, I pushed myself off the bed. I needed to stop being weak, and the first step—pun intended—was to get out of this bed. The dream that woke me lingered and, with it, the strange awareness I'd had since I opened my eyes that first day in the bunker. It was as if I weren't completely alone, even when there was no one around. I thought it would fade, but as the days passed, it only grew stronger.

I knew it wasn't a figment of my imagination. I knew it from the way Cannon watched me as he spoke to me. It wasn't in my mind. I could feel Caleb.

The shaman had confirmed it, we were connected, and as I felt Caleb, did he feel me?

My knees were shaky, but slowly, so very carefully, I edged away from the bed. One step then two, I inched closer to the bathroom. I was panting by the time I got there, which with everything they had told me, irritated me the most. I wasn't hurt anymore, so why was I being so pathetic?

At the door to the bathroom, I stopped in sudden revelation. I may have been healed from my injuries by Caleb's blood, but I was still *me*. Which meant I still had ME, and as my frazzled brain accepted my revelation, the aches and pains I could feel suddenly made more sense.

I wasn't crazy.

Okay, I was perhaps more unhinged than any other twenty-six-year-old female, but I had shit happening that was *supernatural*.

In the bathroom, I answered the call of my bladder, and then while washing my hands, I decided to also wash my face. Eyeing the shower, I wondered if I had the strength to do it. I needed to feel clean.

Flicking the lock on the door, I pulled off my jammies, and after letting the water run, I stepped under the spray of water. The first few moments were honestly the first time I felt truly like myself. My body relished the heat, and my mind felt clear. My toiletries were in the bathroom, and reaching for my usual body wash, I started the slow methodical process of washing.

As I fell into the easy sense of the familiar, my mind wandered back to Caleb. Even here, I could still feel him. Not in the literal sense. It wasn't as if I could feel his actual touch or hear him or anything like that, but I knew I was connected to him. I hoped no one ever asked me how often I reached out for it, trying to feel him.

Trying to find him.

Strangely, the reality that I was inexplicably linked to him didn't scare me as much as the fact he had healed me.

Standing under the warm water for several minutes, with my head tipped back, I savored the quiet. I could learn to ignore the thrum under my skin. Couldn't I? I was pretty stubborn when I wanted to be. I could ignore him.

Eventually.

Hearing the door into the main room open brought me

back to the here and now. Reluctantly, I turned off the shower and took my time drying myself. I hadn't brought in clean jammies since this had never been my plan, so I pulled on my old ones and opened the door.

Doc was on the seat by my bed. His hair was mussed like he'd just woken up. His face was its usual calm mask, but I saw the flicker of concern in his eyes as he watched me walk slowly across the room.

"What woke you?" he asked me as I lingered by the bed, hoping my clutching of the rail went unnoticed. "You okay there?" He gestured to my firm grip, and I knew he had missed nothing.

"Yeah, a little bit unsteady, but doing okay."

"Dream? Nightmare? Weather?" he asked, pulling me back to his first question.

I shrugged, turning to look at the snow-laden window. "Does it matter?"

When I turned back to him as he sat in silence, I noticed his gaze had sharpened. "I know it's a lot to process, Willow. Physically, you're healing well, but emotionally..."

The unfinished sentence hung in the air between us. I didn't need him to complete it. I knew exactly what he meant. I hadn't had the chance to process everything... Sure, I'd been laid up in bed recovering, with nothing *else* to think about, but my mind was still stuck on that night. My attention was still fixed on the fact that I could feel the bond between us growing stronger every day.

"My ME is what I've been feeling," I told him, changing the subject. "I think I was so focused on the injury I forgot that I have a chronic illness." I gave a self-deprecating shrug. "Maybe wishful thinking on my part that when Caleb healed me, he healed *all* of me."

Doc sat back, his frown marring his smooth complexion. "It's possible that his blood could only heal his injury," he mused. He met my confused look with a look of excitement. "Which is what we knew; shifters *can't* heal humans, and if you are feeling you're ME, then it's proof he hasn't healed you. But the injury that Caleb caused you, he fixed that. Isn't that fascinating?"

"Honestly? No." My unenthusiasm didn't stop Doc's.

"When Caleb gave you his blood, he gave you a part of himself, something powerful. *Blood* is powerful, it's what keeps us alive after all. His blood in your system created a connection—"

"We were already connected." I ignored his look of surprise. "Have you forgotten that I've been drawing Caleb since before I met him?"

Doc was nodding before I finished speaking. "Yes, I know, and I maybe overlooked that when I've been thinking about this. But you're right, the connection was there, and his blood makes it..."

"Makes it?"

"Tenable?"

"What do you mean?" I asked him carefully.

"You're already linked, but the blood makes the connection you two had before more binding. Maybe?" His look was appraising. "Well, I'm way out of my depth, but I think...I think it would be fair to say that what's between you now, the bond, it won't be easily broken."

I swallowed hard, my throat too tight to speak. Bound to

him. Doc's words echoed in my head, making my heart race again. I wasn't sure if I was supposed to be relieved or terrified.

"So...I'm stuck? Like this? Forever?" From the sound of my voice, I had failed to keep the panic from it. "That's what the shaman said, but I was hoping science would prove him wrong."

"I don't think it will." He gave me a sad smile. "Maybe I'm wrong. I mean, I have no research to base my theory on. Maybe it's not forever; maybe it only lingers as long as it exists between the two of you. Maybe it's up to both of you to decide what this means."

"Maybe Caleb doesn't care that this has happened." There was more bitterness in my voice than there should have been.

"Do you have feelings for him?"

It was such a non-doctorly question I gaped at him longer than I should. Trying to hide my reaction to the question, I got back into bed, choosing to sit rather than lie.

"Willow, stop stalling."

Busted. I rubbed my temple to ease the tension building there and closed my eyes. "I'm not stalling. Headache." Peeking at him from under my lashes, I saw his unimpressed look. "I don't know why he would leave."

I saw a flash of something—pity probably—crossing his face. "Maybe he's struggling exactly as you are, and let's not forget, he has his demons. I don't know what he's done, but I don't think it would have been easy. He may be struggling as much as you are. Maybe sharing his blood took its toll."

"He doesn't need to deal with it alone."

"He broke pack law," Doc reminded me. "One, you're human, you shouldn't know anything about us. Two, even if you weren't human, blood sharing...it's not common amongst pack."

"Why?"

"You share blood with any of your past boyfriends?"

"Ewww, no!"

"Then why would we?" Doc's grin at my assumption was wide. "We're shifters, we're not debased animals."

My cheeks burned at the reprimand. "Sorry."

"It's fine. You reminded me that you are clueless about our world." Doc looked at his hands, which were linked together on his lap. "Which makes it all the more dangerous."

"Are we snowed in?" I asked suddenly. "Am I here for the whole of winter?"

Doc looked up at me. He looked like I wasn't going to enjoy what he said next. "It's not fully winter yet."

"Right." My eye roll told him what I thought of that comment. "Can I get down?"

"If you leave within the next couple of weeks."

"And I get to leave?" I asked hesitantly. "With everything that's happening?"

"The shaman has been, and he told Cannon he will tell him what he learns." Doc stood, placing his hand on my shoulder. "You've been through a lot, Willow. More than most, and that's before Caleb struck you. You need time to heal. You're getting stronger every day, but you still need time. Rest."

I nodded, knowing everything he said was true, but healing felt impossible when everything inside me was a tangled mess of confusion and fear.

After Doc left, I got back up, and after retrieving a sketch pad, I settled back against the pillows. The dull ache in my abdomen throbbed steadily, reminding me of what had happened. The itch under my skin persisted, pulsing faintly, but it was low, as if he was resting.

The thought made me pause. Was Caleb sleeping? Was that why it was just a slow gentle beat? The idea that I may know more than just being *aware* of him startled me.

What else would we be able to feel? How deep did it run? Would I know what he was thinking? Because for someone like Caleb, knowing what went on in his head would be a welcome perk.

Groaning loudly in frustration, I opened my sketchbook. Then I had to get up and get my pencils. When I was back in bed, I was feeling less benevolent towards the man who was linked to me.

If he were here, we could learn together. If this was something I had to live with, for the *rest of my life*, I wanted to *know* more. Caleb didn't have the right to take that off me by staying away. He didn't have the right to make all my decisions and choose how *I* lived my life.

I knew he would be feeling guilty for what he did. I knew he would be punishing himself more than anyone else could, and I knew he was too thickheaded to listen to anyone else about it.

And there was little I could do about it except tell him that I didn't blame him. If he ever deigned to show up again.

I hadn't lied. Not the night it happened, not the times Cannon or Doc had raised it. I did *not* blame Caleb for what happened to me on that mountain.

But I may never forgive him for leaving me behind.

SIX

Willow

I SAT IN THE CHAIR BESIDE THE BED. THE SNOW WAS so heavy outside that I no longer looked up at the small window. Soft electric light filled the room. I'd been surprised to find the lights were on a dimmer switch, but it was a happy surprise. My sketchbook was on my legs while I rubbed a hand across my abdomen.

The phantom aches still lingered, and I wondered how long it would be before my brain accepted the fact I was no longer injured. I'd been a lot more stable on my feet today. I'd had another shower, even washed my hair, and was now in fresh jammies. I kept glancing at the door, anticipating the arrival of my breakfast. Today was the first time I could say that I had an appetite.

A quiet knock at the door had me sitting up in the chair, my notebook being put on the bed in eager anticipation of being fed. Calling out an invitation to come in, I didn't mask my surprise when the shaman entered.

"Oh!" I hesitated. "Hi." I watched him as he crossed the room, his steps quiet as he approached me, his presence filling the room with an ancient energy. It wasn't until he got closer that I realized I was in the only seat, and I jumped up and scrambled out of the way, flinching at the brief stab of pain at the sudden movement.

His lips twitched as if he could see me, but I knew the heavy thick layer of white across his eyes hindered his vision. Still, I wasn't wholly sure he *was* blind. He was so small he looked frail, but there was absolutely nothing frail about this man. Wispy white hair covered his head, thinning but still there. His skin showed signs of age, but I recalled what I'd been told, that he was a lot older than he appeared. To me, he looked maybe mid-eighties, but I knew he had more years on his clock than it looked.

He sat wordlessly, his cloudy eyes fixed on me, but I knew I was being seen.

"Thank you," he murmured as he settled into the chair.

I nodded, unable to shake the weight of his gaze as he got comfortable in the seat, and I forced myself to not fidget as silence filled the room.

"I hear you are feeling better," he said with no preamble. His voice was low and steady, comforting.

"It seems so," I admitted, my gaze flicking to the door, expecting Doc or someone to come through.

"We are alone, child. I am sure the alpha knows of my presence on his mountain, but we will not be disturbed."

Was that a good thing? "Um...okay?"

"I have spoken to Caleb."

He now had my full attention. The words sent a jolt of electricity through me, but I forced myself to stay still. I wanted to ask the thousand questions that sat on the tip of my tongue, but instead, I held back and waited for him to continue.

"He's hiding," the shaman continued, his words and tone soft but direct. "Running from what he thinks he's done to you."

I swallowed hard but said nothing. There was no need. The shaman seemed to know more than I did about pretty much everything, including how I felt even when I struggled with that myself.

The shaman studied me, one hand on the armrest of the chair, his fingers tapping gently off it. "The bond between you is as strong for him as it is for you."

I nodded, then wondered if he could see that, so I answered hurriedly. "Is it annoying him as much as it annoys me?"

"I don't believe so," he said with a rueful smile on his face. "He didn't mention it was bothering him, so I assume it was not." He seemed to consider his next words carefully. "As we spoke about before, what you're experiencing, what drew you to him from the start, is much deeper. I don't think I need to tell you it's the work of our Goddess?"

"I've been told that," I confirmed, biting back my denial about another heavenly presence other than the one I'd been raised with. I was still very much a Christian, but it wasn't my place to yuck on someone else's faith.

The shaman hesitated. "Ah, you don't believe?"

"I think even if I did, it wouldn't make a difference," I answered carefully. "She is a God to you. You are shifters, I am not."

He looked thoughtful. "Interesting. She is still a deity that cares for all life, as much as your God does."

The mention of God and Luna in the same sentence sent a chill down my spine. I was still very much of the opinion that theology was not for me to get involved with. I knew, for shifters, their belief was absolute. I didn't think there was a Big Bang theorist amongst them. The shifters I had met had spoken of their Goddess with reverence, and for that reason, I had accepted their belief. I was human, I was not part of their world, and because of that, I had no right to voice my opinion of power and divine connections.

But was the shaman saying I *was* someone the Goddess had something to do with?

"I don't think I understand, sir," I said finally, finding my voice, even if it was barely more than a whisper. "Are you saying your Goddess cares about me?"

"I am," he replied. "Her interest is Caleb. His bloodline."

"His bloodline?" I knew I was frowning, my mind trying to wrap around the meaning of his words and how they connected to me.

The shaman nodded, his gaze on mine never wavering. I felt like he could see right into my soul. "Caleb is the last of his bloodline. A strong line, it carries an ancient power tied to the wild nature of the wolf. An alpha struggles most with control, as they fight their inner wolf, their beast. Caleb's bloodline is one of the strongest, very similar to Cannon's, the alpha of this pack where you recover. Being so inherently tied to their ancestral line, they are more prone to be untamed and, as such, run a higher risk of turning feral. Our Goddess knows this. She knows that, without balance, he will lose himself to it. To the calling of the wild."

"This is the same for any alpha?" I asked curiously.

"It is. Most don't even know it's a struggle they face. Cannon, for example, was so focused on overthrowing his father's reign, he never strayed from his calling."

Wetting my lips, I watched the shaman. "But Caleb has no

pack after what Jonah and the other pack did. When he exacted his revenge, he no longer had a purpose?" It was a guess, but I saw the shaman's pleased smile.

"Exactly, by choosing to be alone and shun his brothers, he opened himself to the wildness."

I felt like I would never swallow past the lump in my throat. "And how is this tied to me?"

"Without balance, he loses himself. You've seen it. Luna has seen it. She has chosen you, Willow, to be the balance in his life."

I could only hear the sound of my heart racing, and I feared he was going to have to repeat himself. The idea was...preposterous. No, that wasn't right. It was huge. It was absolutely incomprehensible and strange. So strange. Was this even real? I saw his finger twitch, and I knew he was patiently waiting for me to get over my meltdown. "Chose...me?" He nodded. "But, I'm just—"

"Human," he finished for me, with a gentle but firm tone. "Yes, you are human. I think that's exactly why she chose you. You're grounded in a way shifters are not. You seem to be able to ground Caleb in a way a pack could not. I believe the power you have to tether him, to keep him from falling completely to his wildness, is why he's still with us. Luna's Will is what created the bond between you two, and his blood bound you to him not only to save your life...but to save his."

My mind was racing as the words hung in the air, heavy and profound with the power to blow my mind. "Why me?" I asked him eventually as I realized I was taking huge gulps of air. "Why did she choose me of all people?" I looked down at myself. "I'm no one. Absolutely no one."

"You are Willow, not no one," he corrected me gently. "And

why you? I don't know any more than you do. Our Goddess works in mysterious ways and does not always provide clear answers. Maybe she saw something in you, something that was strong enough to stand between Caleb and the darkness that's so desperately trying to consume him."

"She saw something in me?" I snorted, knowing I probably insulted him, too far gone in my "what the fuck" moment to care. "Was it the debilitating illness? The fact I'm an orphan? Or the complete and totally plain fact that I am not enough?" I felt a swell of anger rise. "Does she know I'm failing? I don't know how to help him! This can't be on me. I don't know what I am doing!"

The shaman wasn't the least bit bothered with my meltdown. He let me rant and then he waited until I was taking huge gulps of air again before he spoke. "You've already helped him, Willow. More than you realize. Your bond is not one-sided. He feels it too, even though he's doing his best to deny it. This is why he ran. He's so scared he's going to hurt you again. He knows what he is capable of. The blood on his hands should never have been yours, and he knows that." The shaman drilled me with a hard stare, a feat for someone who was almost blind. "He knows, without you, he will be lost."

"And?" My snark was lost on the shaman.

"And he's still here, still fighting. For you."

This was madness. Shaking my head in disbelief, I fought the conflicting emotions rising inside me. "You make it sound like I am the one to save him, but that can't be right. I have no powers. I don't belong in your world. In fact, while no one has outright said it, I don't think I'm even *welcome* in this world."

"You belong more than you know," the shaman said quietly. "Luna's choices are never random. You have the strength inside you that Caleb needs. A strength that goes beyond the physical. You may not be a shifter, but you are tied to our world now, to Caleb. You are his balance, and you cannot escape that."

Silence fell between us once more as I tried to process the weight of the words pressing down on me. I'd spent so much time thinking of myself as an outsider, someone who didn't belong here, that I hadn't accepted that the truth was so much more complicated than being a human in a shifter world. The bond between us wasn't something random or born out of desperation or chance—it was something greater. Something beyond either of us.

And I had no idea if I wanted it. Could I be what he needed? After everything that had happened, did I even want to be?

"How do I help him?" I asked, my voice barely audible, the question surprising me as it wasn't what I thought I would say.

The shaman's look softened, and I batted away the thought that for the first time since coming into my room, he looked hopeful. "You don't have to force it," he spoke gently. "The bond will guide you both, but Caleb must be willing to face his demons. To do that, he needs to accept that the beast inside him is part of who he is and not something for him to fear. You, Willow, *you* will remind him of the balance he needs. Remind him that he is more than just his darkness. His actions ten years ago when he exacted his pack's revenge, it haunts him. While he does not regret his actions, he feels the weight of their deaths. Carries it with him. He needs to learn to forgive."

"They killed his entire family," I spoke in his defense. "It will be hard to forgive that."

"I meant he needs to forgive himself," the shaman corrected

me softly. "He needs to forgive himself for the death of his pack, of the pack he killed, and for the harm he has done to you."

My mouth would never have moisture in it again, I was sure. "And if he doesn't?"

The shaman's expression darkened. "Then he will lose himself to the beast and the wild forever."

"Beast? His wolf?"

The shaman shook his head. "No, our wolves are part of us —they want what we want. But the beasts? The darkness all shifters carry? That's different. The more we feed it with hate and self-loathing, the stronger it grows."

Clenching my hands together in my lap, I tried to keep my emotions in check. The thought of Caleb, the man I knew and cared for, turning into something wild and uncontrollable—it was too much. But the knowledge that I might be the only one who could stop it, was even more overwhelming.

"And if I decide to return to my life and never think of shifters or him again?"

The shaman cocked his head to the side, a small smile playing on his lips. "You can lie to yourself, child, but you can't lie to me, or Luna."

Well, what the hell did that mean?

"You love him." He said it so simply, so matter-of-factly, that I blushed crimson. "Your heart will rule your head, child, and I thank you for it."

"Um..." Yup, I had nothing.

"You won't be alone," the shaman added, his voice once more reassuring. "Luna chose you because she knows you are strong enough for this path. Trust in that, and you will be able to trust in yourself."

That may be true, but the knot of uncertainty in my chest

remained. The idea that this was my life, that I was part of something so much bigger than myself, felt impossible. But...I couldn't deny the truth of the shaman's words. I knew the bond was real, I could feel it, and it was growing stronger every day.

Did I love him? I wasn't sure. I knew I *could* love him, and I knew I was so scared of his rejection that I was probably too scared to admit, even to myself, how deep my feelings ran.

"What happens now?" I asked him, breaking the silence.

"I told him to come to you."

Alarm crossed my face, and even in his hindered sight, I knew the shaman saw it because he laughed. "He is stubborn, child. He will come when he is ready, but he will come."

"So...I just wait?"

The shaman stood, giving me a kind smile. "Isn't that what you have been doing?"

He patted my shoulder before he left me in my room, my mind overflowing with all the information he had shared since he started our talk.

Whether I was ready or not, I was bound to Caleb, and the path forward, for both of us it seemed, was one we would have to face together—if he ever came back.

The shaman may believe he was on his way, but I knew the mule-headed male better, and I wasn't holding my breath.

SEVEN

Caleb

THE WIND WHIPPED THROUGH THE TREES, SHARP AND biting, like a warning. I pushed forward anyway, the burning in my legs a welcome distraction as the rough terrain tried to slow me down. I welcomed the pain and needed the burn to keep me grounded.

Because if I stopped, if I let myself think for even a moment, everything would crash down on me, and I would turn back.

I didn't want to turn back.

Now that I had made my mind up, I *wanted* to see Willow. I knew she would be pissed at me—hell, I was pissed at me—but I knew my girl would be fucking righteous in her rage, and I was ready for it.

The forest thinned ahead, the path opening into a clearing bathed in pale moonlight, the silver of the moon reflecting off the crisp white snow. The sight made me pause. My breathing was hard as I leaned against a tree. I caught my breath as I took in the beautiful scenery in front of me. The serenity that spread out in front of me, sheltered from the wind, brought me a moment of peace. When my breathing was back to normal, I felt for the thread that connected me to Willow. It was there, waiting patiently for me to pull at it, and all the while, it was tugging gently as if it was trying to reel me back in.

It had been doing that for days.

Was it Willow wanting me to return to her? The thought gave me hope, but at the same time, I felt myself get frustrated at the thought. My hand curled into a fist as I reminded myself that I didn't deserve her.

I didn't deserve this connection to her, to know she was waiting for me, despite everything I'd done. I wasn't worthy of her. I had hurt her. Lost control and gave into the darkness inside me, and the beast had nearly killed her.

You should have killed her.

The thought tore through me, sharp and unforgiving, and I grit my teeth as I forced the thoughts back.

Forced the darkness back.

My fist slammed into the tree trunk I had been resting against, the bark splintering in protest. Pain ricocheted up my arm, but it was still overshadowed by the guilt that clawed up and twisted at my insides.

Closing my eyes, I tried to steady my breathing once more, this time for reasons much different than why I stopped. Willow's face swam in front of me, the terror and fear in her eyes as she looked up at me as tears of pain spilled over, the way her body had gone limp in my arms as I held her close to me.

I hadn't been ready to let her go.

She didn't deserve to die. She'd never deserved any of this. The moment my blood entered her, I knew I'd gone too far. The second I whispered the words, I knew I had crossed a line that I would never come back from.

My life for hers, I was okay with that.

And yet, here I was, still alive. Still breathing.

Still fighting.

And so was she.

The bond between us hummed, stronger now than it had been before. I found when I thought of her, it got stronger, encouraging me towards her. I could feel her, like a whisper in the back of my mind, and sometimes it soothed me, and sometimes it only made my guilt worse.

I took a step into the clearing, the snow crunching under my boots. Should I have stayed away? Probably. I should have run so far that even this bond couldn't pull me back to her.

But...I couldn't. Staying away from her seemed to be impossible. How many times had I tried? Something always kept me coming back to her. *Dragging* me back to her, forcing me to face the one thing I didn't want to accept.

I needed her.

That thought alone made me want to tear the world apart. I was an *alpha*, I didn't need anyone. I was a shifter—strong, wild, and stronger than most. My lips curled in a snarl, a low growl emanating from me as I once more pushed down the dark thoughts.

Willow... Well, she wasn't *just* anyone. She was human. Fragile. The exact kind of person that shouldn't hold my attention.

Weak.

I should have stayed away from her. But I hadn't.

And then the Goddess made sure that I couldn't.

I cut a straight path through the snow, my thoughts in turmoil as the two parts of me warred with themselves. I briefly wondered if that would be my life from now on, never knowing which part of me was in control. If I even knew what control was.

The shaman's words were also a constant presence, sticking to my head like a thorn in my side that I couldn't dig out. He told me the Goddess had chosen Willow to save me.

I scoffed in the quiet of the night. *I* saved Willow that night. Yes, Luna blessed the magic, but it was my actions that saved her. *My* blood.

My blood kept her alive, and because of that, she would never be free of me.

Or me her.

The very idea of it should grate, but it didn't. A small part of me hoped what the shaman hoped. That by saving Willow, I had somehow saved myself. I'd spent ten years fighting against the wildness, keeping my rage at bay for what I'd lost. Ten years I had been in control. Now, through my own actions, I was tethered to someone who needed me.

Wasn't that the irony? I was bound, by the blessing of the Goddess, to Willow, and there was no escape.

My gaze lifted skyward. The moon hung low, half-hidden by the clouds, its pale light showing me the way. I had the urge to flip it the finger. A swirl of wind caught me, causing me to almost lose my balance, and I could hear the laughter on the wind. Frustration boiled inside me, but instead of raging against the Goddess, I clenched my jaw.

This was how I was going back to her? Furious, frustrated, and wanting to howl at the moon? Willow deserved so much more. She'd been dragged into my darkness and into this world that would rip her apart if she let it.

If *I* let it.

Blowing out a deep breath, I wondered how I would keep

her safe. Again, my inner voice argued with me, telling me she was supposed to be safe the further she was away from me, but I wasn't listening anymore.

I'd failed her once, and now she was a part of this mess, bound to me, in ways neither of us fully understood.

The best way to keep her safe was to keep her *with* me. The Goddess and the shaman both thought this was the answer, and who was I to argue with the divine and her vessel?

That didn't stop the rising panic that was threatening to crush me. These last few months, I had let myself be ruled by my emotions, even when I never realized it. My anger had been simmering for so long below the surface, I hadn't recognized the danger until it was too late. I accepted the beast within myself, I knew it would always be there, and I knew I had a fight on my hands to wrestle back control.

This was who they wanted to go back to her? This was what I was laying at her door, and part of me felt even guiltier for knowing I would do it anyway.

Because the bond was growing every day. It was no longer a thread between us—it was a lifeline.

I also needed to be honest with myself. I needed to see her. I needed to see her with my own eyes, to see the look on her face when she saw me. Because I knew I had to face what I'd done, and maybe—Luna willing—I could figure out how to make things right.

As much as I hated to admit it, and I would probably deny it if asked, the shaman had been right about one thing. Without Willow, I was lost. And if I was lost now, then it would only be a matter of time before I was lost for good.

Looking up to the sky, I watched the last of the moon get swallowed by clouds. Walking in amongst the trees, I felt my steps get heavier than before. Blackridge Peak packlands weren't far. I could already sense the edges of their territory, the subtle shift in the air, as I got closer to their land.

I didn't know what I was going to say to her when I saw her again. I expected her to not want to see me, and after everything, I wouldn't blame her if she refused to talk to me. But the bond between us wouldn't let me stay away, and I could only hope that when I faced her, she was willing to listen.

The tall shifter Ned was waiting at the bottom of the mountain. I wasn't mistaken, he was definitely waiting for something, and I didn't need to guess at who he was waiting for.

He looked me over coldly, his sniff both derisive and dismissive. "Knew you wouldn't stay away for good."

"Disappointed?" I asked as I came to a stop a few feet from him.

"Disappointed I didn't have to travel to your packlands? Nah."

"Why would you be coming to Shadowridge Peak?" I decided to be casual, countering his barely restrained aggression.

"Because you need a good ass-kicking for what you've done to her." He pushed the sleeves of his sweater up. "I don't mind taking this one for the pack."

"You're seriously waiting at the bottom of Blackridge to kick my ass?" I asked, barely believing the words leaving my mouth.

"Damn right I am," he growled. And before I could respond, he lunged, his fist cutting through the air in a blur, aimed straight at me.

I barely ducked in time, his fist grazing the air an inch from my jaw. The momentum threw him off balance, but he recovered fast, circling me with the kind of ease that said he'd been waiting for this moment.

"What the hell, Ned?" I shouted, raising my hands defensively, my instincts kicking in.

"You're reckless, Caleb!" he barked, advancing again. "Do you even think about what you left behind?"

This time, I caught his next punch, the impact vibrating through my arm as I shoved him back. "I was doing what was best," I snarled, furious I had to explain myself to *him*.

"You don't get it, do you?" He shook his head, his lips curling in frustration. "She's not some passenger in your life, Caleb. She's part of it. You're dragging her into this mess and then expecting her to survive it alone!"

I stared at him, his words striking deeper than his fists could. For a second, the tension hung between us, charged and volatile.

"You think I don't know that?" I growled, stepping closer. "You think I don't wake up every damn day knowing I'm the reason she's in this position?"

"Then do something about it!" he roared, shoving me hard in the chest, knocking me back a step.

I stood there, chest heaving, as the truth in his words settled like a weight on my shoulders.

Ned dropped his fists, his voice quieter but no less cutting. "She's stronger than you think, but she's human, Caleb. She has limits."

I nodded once, swallowing hard. "You done now?"

"No."

The punch landed squarely on my jaw, snapping my head to the side. Pain flared instantly, a sharp realization of just how much strength Ned could pack into a single blow. Before I could recover, his follow-up—a short jab to my cheekbone—connected with brutal precision.

The crunch of bone echoed through the night, and I stumbled back a step, tasting blood as it filled my mouth. My wolf growled, pacing beneath my skin, but I forced it back, refusing to let instinct take over.

"Feel that, Caleb?" Ned demanded, his voice a low growl. He was circling me now, his fists still raised. "That's reality, punching you in the face. Wake the hell up!"

I spat blood onto the frozen ground, straightening with a grimace. "You done playing hero, or are you just getting started?" I muttered, rolling my shoulders.

Ned shook his head, his expression dark. "Not even close." He lunged again, and I barely had time to dodge his next punch, the air hissing as his fist whizzed past my ear.

"Dammit, Ned!" I snarled, swinging back on reflex. My fist connected with his side, the impact enough to make him grunt, but he barely flinched. "I don't want to hurt you!"

"You think this is about me?" he snapped, stepping in close and slamming his shoulder into mine, sending me sprawling backward into the snow.

I scrambled to my feet, wiping the blood from my lip with the back of my hand. "You think I don't know what I'm doing?"

"That's the problem, Caleb. You don't!" His voice was raw, shaking with fury. "You're about one bad decision away from losing it completely."

I exhaled sharply, the fire in my chest simmering down as the weight of his words sank in. "Fine," I muttered, my voice rough as I straightened. "Point made."

Ned smirked faintly, though his eyes were still hard. "Good. Next time, maybe I'll let you get the first hit."

"Next time, maybe I'll actually take it," I shot back, wiping the blood off my lip again.

And with that, he turned and walked away, leaving me standing in the cold, the echoes of his words burning hotter than the fight ever could.

She may be human, but Willow had a loyal pack behind her. I wondered if she even knew that. Spitting blood onto the snow once more, I felt the magic of Luna heal, and I started the climb up the mountain.

The black wolf was waiting for me, and I didn't slow as I approached the alpha of Blackridge Peak. Brilliant blue eyes watched me get closer, but I felt no malice.

"Alpha Cannon," I greeted as I stopped a few feet from him. "It's a cold night."

The wolf didn't blink. Instead, he walked around me, his muzzle too close to my neck for my liking, but I held my ground. I'd pissed him off, I knew that. He was an alpha protecting his pack.

I got it, I did. But still...

"You sniff me much more, and I will begin to question your loyalty to your mate."

Large jaws snapped dangerously close to my ear, and then he shifted to his human form. The fact Cannon was taller than me hadn't pissed me off until now.

"You done?"

"You come into my packlands, after what you did, with an attitude?"

He had a point. But also...fuck him. "Where is she?"

"I need to tell her you're here—"

"She knows." I watched as he pulled on sweatpants and a hoodie, zipping it over his naked chest, the cold not bothering him at all. "She can feel me as much as I feel her."

Cannon considered my words and then sniffed dismissively. "I don't give a fuck. I will *ask* her if she wants to see you."

"Fine." I walked towards the bunker when the alpha took hold of my arm and pulled me to a halt.

"You will wait here."

With a sharp twist of my body, I dislodged his hold. "You will kindly fuck off." I saw his eyes narrow and spoke over whatever protest he was about to give me. "I've already had a welcoming party; I'm pissed off and haven't punched *your* pack out of respect for *you*, but do not push me." I held my hand up, stopping his next words. "You know what's between us. You know what I am." I waited for his nod of acknowledgment. "I'm going to see her. You're welcome to be there, but I see her *now*."

"You order me in my own territory?"

Rolling my head on my shoulders, I considered my next words carefully. "It's not an order; I am *requesting* you to be beside me when I see her." I let that sink in. "I'm *asking* for you to be there."

"And I will be, but don't you think she needs some warning first? The choice to decide if she is ready to talk to you?"

"I don't have time for her to think about it," I muttered as we both resumed walking.

"Scared she's going to say no?"

"Fucking terrified."

That earned me a chuckle from Cannon, and I was glad he hadn't pushed the order that I was to remain behind. He wasn't someone I wanted as an enemy. He wasn't someone I would want as a friend either, but an ally? I could use an ally like Cannon.

My fight wasn't only to get Willow to forgive me, I still needed to know who hunted her. And why. The more help I had in that, the better. For Willow. And all I cared about right now was Willow.

"How do you feel?" Cannon asked me, his tone casual, his scent anything but.

"With my fingers."

He hesitated and then I heard his chuckle. I didn't dodge the punch to my arm. "Asshole."

I let the smile slip out in the darkness, knowing full well the alpha could see it.

"So? I'm waiting," he pressed.

"I feel like shit," I told him the truth. "Every day is a battle."

Silence enveloped us as we walked. "You're still fighting," he murmured. "Isn't that a good thing?"

"Is it?" I glanced upward as the moon came out of hiding. "She seems to think so," I told him, pointing to the moon.

"Then you must be doing something right," he said calmly. "Willow is healing well."

"Good."

"She still feels the pain," he added with no softness, but I'd learned quickly that wasn't his style. "Her wounds healed quickly, alarming for a human, I would add." I felt the weight of his side-eye but said nothing.

"The pain?"

"Doc thinks it's her body's way of trying to deal with the healing."

I glanced at him. "By making her feel the pain as if she was still suffering?"

Cannon shrugged. "I don't know. I know little about human pain, but it seems unfair that she gets healed but still has to suffer the phantom pain."

I felt my knees weaken, the reality at his bluntness resonating more than I expected. *Phantom pain.* I knew *exactly* what that was. The feeling of being healed on the outside but still torn apart on the inside. It was a cruelty that I'd never imagined she would have to bear.

"Like she's being punished..." I said, more to myself than to Cannon. My voice was low, broken. The idea that she was being made to feel pain because of me—that it may be some twisted consequence of our bond—cut deep.

Cannon didn't say anything for a moment, but when I glanced at him, I saw the same doubt flickering in his eyes that mirrored my own.

We exchanged a look, the question hanging between us. I once more cast a glance to the heavens, to the pale moon hidden behind the shifting clouds. The shaman had said this was Luna's Will, but was it her Will to make Willow suffer? I was no longer sure.

Maybe Luna wasn't as aligned as the shaman implied.

The doubt gnawed at me, dark and insidious. What if her pain wasn't just a side effect of the healing? What if it was something more deliberate? A cosmic test, or...Goddess forbid, a punishment? For my sins? For what I'd done?

My fists clenched tightly at my sides as the familiar anger rose inside me, hot and sharp. If that was true...if the Goddess was making her suffer because of me, then...then what the hell was the point? What was the point in saving her if she was going to have to live with the pain? Willow already lived with pain, and she didn't need any more of it.

Cannon picked up on my tension. "Maybe it's just a side effect that will fade," he told me, his voice gentler. "Maybe it's just...maybe it's what happens when someone gets caught in something they shouldn't."

I didn't respond to him, and I didn't think he expected me to. I knew deep down that this wasn't just *something* that happened. Not when it came to Willow. This was bigger than the blood I'd given her or the bond we shared.

This felt a lot like fate. My top lip curled. This was the Goddess's Will. Maybe Ned and Cannon were right; maybe I'd dragged Willow into something that she was never meant to endure.

But I was the one she was tied to. And now I had to find a way to make it right.

For her.

EIGHT

Willow

THE ROOM WAS TOO QUIET, THE KIND OF QUIET THAT made every breath feel as if it was too loud. I sat up in the bed, my legs tucked beneath me, my sketchbook lying forgotten on the covers beside me. The night held a strange stillness to it, like the world was holding its breath, waiting for something to happen.

Even the snow had stopped falling.

I wasn't sure what time it was, but I knew it wasn't too late. Time was different here in the bunker. I mean, obviously time wasn't different, it just seemed to pass differently. Some hours rushed past, while some dragged so slowly I could almost feel the seconds passing.

I'd spent most of yesterday mulling over the shaman's words. Between his first visit and his second, I wasn't sure he'd helped. He'd given me a mix of answers and riddles that left me more confused and uncertain than before. The explanation of the bond and the Goddess choosing me, at the time, had made sense. And now...well, now, none of it felt real.

None of it felt like it was me.

But there was something else. Something that I hadn't been able to shake all day.

My gaze dropped to my lap, where my hands lay, my fingers linked loosely, and it wouldn't take a doctor to see the slight tremble in them. I'd been feeling the bond more today. It felt like it was changing, morphing into something stronger. I'd tried to push it down, but every time I did, the itch that I couldn't scratch thrummed under my skin.

It had been subtle at first. I was almost used to the steady hum beneath my skin, but this morning, it started to change. It pulled at the edges of my awareness, like the ghost of a forgotten touch. But throughout the day, it had become more than that.

I could feel him.

Not in the way I felt people when they were close by, but in a deeper, quieter way that was like he was there in the back of my mind. I didn't know if it was my imagination. Maybe since talking to the shaman, I'd bought into his theories. Or maybe this was real? All I knew was that it felt stronger tonight.

The bond felt alive. I could almost hear it whispering to me that Caleb was nearby.

I closed my eyes to contain the wild hope that surged within me at the thought of him coming here.

Or maybe you've finally lost your mind.

Maybe the connection had finally driven me crazy. Did I even know what was real anymore? Between the pain from my injuries, the phantom ache in my chest, and this strange new awareness of Caleb, it was all too much.

Yet, as I sat there, my eyes still closed tightly, I felt it again—*him.*

His presence was like a shadow stretching across the room,

and my heartbeat quickened as a soft flutter of panic and anticipation shot through me.

I wasn't losing it.

Caleb was close. I would bet my life on it.

The bond tightened and became more insistent. My skin prickled with awareness, and I found myself straightening, smoothing down my hair, hoping it looked decent.

A wave of fear washed over me, and I pressed the palms of my hands against my stomach to soothe the churning in my belly. For days, I'd waited for this moment. I'd feared it, longed for it, and demanded it. Now that I thought it was here? I didn't know what to do.

Did I want to see him again?

Yes.

The answer came quickly, unbidden, and without thought. A normal person would question it. A normal person would remember the anger, the hurt, and the sense of betrayal. But either I wasn't normal or I didn't care. There was more to Caleb and me, and it had been growing ever since the day I first met him.

Opening my eyes, I felt the room become smaller as I struggled to control my racing heart. I could feel the weight of his presence bearing down on me, like the storm building on the horizon, and I knew I wasn't ready. Pushing the sketchbook further away from me, I swung my legs over the edge of the bed, my feet hitting the cold floor with a soft thud.

The air shifted around me, becoming tighter, and my breath caught in my throat. My skin tingled with the awareness of him, the bond humming to life.

He was here.

Before I could even process it all, the door pushed open

silently, a slow deliberate push that sent a chill down my spine as the coldness of outside seeped into my room. My blood rushed in my ears as my gaze stayed fixed on the door.

Caleb stood in the doorway, his broad frame filling the space, his face half-hidden in the shadows. His eyes found mine instantly, and for a moment, everything else fell away. The room, the pain, the confusion...it all disappeared, and all that was left was the two of us.

The connection between us snapped into focus, sharper and clearer than ever before. I could feel him. Not just his presence, but his emotions too—faint and distant but there.

His guilt. His anguish. And the raw need that coursed through him.

My chest felt tight as I drank him in, my body a mess of emotions surging inside me all at once.

I didn't know what to say.

I didn't know what to do.

I wanted to cross the distance, run to him, throw my arms around him, and never let go, but my mind was screaming to keep my distance.

I saw his eyes darken, his jaw tightening as if he could feel the hesitation, my confusion. He took a deliberate step into the room, murmuring something too low for me to hear as he pushed the door closed, and I wondered who he had locked out. The small sound of the lock clicking echoed in the silence between us.

"Willow," he greeted me, his voice low and rough around the edges.

Just hearing him say my name sent a shiver down my spine, goose bumps breaking over my skin. I swallowed hard, my throat dry as I struggled to speak. I felt frozen, and I was scared of what would come out if I spoke.

Caleb didn't seem to expect me to speak. He was looking me over, looking for what? Signs of my injury?

The bond was strumming between us. It felt alive and electric.

Happy.

That jarred me. It really felt like a living thing, pulsing with every beat of my heart. Did he feel this too? Was it as strong for him as it was for me?

I wanted to ask him, and I finally managed to speak, my voice barely a whisper. "Why are you here?"

I felt my eyes widen in shock. That was not what I had thought I was going to say.

Caleb's eyes flickered with something—regret, maybe? Or shame? It was hard to tell in the shadows, with the light behind him. He took another step forward, carefully, deliberately keeping his movements slow, like he was afraid of scaring me.

Or maybe he was afraid to come closer.

"I needed to see you," he said, his voice thick with emotion. "I tried..." He blew out a breath. "I tried to stay away, but..." His hands raised and then fell to his sides helplessly. "I couldn't stay away."

The air between us was thick and heavy with so many unspoken things. My heart had leapt at his words, but my body had remained rooted to the spot, wary. It knew he had almost killed me. It knew that it was his blood that was the only reason I was still standing. Still breathing. Once more, I saw the wildness in his eyes as he fought his demons that night, never realizing until it was too late, that the only thing he was striking as he fought...was me.

"Should you have come?" Even when the question left my mouth, I knew the answer was yes. I'd been waiting for this. For him. I'd been aching for him no matter how much I wanted to deny it.

"Honestly?" he asked, his voice a low rasp that made me want to drown in it. "I don't know." His look was steady as he watched me. "But I couldn't stay away any longer."

Did he know what that did to me? That admission of weakness from him? My stubborn body finally gave in, and I took a step forward before catching myself.

"Caleb..." My voice was barely a whisper, and even as his name left my lips, I longed to be closer to him. The distance, the pain, the betrayal...it was all still there, lingering in the space that separated us.

But so was *everything* else. That primal and desperate need that pulled us together even when I didn't want to admit it. But I couldn't *deny* it.

Caleb's eyes darkened, and an emotion crossed his face that set my heart to racing. The way he looked at me like I was the only thing that was tethering him to this world was causing havoc within me.

"Caleb..." I took a step back. I had to keep my walls up; at this rate they were in danger of crumbling completely. "Don't do this to me..."

"What am I doing?" he asked softly, his voice one of confusion and something else, something that reminded me of our time in the car. "I never meant to hurt you," he spoke softly, gently, but the guilt was heavy. "I'm so sorry."

My feet reclaimed the step forward, and I no longer knew who was in control, my brain or my heart. The pull towards him was like gravity, impossible to fight as I moved closer.

Now I was right in front of him, so close that I could feel the heat radiating from his body. My heart was pounding out a wild, frantic rhythm that matched the chaos in my mind. I didn't know what I wanted. I didn't know if I should push him away or pull him even closer. All I knew was I couldn't stand this distance between us.

Caleb's gaze dropped to my lips, and my breath caught in my throat.

"Why don't you hate me?" he murmured, the words sounding harsh as he focused on my mouth. His hand reached out, hesitant, doubting he had the right to touch me, but the pull between us was pulsing.

"I could never hate you, Caleb." My voice was shaking. It made me sound vulnerable, but he heard the truth in my words. It was true, I didn't hate him.

His thumb brushed across my cheek, the roughness of his skin sending another shiver down my spine. My body once more betrayed me, leaning into his touch even though I wanted to step back. It was too soon. There was so much more we needed to talk about, but...Caleb was *here*. He had come back. He was here for me, and the way he was looking at me...

"Willow—"

Before I could second-guess myself, I closed the distance between us. Pushing up on my toes, I pulled his head down at the same time, and my lips crashed against his in a kiss that felt like a mix of desperation and surrender.

The kiss was raw, full of everything we hadn't said, everything that I hadn't been able to put into words. Caleb's hands gripped my waist, pulling me closer, keeping me tight against his hard body as I clung to him. It felt like he was the only thing keeping me from falling apart.

His mouth moved over mine, soft but firm, punishing but begging for forgiveness. Our tongues tasted each other, and I felt his hand slip down and squeeze my ass. I wanted to climb his body like a tree. I wanted to lie back and have him claim me once more.

Caleb caught my lower lip between his teeth, and my hands tugged at his hair, the moan drowning in my throat as he lifted me and my legs wrapped around his waist. Caleb turned, and I was pressed against the wall. I felt his hand cup the back of my neck as the other trailed down my side, leaving a trail of goose bumps behind it.

I was gasping as Caleb dipped his head to taste my skin. His lips moved over my neck, nipping at my pulse. My back was pressed even harder into the wall, but the dull ache was nothing as the fire between us consumed me. My hands knotted in his hair, pulling him up, back to my mouth. Our tongues twisted together as the kiss deepened. I felt his warm palm push my shirt up, his fingers skimming over my back and dipping under my pants.

My head tilted back when Caleb's fingers skimmed over my bare ass, trailing back over my hip to the front, dipping lower, finding my wetness. His groan against my neck as he kissed a scorching trail down my throat was going to be my undoing. I was sure I was going to combust when his thumb brushed over my nipple, and as much as I wanted to lose myself in him, part of me couldn't forget.

The ache in my abdomen was the memory of what he'd done. As much as I wanted this, it wasn't that simple.

Breaking the kiss, my breath coming in sharp gasps, I pulled back, my forehead dropping to rest on his shoulder. Caleb's arms tightened around me for a moment, and then he loosened his grip, letting my legs fall from his waist, and he supported me as I lowered them to the floor.

My fingers twisted into the fabric of his shirt, hating myself for stopping but knowing I was doing the right thing. "We can't..." My voice was throaty, the lingering passion making me sound husky. I pressed my head into his chest. "We can't pretend that nothing happened."

"I know, and I don't want to," he told me, the strain in his voice evident. He pressed his lips to the top of my head. "But I can't pretend that I don't need you. I've tried that, and it damn near tore me apart."

Tilting my head back just enough to be able to look up at him, I could feel my heart still pounding against his. Caleb looked down at me, his eyes searching mine, open and filled with a vulnerability I hadn't seen before. I knew he was telling the truth. He *did* need me.

Just as much as I needed him.

But that didn't make everything okay.

"I don't think I can trust you," I told him, hating the way the mask fell over his face so quickly. "I don't know if I trust *us*. Or this bond."

I saw him wince, but he didn't look away. "I don't expect forgiveness," he admitted, standing back, putting space between us. "I know I fucked up. I never, ever meant to hurt you. I'll do whatever it takes to make you trust me, just..." He ran his hand through his hair. "Try not to shut me out."

I could hear the sincerity in his voice. I couldn't remember a time when I felt that he was this honest with me. I wanted to cling to it, but I also remembered waking up alone after he had stabbed me with his claws.

"We have a lot to think about," I told him. "So much to try and make sense of."

"We do." He was watching me carefully, waiting for what, I wasn't sure.

"I think it's good you're here," I told him honestly, "but this"—I waved my hand between us—"I don't think this is a good idea."

He nodded, his eyes guarded as he took a small step back, giving me even more space. "Whatever you want."

If I knew what I wanted, then this would be a heck of a lot easier.

"I truly am sorry I hurt you," he said, his voice sounding firmer, solider. "It was never..." He pushed his hair back in frustration. "You were never meant to get hurt."

"I know." And I did know, it's what I'd been trying to tell the others. "I know you weren't yourself when it happened."

He broke eye contact, his glare fierce as he fixed it on the unoffending nightlight. "It will *never* happen again."

I wanted to ask if he was sure, but instead, I simply acknowledged his words with a dip of my head. It felt like a promise, but it didn't fix anything. He was still haunted, and I was still bonded to him.

"How did you do it?" I asked him, walking back to the bed and leaning against it, glad I no longer sounded like a panting hussy.

"Do what?" Caleb asked me carefully.

"Heal me." I kept my gaze trained on him, ready to read his tells. Not that he had many. "How did you know your blood would save me?"

Caleb

THE QUESTION HUNG IN THE AIR BETWEEN US, SHARP and heavy, like the weight of all the unspoken things between us. My throat tightened, and for a moment, I didn't know how to answer her. The kiss we'd just shared still lingered, I could still taste her, and I still wanted to reach out and kiss her again. My body craved her, and I was having a hard time adjusting from the need to claim her to her desire to talk, like she just hadn't been wrapped around me, dripping wet for me.

She sat on the bed, pushing herself back, her legs folded under her, and I tried not to notice her slim legs or the stretch of the material as it clung to her curves. When I looked up at her, her eyes were on mine, unwavering. She was strong, stronger than perhaps I gave her credit for. But she was also vulnerable in a way that made me want to protect her from everything.

Especially from me.

"Caleb, are you listening?" Her voice was soft, but there was a touch of steel underneath. "How did you know your blood would save me?"

I didn't. That was the truth. I hadn't known anything in that moment; all I'd had was the desperate fear of losing her and an old cautionary tale from a grandmother who walked too close to the wild side for my mother's comfort. A spell so old and forbidden that only the old ones knew of it.

"I didn't know," I told her quietly. It wasn't even a lie. I had been clutching at anything to keep her with me. I hadn't even known I remembered the words of the incantation. I wouldn't bet my life on remembering them now. "I acted recklessly." Also true.

Willow blinked, her surprise flickering across her face. I could tell she hadn't expected that answer. Hell, I was no longer sure what she did expect. But she deserved the truth, as much as I could share, and no one ever claimed the truth wasn't ugly.

"You didn't know." Her voice trembled slightly, though she was doing her best to keep it steady. "You didn't know it worked?" Her eyes took on a harder edge. "When you left, you didn't know I was still alive?"

I ran a hand over my face, the familiar burn of guilt settling in my chest. How did I explain it to her? How did I tell her that I was lost to the darkness and no longer in control? That the beast within me had been on the verge of taking over?

But...she wasn't asking me about that. She was asking why I had given her blood, why I had made a decision that was contrary to everything she knew and had been told about shifters.

"I had no choice," I told her honestly. My voice sounded rough and I hoped she didn't hear the self-loathing that haunted me since that night. "You were dying, Willow. I couldn't let you die and do...nothing." I looked up, my eyes locking onto hers, hoping she understood. "I wasn't thinking straight, I just knew..."

"Knew what?" The steel was in her voice now, and I deserved it.

"I knew I couldn't lose you."

She flinched, looking away from me, but not before I saw the confusion in her eyes. The uncertainty.

I felt the flicker of something deeper, the unspoken connection between us that had always been there. Not the bond, or the link, or whatever the fuck we were calling it today. The more basic connection, the attraction.

"Did you know your blood wouldn't change me?" she asked me suddenly. "That I would still be human?"

"Of course." This part, I fully understood. You couldn't *turn* someone; that was a Hollywood storyline, not reality. What you could do was tie their life to yours. I'd be damned if I told her that, though. "You have to remember," I told her, stepping closer, "it wasn't just my blood, Willow. The connection between us is the Will of Luna, and there was more than my blood at play that night."

Willow was watching me, studying me, probably trying to sniff out any of my usual bullshit. I watched her back, calmly, watching the frown line deepen as her confusion grew.

"You believe your Goddess stepped in and that I'm here as some form of divine intervention?"

Divine intervention, and some really dark blood magic.

Despite that, I nodded. "I do."

Willow sniffed. "The shaman believes your Goddess is behind all this." She looked down at her pants legs, smoothing them over her thighs, distracting me slightly. "He says that the blood and the bond are what healed me. He says because I'm human, it's why Luna chose me. He says I ground you when a pack cannot."

I knew I was frowning. "The shaman says a lot," I mused. "So, he told you that my blood healed you because of the bond, and it's what the Goddess wants?"

I watched her nod, her movement hesitant, as if she was picking up on the fact I may not be a believer. "You're an alpha," she whispered. "Your bloodline is important. The Goddess doesn't want to lose that."

And how in the hell did tethering me to Willow preserve my bloodline? Seriously, was anyone buying this shit? I saw her eyes widen, doubt swirling in her green eyes as she tried to tell me that there was some greater reason behind all this than the actual truth.

"Is it not true?"

How did I answer that? Truthfully? Fuck no. "I don't know." Which *was* true, I wasn't one hundred percent sure that it was bullshit. I also wasn't one hundred percent sure it wasn't. "I know that you're alive"—I gestured to her midriff—"and healed. And that's all that matters."

"That's all that matters?" she asked skeptically.

I held in my sigh. I wanted to tell her I'd been asking myself the same thing. I wanted to tell her none of it made sense. That we were even connected to begin with still made no sense to me. I wanted to tell her that the pull I felt towards her, the need to protect her, to *be* with her, was stronger than anything I had ever felt in my life.

And that feeling terrified me.

"You being alive, unharmed, is all that matters," I told her instead. "I won't ask for forgiveness—I don't deserve it—but I want you to know that I am so thankful that you are."

"Thankful." Her gaze hardened. I saw the way her shoulders straightened, the way her eyes narrowed. "You're *thankful*."

Fuck. What had I said wrong this time? "You think I'm not grateful?"

Anger flashed in her eyes, and I had no clue how I had made this worse. "Thankful. Grateful. Any other adjective you want to throw at me?"

I knew my face showed my surprise at her outburst. "What have I said to piss you off?" I asked her cautiously. "I never meant to hurt you. The fact I almost killed you, the fact you're still here, yes, I'm eternally grateful." Shoving my hands into my pockets, I watched her. "You should have never been involved in this, and the fact that you can walk away is all that matters."

"Walk away?" Well, that went down like a red flag to a bull. She was on her feet. "You think with this connection between us, I can *walk away*?"

So that was what was wrong? She didn't want to be tethered to me? *That* I understood. "I know it's going to be difficult to start with, but hopefully, with time, we may not even notice it anymore."

I'd never seen Willow so close to losing her shit completely, but I was pretty sure she was about to explode.

"What does it feel like for you?" she asked me suddenly. "The bond. Describe it."

I shook my head helplessly as I thought about it. "I dunno, a...a pull."

"A pull?" Her arms folded across her chest, and her foot began to tap against the floor. "That's it? What kind of pull? A strong pull? Weak? Warm? Comforting? Irritating?" The last was asked with a look that didn't need further explanation.

I shrugged. "Just a pull."

Willow screeched and I ducked to miss the sketchbook as she hurled it across the room at me. Wildly she looked around, and I knew she was looking for something else to throw. In two strides, I had her arms pinned to her sides, trying to avoid the thrashing of her head from side to side.

"Will you calm down?" I asked through clenched teeth as the little vixen kicked me. "What the fuck is wrong with you?"

With an almighty shove, Willow broke free, putting distance between us. She faced me, her chest rising rapidly as she panted, her glare fixed on me. "A pull?" Her voice pulsed with anger. "I go through all *this*, and you feel *nothing* but *a pull*?"

She actually let out a growl, and when she saw me start to smile, I hastily wiped my face clear of emotion.

"Is this the part where you tell me what it feels like for you?"

Willow shook her head, turning her back to me and wrapping her arms around herself. "Why? You obviously don't feel the same." The amount of bitterness in her voice made me frown.

Slowly, I approached her. Her back stiffened as she heard me approach, but she didn't turn around or stop me. Tentatively, I reached out, my hands landing lightly on her shoulders, feeling her tense beneath me. My grip tightened and relaxed as I rubbed her shoulders.

"The pull I feel, it's constant," I admitted softly. "It tugs at me every second." I moved her hair aside, my nose trailing over her neck, inhaling the fresh scent of her. "It used to be...fragile," I explained as I searched for the right words. "Now, it's stronger than rope. Thicker, too. It feels unbreakable." My lips tasted her skin. "It's within me, buried deep, right here." My hand slipped between her arm and her side, trailing over the material of her top, loving the sound of her quickened breathing, coming around to her front, and resting lightly on her chest, between her breasts. "Right here," I said, pressing lightly.

I heard her shaky inhale and stepped closer to her, pressing her firmly against me. "It sits there, every moment of the day, reminding me that you're here." My head dipped, my forehead resting on her shoulder as I covered her back with my body. "Telling me you're *mine*."

"Caleb..."

I squeezed my eyes shut. "I know what I did to you." No, that wasn't right. "What I've *done* to you. I will spend the rest of my life fighting for your forgiveness. I don't deserve it, I know that, but I will earn your trust again, Willow. I swear it."

I felt a tear drip onto my hand, and I fought the urge to spin her around in my arms and kiss her tears away. Instead, I loosened my hold and stepped back. "That's what it feels like," I mumbled as I moved away. "That's the pull I feel."

Willow turned, her eyes soft and wet with more tears. She sniffled, rubbing her nose with the back of her hand. "You could have led with that," she protested weakly.

My smile broke free, and I saw the answering flush of her cheeks. "I'm not good with words," I mumbled, feeling self-conscious. Open. Exposed.

Willow blew her nose, her eyebrow quirking at my confession. "If you say words like that," she told me with a light chuckle, "you'll have anyone eating out of the palm of your hand."

It was meant as a joke, but it made me frown. "I meant them."

Her smile faded as she noticed the change in my demeanor. "I know," she told me gently. "I know."

We stood like that for a moment, the pull tugging at my insides insistently, as if it wanted me to close the short gap between us.

"It's why you're here?" she asked. Stooping, she picked up her thrown sketchbook.

"A bit," I admitted. "And I needed to see you with my own eyes. See you standing on two feet."

"I'm okay," she assured me. "Thanks to you."

"Not just me," I reminded her.

Willow rolled her eyes, but I knew she was more than aware that there was something more happening here.

"You okay?" I asked her.

"I don't know," she answered truthfully. "I don't know how to live with...this. This connection. Doesn't it feel like it's too much to you?"

Her words hit me harder than I expected. Was she rejecting the bond? Panic flared within me at the thought of what would happen if she succeeded. "I know it's a lot." I kept my voice calm and measured. "But I'm here, you're not alone. I'm not going anywhere."

Her eyes searched mine, and for a second, I saw the flicker of vulnerability. She was scared. Scared of what this bond meant and scared of how it could change her life.

And if I was honest, I knew she was scared of me. Of what I was capable of.

"I will never hurt you again," I told her, moving until I was standing right in front of her, looking down at her. "I can't promise you much in this life, Willow, but I promise you that. Never again."

Her breathing was shaky, but she never pulled away. The tension thickened between us, less about fear and more about everything else that remained unspoken between us.

"I never blamed you," she told me softly, her gaze dropped to the floor. "But..."

"But you don't trust me," I finished her sentence. Reaching out, my finger slipped under her chin, tilting her head back so she had to look at me. "I will earn that back. I'll fight for it, for you, every damn day."

I saw the battle that played out inside her, felt her struggle through the bond that tied us, as she struggled between her heart and her head. I knew she wanted to believe me. I could see it in the way she looked at me, in the way she never pulled away from my touch. But I could also see the hurt, and I knew she needed to work through it all.

Letting my hand drop from her chin, I stepped back so I wasn't crowding her, giving her her space. Knowing that she needed it. This wasn't going to be easy. I knew that, but I meant what I said. I wasn't going to lose her. I'd come so close to losing her that I would *never* let that happen.

"You need time," I told her, "and I know that. When you're ready, I'll be waiting."

"You're leaving?" I felt the spike of worry through the bond, and it almost made me smile.

"I'll be here," I assured her. "We have a lot to figure out, and I also need to know who was chasing you. Hunting you. There's still so much we don't know."

"I need to go home," Willow whispered, almost apologetically. "I have the art studio, my home, my friends."

"Then you'll go back to Whispering Pines." It wasn't ideal,

but some time and distance between me and pack couldn't be bad.

I saw her swallow. "And...where will you be?"

"With you."

I could almost feel the relief she tried to hide. She wasn't ready to let me in completely, not yet, but she wasn't willing to let me go either.

And that was enough. For now.

TEN

Caleb

I sat in the chair, in the corner of the room, saying nothing as Willow made her case to leave Blackridge Peak to Doc.

"I want to go back home," she told him, her voice calm but firm. She stood a few feet away from me, arms crossed, her gaze steady on Doc, purposely not looking my way. Her whole stance was daring him to argue with her, and I hid my smile behind my hand as I knew that he would.

"No."

Willow's eyebrows shot up, glancing at me once, but I said nothing, and she looked back at Doc. "What do you mean no?" She took a deep breath. "You can't just say no." Her tone was getting sharper. "This is my life, it's *my* decision."

Doc shot me a look, but I remained silent. Did he think I was going to go against her wishes? Had he learned nothing? This was Basic Female 101. I wasn't going to say a word.

I watched him try to temper his words. "You're not ready, Willow." He tried so hard to sound patient. I wondered if he knew he was failing? "You're still learning how to deal with all…" He waved his hand towards me. "This."

I was a *this*? Interesting.

"I feel fine."

My stubborn, determined girl. My lips twitched and I knew Doc saw it.

"Is this your idea?" he accused me, his frown of disapproval clear.

"This is *my* choice," Willow ground out, refusing to back down. "It has nothing to do with Caleb."

It had everything to do with me, and we all knew it.

Doc pinched the bridge of his nose as he took a deep breath. "You don't know what's out there. You don't know if the shifters after you are still after you. You don't know who was targeting you." He inhaled deeply, calming himself. "You don't even know *why*. Until we figure that out, you can't just go running back there. It's not safe."

"I'm not running," Willow snapped. "I'm trying to get my life back on track. I can't stay in your bunker forever, hiding away like some, like some, *damsel*. This is my life, Doc."

"You're being naive," Doc snapped back, equally as frustrated as she seemed to be.

I saw her reaction to his words, and damn, I wished I had popcorn. Shit was about to go down.

"I'm being *naive*?"

Yup, she was going to lose it.

"You think I don't know that the danger is still out there?" Her voice was getting higher, her eyes narrowed in anger. "You think I'm running away? You think I'm being reckless?" She didn't give him the chance to respond, her hands on her hips.

"Think what you like, but I *can't* go on like this. I have a business. A life. Responsibilities. I appreciate everything you have done for me, but, Doc? Me and this room, it can't go on forever."

Doc's teeth ground together, and I watched as he struggled to find the words. "I've known you a few months, and of that few, you have been in the hospital *twice*."

I wondered how much control it took for him not to look at me as he spoke.

"You are not safe, Willow," he added.

I couldn't call him a liar, every word was true, and the unspoken allegation that this was my fault was probably a correct one. Doc's words didn't bother me, but they bothered my girl.

"Is anyone ever safe?" she demanded. "I'm not helpless," she added, finally looking at me. "This isn't his fault," she said emphatically, glancing at me before turning back to Doc and playing her trump card. "And Caleb is coming with me."

She looked at me with such faith that my smile broke free.

"Well then, that's alright, then," Doc spat. "Are we forgetting that Caleb is the reason you were in that bed this time?"

He went there. Interesting. I may need to look into his relationship with Willow after all.

"I know you want to protect me," Willow said, her voice soft now. "And you have, Doc, and you have done so much for me, and I thank you for that." She inhaled deeply. "But I can't live in this world of yours. I can't constantly look over my shoulder, waiting for the next attack. I need normal. I *need* to go home."

"And Caleb brings you normal?"

I'd had enough. "You sound jealous," I mused, speaking for

the first time. "Is there more to this than you being a healthcare provider?"

"A healthcare provider?" he snapped angrily. "I'm her *doctor*."

"And she's no longer sick," I reminded him plainly. "Willow is healed, she's not a shifter, she is not pack, and she wants to go home. She told you as a courtesy, but you can't stop her."

"And you think you can protect her?"

"She wants to go back, and I'm going with her," I told him.

His eyes flicked between the two of us, the tension between us thickening as he processed what she wanted.

"I need to talk to the alpha," he said, heading for the door.

"You're talking to him," I reminded him with a slow drawl. "Willow wants to leave. End of conversation."

He stood there, fuming silently, and then he marched out of the room, the door slamming behind him.

"He's just protective," Willow murmured. "It's nice that he cares." She glanced at me, her cheeks reddening.

"You like that he cares...so much?" It was the best way to word it. Did Willow want his attention? Did she relish it?

"It's nice to have *friends*." She emphasized the word *friends*, and I felt the knot inside me loosen. "It reminds me that I'm normal."

Normal. I almost laughed at her. There was no *normal* for Willow anymore, not after everything that had happened. And definitely not with her tied to me. But I understood what she was striving to return to. The *feeling* of normalcy was the reason she wanted her old life back, why she wanted to go back to her store. She wanted something that didn't feel like it was controlled by shifters or packs or, dare I say, me.

"It may have actually made him worse to tell him I was

accompanying you." I stood from the chair, stretching languidly. I could feel her eyes traveling over my body, thinking I wasn't aware of her appraisal. "You're drooling," I teased lightly, watching her eyes snap to mine, her cheeks flaming at being caught.

"Ass." Turning away from me, she pretended to busy herself straightening her bed. "You know, you coming with me," she began, "it's not really giving me space."

"Mm-hmm, space means nothing to our connection. I may as well be close at hand." I watched her hands still as she listened. "Doc was right, you're still being hunted, Willow. I know you want to go home, but going back without me? Not an option."

"I'll be careful—"

"I know. I'll make sure of it."

"So, you're going to hover over me all the time?"

I swallowed the words I wanted to say, the ones that would have told her I wasn't hovering, I was protecting her. But they sounded hypocritical when I was the one who'd brought the most danger to her. Instead, I gave her a wicked smile, my gaze trailing slowly down her body. "I could hover over you all night long," I told her suggestively.

"Hound," she muttered, looking away from my heated gaze.

"Wolf," I corrected. She wet her bottom lip, refusing to meet my eyes. "I'm not taking away your choice," I reminded her. "But leaving you alone, it's not an option. Not until I know who's behind your break-ins and for putting you in the hospital." I saw her arch her brow. "The first time," I clarified. "Until you're safe, I stay."

"And if you figure it out, what happens then? What

happens when I'm *safe*." Her fingers clipped out the air quotes, and I hid my smile at her sass.

"I don't have an answer for that," I told her honestly. There was no *after* in my head anymore when it came to Willow. "Let's focus on one thing at a time, okay?"

She let out a slow breath, her shoulders sagging a little. "One thing at a time," Willow repeated. "And dare I ask...but... us? I can't keep feeling like I'm trapped in something I don't understand."

"Trapped?" Her words hurt more than they were meant, I was sure. "I would never want that," I said slowly. "I'll give you your space, but I will not leave you."

Her small weary smile didn't reach her eyes. "That's the best I'm going to get, isn't it?"

"I'm not a miracle worker," I said, sitting back down, trying to give her the distance she wanted.

"You miraculously healed me," she murmured, her lips twitching, and I wondered if she knew how amazing she was. Here she was, making jokes with me, defending me in front of Doc, when I was the reason she'd almost died.

"After being the reason you needed healing to start with."

Her frown marred her features, a reminder that things were not clear between us.

Willow leaned against the bed, her hip resting against the rail as she tried to appear casual. Her attempt failed miserably, and it accentuated how badly she failed when she crossed her arms in that stubborn way that made me want to tear my hair out and also pull her closer.

"Should we address the elephant in the room?" The challenge was clear in her eyes. She was definitely feeling feisty this evening.

"There's an elephant?"

She shot me a look and I stopped myself from grinning at provoking her. "I need to know something."

I suddenly didn't like where this was going. "And what's that?"

Her gaze flicked over me, trying to read me. "The connection between us..." She hesitated, her tongue flicking out to wet her lips. "It's getting stronger, isn't it?"

"Yes," I admitted. "Doesn't help when you keep distracting me with that tongue." I didn't hide the roughness of my voice. She needed to know how she affected me.

Willow immediately clamped her mouth shut, her lips pressing into a thin line. "Sorry." She had nothing to apologize for. "With you so close, it's even stronger. It's like I can reach out and touch it."

I nodded because I felt the same. The pull to be near her, to protect her, to just...be with her. The physical need to touch her, claim her, consume her. It was getting deeper, burrowing inside me, taking root.

"It's the bond," I explained after a moment, the words heavy. "We both know when I gave you my blood, it strengthened the connection, and I guess...being so close to you only makes it"—it was my turn to wet my lips as my mouth ran dry—"harder."

Heat pooled in her eyes, and I fought back the groan as her scent permeated the room.

"I don't think it's just the blood," I carried on, focusing on anything but the signals her body was giving me. "We were already attracted to each other." I motioned between us. "This pull was there before it got more complicated."

"You're saying it was always going to happen?"

"I know you were in that car with me," I murmured, seeing her flush again. "I think the blood just accelerated what we already felt."

She didn't say anything, but I could see the questions swirling behind her eyes. I wanted to explain more, to tell her how a bond like this worked and how it would affect us, but the truth was, I had no idea how to explain it. Because I didn't understand it myself. Not when she was human. The things we were feeling shouldn't be like this when she wasn't a shifter. This was more like a mate bond, and I knew we could never be mates.

"Can we stop it?"

Fuck no. My possessiveness shocked me, and it took me a moment to control my reaction, which Willow completely misinterpreted.

"I didn't mean to offend you," she spoke quickly. "I just wondered if it was something we're stuck with."

Again, the words shouldn't have hurt, but they did. The idea that she wanted to stop what was happening between us, that she didn't want to be mine, was a blow I wasn't prepared for. But I kept my expression neutral, not letting her see how deep her words cut.

"The bond is part of us," I said, my voice steady. "There's no stopping it."

Willow frowned, her gaze moving off of mine. "So, what are you saying? We're tied together. You and me? Like it or not?"

I knew why she would feel like that. I mean, who wanted to be tied to the man who shredded his claws into her? I couldn't blame her. This wasn't what she would choose, I understood. She probably felt trapped. I would too if I were in her shoes.

"I know it feels like a lot," I said, taking a step closer to her.

"But it doesn't have to be a bad thing. Our connection, it's about protection, not about controlling you. It's something more—"

"More how?" She looked up at me, her expression a mixture of confusion and something else, something that looked a lot like desire. "What are you saying, Caleb?"

How did I put into words the way I felt about her? The pull, the need, the *want*. It was more than the bond, it was *her*.

It had always been her.

Everything about her called to me in a way I'd never experienced before. But how did I *say* that? Me? The man who punctured her abdomen and almost killed her. I didn't have the right to lay that at her feet, not now. Probably not ever. Not when she was still trying to figure out her place in her new reality.

"I'm saying..." What the fuck was I saying? "I'm saying I'll be there no matter what. Bond or no bond, you have my protection."

Those light green eyes of hers searched mine like she was trying to figure out what I was holding back. But I held her stare, saying nothing, because the last thing I wanted to do was make her feel like this wasn't her choice.

"You make me sound like a burden," she said, not bothering to hide her disappointment. "I don't want you to feel like you're tied to me because of some bond."

"You're not a burden." Frustration flared within me. Didn't she see how poorly I was hanging on to my control and not taking all her clothes off and sinking inside her? She wasn't an obligation, she was a temptation. "I want to be where you are."

Her breath hitched, and I cursed inwardly at letting that slip. Her eyes were wide with emotions she wasn't ready to admit and I wasn't admitting to feeling. At least, not out loud. I closed the distance between us, close enough that I could feel the heat of her body, the smell of her skin, the scent of her arousal that was going to drive me to the edge.

"Caleb?" Her voice was shaking and I felt the vibrations in my blood.

Reaching out, I cupped her face gently. My thumb brushed over her bottom lip, plump and juicy. I wanted to sink my teeth into it. I shouldn't be touching her, but the need to make contact with her skin was stronger than the logic to step back and not overwhelm her.

"I'm here, not because of a bond, but because I *want* to be. Understand?"

Her gaze dropped to my lips, a look of hunger in her eyes that made my pulse quicken. She was letting me in, letting me see her desire, and it made me want to close the distance, pull her into me, and kiss her until there was no doubt I was here for her. *Only* for her.

But to do that would be the complete opposite of everything that I had just told her. Told myself.

I dropped my hands, stepping back, barely holding on to my control. "We'll figure this out," I told her. "Together, right?"

Willow cleared her throat, her chin dropping, avoiding my eyes. "Yeah, of course. We make a good team."

A team? We were so much more than a team.

Willow focused on the wall. "You should get some rest," she said quickly. "I think the snow's finally stopped. We can talk more later, but if we want to leave in the morning, we should rest."

I dipped my chin in acknowledgment. The tension lay between us, thick and unresolved, but that was enough for tonight. She was doing so well, so strong. I walked to the door.

Glancing back at her, I saw her arms wrapping around herself like she was holding herself together.

"Where will you sleep?" she asked suddenly.

"I'm resourceful," I said with a smile. "Don't worry about it."

Willow looked at the chair. "Um, if you wanted?" She didn't meet my eyes. "The chair will be free."

"If you don't mind?" I asked, dropping my hand from the door handle.

"No, of course not. It's not like we haven't slept in the same place before."

"Then I guess I'll take the chair."

Willow gulped but pretended this wasn't a dangerous situation. "I'll just wash up first," she mumbled, practically running to the bathroom.

After she flicked the lock, I smiled as I heard her muttering to herself in the bathroom. Shirking off my jacket, I kicked off my boots, getting comfortable in the chair.

I could sleep in the same room and not touch her. I'd done it before. This would be fine. I wasn't an animal. I could control my impulses.

Closing my eyes, I was sure I had everything under control until my eyes snapped open, my body tensing.

From across the room, originating from the bathroom, came an unmistakable scent.

Fuck.

ELEVEN

Willow

I LEANED AGAINST THE BATHROOM SINK, GRIPPING the cool porcelain with shaky hands, trying to steady my breathing.

This was insanity. None of this was normal.

I'd turned the water off, but I hadn't moved. My pulse was racing, my skin was tingling, and it wasn't from the cold. Leaning over, I turned the shower on. Looking down at myself, I saw my nipples peaked and clearly visible through my shirt. Stripping off my jammies, I stepped under the water, letting the warmth soothe me.

My body felt tense, a familiar itch scratching along my veins. Not the itch from the bond, this was a deeper, more primal need. I craved something.

Caleb.

He was so close, just in the other room. I could feel him like a second heartbeat, pulsing almost in rhythm with my own. The need for him was impossible to ignore.

Exhaling slowly, I tipped my head back, letting the water flow over me. I'd wash my hair and ignore any other *urges* I may be having. My fingers dug deep into my scalp, massaging methodically as I envisaged strong, long fingers entwined in my hair, holding my head where he wanted it. Wrapping my blonde hair around his fingers as he held my head in place, as his cock thrust into my mouth.

"Jesus," I groaned. "Pull it together," I scolded myself. My body felt warm, and not from the hot water. Rinsing my hair, I picked up my body wash, trying to be quick, wanting out of the shower now. Despite my wishes, my hands moved slowly over my skin, tracing patterns on my skin that I remembered his hands making when we were together that one time in the car.

My fingers rubbed circles over my scars before sinking lower, tantalizingly close to where I needed to feel Caleb's touch. Biting my lip, ignoring the small, breathy gasps I was making, I slipped one finger between my lips. I was so wet. My body was completely betraying me in ways I hadn't expected. In a way I wasn't ready to deal with. My eyes closed as I gently rubbed the ache between my legs, my knees weak as desire pulsed through me.

God, I needed him inside here with me. I needed him to touch me, fuck me. My head tipped back again as the sensations built steadily.

I felt so restless, so…hungry. I could *feel* him, his presence humming insistently in the back of my mind. The heat between us only seemed to grow the more I tried to deny it.

My fingers were slick with my need. Holy shit, I was so close. My teeth bit at my lip as I fought the groan I wanted to moan, but I couldn't let him know what I was doing in here.

The loud thump on the door caused me to yelp in surprise, my hands flying up in fright.

"I need the bathroom," he said gruffly through the door. "Will you be much longer?"

I couldn't speak. Desire coated my tongue. My clit still throbbed with unfulfilled need.

"*Willow*?" His voice was sharp. Tight.

"No!" Hastily rubbing my hands under the water, I turned the water off. "Give me a minute."

The mirror was fogged over, but as I dried off, I could feel the flush of my skin, and I hoped to God he thought it was from the heat of the shower.

And then I remembered his sense of smell.

Oh shit. And now I knew why he had sounded so...strained. He could smell me. Now I wanted to stay in here for a whole different reason.

Wetting a washcloth, I pawed between my legs, hoping to clear any sign of my arousal. This was so embarrassing. What the hell had I been thinking?

He was a shifter for fuck's sake.

I took a deep steadying breath and stepped away from the sink. I couldn't hide in here forever. Wrapping my towel around me, I picked up my jammies, and with a quick prayer it wouldn't be awkward, I opened the door.

A solid, immovable *force* stood in front of me, his eyes burning with a heat that instantly spiked my own. Caleb didn't move, his nostrils flared, and I heard a soft groan as his eyes burned a path down my body.

I just stood there, my heart beating too fast, watching the rise and fall of his shoulders. The room was dim, shadows danced around his silhouette, and I felt the bond between us, strained so tight that it was almost vibrating.

"Caleb," I whispered, unsure why I was whispering but needing to break the silence between us.

He still didn't move. I recognized slowly that he was holding himself in check. His eyes burned into mine. "Go to bed, Willow." His voice was low, gruff, but controlled.

I hesitated. The bond beat like its own heartbeat between us, and I knew he felt it too, as it grew stronger and stronger. My body ached with desire. Need. I didn't want to deny it.

I wanted to be closer.

"Caleb—"

His hands flexed and I remembered the last time he had been in front of me, barely holding on to his control.

I stepped back automatically, and I saw the flash of pain as he recognized why.

"Go to bed, Willow," he told me again, his voice tinged with regret. "I won't touch you."

He was past me and locked in the bathroom before I had the chance to explain. Standing there, clutching my towel, I stared at the closed door. "I didn't mean that," I told the door softly, knowing he could hear me. "I'm sorry."

Crossing over to the bed, I felt something inside me twist. We'd been through hell together, nearly lost each other, more than once, and the weight of that was enough. I didn't need to add to our misery by overreacting to a man I cared so much for.

Quickly, I dropped my towel, pulled on my jammies, and scrambled under the covers, hoping that layers of cotton would smother my lingering smell of arousal to the sensitive shifter's nose. Turning with my back to the door, I focused on the wall.

I heard the toilet flush, the faucet turn on, then off, and then the snick of the door as Caleb entered the room.

"I don't want to fight," I whispered, my voice barely audible.

"We're not fighting," he assured me.

I felt my throat tightening. "You're mad at me?"

I couldn't see him, but I could almost feel him stiffening at the question. For a long moment, he didn't answer. When he finally spoke, his voice was rough, full of something raw that made my pulse quicken. "I'm not mad. We're trying to figure our shit out, not make things worse."

Worse? Is that what he thought this was? Something that was broken? Dangerous? Something we needed to tiptoe around? I opened my mouth to ask, but he spoke again.

"Smelling you when you're...riled up...it's hard."

"Hard?" My thirteen-year-old self snickered. "How hard? Really hard?"

I heard his groan, but I also heard the amusement. "You're a child."

I grinned at the wall, the tension leaving my body. The bond between us flexed; it felt like...approval.

"Even with you in the room, I can still feel it pulling at me," I confessed. Caleb grunted in agreement, cementing the fact that he felt it too. "Do you know what this is?"

"No."

I didn't believe him, but I also didn't want to fight. "I don't think we can ignore it."

His sigh was loud in the quiet. "No."

"Are you sure you're not ignoring it?" I whispered, my face half-hidden in my pillow.

The chair thumped off the wall, and I tensed, knowing he was on his feet. He was behind me, and then he was moving onto the bed beside me, the bed creaking in protest at the added weight. Caleb was a big man. Solid. A large arm wrapped around me despite the layers that covered me. I could see the tension in his muscled arms, but I didn't resist as he pulled me tight into his body.

"I'm not ignoring it," he ground out, his voice low in my ear. "I *can't* ignore it. I'm not dead. That's the only way I could ignore it, and with how sweet your pussy smells, even then, it would be impossible."

My face flamed at his words, and I bit my lip as my heart galloped in my chest. "I washed myself," I whispered in protest.

I was moved onto my back, the covers still separating us, but as I stared up at him, the look in his eyes made my breath catch. The heat was undeniable. Raw. Wild. But I saw something darker.

Guilt.

I wanted to reach for him, but he pressed the blankets tightly around me, prohibiting any movements.

"If I give into this," he told me, his voice gravelly with emotion, "I won't be able to stop."

My body was shaking with need, but I didn't want to back down, and I also wanted to respect what he was saying. It was so complicated, and we both had things we needed to resolve, but I also knew I wanted him. I didn't want to be without him. Despite everything I had said earlier, I *wanted* him.

"If you won't be able to stop..." I dipped my eyes from his fierce gaze, taking a moment to consider my next words. Looking up at him from under my lashes, I sealed my fate. "Don't stop."

Caleb stared at me for a long moment, his eyes searching mine, and I could see the war that raged inside of him. He was fighting this.

Fighting *us*.

I was tired of fighting. "Caleb…"

His breath was uneven, his fists still clenched on either side of me as he leaned over me. His gaze dropped to my lips, and his body leaned into mine, despite his restraint.

Just when I thought he might pull away, he closed the distance between us in one swift movement, and his lips found mine, opening over mine, and he swallowed my moan as he made me forget everything. The room, the tension, the fear—all disappeared the moment his mouth claimed mine. It wasn't just a kiss—it was a release.

I melted into him, my hands struggling to fight free of the blankets as I kissed him back, my body straining to be closer to his. The bond pulsed between us, and I could feel the connection deepening, weaving us together in ways I couldn't explain.

Caleb growled low in his throat as he pulled me closer. His hands, finally freeing me of the blankets, slid down my body, resting on my waist as he kissed me harder, deeper, like he was afraid I might move away if he didn't hold me tightly enough.

Our tongues moved against each other, and my fingers sank into his thick heavy hair, rubbing the soft strands between my fingers as I arched into his kiss.

I lost myself in him. In us.

I felt him push my top up, his hands exploring my body, and I felt him come to a stop. Caleb jerked his head back, his body immobile as his fingers traced over the scars on my abdomen. His touch, which had just been so urgent, now slowed, trembling slightly as he brushed over the rough skin that told the story of my survival.

His breath hitched, and I felt his grip loosen as if he

couldn't trust himself to be so close to me. The wildness in his eyes was gone, and all that was left was regret.

Shame.

My heart sank as I realized what was happening. He was feeling what he had done, feeling the scars on my abdomen that he had caused.

"It's okay, Caleb," I whispered desperately as I reached out for him, my own hand trembling as I reached up and cupped his face. I needed him to understand that I was still here.

But he shook his head, his jaw tight, and the tension radiating from his body was palpable. He was still holding me, but the way in which he held me had changed. Just moments ago, his touch had been almost feral—wild and uncontrolled, like he was on the edge of something he couldn't come back from. Now, it was different, cautious. Unsure. He was holding me like I might break, as if I were fragile.

Damaged.

"Don't look." My voice cracked, a plea of desperation slipping from my lips. It was a stupid thing to say, but I couldn't stop the words from spilling out. I didn't want him to look at the marks he had left on my skin. I felt his fingers flex against me, against the reminder of what had been done.

Caleb's head dropped, shielding himself from my gaze. His breathing was heavy and ragged, for completely different reasons than seconds before. I could see him fight to control himself, saw the effort it took in the way his chest rose and fell.

Worse, I could feel it in the bond—the guilt, the shame that he couldn't shake. It was a suffocating weight, wrapping around us both like a weight neither of us could bear.

"I need to see," he rasped, his voice hoarse, full of the agony I knew he had been carrying since that night. His eyes flickered to mine, and seeing the self-loathing made my heart squeeze with pain. "I almost lost you, I need to see."

"No." My chest was tight, breathing was painful. Shaking my head, I brushed my fingers over his cheek. "This wasn't your fault. You *saved* me. *You* brought me back."

But I already knew he wasn't listening. His eyes dropped to the bottom of my shirt, and with a slow, deliberate push, he lifted the top up, exposing my stomach. I heard the sharp intake of breath, and I turned my head away as I felt his fingers trace the line of my scars. His fingers trembled as they caressed the healed skin. "I never should have done this to you. It should never have gotten so far. I let my darkness—" He stopped, his voice cracking, the pain in his voice sending a shiver down my spine.

"I'm still here," I whispered, still trying to reach him, still trying to pull him back from spiraling back into the darkness. "We're both still here," I reminded him, my throat thick with emotion.

He looked up at me then, his gaze locking with mine, and for a second, I saw a flicker of something else in his eyes. Hope? Or maybe the realization that we were still here, together. But it was fleeting, and before I could hold on to him, he was pulling away, his face hard. Guilt wrapped around him like a shield.

"You don't understand," he muttered as he got off the bed. "I could hurt you again. You're not safe with me, Willow."

"That's bullshit, and you know it," I snapped, pushing my shirt down and sitting up in bed. "I am *not* afraid of you, Caleb."

His jaw flexed, his eyes burning into mine, a mix of frustration and longing swirling together. "Well, then you're an idiot because you should be."

Anger had me pushing myself off the bed, closing the distance between us, my fingers jabbing into his chest. "I am *not* an idiot," I whispered fiercely. "I *trust* you."

His breath caught, and for a moment, the tension between us was so thick I could choke on it. Our bond hummed between us, tugging at us, pulling us closer. I could feel the heat radiating from him, the barely restrained power coiling beneath his skin, and I knew he was resisting it. Resisting the pull between us.

The instinct to protect.

To possess.

I was fighting it too, but for a different reason.

Because despite all the stuff that had happened, despite the scars on my body and the uncertainty of what lay ahead for us, one thing for me was constant.

And that was *him*. Caleb.

I still wanted him. I needed him.

Him. No one else.

And I needed him to understand that.

I stepped closer until there was hardly space between us, my fingers curling around the edge of the fabric of his shirt, pushing it up, exposing his rock-hard abs. My fingers danced along the grooves of his body, dipping over the hard planes of muscle. "You didn't lose me," I told him, pleased my voice sounded steady, because my heart definitely was not. "You didn't hurt me on purpose," I whispered. "And you would never hurt me on purpose."

He stared down at me, his breathing uneven, his eyes flicking between mine, searching for the lie. His hands hovered near mine, hesitant, like he was afraid to touch me again.

"I never meant to hurt you." He sounded broken and I knew I was going to cry. "But I did, and I could do it again."

"You won't." Taking his hand, I guided it to my stomach, pressing his large hand against my abdomen, ignoring the twinge of pain. Quickly, I dropped my hand from his, but Caleb kept his pressed gently against my puckered skin.

With confidence I didn't think I had, I pulled my shirt up, over my head, exposing my chest to him, dropping the shirt on the floor.

"Look at me," I instructed him. Taking his hand once more, I pulled his fingers over my skin. "Look at me and touch me. I'm not a shifter," I reminded him. "I don't lose my scars. I want you to look at them, really see them." His eyes were glued to my body.

Gently I took his hands, bringing them up to my chest, making him feel the weight of my breasts. For a second, he didn't move, but I felt his fingers flex, and slowly, his hands curled into my body, cupping my breasts, his thumbs stroking over my nipples. His gaze was fixed on my body. I watched as his attention seemed torn between my breasts and my scars.

"Touch me, Caleb," I told him. "I'm yours."

TWELVE

Caleb

Her words shattered the last of my resolve, but I was hanging on to my control. Barely.

Touch me. I'm yours.

I stood frozen, as if time had stopped, the words echoing in my head. On replay. Over and over, searing into my skin like a brand. She was offering me everything, *trusting* me despite what I'd done—despite the darkness that lived within me.

She trusted me. But I didn't trust myself. Not with her. Not with this.

I stared at her, my chest heaving as my instincts to claim her warred with the guilt that gnawed at me from the inside. Willow stood before me, bare, vulnerable, yet her gaze was steady, her posture straight and proud. But all I could see were the scars I'd caused. They marred her perfect skin because I'd failed her. And yet, here she was, asking me to touch her as if none of it mattered.

"Willow..." I couldn't even finish the sentence. I didn't even know what I was trying to say. My head was spinning. My body was torn between the need to cover her body with mine or to turn away and talk sense into her.

She shouldn't be asking this. She shouldn't *want* this.

Her hand reached out, taking hold of my right hand, and she guided it slowly and deliberately to the scar on her abdomen. The deepest one, the one that had almost taken her life. Her skin was warm beneath my fingers, but I could only feel the cold rush of fear. The memory of her blood on my hands, of that moment when I thought she was gone forever, it haunted me.

And now she wanted me to touch her?

"I won't break, Caleb," she whispered, her breath shaky but her gaze warm and steady. She wanted to convince me, but I wasn't convinced.

Pulling back, I didn't expect her grip to tighten, keeping my hand where it was, forcing me to feel her.

See her.

"Look at me," she directed softly, her gaze locking with mine. "I'm right here. I survived. *We* survived."

"You don't understand," I protested, my heart hammering against my ribs. "You shouldn't have *needed* to survive."

"But I did." Her tone was firm. "And now, I need *this*, I need *you*."

Her voice was filled with so much certainty, like she could see right through me, like she knew I was falling apart inside. And maybe she did. The bond between us had begun to feel like a living thing, threading between us, tying us to each other in ways I didn't understand.

I hated the tremble in my fingers as they rested against her skin, feeling the ridges of the scar beneath them. She was soft, warm, and alive. My memory raced with the night I almost lost her. The night I failed her.

"Willow, you can't—"

"Yes, I can," she spoke over me. Her palm pushed my hand into her skin firmer. Making sure my touch held. "You need to believe in us, believe that you won't hurt me." Her voice sounded a little breathless, and I realized how vulnerable she was too.

She was being strong, and she was asking me to be the same. I couldn't breathe. I wasn't safe. I knew that. She had to know it too. The animal in me, the part that wanted to claim her, to mark her as mine, was there, and I knew it would always be there, lurking beneath the surface. And after everything, having lost control before, did I really trust myself not to lose it again?

I knew she could see the doubt in my eyes, feel it through the bond, and yet she never wavered. Gently, she guided my hand across her stomach, up over her side, and along her ribs, showing me that she wasn't afraid of my touch.

"I'm yours," she said again, her voice barely a whisper, although it had the power to wrap around me like a noose. "You know I am."

A low growl rumbled in my chest, my instincts reacting to her words before my mind could catch up. The bond flickered, pulling us closer, and the need to possess her once more roared to life. My hand moved on its own, tracing over the curve of her waist, relishing the softness of her skin beneath my calloused touch.

My fingers ghosted over her hip, rising higher, brushing over the curve of her breast. Willow sucked in a breath, her eyes fluttering closed for a moment, and the sound of it shot straight to my cock like a lightning bolt. I could feel my resolve unraveling bit by bit, my control slipping as the sense of wildness rose to the surface.

My eyes closed tight as my instincts screamed at me to step back. What if I lost control again?

Lips brushed mine, causing my eyes to fly wide open. I met her gaze, her eyes wide and full of certainty. "Kiss me."

That was all it took for the last of my restraint to snap.

Her mouth opened willingly, my fingers dug into her soft flesh, and I was already pushing her pants down.

"Get on the bed," I ordered, pulling my shirt over my head and tossing it to the side. Willow did as she was told, and I grabbed the bottom of her nightwear and tugged them down. I could smell her arousal, and I couldn't get enough. Her taste, her scent, everything about her drove me to the brink of madness, and I was done fighting it.

Following her onto the bed, my hands roamed over her body, learning every dip and bump of her skin, memorizing the feel of her, the way her body arched against me. The breathless gasps she made as I kissed her deeper, harder. My lips captured the swollen peak of her breast, and I loved the throaty moan that spilled from her lips as I licked and sucked.

Willow's head tilted back, her eyes closed in appreciation as I feasted on her breasts, switching from one to the other, savoring the taste of her skin. The small desperate sounds that escaped from her lips only fueled my fire. My hand trailed down her body, teasing, until my fingers found their way between her legs. I couldn't stop the smile from spreading across my face when her body jerked at my touch, her legs falling open as I stroked her. She was already slick with need, and the realization that my girl was ready for me sent a wave of primal satisfaction through me.

Her hands tangled in my hair, her body moving, seeking more. The bond between us pulsed with an energy that made the very air around us crackle with it.

Willow's hips lifted. Her hand slid down her body, resting on top of mine, pressing against it, and I growled low in my throat, the sound vibrating through me as I slipped a finger inside her. Her sharp intake of breath was followed by a soft moan, her body tightening around me, and I felt myself losing myself in her as I watched her writhe with pleasure. Every movement, every inhale, every plea for more fed the beast inside me. The wild part of me that had always craved her, even before I realized what this was between us.

"You're so fucking perfect," I murmured against her skin, my lips trailing down her neck as my fingers continued to move inside her, slow and sure, coaxing her higher with every stroke.

Willow's grip tightened on my forearm, a soft whimper on her lips as her body arched up into my hand, trying to get closer to me, pulling me even deeper inside her. "Caleb...more... please..."

It was too much, and I couldn't resist her. I wanted her to have everything, and I added another finger, stroking her deeper, faster, watching as her face contorted in pleasure, her breathing even more rapid now, her body tightening around my fingers with every movement. Her slick heat coated my fingers, I was drowning in her scent, and her moans filled the room. All of it was driving me to the edge, right along with her.

I pressed my thumb against her clit, circling it slowly, a contrast to the rhythm of my fingers. "Oh my God, Caleb." Her voice was thick with need, her body close to release. So close.

I dipped my head, my mouth returning to her breast, sucking and nipping at her sensitive skin as my fingers plunged into her over and over, bringing her to the brink. Her muscles tightened, and her legs trembled as the climax built inside her. Her hands clutched at anything—me, the bed, her hair. She was on the edge, and I was right there, waiting for her to fall apart.

And then she peaked, her back bowing off the bed as she came, her cries filling the air as her body convulsed around my fingers. I held her through it, my lips brushing against her skin, murmuring soothing platitudes as her pleasure rippled through her. Willow clung to me, her breath coming in broken gulps, her body shaking in the aftermath.

She coated my fingers with her climax, and I pulled my fingers from her slowly, savoring the way her walls still quivered. Bringing my fingers to my mouth, I tasted her, watching her come down from her high. Willow's eyes fluttered open, her gaze heavy-lidded as she watched me hungrily lick my fingers clean of her.

"Caleb..." Her voice was barely above a whisper, her eyes locked on mine, the bond between us alive and electric.

My lips found hers in a kiss that was both gentle and possessive. Willow kissed me back with the same intensity, her fingers threading through my hair, pulling me closer over her body until I was settled between her legs.

I broke the kiss just long enough to rest my forehead against hers, my breathing heavy as I tried to calm down the wild storm inside me. "You're so fucking beautiful," I whispered, dipping in to take another kiss. "You're mine," I whispered against her lips, my voice rough, filled with the truth of it.

I kissed her again, deeper this time, pouring everything I couldn't say into the press of my lips, the brush of my tongue.

She responded instantly, her body soft and pliant beneath me, her fingers clutching at my shoulders as if she were afraid I'd pull away.

But I wasn't running from her anymore.

My body moved, the heat of her still radiating through me. Her legs wrapped around me, pulling me closer, her hips lifting, telling me her desire.

"You need to take your jeans off," Willow said as she kissed along my jawline. "Now. Like, right now."

The scent of her arousal filled the air, surrounding me, making it almost impossible to think of anything but her. The way she tasted on my fingers, the way her body moved under mine, the way our bond was singing in my blood, pushing me to madness.

Moving down her body, I kissed her skin. I could feel her heartbeat on my lips as I kissed her chest. The desire to claim her in every way possible tore through me. My movement hesitated at her scars, seeing the visible signs of what my loss of control could do.

And here I was, on the brink of making the same mistake.

She deserved so much more than this. More than me.

But Willow sensed my hesitation, and with a roll of her hips and a firm push against my head, she shoved me down her body. My mouth tasted her, her pussy so wet my tongue glided through her wetness. Covering her clit with my mouth, I moved my tongue over it. Looking up, I saw Willow propped up on her elbows, watching me as my tongue slid over her clit slowly. Pushing two fingers into her, I continued to tease her clit as I watched her chest heaving, her walls contracting around my fingers.

"Caleb." Her moan was throaty, heavy with lust.

Pushing her legs wider apart, I replaced my fingers with my tongue, tasting her sweetness as it painted my tongue. Willow's hands were twisted into my hair as she rocked against my face.

"Oh God..." Her whispered pleas went unanswered. "Oh shit, Caleb, oh fuck, there..." Her body squirmed under my tongue, and I moved back to her clit, my fingers sliding inside her pussy easily because she was so soaked. "Caleb!"

My mouth wrapped around her clit, and I sucked hard while my girl cried out as her climax swept through her. Her legs clenched, squeezing my head as she thrust her hips against me, and then just as suddenly, she pushed me away, whispering it was too good.

Grinning, I took a moment to shed my jeans, the need to be inside her driving me forward. She had already reached for me, not giving me time to think as she pulled me back down to her. A soft moan escaped her when she felt my cock rub against her.

My control was close to snapping.

"Willow," I rasped, my voice barely recognizable. I wanted to warn her, tell her I was close to losing it, how badly I needed her, but I couldn't think. All I could do was feel.

I thrust against her, and her nails dug into my shoulders as her hips lifted, seeking more. I needed to slow down and give her time, but she wasn't asking for that. She was meeting me with equal hunger, her hands roaming over my back, clutching at me.

I knew I couldn't deny her. Not now. Not ever.

My mouth moved down her neck, tasting the salt of her skin as my hands gripped her hips, holding her steady as I positioned myself at her entrance. I felt her trembling beneath me, her breath coming in shallow pants, and I could feel the same tension building inside of me, threatening to break me apart.

"I need you," she whispered, her voice heavy with desperation, and the sound of it drove me past my final limit.

"I've got you," I promised, my voice hoarse.

I pushed inside her, slow and steady, savoring the feel of her around me, the way she gasped, the way her body tensed before she relaxed. The way her legs tightened around my waist as I sank into her completely. My vision blurred, and the sensation of being inside her again, of being so connected to her, threatened to overwhelm me.

I paused, giving her a moment, my forehead pressed against hers as we both caught our breath. Willow's hands cradled my face, her eyes locking onto mine, and in that moment, I could see everything. Her trust, her desire, the love she'd hinted at, all of it was there, and it echoed through our bond, binding us together in a way words never could.

"Caleb." Her voice was shaking, and I kissed her again, biting her bottom lip, dragging it between my teeth, unable to stop myself.

Then I started to move.

Slow at first, relishing every inch of being inside her, the way her body clenched around me, the way she breathed my name like a prayer. I moved against her until the need grew more intense, more consuming, and I couldn't hold back.

I picked up the pace, my hips driving into her, each thrust sending a shockwave of pleasure through both of us. Her moans filled the air, her fingers digging into my back as her body moved in perfect rhythm with mine. Her legs tightened around me, squeezing me.

"Willow," I groaned, burying my face in the curve of her neck as the pressure built inside of me, threatening to consume me. She was everything—everything I ever wanted, ever needed

—and having her under me like this, completely and utterly mine, was more than I could ever have imagined.

I felt her pussy as it tightened around me, her breath coming in short, broken puffs of air, and I knew she was close. I could feel it in the way her body moved, the way her nails raked down my back. Her soft cries turned into something more desperate, more primal.

"Come for me," I whispered, my voice gruff with command, and she shattered.

Her back arched off the bed. Her pussy clenched around my cock as she screamed my name. Wave after wave of pleasure rocked through her as her walls gripped me tight. The sight and feel of her coming undone was enough to send me over the edge right along with her.

I thrust into her one last time, my body tensing as my release ripped through me, everything else fading around me, as the pleasure hit me like a bolt of lightning. I pressed close, breathing in the warmth of her skin, as I groaned her name, emptying myself inside her, her pussy milking my cock, the bond flaring with an intensity that added to the pleasure.

We stayed like that, tangled together, as our bodies trembled in the aftermath. I could feel her heartbeat slowing, matching the rhythm of mine, and I felt contentment.

This was everything.

It was trust and love, and even as I held her, the weight of it settled over me. With a groan, I rolled us so I was spooning her and she was curled up in front of me.

Placing a kiss on the top of her head, I heard her sleepy yawn, the sound soft and content. My wolf rumbled his approval, a deep vibration that echoed through my chest as I held her, sated and safe in my arms. All that mattered right now was this.

Tomorrow, we'd face our next challenge, but for tonight, she was mine.

And I wasn't letting go.

THIRTEEN

Willow

My eyes opened in the dark room. The small window high up had snow against it, but also soft light. I lay in Caleb's arms, my cheek pressed against the warmth of his chest, listening to the steady beat of his heart beneath my ear. This was the first morning in a long time that I'd woken up feeling like this—safe, calm, and dare I even say, relaxed.

I didn't feel the weight of fear looming over me, and I couldn't remember the last time I'd been free of that feeling.

Caleb's arm tightened around me, pulling me closer, and I couldn't help the smile that tugged at my lips. After everything that we had been through, this felt like a moment of peace I never thought we'd get.

A niggling thought at the back of my mind cautioned me not to get used to it; the track record Caleb and I had wasn't great.

I moved slightly, my fingers gliding over his skin, tracing the soft hair on his chest. It was not a blanket, not like a man-rug. It was just a few sparse hairs that broke up his smooth skin. As much as I wanted to stay like this—wrapped in him, safe in a cocoon away from everything else—I knew we couldn't hide forever. There were still so many things we needed to address.

I fought back the sigh, pulling myself out of my thoughts, and shifting slightly against the warmth of him.

"You're thinking very loudly," he murmured, his voice thick with satisfaction, the kind of smugness you sometimes felt after you woke up after a really good sleep. His large hand rested over the curve of my hip, keeping me close. "You good?" His voice was low and rough, making something warm settle deep in my belly.

Looking up at him, I saw the dark of his eyes, heavy still with sleep. I smiled at him. It was so hard to stop smiling. "Just thinking of all the things we need to do. But honestly, I'm looking forward to going home."

Caleb didn't say anything, his hand tightening on my hip for a brief moment before he let go, sitting up on the bed. "I'm sure you are."

The easy comfort of the morning started to fade, but I didn't let it ruin my good mood. There was a lot to do. We needed to learn what it was between us, and we needed to learn who it was that broke into my home and why. And we needed to talk about Caleb and the darkness that threatened to consume him.

"Do you think they'll think we're running away?" I asked him, sitting up and watching Caleb walk in all his naked glory to the bathroom.

"Do we care?" he asked, looking over his shoulder.

"Caleb," I reprimanded him gently, getting out of bed. "They're only trying to help us."

He held my stare, his gaze softening. "They won't like it,"

he conceded, walking back to me. "They don't have to." He dropped a kiss on my lips. "Stop worrying."

I wished it were that simple. Caleb could act like he didn't care what the others thought, but I knew he wasn't as blasé as he made out.

"Cannon won't like you leaving without seeing the shaman," I told him. "Doc won't like me leaving." My sly grin held his attention. "Ned will be pissed he didn't get to kick your ass."

Caleb raised an eyebrow as he reached for me. "And why would he think he *could*?"

I giggled as I dodged his hold. "I may have told him to find you and kick your ass."

Caleb's eyes widened and then narrowed. I saw his intent and yelped as I darted to the bathroom and was easily caught by strong arms. I screamed in laughter as he carried me into the bathroom, tickling me, kicking the door closed behind him.

"What's happening?" I asked him, seeing his smirk.

"Shower time," he answered.

"Why, sir, are you saying I'm filthy?" I said, feigning mock outrage.

"No," he told me, his eyes darkening. "But you will be."

It took us a little bit longer to get dressed because we kept stealing kisses, and I kept smiling because he had that effect on me. He made me happy. Something that kind of took me by surprise but also something, I thought, deep down I had hoped for, and I was pleased I was right. All of which meant I was also a little reluctant to leave this room.

We'd had one night—one moment of respite—but reality was already creeping back in. Inside this bubble of content-ment, we were uninhibited and protected in our self-confinement. I didn't think either of us expected *this* to continue like we were now, once we went beyond this door.

Caleb finally got sick of me stalling and simply opened the door and walked out of the room. I had no choice but to follow him, and as I caught up, he gave my hand a squeeze when he caught it in his.

We found Doc in a room near the main door of the bunker. It was a lab, and for a bunker three-quarters of the way up a mountain, the amount of equipment in it was impressive.

Doc looked like he'd been up all night, and I was certain he was wearing the same clothes as yesterday. He looked up from the computer as Caleb leaned against the doorway, with me hovering uncertainly beside him. I didn't want to argue with him again, so I was hoping for an easier conversation this morning than we had last night.

"Cannon says the shaman told you to make amends," Doc started with no preamble. He glanced at me, his gaze dropping to our linked fingers. "I'm going to assume you did that."

"Not that it's any of...*anyone's* business, but Willow and I have reached an understanding."

I winced at the coldness in Caleb's voice. Just moments ago, he was warm and approachable, and now he was his same stand-offish self. Doc looked between us again, and I knew he wanted to say something, but he turned back to his screen.

"You're going back today?" he asked as he scrolled down a chart of some kind. Nosiness had me moving closer, but Caleb tugged on my hand, slightly preventing me from going into the room and peering over Doc's shoulder.

"I'll speak to Cannon first," Caleb told him, "but yes, we'll be off the mountain by afternoon."

Doc nodded. "Before you leave, Willow, I'd like to take a few more samples, if that's okay with you?"

"Why?" Caleb's tone was firm, and I saw his eyes narrow.

"It's okay," I spoke quickly, trying not to roll my eyes at the man beside me and his Neanderthal behavior. "Since Doc's been my doctor," I said with a warm smile at Doc, "I've been better. Healthier."

Doc loosened up a little, and I was pleased the tension lessened slightly. "You are an obedient patient," he praised me. "Keep it up and keep your stress levels down, and hopefully we will keep the ME flares down."

Caleb looked at me in question, and I saw him thinking about it. "It's not all stress related," I murmured, but I knew Doc heard me. "I'll be back before we leave," I promised. "And you can get what you need, okay?"

We said our goodbyes—well, I did, Caleb merely grunted and walked away. Outside, I was amazed at how much snow had fallen. Everywhere was covered in a blanket of white.

It felt like we could be safe here, but this was not where either of us belonged. The reality for Caleb and me right now was that we weren't safe. Not here, maybe not anywhere.

Pushing my hair behind my ear, I tried not to look at Caleb as we headed towards the town that was Blackridge Peak. I'd been here once before, the day that Caleb left me, and just like my encounter with Doc, I was hoping this visit went a little smoothly than the last.

"I have questions," I told Caleb as we walked over the snow, and I knew he was being patient by going at my pace.

"When do you not have questions?" he asked with a gleam in his eyes.

"Har har." I tried to contain myself to just a few. "What do you think is waiting for us when we leave here? Do you think Whispering Pines will be okay for us? How do we start looking into the people who did the break-ins and followed me? And..."

"And?" His lips twitched with amusement.

"And do you intend to return to Shadowridge Peak?"

He lost the hint of a smile, but he considered the question carefully. "There is a lot of my past on that mountain that I don't want reminded of," he said quietly, slowing us down as we walked. "You saw firsthand what can happen there." He looked away from me, his gaze fixed north. "You paid a price that you should never have had to pay because of..." Caleb rolled his shoulders, his uncomfortableness evident. "Because of what lies in wait for me on that peak."

"Then we need to make a plan," I said with a confidence I wasn't feeling. I felt his eyes on me as I continued. "We can't keep guessing about what's waiting for us, so we need to start making lists or inquiries as to who in the world I could possibly be of interest to. You said before, you had connections; can we use them?"

He was watching me, a calculated look in his eye, one I was familiar with, and it usually meant I wasn't going to like what he said next. "I can, and I have."

"You have?" We had stopped walking to Cannon's house and stood in the middle of a snowy path. Only a few people walked the streets, and I was trying to pretend I wasn't noticing them notice us. "When?"

"When I came to get you."

"Which time?"

His huff of laughter at my cheekiness made me grin. "*This* time. I've reached out to an old...friend. I'm waiting to hear back."

"Oh." I hadn't expected that, and I wanted to ask more, but he was obviously uncomfortable, and I didn't want to push it. We had enough time to discuss it later when he was ready. This conversation was the first time we'd spoken about Shadowridge Peak since last night, and I selfishly didn't want to ruin the morning completely.

Caleb was looking past me, and I turned to see what held his attention. There was nothing that stood out to me, just a few of Cannon's pack looking our way as they went about their morning. When I looked back at Caleb, I saw his jaw was tight and his brow was furrowed in a frown. The hard look in his eye sent a chill down my spine.

"What's wrong?" I asked him quietly.

"We're exposed here. Come on, let's go see Cannon and get off this mountain."

"What are you seeing that I'm not?" I asked him as we resumed walking, trying to be quiet because I knew how well shifters could hear.

"It's nothing," he assured me, his fingers tightening around mine. "Do you still have the drawings of the shifter that followed you?" he asked me suddenly.

"Probably, well, I wouldn't," I corrected quickly, "Cannon or Ned should though. Why?"

"Because we need to find who's been targeting you," he said, his voice darkening. "Whoever they are, they've been careful, really careful, but sooner or later, they'll slip up. The fact you've seen them may be the best clue."

"Yeah, let's hope so." We were walking through the town now. Cannon lived right in the center, and we passed a few more people on our way. I began to notice the looks because this pack was not hiding their disapproval.

"Do these people know you?" I asked Caleb, my voice barely a whisper.

"No." His scowl was etched deep now, and I wasn't sure why.

"So, it's me?" I guessed. "Why are they staring like they've never seen a human before?"

"Ignore them."

Well, that wasn't helpful, or comforting. "Are we walking into a fight?" I asked in the same whisper.

"No." He gave me a smile that didn't reach his eyes. "Don't worry about it. We'll be gone soon."

He was right. If they didn't like a human on their mountain, I got it, I did. I had taken up pack resources, so maybe I had outstayed my welcome. If I had ever been welcome to begin with. My gut told me it was more than that, but my head told me to tackle one problem at a time.

The door to Cannon's house opened as we walked up the path. A stunning woman about my age stood there in leggings and a T-shirt, but her lack of winter clothing didn't draw my attention, it was her pure white hair. She looked at me from head to toe and then did the same to Caleb.

She and Caleb shared a look, and I was going to attempt to break the awkward silence when she suddenly stepped back.

"He's in the study, he's expecting you," she told him. Her eyes flicked to me again, and once more, I received a once-over.

"Hi?" I wasn't a confrontational person, but I also respected good manners.

I didn't expect her to grin or look at Caleb with amusement. "Hi," she told me. "Nice to see you on your feet again," she added. "You look well." Her amusement was clear as she carried on. "Relaxed."

"Kezia." Cannon's voice came from behind her, and then he was in the doorway. I watched in fascination as he slipped his arm around her, pulling her back into his body. It was possessive but also oddly endearing. "Excuse my mate," he grumbled. "Manners of a goat sometimes."

"I was just saying they looked well rested," she told him, looking up at him with a smirk.

I didn't hear his reply, but her look turned heated, and Caleb cleared his throat.

"Do we do this here or inside?" he asked them both.

"Come in," Cannon told him. His mate hesitated, looking between us again. "Go, it won't take long, I'll join you," he assured her.

Kezia looked like she wanted to argue, but instead, she shrugged and went back inside. She came back almost as quickly.

"Travel safe," she told me. "It really is good to see you well." Her attention switched to Caleb. "Not everyone will understand," she said seriously. "If it doesn't matter to you now, make sure it doesn't matter then."

I felt him bristle, but she was gone again, and Cannon was looking between us both with a frown. "You better come in."

"What is happening?" I asked Caleb as we followed Cannon inside.

"It's nothing."

When we were in his study, a place I remembered well, I sat as Cannon closed the doors. Like last time, Caleb chose to stand.

"It's not nothing," Cannon said with a hard look at Caleb. "It's a whole lot of something, and you know it."

"I didn't ask for your opinion."

"I don't give a fuck if you did or not. I'm giving Willow my opinion because she deserves to know. This"—he gestured between us—"won't be accepted by some."

"What is 'this'?" I asked, talking quickly before Caleb lost his temper. "Is Caleb not welcome here because of what happened with his pack?"

Cannon looked momentarily perplexed at my question and then shook his head. "His pack? No. This has to do with you. Both of you."

"What has?" Why did I feel like I wasn't going to like the answer?

"Humans and shifters aren't favored by Pack Council," Cannon told me bluntly. "Shifters stick to shifters. It's not accepted overall to go outside of the...species," he added.

"Excuse me?" I knew my jaw was slack.

"We're a different species to human. We don't generally have relationships with humans." He was so forthright in the way he said things, even when there were gentler ways of telling someone that the guy they were falling for didn't have a future with her.

"But Doc is mixed," I blurted. "He's human and shifter."

"Yes, he has *some* shifter in him, but he also has very few of the benefits of being a shifter." When he saw I didn't understand, he sighed deeply. "He can't *shift*, Willow. He will never have a son or daughter who is a shifter. Shifters that have relationships with humans are usually just using them for sex. Nothing more."

I felt sick. Caleb's angry snort didn't help.

"She doesn't need to know this right now," he protested. "We have more important things happening."

"Using them for sex?" I asked, feeling completely adrift.

Caleb crouched down to look at me. Reaching out his hand, he cupped my cheek. "Not me." When he saw I didn't believe him, his frown deepened. "*No*, Willow. It's not *just* sex," he assured me. "I'm pissed off you think it would be," he added, leaning forward to brush his lips over mine. "You and I, this is happening. Anyone who doesn't like it?" He stroked his thumb over my cheek. "They can fuck off. I don't care about what anyone thinks, only you."

My mind was still reeling. "I mean, I'm not saying I was expecting you to put a ring on it or anything. I'm not a crazy psycho. We have *so* much shit to work through, but..." I looked up at Cannon. "Can Caleb get in trouble for this? For me?" My eyes widened. "Is this why I'm being targeted?" When Caleb went to speak, I placed a finger over his lips. "Cannon, I'm asking *you*."

"I don't know," he told me simply. "It's unlikely because you and Caleb didn't have this relationship when it happened," he said as he looked directly at me. "But I won't lie and tell you it could—it probably will—bring problems in the future for you, both of you."

FOURTEEN

Caleb

She was avoiding looking at me, and I wanted to rip Cannon's flapping tongue from his body. Willow didn't need this kind of shit in her head right now. We had other problems, *bigger* problems. Problems that were *actually* problems, not this.

Willow was mine, and I didn't give a fuck what anyone thought of that.

"Look at me," I said gently, willing her to lift her eyes from where she had them trained on the floor. "Willow, *look* at me."

Slowly her gaze lifted, and I saw the confusion and the hurt there. She needed reassurance, something to ground her. I could give her that. "You're stuck with me," I teased her gently, hoping to see a hint of a smile. "We're linked, Willow. You and I, we're bound together. Luna put us together for a reason. Luna doesn't care that you're human, and neither do I."

Willow bit the corner of her bottom lip, her eyes darting to Cannon. "What if it was only to help each other, not sleep with each other?"

"Are you ready for the 'until death do us part' step?" I asked her bluntly. Her eyes widened in alarm at the very thought of it, which I tried not to take as an insult. "Exactly, it's too soon for this to even be a concern for you. You take it one day at a time. If this is your ever after, then this is your ever after. Okay?"

Hesitantly, she nodded, and I gave her one more brief kiss before I stood and turned to Cannon. The look I gave him told him to shut his mouth, and wisely, he heeded my unspoken request.

"We're leaving," I told him bluntly. "Heading back to Whispering Pines. I've reached out to an old...friend." I ignored the quirk of his eyebrow. "I *will* find out who's targeting her and why." His face gave away nothing, but I sensed something off about him. "You know something?" I asked. "What is it?"

Willow was looking up at him with a look of curiosity and confusion. "Do you?"

Cannon sucked his teeth and then gave a half-hearted shrug. "It might be nothing."

"It might be something," I countered. "What?"

He glanced at Willow but chose to continue. "You told Willow you thought someone, or someones, were trying to get you off Shadowridge Peak. To give up your claim to the mountain."

I hadn't really wanted her to share that information, but after what I did to her, why would she hold my confidences? "And?"

Cannon gave me a flat stare. "I don't want your packlands; I have my own," he said with a slight reprimand. "But...it's possible there are packs, or a pack, that would want you to give up the claim."

"Who?" I demanded.

"I don't know." He held up his hand. "Don't start on me,

Caleb. I'm telling you the truth, I *don't* know. But I am looking into it."

"Then I'll look into it with you."

"And Willow does what? Stays on a mountain peak for the whole of winter?" he asked me, and I could see he was losing his patience.

I was losing my patience.

"They targeted Willow," I told him through clenched teeth.

"I know, and they will pay. We do not hurt humans." Cannon looked at her, noting how quiet she was. "I will do everything I can to ensure you are safe, Willow."

She nodded, but I wasn't sure she was really listening. "How would they know I was even connected to her?" I asked him. "The drawings? The visions she has? They wouldn't know about them. Unless someone told them." I knew I was borderline accusing him and was rewarded with an angry glare.

"I didn't fucking tell anyone," Cannon said through gritted teeth. "I won't tell you again."

"Then how do they know about her?" I asked, equally pissed off.

"You."

We both looked at her. She was sitting almost curled in a ball, her arms wrapped around herself, her gaze on the window.

"You kept coming back to Whispering Pines," she said. "Coming back to *me*. Perhaps they thought they could target someone you cared about—or they *thought* you cared about—to get your attention. They wouldn't need to know the reason was nothing like that—"

"Then." I looked down at her with a challenge in my eye when I cut her off. "They wouldn't know our relationship wasn't this *then*."

Cannon's gaze was steady. "So, this *is* about you." He looked at Willow with a hint of sadness. "I think you're right," he told her. "It was never about what you could paint, not to them."

"The two may not be connected," I corrected him, "but they're still two things we need answered. Who are they, and what did they hope to achieve?"

Cannon was thoughtful, his gaze directed on the door. "New pack? It's a good packlands, secluded, and a nightmare to get to in winter. Plenty of game."

"Haunted by the dead," I added drily.

"Only for you," he quipped back. "It makes sense."

It did. I hadn't been mad with the darkness, I'd been right. Someone was trying to take over Shadowridge Peak and was using Willow as collateral damage.

"I want her back in Whispering Pines," I told Cannon. "Agreed?"

He nodded. "Surrounded by humans is the safest place for her right now."

"I want to stay and help," Willow protested. "I can do sketches of the ones I saw."

"I'll need those," I told Cannon. "I may know them," I added, and I saw his agreement. Turning to Willow, I held out my hand. "You're going home. I'm coming too," I assured her. "I won't leave you alone."

She slipped her hand into mine, and I pulled her gently to her feet. Willow still looked scared, and when she asked if she could use the bathroom, Cannon showed her where it was.

When he came back, he left the study door open and stood close to me, his voice low so she would never hear him.

"When you told her that if this was her ever after, you placed a lot of emphasis on the *if*."

"So?"

"No *so*. I just found it interesting that you didn't mention this was already yours."

Observant bastard. "And?"

"Your choice is your choice, Caleb." He watched the hall for Willow. "But if a human is who you choose to stay with, she will never give you an alpha. She will never birth a shifter."

"Your point?"

"Why are you fighting for packlands if you don't plan on having a pack? Or children who will carry on your alpha line?"

"They're mine. Both of them," I told him, my voice a low growl, my shoulders set with determination. "I'm the alpha of Shadowridge Peak. If they want to challenge me for the right to be alpha, then they challenge *me*. They do *not* target my woman."

Cannon grinned. "Well, thank fuck you've finally said something sensible. You suddenly sound like an alpha. Welcome back."

ALPHA CANNON OF THE BLACKRIDGE PEAK PACK WAS a dick.

He had gone to "fetch" something, and while he was gone, some of his pack just *happened* to be passing by.

I waited patiently in the corner of his hallway as Willow said her goodbyes to his betas and Doc, who claimed he was her physician. He was part shifter, and because of that, he smelled wrong. I also didn't like the way his eyes lingered on my girl with more than clinical assessment, and I wondered if he would heal if I plucked his eyeballs from their sockets.

I didn't like him.

You don't like anyone.

My inner voice sounded suspiciously like someone I missed listening to. My mother.

I hadn't felt her presence on Shadowridge Peak when I returned, and I hoped that meant she was at peace. My father's presence had also been missing, and I was sure the Goddess Luna had called her alpha and his mate home. The ones I had felt, the ones I had sent to the afterlife, I was sure Luna wouldn't want them in death to join the eternal hunt anyway.

"The Jeep's ready to take you," Cannon told me, coming to stand beside me. "It's got a tracker. My brother has already disabled it." He saw my look. Wordlessly he handed over the plastic casing. "As I said, my brother disabled it."

That made me grin, and I heard his huff of amusement beside me. "You're even pricklier than I am," he mused under his breath. His attention was fixed on Willow, who was smiling at something Ned said. "She's good for you."

"You approve?" I heard my sarcasm and didn't blanch when he gave me a dirty look at the attitude.

"She can't be your mate, we know that," he told me, dropping his voice even lower. "But Luna has chosen her, and I don't argue with the Will of the Goddess."

"She has chosen her," I agreed. "If Luna decides she hasn't chosen her *for me*"—I shared a look with him—"then I have no problem arguing, Goddess or not."

"She's still human," Cannon cautioned. "You're going to meet some resistance among some packs."

"Yours?"

He shrugged. "My pack's one of the more open-minded." I remembered some of his *pack* staring at Willow and me outside. I wouldn't bet my next meal on the open-mindedness of his pack. "And...you can still always meet your mate."

Seeing Willow looking over at me, I knew she was eager to start the return journey. "I've been an alpha for ten years," I told him, keeping my eyes on the woman who held my attention most of the time. "Luna wanted my attention, she got it." I turned to look at Cannon. "With Willow."

He didn't look like he agreed, but he didn't argue.

What could he say that I hadn't already considered? She wasn't a shifter, so why would the Goddess send me to her? Humans and shifters weren't meant to mix. They couldn't reproduce. No shifter was born from a human mother. Half-breeds like Doc showed us that. The shaman had said the goddess was worried about my bloodline. Willow wasn't the answer to that problem. She never could be.

Maybe they meant my father's legacy would be besmirched if I were the last of his bloodline and I went rogue, letting the darkness consume me. Even so, Willow, the *human*, saving me had no endgame that I could see.

Did I think she was my mate? No. I knew better. Did that mean she wasn't mine? No. Willow Harper belonged to me, and I wasn't going to let her go.

I watched her say her goodbyes and then walk over to me. Her smile held a hint of sadness, but her eyes were filled with the excitement of returning home. "I'm ready." Her smile dimmed a little when she looked at Cannon, and I knew the alpha beside me unsettled her. "Thank you, for everything."

"I'm sure we'll see you again," Cannon said smoothly. "You are always welcome on Blackridge Peak."

She didn't hide her surprise, and I didn't think I did either. Helping her at the Will of the Goddess was one thing; offering her to return if she wanted to, was more than I expected.

"Um...thank you." Her eyes flicked to mine nervously, and I reached out and took her hand, which she gripped readily. "But I think my hiking days are done," she added with a nervous laugh. "Mountain living is too off grid for me."

Cannon felt me stiffen beside him, and when he turned to look at me, I could hear his unspoken *told you so.*

Saying nothing except *goodbye*, I led Willow out of the house and down to the Jeep that had been provided for us by the alpha. The terrain was steep, not as steep as my own peak, but it meant that vehicles struggled to get close to the town.

Willow stayed close to me as we walked to the parked Jeep. She didn't lift her head to look around, keeping her eyes on the ground in front of her. I knew if I asked, she would tell me she was watching her footing. I knew it was bullshit. She didn't want to see any frowns from pack who didn't like her holding the hand of a shifter.

For that reason, I looked at every pack member we passed until they dropped their stare.

This was Cannon's pack, but I was still an alpha, and I would be shown respect. If I wanted to hold my woman's hand, I would.

"Are you intending to melt the snow by glare alone?" I teased her as we walked further from the town.

"Will it work?" she asked, forcing lightness into her voice, but she failed to hide the bitterness from me.

"No." Pulling her closer, I looked down at her. "You can never please everyone," I told her gently. "You're letting other people's prejudices rule you."

"I know why shifters would want to keep quiet," she spoke quietly, keeping her voice deliberately low to avoid shifters' hearing. "But, having met a few of you, I didn't think that *I* would be considered the threat."

"Mm-hmm, you're definitely scary, especially without your morning pot of tea."

That earned me an elbow to the ribs. Which, as usual, was ineffective.

"Do you think they really are after you, and I was nothing more than bait?" She was already frowning as she thought about it. "It makes no sense. It's so random to pick me to target."

It did seem random. Until you thought about it and realized there was no one left that I cared about.

But I cared about Willow.

Even those first few weeks, I hadn't been able to stay away. The drawings mattered and were the reason I was in Whispering Pines, but the reason I kept returning? It didn't take a genius to work out it was because of the woman beside me.

I hadn't wanted to admit it then. Hell, I'd fought it with every part of myself. But now? With the way her scent was wrapped around me like a drug I couldn't quit, the truth was inescapable. Willow was more than a human woman I should have stayed away from.

She was the reason I couldn't leave.

I glanced at her from the corner of my eye, watching her as she picked her way through the snow. She was trying to keep up with me, not knowing I was moving at a fraction of the speed I would normally walk over this snow. Her careful steps, the look of concentration on her face, the shadows under her eyes as her body still healed from her wounds, even with all that, she still made the world around me seem...softer. Less harsh. And for a while, I'd been so sure of myself that I could keep her untouched by everything in my world. That I could keep her safe by keeping her in the dark.

But I couldn't have been more wrong.

I'd dragged her into this, and whether I liked it or not, she was part of my world now. My enemies knew it. And they would use her to get to me; they already *had* used her.

The trashing of her home and store lured me off Shadowridge Peak. Running her off the road and putting her in the hospital brought me out of the shadows.

They used her to get my attention, and that's why I wouldn't—that's why I *couldn't*—walk away from her again.

The very thought of her being hurt again...of losing her... twisted something deep in my chest. I already carried the guilt and shame of what I had done to her. My claws covered in her blood would haunt me for my lifetime. I knew that. I accepted it.

I'd suffered loss, more than I should have, but losing Willow? When I felt like this for her...it terrified me in a way that nothing else had.

"You okay?"

Her soft voice brought me out of my thoughts, I looked down, seeing the concern in her eyes. "Yeah, just thinking."

"Looked painful," she quipped.

Her squeal of laughter as I chased her with a handful of snow made me laugh.

I saw the Jeep, and soon we were both in. Willow immediately adjusted the heater after I started the engine. I knew I couldn't get lost in my head. Right now, I needed to focus on keeping her safe. There were still too many unknowns, too many threats to her.

But later, when the dust settled...when the danger was over...what then? I knew there was no future where I could just walk away from her. The joy of being with her outweighed everything else.

Surely this was what the Goddess wanted.

Right?

FIFTEEN

Willow

IT WAS SO STRANGE BEING BACK.

My house looked exactly the same as it had when I left. Everything was tidy and in its place. It was neat, lifeless, pretty much how it always was. Standing there, I realized that my home looked unlived in. Empty. It wasn't a perfect picture of how clean a house was before you went on vacation; it looked like this every day.

Had it always looked like this, or was I seeing it differently now that *everything* was different?

Because everything *was* different.

Glancing at Caleb, who was standing in the kitchen and scanning the room for threats that didn't exist, I knew he was the reason everything had changed. My home, my sanctuary, felt too small with him in it. His presence filled the space, making it hard to look at anything else.

I could pretend this was normal, but did I even know what normal was anymore?

Caleb hadn't mentioned sleeping arrangements on our

journey back to Whispering Pines, and neither had I. What was I supposed to suggest? The bed? Too forward. The couch? Ouch. The very thought of a six-foot-plus, fiercely protective, intense shifter crashing on my couch was just a reminder of the world I'd become entangled in.

And now, said shifter was my...what? Roommate?

Unbidden, I started to smile at the thought of it. If someone had told me two months ago that I'd be sharing my living space with Caleb, I would've laughed in their face.

Yet here we were.

His intense stare caught mine and we stood a few feet apart, saying nothing. The silence between us wasn't uncomfortable, but it was filled with things we were holding back. Like the night we slept together in the bunker. We hadn't had sex again, but Caleb wasn't shy in offering light kisses when he felt like it.

When he felt like it. Was that harsh?

I never felt like he felt *obligated* to kiss me. But I did think we were both trying to figure it all out.

"It was a long drive," he spoke suddenly. "Do you mind if I shower?"

"Um...no, of course not. Are you using the main bathroom or mine?" Wow. Awkward.

"Which one would you prefer me to use?"

Loaded question, and I floundered as to what the right response was.

"Whichever one you want. The pressure's good in both of them." *Pressure? That's what you're going with? Water pressure?*

He didn't say anything, and only moments later, I heard the bathroom door in the hall close.

"Right, the main one, then." *Did it mean anything that he picked that one?*

Why did I feel that his choice of bathroom added to the tension? But yet I also felt relaxed knowing the door was closed and I could breathe in my own space without his eyes on me.

What was I doing?

How was I going to *live* with him if this was how I felt after one hour of being in the house together?

What the heck did I tell Lily? I wasn't sure I could explain Caleb to *myself*, so how could I tell my friends? And expect them to believe me? The fact he was staying here, in my house, was out of character for me, and where did he sleep?

I could hear the questions now, and I knew I had no answer for them.

I had heard him in Cannon's study...library? Shaking my head at being so easily distracted, I thought back to what he said in the whatever-it-was room. When he asked me if this was my "ever after," I hadn't expected the question, and I'd frozen when he asked it. Because all I could think of was, *was I his?*

What was I to him? Someone he needed to save?

Why was he really here? To find the ones who were pursuing me to get to *him?*

Were we together? Or were we two people who slept together?

I hated the way the last question made me feel. I mean, we'd been alone for hours, and I hadn't brought it up.

Neither had he.

In defense of the situation, I'd slept for most of the journey because I was still recovering from my wounds. Which brought me to my next fear...was he only here because he felt guilty about what happened on Shadowridge Peak?

Then add onto *that* I was struggling with how this relationship—if you could even call it that—was viewed by his fellow shifters. Shifters didn't approve of mixed-race relationships. I wasn't an idiot; it was obvious as to why. If Doc was part-shifter because his father was a shifter and his mother was human, then reading between the lines, it meant that babies born of a human woman to shifter men didn't birth shifters. I also remembered my earlier thoughts that Luna was not a very forward-thinking Goddess; her emphasis was on continuing her species of shifters.

I wasn't planning any baby showers in my immediate future, but Caleb was an alpha. Was it not his duty to his pack to give them shifter babies?

But he didn't have a pack.

Which is why this shouldn't be the thing bothering me as much as it was. But how could I be with him when some of his society didn't think we belonged together?

Ugh...these thoughts were harder to shake off than I expected. Was he only here because of this bond between us?

I hated that *that* question was the one I feared the most.

Tea. That's what I needed, a good strong cup of tea. Waiting for the kettle to boil on the stove, I busied myself with getting cups, the teapot, and the tea leaves for the pot ready.

I was pouring myself a cup of tea when the bathroom door opened, and soon he was walking into the living room, a walking temptation. Shirtless, with a towel slung around his shoulders, his hair damp from the shower, wearing dark jeans with the top button undone. I forced myself to look away before I started imagining things I definitely should not be thinking about.

"Do you think we need to talk?" I blurted before I could stop myself.

Caleb paused. He had been reaching for the teapot, his eyes locking onto mine. "About?"

"Our story? Your alibi? What we're going to tell my friends?"

He poured himself a cup of tea, blowing across the cup delicately as he raised it to his lips. "Tell people? Why do we need to tell them anything? It has nothing to do with them."

"Of course it has!" My voice was sharper than I intended, but when he said such ridiculous things, could he blame me? "People will ask questions, Caleb. You're going to be living in my house. My friends, my neighbors...they're going to want to know why you're here! They *know* I only have one bedroom!"

He looked so calm, completely unfazed. "Why are you getting excited about this? Let them ask."

I felt like I had stepped back in time. He was once more an infuriating man who drove me to the brink of frustration. "It's not that simple."

"Why?" He sipped his tea. "I don't really care what anyone else thinks or asks. We know the truth."

I opened my mouth to ask if we did, but the words died on my tongue. He had a way of simplifying things that could almost feel dismissive in the way he approached them. But it wasn't that easy. How did I explain to my friends that this man, who only one of them knew about, was now living with me?

I couldn't tell them *what* he was or why I had been targeted. It was such a mess. I had been so eager to come home, but I wished I'd had the foresight to plan better.

Or dared to ask in the car.

Hindsight truly was brutal.

The knock on the front door made us both look at each

other and then towards the door. Neither of us moved, and when the knocking got louder, I jumped up to answer the door, only to meet an immovable wall.

"I'll go," Caleb told me. "You don't know who it is."

"Neither do you," I whispered furiously, hurrying after him. "You can't open my door in just jeans and all those abs out for anyone to see!"

Caleb looked over his shoulder at me, and I saw his smug smirk. "Hopefully, it encourages them to go away," he said with a wink.

"It's probably Lily!" I whisper-hissed, though I think I sounded more like a hissing feline than saying actual legible words.

Caleb opened the door without even using the spy hole. The audacity of him taking ownership was not lost on just me.

Lily stood at my front door with her mouth hanging open as she took in six-foot-three of muscled perfection. She recovered a hell of a lot quicker than me, her mouth snapping shut, and the most ferocious glare transformed her face.

"*You!*"

Caleb turned slightly so he could see me as he kept her in his sights. "Willow, you have a visitor."

Lily seemed to realize I was in the room, because her scowl vanished, and her squeal of delight caused not just the shifter in the room to wince. "Oh my God, you're home!" She brushed past Caleb with barely a glance and launched herself at me, causing me to stumble backward.

I felt his hand at my back, steadying me, and I saw Lily look up at him and immediately drop her arms. "Your wounds, I'm so sorry!" Which was immediately followed by the realization I was not in a hospital bed. "Should you be out? You were so badly beaten up!"

Her innocent question caused Caleb to flinch again, but this time for a different reason.

"I'm better," I assured her hurriedly. "Healing really well." Flicking my eyes to Caleb, I tried to catch his eye, but he was avoiding me, staring at the floor with a frown on his face.

Lily missed nothing at the best of times. She turned to look at Caleb. "So...what's going on here? Are you two...?" I saw her check him out. "Why are you half-dressed?"

"I just got out of the shower."

"Why?" she demanded.

I saw the look that came over his face and knew he was about to deliver a witty reply that would not go down well, so being a good friend and always ready to avoid confrontation, I jumped in.

"How did you know I was home?"

Now, she was frowning at me. "Oh, you mean when you *never* told me?"

Yup, here we go.

"It was Noel's turn to water the plants," she said. "He said he saw 'some guy' come out of a Jeep and go into your house, and did I know who it was?"

She left the question hanging in the air, and I could feel the heat rising in my cheeks.

"It's just Caleb," I muttered. I hated how weak I sounded.

"Right." She looked between us, her eyes once more roaming over his bare chest. "Just Caleb. *Friends*, right?"

Caleb didn't say anything, but I could feel the tension rolling off him in waves.

"Well, you're obviously *busy*," Lily said, breaking the

sudden awkward silence. "I just wanted to check in and see how you were." She sniffed delicately and I knew I was going to get it later. "It's only been about a week since I saw you, but you look so much better." Her smile was genuine, but I knew the glint in her eye well. "Call me...*soon*."

I gave her a tight smile, grateful for the out she just gave me. "Thank you for stopping by. I'm...sorry I didn't tell you. It was kind of sudden, and then I slept most of the way home—"

"Willow." Caleb's voice was low, but it was enough to stop me from babbling.

"Yeah, right, sorry." I forced a smile when I saw her eyes narrowing. "It's all good, we're good, just trying to settle back in."

"Mm-hmm." She turned to leave. "You need groceries. *If* I'd known you were coming home, I would have stocked your fridge."

"I can do that," I called after her, my cheeks burning again, but no idea why. "Wait!" She turned at the door, an eyebrow raised expectantly. "I have plants?"

She grinned, shooting Caleb a smug look, and I wasn't sure why. "Yeah. You have plants. Speak soon."

She left with a grin, and I wasn't sure why she suddenly looked victorious.

"What just happened?" I murmured. "That was super awkward."

Caleb's voice rumbled close behind me. "You didn't have to lie."

Turning to look at him, I hadn't realized I was so close to him. "I didn't lie. I just..."

"Lied."

"Didn't tell her everything," I snapped back.

He took a step closer, and I really wanted to demand he put a shirt on. All that flesh on display was distracting.

"So that's how you feel?" he asked me, his face unreadable. "You need to hide what we are?"

Shaking my head, I took a step back. I didn't have an answer. The truth was, I wasn't sure what I would call us yet. And until I figured that out, wasn't hiding the easiest option?

I didn't say that.

Instead, I walked towards my bedroom, pushing the door open. I saw the new additions to the room. Several potted plants were dotted around my space, making my bedroom more...homey.

"You didn't answer."

I jumped ten feet in the air as the stealthy shifter scared the shit out of me by sneaking up behind me. "Caleb!" My heart was pounding. "Do *not* do that!"

His look was unrelenting, and I took a deep breath, searching for an answer that would make sense, for both of us. "Caleb, it's not about hiding. It's about...I don't know." I shrugged helplessly, frustrated at my tangled thoughts. "It's just you're...you. And I'm me. And in your world, that means something different. *We're* different. And I need to have answers before I think of questions, and I don't have any answers."

He crossed his arms over his impressive chest, his gaze fixed and unblinking. Completely ignoring the fact he was making me drool at the sight of his physique. "You don't need answers, you need *honesty*. Be honest with them...and with yourself."

"Honest with them?" I challenged. "So, tell them you're a shifter, and some of your *species* don't like it when one of your kind sticks their dick in one of my kind?"

Caleb's eyes narrowed dangerously. "Is that what you think this is? That it was about sex and only sex?"

I hated his crude words, and I dropped my eyes, suddenly feeling exhausted. "No, of course not."

"Then why are you acting like this? Do you want an excuse to step away from this? From us?"

The simplicity of his question struck a chord in me. But as much as I wanted to believe it, things weren't that straightforward. Looking up, I took in the hard lines of his face, the intensity in his eyes as he watched me. My mouth went dry as I considered my words.

"It's that easy for you?" I asked carefully.

His expression softened, and he closed the distance between us. "Yes. I know what I want." Reaching out, he tucked my hair behind my ear, his fingers rubbing a few strands between them as his hand dropped softly. "I'm not ashamed of that. Or you."

His words settled around me like a weight. A weight that pulled me closer to the truth I was too chicken to face. But Caleb wasn't hiding, and he wasn't pretending. His being here wasn't just a commitment he felt he owed or empty words. It was *action*. He wasn't wavering on what he wanted or letting the doubts of others cast a shadow over his own feelings.

I didn't know what to say. All my life, I'd relied on myself and my own logic. But with Caleb, my expectations were different. *He* made me different. Being with him meant stepping outside my comfort zone, and it meant trusting him.

I wasn't sure I was there yet. He had a tendency to disappear on me.

Caleb moved back, giving me space, and for the first time since returning home, I realized how much I wanted him here.

And admitting that to myself terrified me.

"Hey..." I began, but I didn't know what else to say. "I..."

"You've got time," he said gently. "Just don't take too long. But also...take as long as you need."

With that, he turned and walked down the hall, leaving me to confront the questions that haunted me, and no one to ask them.

Except for the plants.

SIXTEEN

Willow

OUR EVENING HAD BEEN QUIET. NOT MUCH WAS SAID, but it hadn't been oppressively suffocating. Caleb had slipped out mid-evening to "let his wolf run" as he called it. If I was asked if I breathed easier when he was gone, I wouldn't have been truthful. I also wouldn't have been lying.

So yeah, there was that.

He also saved the awkwardness of the "where do I sleep?" because he was still gone when I went to bed. He'd told me not to wait up, and I hadn't. My body was healed, but whether I was still suffering from mental unawareness of my healed body, or perhaps it was more basic and it was simple PTSD or my ME, but either way, my body ached.

I woke up alone, the other side of the bed as it was when I went to sleep, but I knew he was in the house because I could hear him moving around.

Unless it wasn't him.

The fear that followed that thought almost made me throw up on my covers. The quick rap of knuckles against my bedroom door had me calming down.

"You awake?" His voice was deep and gruff. "Your scent changed."

My scent changed. The fundamental differences between us were once more highlighted by his use of his natural shifter abilities.

"Yeah, fine. Sorry, I'll be out soon."

Why had I apologized? Shaking my head at myself for being an awkward ninny, I got out of bed and trotted to the bathroom. After a quick shower, I pulled on a pair of soft lounge pants and an oversized baseball T-shirt. Extra thick fluffy socks completed my cozy outfit, and with a quick brush of my hair, I went in search of coffee. And Caleb.

Walking into the living room, I found myself watching him from across the room. He moved through the kitchen space with a predatory grace that felt so at odds with the easy familiarity of my own home. His movements were sure, perhaps a little too quiet, and at times cautious—as though he didn't belong.

I couldn't deny it was strange to see him here, in my kitchen, looking out of place against the backdrop of my pale beige and white kitchen. I knew better than to think he wasn't aware of me in the room, but his gaze kept flicking to the windows as if he were wishing he was outside instead of in. Or maybe I was doing him a disservice? Maybe he was on guard, waiting for whoever had been after me to leap out of the woods behind my house and attack me.

"Coffee?" he offered, pointing to a cup on the counter, and I was grateful for the break in the silence.

Was that my mug? How had he known that? "Yeah." I blinked slowly, wondering why I was being weird. "Thanks."

Padding over to him in my fluffy socks, I saw him look

down and thought I saw a ghost of a smile as he regarded them. As I took the cup from him, our fingers brushed, causing a jolt to run up my arm at the contact.

The effect he had on me was something I couldn't explain. I had tried—and failed—to reason it out. I'd also tried to ignore it, but that hadn't worked, as both times I'd slept with him happened when I'd been trying to deny the connection that existed between us.

I also realized that seeing him in my kitchen, in familiar surroundings, wasn't dulling the connection. If anything, it was making it sharper, more undeniable. There was no escaping the pull that I had to him.

"Are you planning on going to your studio today?" he asked, leaning against the counter with a casualness that looked alien on him.

I wasn't being harsh, the guy was intense. *Casual* and *Caleb* in the same sentence was unnatural.

Nodding, I took a sip of coffee. "I am, it's been too long. I know Lorna will have done an amazing job, but I need to get back into a routine."

I noticed that something I said didn't seem to sit right with him. His gaze dropped to the floor as if something I said dissatisfied him. Setting his coffee cup down, he turned and began opening cabinets, scanning the lack of contents with a bit too much intensity.

"Yes, I know, I need to go to the store." I sounded too defensive.

"You've not been here," he said reasonably. "But even when you *are* here, your food stock is sadly lacking," he mused, and I tried not to bristle at the insult. Intentional or not, it still stung. "I'll make a list, in case you're not able to get out or something."

Or something?

"Caleb, it's a grocery store run. Not much call for a survival mission in Whispering Pines," I said with a forced laugh, but I stopped when I saw his expression.

There was no humor in his eyes, just that raw intensity, that ever-present wariness. Did he know he was scanning the perimeter of my kitchen like it was hostile territory?

"Of course," he murmured. "I was thinking of your ME."

Oh, well, now I felt like a dick.

"I'll finish my coffee, change my feet, and then we can go together. If you want? Or I can go myself?" Did shifters shop? Or did they just eat the neighboring wildlife? Cheeks burning at my ignorance, I gulped my coffee.

"I'll go with you," he told me, making no mention of my sudden behavior change, but I knew he saw it.

He noticed everything.

"I'll be two minutes." Putting my coffee cup down, I hurried to my bedroom door, closing it firmly behind me as I leaned against it for a moment to catch my breath.

What the hell was wrong with us? This was *Caleb*. I *knew* this man. I'd had *sex* with this man. *Twice.* I'd slept beside him more times than I could count. As man *and* wolf. Why were we acting like strangers?

After pulling off my socks and lounge pants, and dressing in jeans and boots, I left my room, determined to make the weirdness between us disappear.

Grabbing my phone and keys, I gestured for Caleb to follow me. "Come on, you, let's go get some fresh air and food. Maybe if I feed you properly, you won't keep pacing in my kitchen."

Caleb opened the Jeep as I locked up, and following my directions, he drove us to the grocery store. I watched him as he scanned our surroundings the whole way. He took note of everything—cars, houses, pedestrians. I wasn't sure if he was looking at them out of curiosity or if he was analyzing them all as potential threats. Whispering Pines was a quiet town with a good tourist population, but trying to see it through Caleb's eyes, it felt foreign.

"Do you like it here?" he asked suddenly, nodding towards the tree-lined street that led to the grocery store.

"I do," I answered easily. "There's enough trade to keep an artist in business," I jested slightly. "A good tourist trade to matter and make a difference, but not too much to take away the sense of the familiar, if you know what I mean?"

"I don't," he admitted, glancing at me curiously.

I thought about how to explain it. "Mostly everyone knows everyone, local, I mean. But we have enough passing trade from the hikers and such that it keeps the day-to-day fresh. Sure, I may see the owner, Phil, from the bakery everywhere I go," I teased, referencing my first conversation with Caleb, "but I also see new people all the time." Seeing he didn't like that idea, I hurried on. "Whispering Pines is a tight community, but in a good way. We're not living in each other's pocket, but we're aware of where the pockets are if we need them."

I thought about the meeting in the town hall over the break-ins and my own break-ins added into that.

"When they broke into my store and my house, the community pulled together to help me. I got packed off to Lorna's, and the community banded together to fix the mess." Looking at the shoppers as they came and went into the grocery store as Caleb parked the Jeep, I sighed. "I don't think you would get that elsewhere." I thought about it. "Or bigger towns."

I saw him give a slight nod, his eyes lingering on the unfamiliar faces for a different reason.

"Whispering Pines is small enough for that sense of community but big enough not to have *everyone* know your business," I clarified. "And not too big that no one knows who you are."

He sniffed dismissively. "Sounds like a pack."

The idea surprised me. Did it? Was that what community was? Pack-like?

"You ready to do this?" he asked, eyeing the grocery store.

"It's just grocery shopping," I chided him with a roll of my eyes, "not a military operation."

He closed his eyes briefly at the slight reprimand. "This is just...different."

"Different how?" I asked, genuinely curious.

Caleb's steady gaze met mine. "From what I'm used to."

His reply left me with a faint sense of unease. A harsh reminder—as if I needed one—that this wasn't his world any more than his was mine. Had I given any thought before this about how the divide between us was so...wide?

"Come on," I said with forced cheerfulness. "Let's go food shopping."

The groan he made was pretty much the same groan *any* man made when told they were going grocery shopping.

Maybe the divide wasn't as wide as I thought. Grinning, I collected a cart while Caleb surveyed the store with a look of distrust and trepidation.

Grocery shopping with Caleb was strangely fascinating. He put more fruit and veg in the cart than I would. He added way more meat than I would, and when I added the snacks I usually bought for Alistair, he picked them back out of the cart.

"Still don't know if he's the reason your house was broken into by not being *broken* into," he grumbled. "It's how I found your key, remember?"

I'd told him about the other break-ins in town during our recent time together, and he'd said nothing, but I knew he had taken the story of my awkwardness when confronted with the townspeople and stored it away to analyze later.

"He's just a boy," I reminded him softly. Putting one bag of chips back in the cart.

"Who's vandalizing other people's property," he reminded me, but he let the bag of chips stay in the cart.

By the time we got back to my house, I could tell he was still as tense but seemed tired.

"You didn't sleep, did you?" I accused him as he started unpacking the groceries. His quick glance up at me confirmed my suspicions. "Caleb! You don't need to stay up all night and guard me. Honestly, you're *just* as scary being woken in the middle of the night as you would be patrolling outside."

I saw his lips twitch, but he turned away to open the fridge, hiding from me if he smiled at my words.

Clearing my throat, I tried to think of ways to put what I was going to say next. "You don't need to sleep on the couch if that's what you're worried about?"

He half turned to look at me as he placed two thick steaks in the fridge. "Why would I be worried?"

Right? Why would he be worried? "You know, because of... um...stuff."

Closing the fridge door, he turned to look at me, his arms resting loosely beside him. "Define *stuff*."

Define stuff, sure. Easy. Excuse me while I can't think of anything to say.

"You know, us."

One perfectly sculpted eyebrow rose. "I know *us* very well." His gaze raked over me, hot, filthy, and full of promise.

My cheeks were burning, but also, I felt slightly indignant. "Then *why* did you spend all of last night outside?"

A slow smile crept across his face, and his eyes were hooded with victory. "You want me in your bed at night, Willow?"

Did I? Yes.

"Yes."

He crossed the room so quickly that I gasped at his speed, and he used the opportunity to claim my mouth with his. The kiss was gentle at first, warm and familiar, but I sensed the hesitancy as Caleb tested the waters. It lasted a moment because any uncertainty dissolved, and the kiss deepened, filled with the unspoken passion that existed between us. All that mattered was our connection, the bond between us, and the undeniable pull we had towards each other.

The kiss gained urgency. Caleb's hands slipped into my hair, fingers twisting gently as he pulled me closer, tilting my head so he could deepen the kiss even further. I was no better, my hands curling into his shoulders, gripping him tight.

We were hungry for each other, mouths opening, tongues dueling as if we'd been starved, and the tension that had lingered between us melted away as we lost ourselves in the kiss. Every touch felt amplified, every sensation more vivid, and it wasn't long before my clothes were removed as quickly as his.

Picking me up, he placed me on the counter, my legs parting naturally for him to fit between. Caleb's lips nipped and sucked at my neck, his fingers dipping between my legs, testing my readiness. Gripping his cock, I guided him to my entrance, not caring about foreplay, I needed him inside.

Caleb inside me made sense. Caleb fucking me was one of the *only* things that made sense.

He pushed forward, and my head dropped back as I felt the deliciousness of the slight burn of his thick cock stretching me.

"Caleb." My voice was husky and filled with need. A need he recognized as he started to move inside me, claiming my mouth again, smothering my moans of appreciation.

He wasn't gentle, but then, neither was I. My fingers dug into his shoulders, nails dragging over his smooth skin as he picked up the pace between my thighs. He pushed me backward until I was almost lying on the kitchen counter, his body following me down as he drove into me.

"You feel so good," he murmured against my breast, his mouth capturing the stiff peak, his tongue flicking over it lazily. Caleb moved his hand down to rub my clit in smooth circles, applying the perfect amount of pressure to make me squirm greedily beneath him. Wrapping my legs around his hips, I pulled him in tighter. "You were made for me, Willow." He groaned as my inner muscles pulsed around him, gripping him tighter. "Fuck, do it again," he ordered. I looked up at him and saw his head tilted back, his eyes closed, and his expression twisted into one of lust and desire.

Knowing I did this to him filled me with intense satisfaction. The idea of us both letting go like this filled me with a wild, insatiable *need*. He made me *crave* him. All I wanted was his cum spilling inside me, filling me.

Caleb gripped my hips suddenly, pulling me closer to the edge of the kitchen counter. Pushing my legs wider, he looked down at me with a wildness that made me shiver with anticipation. His pace was relentless, and all I could do was lie there and take it.

Relish it.

"Caleb..." The needy whine in my voice made me sound unrecognizable, but he knew what I wanted.

Bending swiftly, he nipped at the underside of my breast. "I know," he growled. "I know what you want." His look was fierce but stunning.

I never wanted this to end, but my body was ready to let go. My climax was building fast, and I wasn't sure I was ready for it, because I knew my orgasm was going to be a big one.

"Come for me," he demanded as he pushed into me over and over. "Come for me. Show me who you belong to."

Jesus Lord, I was going to combust.

My cry of disappointment when he withdrew, leaving me empty, turned to a cry of pleasure as his mouth and fingers replaced his cock. His tongue moved over my clit, his mouth sucking on the tight bundle of flesh, and his fingers sawing into me made me lose control. It was all I needed.

My scream echoed around us, my hands fisting his hair, pulling him into my pussy as he feasted on my orgasm, his mouth and tongue delivering a climax that shook me to my core. The intensity of it never lessened, not when he replaced his fingers with his cock once more. Not when he fucked me with a force that was almost brutal but was *still not enough*.

He lifted me effortlessly, and my back was slammed against the wall as he fucked into me. My orgasm was never-ending, or maybe I was on the next one, or the next, I didn't know. I was losing count. My body was limp, and I was barely holding on as pleasure crashed over me in continuous waves.

Caleb's sharp bite at my shoulder brought a moment of pain, and then I was lost in another orgasm, dimly aware that he was roaring out his release. His head dropped to burrow in the crook of my neck as he shuddered and spilled inside me.

Later—minutes, hours, who knew—I opened my eyes and realized we were in a tangle of limbs on the couch. When did we move?

Tilting my head back, I looked up at him, realizing he was asleep. His face was the picture of contentment. The small smile on his face was gentle and peaceful.

He looked so striking when he was relaxed. Don't get me wrong, he was gorgeous—grumpy or furious—but like this, unguarded, he was breathtaking.

My body was tender, and my core felt slightly bruised, but something deep inside me was immensely satisfied. I vaguely recalled Caleb using a warm wet cloth on my lower body, so there was no awkward stickiness between my thighs serving as a reminder of what we'd done, not that I needed it. My lower body still pulsed with the aftereffects of having great sex...*really* great sex.

But I didn't want to leave the comfort of his embrace. Here, like this, my head didn't have a thousand questions lined up waiting to be answered.

Wrapped in his arms, I didn't feel like I needed to hide our relationship. I didn't need to question it. I didn't need to question *him*. I was still relishing the touch of a man who had laid claim to my body as he was claiming my heart.

Here, on my couch, nothing mattered except us.

Call me stupid or a coward, call me whatever you wanted, but right now, right here, I was happy to ignore everything else that posed a threat to *us* and simply bask in the aftermath of our lovemaking and savor the feeling of being safe in Caleb's arms.

He said I was made for him? I was beginning to think he was right.

SEVENTEEN

Caleb

WATCHING WILLOW EAT MADE MY WOLF HAPPY.

Watching her eat meat that I cooked for her was deeply satisfying. She'd frowned when I suggested cooking her steak rare, her nose wrinkling up in disgust. When she told me she ate her steak cooked "well done," I'd questioned her sanity.

We'd compromised on medium-well, which in reality was more medium-rare. However, she was eating every scrap like she hadn't been fed in days. Not only was she eating it, but she was savoring it, licking her lips as she gobbled her meal greedily.

"When was the last time you ate?" I asked her in amusement as she licked her lips.

"You made a sandwich earlier, after..." Her cheeks reddened, and she looked away from my knowing grin.

My *smug* grin. After fucking her on the counter earlier and carrying her to the couch where we'd both fallen asleep, I'd woken up, carried her to her bed, and started all over again.

Now it was evening, and we were both hungry after round three in her shower. I made a note to get her a new shower curtain. Taking a bite of my steak, I wondered if there was anything better in this world than Willow's snug pussy wrapped around my cock.

Taking a sniff of the air as I chewed, my wolf rumbled with happiness as I smelled my scent all over her. She's never washing that off, I thought, knowing how arrogant that sounded and not caring. My scent was embedded in her skin. The only way she would be free of it was if I never touched her again, and I knew that was never going to happen.

She was *mine*.

This morning and afternoon had proved that. I would find the bastards that hurt her, and when I was done with them, I would ensure no one ever hurt her again.

Including me.

When the threat to her was removed, I knew the right thing was probably to remove myself as well. But I couldn't.

I *wouldn't*. I would do better by Willow. I would be the man she deserved.

I knew the fears Willow had regarding how other shifters would view us. Some of my kind didn't approve of blurring the lines. Humans were supposed to be separate from us, they were not part of our world. They didn't share our abilities; they didn't have the grace of Luna in their blood.

But Willow did.

I knew she did. She had *my* blood in her system. I couldn't explain it, but the connection between us was growing the more we were together. I knew it wasn't a mate bond—the simple fact was that a mate bond couldn't exist with a human.

But our bond was *something*.

It was and I could feel it becoming *more* every day.

All of which satisfied my wolf, because it confirmed that the woman across from me belonged with me. I may never be able to call her mate, but I could call her mine.

Willow looked back at me, clearing her throat. "I had a few texts from Lily earlier," she began carefully. "They noticed we never made it to the studio today." Her slight frown as she spoke did nothing to quell my sense of self-satisfaction at how she spent her day instead. "They are expecting me tomorrow. I told her I would be in."

I didn't like it, but I couldn't stop her. This was her business after all. "Sounds good," I told her as I ate a fry. Why I needed to eat fries with a steak was alien. I wanted meat, and for a side, more meat would do. Instead, I had thin strips of a vegetable my wolf didn't want or need. "What time do we leave in the morning?"

"We?" Willow was looking at me in surprise, her fork half-raised to her mouth. "You're still coming?"

"Why wouldn't I be?" Was she serious? After today? After laying claim to her tight body over and over again, she thought I wouldn't be as protective. As *possessive*?

"Oh, I thought, you know…"

"I don't know," I answered smoothly. "The threat to you is still out there. *My* enemies are still out there."

"I know." She dropped her eyes, and I wanted to tell her to lift them again and challenge me as she so obviously wanted to do.

Challenge me? What kind of shit was I talking about? That wasn't me. A shiver of fear danced down my spine as I realized how I sounded to myself.

Unhinged.

Wild.

Feral.

Fuck, I was slipping. Again. Taking her this afternoon had loosened my control. I needed to be better.

Stronger.

For her. She could never be near me if I lost control again. And I knew I could never be without her being near. I needed to rein it in. My teeth ground against each other as I tried to pull control back from my inner darkness.

I claimed Willow. *Only* me. The beast that lived within me, that clung to the shadowy edges of my consciousness, it could fuck off.

Willow cleared her throat again. Either she had something stuck in her throat or I was making her nervous. I didn't want it to be the latter, so I forced myself to eat another fried stick of potato.

"If you come with me, I'll introduce you to Lorna and maybe her husband, Noel."

"Sounds good," I lied easily. "It would be nice to meet the people who took such good care of you when I wasn't here for you." That wasn't a lie. I *was* appreciative of the people who had cared for her.

"We could go for dinner," she suggested tentatively. "It will maybe help them understand...us a bit better?" She took a hasty sip of water. "And Lily too."

The suggestion seemed to hang in the air between us. I couldn't think of anything worse. "Dinner, huh?" I cut my steak with more savagery than was perhaps warranted.

She nodded eagerly. "It could be good, Caleb. I need them to know you."

"You need them to *like* me, you mean." I saw her disappointed frown and felt like a dick. "Alright, dinner it is."

She gave me a look that lingered too long. It looked a lot like doubt, but then after a moment, I saw her smile, warm and soft, like her. She held my gaze for a second or two longer before returning to her meal.

"Thank you," she murmured. "It'll be good," she said again, and I wasn't sure which one of us she was trying to convince. Maybe both?

Her words settled around me as I watched her eat. I wasn't sure why she thought meeting her friends was a good idea, but the hope in her eyes was hard to ignore.

"You don't need to thank me, Willow," I chided her gently. "This is what people do." I saw her smile again, but I was wound tight beneath my own calm tone.

People. Not shifters.

Pack ate together as it was. It wasn't a formal affair. Or an event. It was simply mealtime. I was already dreading that I was going to make a mistake.

Dinner with her friends. People who were already protective of her, which was good, but not when it came to the fact that they would be protective *against* me. I would need to be on my best behavior as I pretended to be *normal*. The very thought of it left a bad taste in my mouth. It all felt so...human.

This quiet town, where they all knew each other, where dinner conversation would involve talking about people I didn't know, about the weather, and whatever mundane shit they filled their day with. It hadn't struck me until now just how something so simple could cause a problem for us.

Her gaze was steady, unwavering, as she ate, as if she knew I didn't want this, as if she could hear my hesitations as they ticked over in my mind. The simple fact that she knew I was having trouble over this, even though I thought I hid it, just confirmed how much Willow had already sacrificed for me. I owed her my best attempt. Even if I hated the idea of fitting into this life, I would do it for her.

"You don't need to worry," I assured her. "We will show your friends that I am going nowhere." I didn't tell her that my instincts were at war with my words. I wanted to shout this wasn't where I belonged. But I *did* belong with her.

When I was with her, just her, it was simple. When we were wrapped around each other, nothing else mattered. But then reality came along and reminded me that this world was sometimes as foreign to me as my world was to her.

Willow looked pleased and when she stood up to gather the dinner dishes, I watched her, appreciating the gentle curve of her ass and the way her hips swayed slightly when she walked. She wanted me to meet her friends; she wasn't hiding me. I needed to recognize the trust she put in me. After what I did to her, I didn't deserve it. But I knew I wasn't going to shatter that for anything.

I would spend the rest of my life making it up to her, for hurting her. For using blood magic to save her.

I stood, picking up my glass and taking it over to her, where she stood by the sink, rinsing plates. Our fingers brushed, the thrill of her touch rushing through me.

"You don't have to come, you know. It's maybe not fair of me to ask. We're, well, it's kind of sudden."

Which is exactly why I'd burn the fucking world for this woman if she asked.

She expected nothing from me, even when she gave me *everything*. Even after all the shit I'd put her through. Hospitalized her. Ripped her apart with my claws, yet she stood here telling me she understood if I didn't want to have one meal with her friends.

One meal.

She had almost died in my arms, and I was balking at dinner?

Goddess, I was a colossal prick.

"I want to be introduced to your friends," I told her, gathering her in my arms, ignoring the fact her hands were wet. "I want to hear their stories, I want to meet their challenges to see if I am good enough for you, and I want them to know that I'm not, but I will work hard every day until they think I could be."

Her gaze was so soft as she searched my eyes. Reaching up, she cupped my cheek. "You're too hard on yourself. They're going to love you."

Like I do—it felt like it hung unspoken between us. Or maybe I wished for more than I was due.

I meant it though. No matter how long it took, I would make myself worthy of her.

WHY THE HELL HAD I AGREED TO THIS?

The day had passed too quickly, the threat of this meal hanging over me like a hangman's noose as I stood on the gallows. We'd gone to her store in the morning. The older woman, who I remembered was one of Willow's students, had been running the store in her absence.

She had a *lot* to say. The woman didn't draw breath. Two hours into being back in the store, Willow coaxed me to leave. I think she knew her friend Lorna was close to no longer breathing because I was going to gag her.

She'd moved Willow's store around a little, and I knew my girl wasn't overly happy with the changes, but I saw her bite her tongue, and a few times she went to a different place than where she thought something should be, only to be directed *in her own store* to the right place. Lorna's husband was a carpenter, and extra shelving and cabinets had been added to one wall and also in the kitchen.

Yet, Willow didn't say a word and bit back all her hurt as she adjusted to her new store layout.

This was why I wanted to decapitate Lorna, but being the good shifter I was, I watched my girl, saw the way she graciously accepted the help, and respected what she wanted.

Willow urged me to go "for a walk," which we both knew meant "shift and run." Lorna had screeched at the idea of "a nice meal out," and despite declaring she had nothing to wear, she adamantly insisted she would do her day's work before she went home and ransacked her closet.

Willow caught my flat stare, and it was at that point I was led to the back door and encouraged to "run it off."

Now, here we were. In an Italian restaurant, crammed into a booth with the stench of garlic lingering audaciously in the air. The place was small and cozy. If I were being overly critical, I would call it cramped, but it was full of people, and the low hum of their chatter and laughter filled the restaurant.

Lorna and her husband, Noel, were across from us, with Lily's dad beside them. Lily was against the wall, with Willow between us, as I took the outside seat.

The scent of cooked meat, melted cheese and spices suffocated me. But overriding all of that was the scent of garlic. I could hardly scent Willow, and she sat beside me. I was not ignorant of the openly curious stares from the three humans across from me, or the constant wave of suspicion that assaulted my senses from Lily.

I knew it was going to be a long night. Reminding myself this was for Willow, I vowed I would get through it, but when the server came to the table to take drink orders, I ordered a beer before anyone else spoke. I felt Willow press her leg against mine, and my hand automatically dipped under the table, placing my hand over her thigh, letting the touch of her ground me.

She slipped her hand into mine, squeezing gently as she listened to her friends discuss the menu. I could feel her pulse as my finger soothingly traced over her wrist. It soothed me, at least.

She leaned in and whispered, "They're just curious, don't worry."

I gave her a small nod, but my senses were on high alert, cataloging every voice and every movement in the restaurant. I could feel their stares as they drew Willow into the conversation, their unspoken questions sitting impatiently on their lips, waiting for the right time to be asked.

"It's so good to see you, Mr. Summers," Willow spoke to Lily's dad, and I picked up on the hint of shyness she had when she spoke to the older man. He was dark-skinned, darker than his daughter. Willow told me he had a timber mill on the outskirts of town, and the first thing I'd noticed when I shook his hand was that he'd never logged timber in his life. His hands were smooth and soft. "I don't remember the last time we all went out," she added.

"Well, this is the first time you've been out to dinner with me," Lorna added in, making herself somehow the center of attention again.

Willow's smile was warm and filled with affection, and I

tried to banish the thoughts of never wanting to be in the woman's presence again.

Good Goddess, she was grating. My hand was squeezed beneath the table, and I tried to relax my shoulders.

She had done a lot for Willow, and I was grateful for her. I needed to see the qualities that Willow would see in her. Maybe then I could see the good things in the woman.

Other than the need to smother her in her sleep.

Hiding my grin behind my bottle as I took a swig of beer, I caught her husband's eye, and somehow, I saw my thoughts reflected in his eyes. He gave me the weary smile of someone who'd been there, done that, worked through it, and resigned themselves to the inevitable that this was his life.

I tipped my bottle to him slightly and saw a genuine smile before he took a drink of his own beer. He had chosen draught beer. It was cloudy and had a huge foamy head, and I knew I was happy I took a bottle.

"Okay, I've been patient enough," Lorna declared suddenly, her eyes wide with excitement. "Tell me all about yourself, Caleb."

Fuck. Was this what hell felt like?

EIGHTEEN

Caleb

I COULD FEEL THEIR STARES ON ME. EVEN LILY HAD twisted in her position at the end of our bench to somehow be drilling me with eyes.

"What do you want to know?" I asked, trying to fake a smile that looked open and genuine.

Willow jumped in. "Now, Lorna, I told you earlier not to pester Caleb with questions. I promised him you all would be kind and *gentle*." Somehow, I didn't need to see the look she gave Lily to know it was pointed. "Caleb's staying with me for a while."

For a while? I didn't blame them for the unspoken questions. It wasn't exactly a ringing endorsement. It hardly said our relationship was a solid one. But how else did she explain me?

Lily's dad, he was very easy to read. He'd been looking at me with suspicion since I first met him. "What do you do for work?"

I was guessing *drifter* wasn't going to win any favors. "I like to move around a lot," I told him. I wasn't going to lie, but I also wasn't going to be completely truthful. "I pick up what work's going as I move around." His gaze flicked to Willow briefly, worry etching into the lines around his eyes.

"You have no trade?" he asked me, his tone taking on a slight edge.

"Did criminal justice at college, didn't go to law school." I preempted his next question. "Joined the army instead. Did two tours, came out, felt like my service wasn't over, went back for one more tour." Lorna's husband and Lily's dad were both watching me, and I saw the suspicion shift to respect, albeit in Lily's dad's case, it was grudgingly. "Got back after the third one, knew I'd seen too much, done too much to then face conflict every day at work, so the skills I learned in the army, I worked on them. While I'm no tradesman, I can fix things. Build things. It keeps me honest."

"Hard work is the most honest," Lorna's husband said with a salute of his beer.

"Noel," his wife admonished him, flicking a worried glance at Lily's dad.

"I missed your name," I told him bluntly, knowing damn well that Willow introduced him as "Lily's dad."

"Raymond."

"Thanks," I murmured, feeling Willow squeezing my hand.

"So, you have no job right now?" Lily asked, leaning forward.

"Didn't say that," I countered with an ease that belied the tension I was feeling. "My job right now allows me to work from home." Which wasn't a lie. Protecting Willow *was* working from home. Her home. But they didn't need unnecessary details.

"And how long are you here for?" Raymond asked, his eyes still shrewd.

"For as long as Willow wants me here," I countered smoothly.

I heard Lily's impatient huff and Lorna's murmuring to her husband about how sweet that was. But I kept my gaze locked on Raymond's, knowing the answer didn't satisfy him. His jaw clenched, but before he could say anything else, Willow leaned forward, her hand on the menu.

"So, what's everyone having?"

As discussion picked up about who was ordering what and what appetizers could be shared, Willow leaned into me, and I could feel her unease, but despite that, she forced a smile. "You're doing great," she said quietly, low enough for only me to hear.

Lorna asked her if she wanted to halve a pizza with her, and Willow turned back to the conversation.

Even with her encouragement, it was hard not to feel like an outsider. Ostracized. Every glance in my direction felt like a spotlight on how different I was. When Noel asked me where I was from, I gave him the vaguest answer I could manage without lying outright. Small town, moved around a lot, definitely an American. That seemed to satisfy him, but a glance at Raymond told me he wasn't buying it.

Food ordered, it arrived not long after. The bonus of Italian cooking, everything was fresh and cooked quickly.

Willow ate her chicken parmesan quickly, and I caught the slight look of surprise on Lily's face when Willow leaned over and asked for a bite of my veal.

"But it's a baby cow!" Lily protested.

"Mm-hmm, meat, yummy, I want some," Willow said, looking directly at me, but the look of hunger in her eyes had nothing to do with the meat on my plate.

The dinner dragged on, and I listened to her friends tell her about the town gossip that she'd missed. Though I was confident Willow would have missed this had she been in town these last few weeks. Even now, she looked bored at their retellings of what had happened. The only piece of gossip, if that's what it could be called, was that Alistair's dad had figured out the pattern to the break-ins and gave his ass a kicking. Then dragged his son to every house and made him apologize and offer to make amends.

The sheriff had deemed that appropriate punishment.

Alistair's dad had also kicked his wife out and was going to be staying more permanently in Whispering Pines. Willow looked both sad and happy for her young friend, and I wrapped my arm around her as she listened.

The only highlight of the evening was watching her smile and laugh with her friends, her cheeks flushed with happiness and the heat of the room. There was something about seeing her so content that made me...protective.

But as much as I enjoyed seeing her enjoy herself, I couldn't settle. I couldn't shake the feeling of being watched. Raymond didn't drop his stare, and neither did his daughter, but it was more than that. It was irritating me, and despite having my back to a wall, I still had the urge to look over my shoulder.

When the bill came, it devolved into a three-way argument between the women. Lily thought couples, or father-daughters, should pay a third. Lorna wanted everyone to pay their own for fairness, and Willow wanted to pay for it all. Raymond excused himself to go to the restroom, saying Lily's vote would be the same as his.

When he came back, he'd settled the bill. Lorna gushed at his generosity, Lily rolled her eyes, Noel murmured his thanks, his ears turning red with embarrassment, and Willow seethed beside me. Her "thank you" was neither heartfelt nor sincere.

Which was why I was going to fuck her to oblivion when we got home. Willow had invited them out, so it was for her to pay it all if she wanted. Taking that choice from her by an underhand move was shitty.

His intention may have been good, but I'd seen my girl bite her tongue too many times today.

Dipping my head to her ear, I spoke so lowly Willow may not have heard me. "You're going to come on my tongue so much tonight I'll never be thirsty again."

My girl stiffened in surprise at my words, and the little intake of breath got my cock hard as her scent overpowered the stench of garlic. If I'd known making her wet was a relief for my nostrils, I would have whispered dirty promises in her ear all night.

The evening had finally wound down. Lorna was still talking—when was she not?—but I felt myself finally relax a little. Willow was pressed into my side, almost subconsciously, as if the tension and the pretense of the night had taken a toll on her too. Lorna and Noel had accepted my presence, Lily too, although I knew she resented the fact she was softening towards me. The only one who was pissing me off now was her father.

Eventually, Willow's gaze met mine, a hint of relief in her eyes. "I'm ready to go if you are?" she murmured softly, the question just for me.

"More than ready," I replied, a touch of humor in my voice, and welcomed seeing her bright smile.

We said our goodbyes, and as we stepped out into the cool night air, I took a deep inhale of the pure air. Willow's hand slipped into mine, settling me once more as she tugged my hand to look at her.

"Thank you for this," she said quietly. "I know that was a lot for you, and I know it wasn't easy. I really appreciated it."

Pulling her a little closer, I dropped a kiss on her lips. "For you, I'd face worse." Leaning down, I pressed a gentle kiss to her head, knowing how true my words were.

We started the walk home, when Lily came barreling out of the restaurant, yelling for Willow.

What now? I was tempted to keep walking and pretend we hadn't heard her. But my good, sweet girl stopped and turned.

"Lorna wants to know who's opening the store tomorrow. She's turned hysterical, thinking she's out of a job." Lily rolled her eyes at the overly dramatic woman. Like she could speak? "How much liquor was in the tiramisu?" she snarked, leading Willow back into the restaurant.

I would face worse for her—I *just* told her that—but the Goddess herself could not make me walk back inside that restaurant tonight.

"Willow?" I called after her.

She turned back, her hand on the door, understanding in her eyes. "Stay out here. I'll be two minutes, once I've calmed her down."

I could see inside the restaurant from out here. I could see everything and not have to *hear* everything; it was a win-win for me.

"I will make it up to you," I promised, relishing her flushed look at my dark promise.

Looking around, I could still feel the sense of being watched. I couldn't scent anyone out here though. There were a few pedestrians. It was a nice evening for the time of year, but there was no shifter in the air.

Cursing the lingering scent of garlic, I turned to look up the street. Nothing. Frowning, I turned to look back into the restaurant and saw the party of five all heading to the door and Lorna apologizing profusely for being overly emotional when she was tipsy.

She'd had one glass of wine. The thought made me smile despite her annoying traits. I could see why my girl loved her, and I knew she would probably grow on me. Whether I wanted her to or not.

Once outside, we grouped into our respective pairs, more hugs between the women were shared, and we finally, *finally* started the walk home.

Willow leaned into me as we walked, and I was ready for a pleasant walk and a long night of owning her body when a whisper on the wind made me falter.

"I know what you are."

Turning to look over my shoulder, I met Raymond's dark gaze as he held the passenger door open for his daughter, who wasn't paying attention to where her father's focus was.

He dipped his head in acknowledgment, and as I turned back, holding Willow closer to me, I made the mental note to make a house call to Raymond Summers when his daughter wasn't home.

STANDING OUTSIDE THE LARGE BUT MODEST, slightly weather-worn house, I shifted my weight, hearing the porch creaking as I listened for any signs of life inside. The street was quiet, no one around to witness my unannounced visit. I'd dropped Willow off at work, and then I'd watched Lily leave for work, her father conspicuously absent, but I didn't know them well enough to know if they traveled to work together.

I suspected that Raymond Summers had opted to stay at home today. This would be a conversation that was best kept private.

Rapping my knuckle against the door again, I heard footsteps approach from inside. The door opened and Raymond stood there, his look one of expectation, and when he glanced at his watch as if to ask what had taken me so long, I snorted as I walked past him into his house.

"Come in, why don't you," he murmured, closing the door behind him.

"Thanks, don't mind if I do," I replied, failing to keep my own bite from my words. "Where do you want to have this *talk*?"

Raymond looked me over from head to toe, weighing me up, and I got the impression he found me lacking.

I didn't give a fuck.

He saw that very clearly, and I saw the ghost of a smirk before he gestured to a door behind me. "The study, I think."

He led the way, and I followed him inside to a room with dark wood and dark navy walls. It was oppressive, and I knew what he'd been aiming for, but in an office this size, all he'd done was make it claustrophobic. Raymond took the seat behind the desk, a weak power move, but I let him have it. I opted to sit in one of the weathered leather chairs.

We sat in silence for a beat, the hum of the recessed lighting and the faint sounds of the road filled the space between us.

Raymond leaned back in his chair, folding his hands, which were laid on the desk, as he waited for me to speak.

I'd played poker with my father, a notorious ball-breaker. Raymond Summers could kiss my ass if he thought I would break first.

"You're not what I expected, Caleb Foster," he started, his voice firm, and when I grinned at the small victory, he gave me a flat, unimpressed stare, but I could scent his irritation, and it made me grin wider. "My daughter, Lily, likes to talk, though, God's mercy, not as much as that woman last night."

The fact Raymond also struggled with Lorna made me decide right then and there Lorna was okay. This time, I saw his slight smirk, and I gave him that one for free.

Manipulative bastard. He was worth the watching.

"When Lily first mentioned the hot guy"—he looked affronted at having to say the phrase—"who was interested in Willow, I admit I didn't pay her any mind. But then I heard you left. Then you came back. Then you left just as suddenly as you arrived in the first place. Then she got her home and business broken into on the same day." He leaned forward, his elbows resting on the desk, his fingers steepling in front of him. "That made me look a little closer. Maybe I put a few things together..."

I waited patiently, acknowledging the words without confirming anything.

The shrewd look he wore last night was back, and his next words were slow as if testing the weight of each one. "I've seen your kind before," he told me carefully, his eyes never leaving mine. "Different places, different people, but it's hard to forget that..."

"That what?" I prompted him, my patience running thin.

"The particular look in the eye." He sat back and considered me. "The unexplained explained."

I felt my wolf stir, but I kept my expression bland, committing to nothing as a low instinctive wariness prickled at my skin. "And what look would that be, exactly?"

His mouth twitched as if my non-confirmation was confirmation enough. "The look of someone who sees beyond what most of us do. Someone who doesn't quite fit." He paused, his gaze unflinching. "I've known about your kind for some time now, one way or another."

"My kind?" I asked, stretching one leg out in front of me casually.

"Shifter."

Fuck. Would Willow forgive me if I killed her best friend's dad?

"You know and have said nothing?"

Raymond shrugged. "Why would I?" His expression hardened. "Never needed to. Your kind has never bothered me or mine before. But Willow...is like a daughter to me. *Family.*" His expression softened slightly when he mentioned her name. "She doesn't know the danger you bring with you."

If only he knew...

"Danger I bring?" He was lucky he'd mentioned the word *daughter* when he declared she was *his;* else we'd be having a very different conversation. "I only want to protect her."

Raymond's gaze sharpened. "By putting her in the hospital?" His look was challenging. "Don't bullshit me about a car accident. I don't know what happened, but the blood my Lily saw, the care that girl needed to be *saved* was your doing." He held his hand up to stop me from speaking. "Even if you didn't cause the wounds yourself, I know it was being tied up in your business that scarred that girl." A flicker of something like pity flickered across his expression. "You may be protecting her, but you're the reason she needs protecting."

My jaw clenched, my fists instinctively flexing as I held my frustration in check. "You don't know shit," I spat out at him.

Raymond leaned back in his seat, his voice quieter, almost resigned. "I'm not the enemy, Caleb. But I also won't stand by and pretend I don't see what's happening right in front of me. You may be here for her, but I've seen what happens when things go wrong with your kind."

"Then you'll know I will do anything in my power to make sure she's protected."

Raymond huffed out a laugh. "Your threats don't work on me, son. Willow will come to no harm from me."

We sat in silence for a moment, a silent truce as we considered our positions. Willow forgave me for almost killing *her*; surely, killing Lily's dad wasn't as bad as that? Was it?

However, the older man's first reaction was to protect her, which not only demonstrated he cared for her but that he was loyal to her. I could respect that. I didn't want to, but I could.

"You want to protect her? Prove it." He studied me, his gaze stern. "Leave her. Leave Whispering Pines and don't come back."

"Never going to happen."

Raymond said nothing, holding my stare, and then he stood, gesturing for me to do the same. I followed his lead as we walked back to the front door, where we faced each other once more.

"She has people who will protect her as fiercely as you do," he told me, his voice low. "No matter who they're protecting her *from*. Don't forget that."

"Are you threatening me?" I asked him, surprised he had the balls to do so.

"No." Raymond shook his head slowly. "That's a *promise*, son."

Making my way down the porch steps and away from the house, I thought of Raymond's words as they echoed around my mind.

Looks like Raymond could grow on me, too... Damn Willow's friends for being so fiercely protective.

Shifters respected pack that protected each other.

Raymond left me with a lot to think about, and I knew I needed to speak to Willow.

And I knew she wasn't going to like it.

NINETEEN

Willow

Whoever taught Caleb Foster how to use his mouth on a woman's body deserved a medal.

He started making love to me right after dinner, drawing one orgasm after another until I was nearly sobbing, almost begging for him to stop. When he finally slid inside me and began to move, my body felt weightless, floating through the waves of sensations he stirred within me. Needless to say, I slept so soundly that I woke feeling completely renewed.

I'd slipped out of bed, careful not to wake him, and as the early morning light filled my studio, I settled into my work.

The charcoal seemed to move almost of its own accord across the page, creating rough sketches that were already half-formed in my mind. Over the past few nights, I'd felt the pull, the need to draw, and I knew that the scenes I was creating were not of my own making. Images of places and times I didn't recognize but that felt unmistakably familiar.

The itch beneath my skin from Caleb's blood had lessened when I was with him. Sometimes I would be aware of a slow hum, but that was usually when I wasn't near him. Like my blood needed him near to cure the need I had for him.

He'd definitely cured me of the itch last night. Pressing my thighs together, I remembered my cries filling my bedroom as he squeezed every moment of pleasure from my body.

But the urge to draw had been niggling me, and this morning when I woke, I knew I wouldn't settle for the rest of the day if I didn't draw. Every stroke of the charcoal brought another scene from Caleb's past to vivid life.

In the first quick sketch, a younger Caleb laughed with others around a bonfire. He looked so relaxed in a way I'd rarely seen him. The imposing log cabin stood in the far corner, so I knew he was on Shadowridge Peak, and the others in the sketch would be part of his pack.

Even from my sketch, I could tell the air around them was thick with the kind of camaraderie and belonging that he had never shown me. The dimple on his left cheek was deep when he laughed as he was in the scene. He looked so happy, *alive*, immersed in a world of shifters.

He belonged there.

In the next sketch, he stood in a vast, open field, the moon high above him, a wolf pup in his arms—was it his? Pushing past the moment of the unknown, I considered him as he stood there. He looked...at peace. Content in a way that pierced me deeper than I wanted to admit.

My chest tightened as I ran a finger over the outline of his form, smudging the harsher line, making it softer. Shading the familiar strong line of his jaw, catching the gleam of happiness in his eyes. I'd never seen this *lightness* in him. He hadn't been simply surviving in his pack, he'd *thrived* in it.

It was becoming clearer, the more I drew, that he had

belonged on that mountain, his world, more than he would ever belong in mine.

I dropped the charcoal as I looked over the three sketches I'd made this morning. Rubbing my hands together as if to shake off the cold sinking into me, I wondered if I could give him what he needed.

A pack.

My stomach twisted as I thought back to what Raymond had said to Caleb yesterday. Caleb had told me everything, and it was clear that Lily's dad hadn't minced his words about what he thought Caleb should do. Caleb hadn't pulled any punches when he told me what happened, and then I think, to make up for the harsh words, he'd sexed me into a stupor. But looking at Caleb with his pack, I remembered what he had said to me.

"It's not like he doesn't care about you," Caleb said, his voice tense, his eyes guarded. "But he's aware of what I am, and because of that, he knows the risks." Caleb shrugged, almost dismissively. But I could see he was angry, in the way he held his back straight, his shoulders squared.

"'Aware'? What does that mean?" I'd asked, feeling indignant on his behalf. "You'd never hurt anyone here."

Caleb had looked at me, the look in his eyes filled with guilt as he remembered he had hurt me. He sighed, his hand rubbing over his face. "That's not the point, Willow. To him, I'm a threat just by being here. That's all he sees, a creature who can bring danger to his world. His daughter's world." He'd looked away, jaw tense. "And can we say he's wrong?"

I'd wanted to argue, tell him he did belong here, that he was more than just a threat, but the words wouldn't come. Because deep down, I'd wondered if Raymond was right. Not about Caleb being dangerous, but about him not truly belonging here. After all, how could he feel at home in a place where he was always watching himself, never being his *true* self?

Feeling numb, I picked up the charcoal again, almost mechanically. The next image flowed from me effortlessly—a scene of Caleb, older, wiser, surrounded by shifters and wolves, the alpha of his pack. The ache in my chest grew as I shaded in his proud, confident stance, seeing how he would've looked in a life where he was free and had a pack to lead.

With a sniff, I hastily brushed away the tears before they had a chance to spill over. Standing, I turned to the door to freshen up before he woke, but he was already there. Leaning against the frame, watching me, his expression unreadable.

"They started again?" he asked, nodding towards the sketches.

"Yeah," I murmured, hoping he couldn't see them. "Been fighting the urge to draw, which meant they came out faster than ever."

He walked into the room, looking over my shoulder easily, as his arms slipped around me, pulling me close to his chest. But I was still able to tilt my head and look up at him, seeing how his gaze softened when he looked at the sketches. A small, almost wistful smile curved his lips. "You've been busy," he said quietly. "I haven't thought of that night in years," he told me, reaching out and picking up the sketch of him at the bonfire with his pack. His friends.

He said nothing as he looked at the one with the wolf pup, and the quiet stretched between us, heavy with unsaid words. I pushed myself closer to him, knowing he was looking at the sketch of him older with a pack. Hating myself for wanting to demand if he was happy here, if he *could* be happy here... with me.

"This is my little sister," he told me, breaking the silence. I moved so I was turned to the sketch pad. He kept an arm around me as he looked down at the drawing. "She was a late addition to our family," he added softly. "Mother called her 'her little surprise.'"

"What was her name?" I asked, looking between the drawing and at him.

"Callie," he murmured, his eyes filled with pain. "She was three when they murdered her."

"Caleb..." Pressing my head into his pec, I tried to hold back the tears. "I'm so sorry."

I felt his lips press against my hair. "Can I keep this one?" His voice was thick with emotion, and I could only nod because I knew I was going to sob if I tried to speak.

We stayed like that for a few minutes, both of us grappling with emotions that I was sure were vastly different from each other.

Eventually, I stepped back, and when I looked up at him, he was waiting, his eyes searching mine, catching the question I hadn't dared ask yet.

"Willow..."

"You look so free here." I gestured to the drawing of his pack. "So at ease." I swallowed hard. "I don't think I've ever seen that."

Caleb let out a slow breath, his hand finding mine, tugging me closer. "My past was...a different time. Who I am in that drawing, I can't go back to that, not even if I wanted to."

"Maybe," I conceded, biting my lip. "But can you say you'll find that here, outside of your world, where you can be free? Maybe there's something left for you on Shadowridge Peak."

Caleb's gaze flickered, something vulnerable flashing across his face. "You want me to leave?"

"No, I didn't say that. But...I don't want to be the reason you feel...I don't know...trapped?" My voice was barely above a whisper. I picked up the third sketch, the one where he was an alpha of a pack. "I don't want to keep you from something you might still need."

His grip tightened on my hand, his expression hardening. "Willow, you don't hold me back. No matter what my past held, it doesn't change what I want now, and I want *you*."

"Really?"

He smiled softly, brushing a thumb over my knuckles. "I want you." Dipping his head, he brushed a kiss over my lips. "I want to sleep beside you every night. I want to wake up beside you every morning."

He kissed me again, his mouth moving over mine with a possessiveness I loved, and as the tension slipped away, I let myself believe that maybe, just maybe, we would find a way to make it work.

THE NEXT MORNING, A SLIVER OF SUNLIGHT CREPT through my curtains, illuminating the room in a warm glow. I blinked sleepily, rolling over to find the space next to me empty, the sheets cool. I sat up, rubbing my eyes as memories of yesterday settled in. Caleb and I had bared pieces of ourselves yesterday morning, maybe things we'd been holding back, but I had felt lighter.

I'd gone to work in the early afternoon and spent the day with Lorna, picking up on work I'd missed. She'd set up an inventory of work from local artists that she wanted me to consider hanging in the gallery. It had become apparent to me she had her own opinion, and after a few conversations, I'd finally just made her tell me her thoughts.

She'd been a student and, let's be honest, a very basic artist, but she had a good eye, and she knew what fit in the gallery. She knew what complemented my style, and I genuinely enjoyed working with her.

Caleb had been in and out during the afternoon, never straying far but never permanent, and I knew Lorna was still someone he wasn't wholly comfortable around.

We'd enjoyed a quiet dinner, then I went into my studio and Caleb went out to "stretch his legs." When he came back, we'd had an early night.

It was a good day.

Now I was awake, a new day, and my bed was empty. Part of me wondered if I'd said too much, voiced doubts he didn't need to hear. But...I also felt a satisfaction that it was out there, and he'd listened to what I was trying to say.

Pulling on a sweater and a pair of sleep shorts, I left my bedroom, the scent of coffee guiding me to the kitchen.

Caleb was standing by the window, a mug in his hand, looking out the window to the trees like he was watching something far away. He didn't speak when I walked in, but his head tilted slightly, acknowledging my presence. As I walked up to him, he wordlessly pulled me into his side, wrapping an arm around me, as if he'd been holding me like this every morning for years.

Putting his cup down, he reached over and placed a steaming mug in front of me. "Morning. I heard you were awake."

"Thanks." I took a sip, knowing that it would be made perfectly. Caleb was thorough in everything he did. I let the warmth settle me, and we stood in silence for a moment before I glanced at him, trying to read his mood. I wasn't sure why he looked so pensive this morning.

Caleb sighed. "I can't stop thinking about what Raymond Summers said," he began, his gaze shifting to look down at me. "I meant everything I said yesterday, but..." His gaze flicked back to the trees, searching for the words. "And you're drawing again. I can't stop thinking this is Luna's doing."

I frowned, instantly on guard. "You think your Goddess is trying to keep us apart?"

"No." He shook his head. "But the shaman and, I think, even Cannon think she has more of a hand in everything. I don't think it's a stretch to say she influences your drawings," he said softly. "And if that's what we accept, then what is she trying to tell us by showing my past or..."

"Your future."

His gaze softened. "This doesn't mean I'm going anywhere. I'm just trying to figure out how to make this work, with us being...us."

"I know," I murmured. I wanted to move away, but I also wanted to press closer. "I think we've both been guilty of forgetting everything that has happened to us over the past few days."

"Yeah," he agreed, his lips pressing into a thin line, then turning to a quick smile. "Not that I'm complaining," he added. "But I've been ignoring the threat to you. You have people targeting you, and I need to find out who."

His words dropped between us, heavy. He was right; reality was knocking on the door, even as we tried to pretend nothing could affect us in this bubble.

It was time to face it head-on.

Moving out of the comfort of his arm, I leaned against the counter, tracing the rim of my coffee mug. "I take it you have a plan?"

His jaw tightened, not liking that I'd moved, but he accepted it. "I've marked boundaries out around the town, marking territory, making it clear I'm ready to defend what's mine."

What did that mean? I had a sudden image of him as a wolf marking his territory. Caleb saw my eyes widen and rolled his in reply.

"You went there, didn't you?" he asked with a shake of his head.

"You peeing in a straight line around the town?" I asked bashfully. "Yeah, I did...sorry."

He muttered something that sounded a lot like *juvenile*, but I wasn't certain. I studied him, seeing the fierceness in his expression that I hadn't seen since he came back. This was the side of Caleb I sometimes didn't feel comfortable with, but it was the side I knew best. This was the fighter in him, finding a purpose in protecting something—and someone—he cared about.

"What are you thinking?" I asked, already dreading the answer. "What's the plan?"

His gaze was soft. A warmth filled my belly as he looked at me, and I felt a sense of relief when I saw a shadow of a smile touch his lips. "Putting 'low-key dinners' on the backburner for a while." His smile grew when he heard my chuckle. "As much as I enjoyed it, let's focus on what's important."

"They'll be devastated at the thought of missing out on

your smooth-flowing conversation," I teased, feeling a bit of the tension ease.

"Yeah, I'll do better," he promised, looking slightly abashed. "But first," he said, growing serious, "I want to get to the bottom of who's using you to get to me."

For a long moment, neither of us spoke, letting the threat settle between us. It wasn't going to be easy, but no part of me wanted to back down.

I wanted Caleb to know I was as willing to fight for him as he was for me. "What are you thinking?" I took a drink of my coffee.

"I want to draw them out," he told me, his gaze steady and clear.

That sounded doable. "Okay, how?"

A determined glint was in his eyes, and I suddenly felt wary.

"How do you feel about being bait?"

TWENTY

Caleb

Willow's eyebrows disappeared into her hairline at my suggestion, a flicker of doubt in her expression. I saw her reservations, and I braced myself for the argument, but to my surprise, she gave a slow, careful nod.

"Bait, huh?" she repeated, her teeth worrying her bottom lip, but there was something steely in her gaze—the kind of courage I'd seen before in her but never truly appreciated. This woman would walk into danger head-on if she thought it would help, and that worried me more than I cared to admit.

"You're not freaking out?" I asked, reaching for her hand. "They've been quiet, but does that mean they've gone away? I don't think so, and we can't afford to wait around, hoping we'll be ready for their next move."

Willow looked down at our entwined fingers and then glanced back up, searching my face. "So...your idea to counter that is you want me to be bait?" She obviously wasn't liking the idea, but she hadn't said no.

"It's not about making you a target," I assured her, though

the irony wasn't lost on me. "It's about controlling the situation. If I set this up right, we lure them out, on *my* terms."

I could see the gears turning behind her eyes as she studied me, her lips pressed in a thin line as she weighed every risk, every possibility. I knew that, more than anything, she wanted to face this down and reclaim her life. Willow didn't want to be looking over her shoulder, and that was why I thought she was considering it. But she also didn't want to act recklessly.

"What if something goes wrong?" she asked, almost reluctantly.

"I will be beside you," I assured her and then thought about it. "Or as close as possible for it to work." I saw a moment of doubt, and something fierce flared in me. "Nothing will happen to you, Willow. Not again."

She nodded slowly, and I could feel the bond between us pulling tighter, making me even more confident that this was the right thing to do. The pull was what kept me close to her, in this town, trying to fit into her life, even as I craved the freedom of familiar territory, like Shadowridge Peak, where I could see any threat coming for miles. But if I couldn't root out these threats and uncover who was coming for her, it wouldn't matter where we were.

"You think it will work?"

I nodded, feeling a surge of relief—and something else. Admiration. She trusted me, and I didn't deserve that, but it was more than that, she was ready to fight alongside me. I wanted to shield her from every ounce of danger, but to keep her safe, I had to put her at risk first.

I knew my plan sounded unhinged, but I truly believed it would work. Sometimes you had to take big risks to win big.

I wisely didn't say that. I knew she was brave and she was

being so strong, but I also didn't want to scare her. I could almost hear my father in my head asking me if I was crazy.

"I've been gathering information," I told her, letting her take a breath. "I've been talking to anyone in town who's noticed anything strange, and trying to piece together something that made sense." I began to pace as I told her what I'd been doing. "You've potentially seen two of them. Can you draw them again?" When she nodded, I felt a surge of pride when I looked at her. "I also have...someone who might have seen them or know of them."

"Who?" Her eyes were wide with curiosity.

"A contact," I replied, purposely evasive. "If there's outsiders who don't belong here, he'll find them."

She opened her mouth to ask another question, but she picked up on my reluctance to share too much detail. I couldn't tell her everything, I knew that. But the fact she was drawing again, scenes of my past—one of a future I would never have—I knew I wasn't imagining the prickling under my skin, sensing our enemies were closing in, or the instinct gnawing at my gut, telling me to get her out of here before it was too late.

And I knew I definitely could not tell her that my wolf was aching to return to my packlands. Even if they were filled with darkness, they were mine, *my* territory.

My packlands. *My* Willow.

Yeah, maybe I'd tell her everything one day, but the fact that I was a possessive asshole, I think she maybe already knew. For now, I needed to focus on one thing at a time.

Reaching over, Willow squeezed my hand. "Okay then, let's do it. What do you need me to do?"

Pulling her over to the couch, I started to lay out my plan so Willow had a clear picture of exactly how I wanted this to go down. She listened intently, a crease furrowing her brow, but she kept quiet as I explained.

"Well, first step is simple recon," I told her plainly. "I've started that, looking at familiar places, your walk to work, the stop you make for coffee, anywhere you'd normally go. Your routine is really easy to pick up," I added. It was how I had known when she wasn't home after all.

"But I haven't been in my routine," she told me. "I've been with you."

"I know, and we need to stop that," I told her, seeing the slight flare of panic in her eyes. "Move through town like you would, keep to your routine, but without me. I'll be close," I added.

"So you stay out of sight..." She looked me over quickly, refraining from mentioning it would be hard for me to blend. "And I just act like there's nothing wrong?"

"Yes." I held her gaze. "I won't be far. The idea is to see who follows you. If they do, I'll be close enough before anything happens to you."

"That's not as reassuring as you think it is," Willow murmured, smoothing her hands over her thighs. "Alright, so I go about my day...then what?"

"If, and I appreciate it's an if, *if* we get a lead, we'll escalate." She didn't react to my use of the word *escalate*, so I continued. "I'm talking about a more deliberate move to draw them out— maybe a rumor, something that would get back to them."

Willow bit her lip. "You mean, like I'm leaving town, so they think this is their last shot?" She sounded doubtful, so I didn't tell her that sounded like a good idea.

"Or...that *I've* left town," I told her slowly, trying to keep my tone calm so as not to alarm her. "They're already watching us, Willow. I can feel their eyes on me. Us. They'll take the bait if they think I'm gone. They won't know when I'll be back, so they'll act."

She looked away, staring out her window, and I saw a flicker of fear cross her face. She was so much stronger than she knew, but she wasn't oblivious to the risk involved.

Glancing back at me, her eyes clear, she folded her arms across her chest. "And what about you, Caleb? When they realize that you're here to protect me after all?"

"Then there'll be a fight," I told her firmly. "They may not know exactly what I am, but they'll know enough to be cautious. As long as I'm here to make sure they never get close to you, they'll learn real fast what happens when they try." I held her gaze. "I've killed two of them already; I'm just getting started."

Willow's lips quirked in a small, wry smile. "Well, that sounds incredibly bloodthirsty." Blowing out a breath, she shrugged. "Intimidation first though, right?"

"Sure." I saw her flat stare and smiled. "I'll do my best, but I won't promise. They want to hurt *you* to hurt *me*." I became serious once more. "Never going to happen, Willow. *Never.* If intimidation doesn't work, then we end this the other way."

Willow looked down, her focus on her crossed arms, and then she unfolded them, clasping her hands instead. I could see her mind racing, torn between accepting the plan and the fear of what could go wrong.

"Okay," she finally said, her voice soft. "We do this, but I need to know you'll have an escape plan if things go sideways."

"You'll be fine." I reached out, covering her hand in mine, the warmth of her skin settling me like nothing else could. "But you—if *anything* ever feels wrong, anything at all—you go to the most populated place, and you stay there until I tell you it's safe. No second-guessing it."

She nodded, but there was a hard determination in her eyes. "I didn't mean me, I meant you. Do *you* have an escape plan? Who has your back in this, Caleb?"

I didn't have an answer. I'd been so focused on making sure she only knew what she needed to. The more dangerous parts, the corners I might cut, those would be on me. But to ask who had my back? I wasn't prepared for that.

"Um…"

"No one?" Willow's eyes narrowed. "What about this 'contact' you have?"

"I wouldn't feel comfortable asking him," I told her honestly.

"Fine," Willow said with a tone I'd never heard from her before. "I will. Who is it?"

Fuck.

"Does it matter?" I asked quietly.

"I'm risking myself for this plan, but I have you protecting me. Who's protecting you, Caleb? I want to know. If we are drawing these people out, if there *are* people to draw out, then I want to know you're covered just as much as I am."

Leaning forward, I caught the back of her neck, pulling her forward, my lips claiming as my mouth devoured hers, as I poured everything I felt about her into that kiss.

When I pulled back, I looked into her eyes. "You're amazing, Willow Harper, do you know that?"

Her cheeks were flushed, and I knew it would be a mix of pleasure and praise. "Nice try," she whispered, leaning up to me and kissing me softly. "I still want to know his name and meet him."

"His name, maybe," I conceded. "You don't need to meet him."

She was going to argue, but I got off the couch, pulling her after me. "Come on, you need to get ready to go to work. We need to let as many people know, this morning, that I'm leaving town for a few days and you'll be alone."

"I'll find out," she taunted as I led her to the bathroom.

Her confidence was so much more than when I'd met her. I wondered if she knew how much she'd blossomed in such a short time. In the shower, I reminded her how precious she was to me.

She was all that mattered. I would find out who was targeting her, and if it meant letting a little of the beast within me loose, then so be it.

⸻

THE WORN FLOORBOARDS CREAKED UNDER MY BOOTS as I stepped into the dimly lit bar. The scent of cedar and old leather hit me, mingling with the familiar scent of whiskey. Across the room, seated alone at a corner table, was a man I hadn't seen in years, but he was instantly recognizable. Eamon looked up as I approached, his sharp eyes cutting through the low light, the all too familiar smirk tugging at the corner of his mouth.

"Caleb Foster," he said, looking me over as he leaned back in his chair. "Heard you'd gone loco. I didn't think you had it in you."

I sat down across from him, crossing my arms. "Your mouth's still spouting out shit, I see."

Eamon chuckled, raising his glass to me. "What can I say?

You're so fucking straightlaced, when I heard you'd lost your mind, I had to check what I was drinking." He took a deep pull of his whiskey. After setting the glass down, his tone sobered. "So...is it true? You've shacked up with a human?"

I kept my expression unreadable. "Not here for the small talk, Eamon. I need your eyes and your instincts."

"See, there he is, straightlaced, all-business Caleb Foster." He sniffed like he'd smelled something bad. "A human, man? Like for real?"

"You got a problem with humans?" I asked him with a raised eyebrow. "How's Britt?"

"Fuck you," he muttered, downing the rest of his drink. "She was my best friend."

"Yeah. Sure. Heard her screaming your name *real* friendly like far too many times," I told him. "You want to throw shit, or you want to get to it?"

His eyes danced with laughter, his grin growing. "I'll take all business for twenty." He nodded to the bartender, raising his glass in one hand, holding up two fingers with the other. "Alright, Alpha, what do you need?"

"Don't call me that," I grumbled.

"Why? You're still an alpha." His hard eyes held mine. "No matter the fact you have no pack, that's your choice."

I glanced around the bar before answering. Even here, among strangers, it felt risky to speak so openly, but if there was anyone I could trust with Willow's safety, it would be Eamon. He had never run from a fight, and his loyalty was to himself, but once...once it had belonged to me.

"Willow is human," I confirmed. "She's gotten tangled in something, and it's putting her at risk."

"I heard she was tangled around you," he told me, pausing while two glasses of whiskey were placed in front of us.

"Will you shut up?" I hesitated as I registered what he'd said. "You heard? Heard from *who*?"

"Shifters talk, always have. Talk travels." He took a drink, and when I didn't resume my conversation, he sighed dramatically and leaned forward. "You were on packlands with a human; *everyone* who's a shifter knows *that*."

"That may be so," I admitted. "But who did *you* hear it from?"

Eamon considered me as I waited. "One of the males from Blackridge Peak was running his mouth at a drop-off a few weeks ago. Said you and her took the tourist route to the ridge, and when you got there, your scent was all over her."

Because we'd had sex in a car, my scent *was* all over her. "His name?"

"No clue." Eamon shrugged. "Know his pack, know his alpha, he was with the alpha's brother. He shut him up before I could."

"Willow is important to me," I told him through a clenched jaw. "Her knowing me is putting her at risk. I don't need gossiping pack to run their mouths about her." I felt my anger building. "I need her safe, Eamon, but I can't watch her every second."

"Which is where I come in?" he guessed. His curiosity was piqued, and I knew I had him. "You want her involved in this?" The look in his eyes shifted from amusement to serious. "You serious about her? A human?"

I held his gaze. "This is more than that. Willow's tied to... something." I hesitated, unsure how much to reveal. "She's connected to things she doesn't understand, and honestly, neither do I." I lifted the glass and downed the whiskey in one go. "There's something about her, something worth protecting."

Eamon watched me, his gaze intense. "Alright. So, what's the plan?"

Briefly, I ran through what had happened up to this point. Eamon listened, his demeanor changing as he took his task seriously.

"So it's a trap?" he surmised. "You're using this girl—who's *important* to you—as bait?"

I felt the sting of rebuttal in his tone. "It's a trap," I confirmed. "We need her to go about her life as usual, but I know she's being watched. I don't know who or why. Or even how many. But if they think I've left her vulnerable, then they may strike. I need you close. Keep an eye on her, but keep your distance. I'll track down anyone suspicious."

Eamon nodded, his expression thoughtful. "And this Willow, how much does she know? *Really* know?"

"About this? She knows it's a trap to draw out my enemies."

Eamon rocked back in his chair as he watched me, letting out a low whistle. "Your enemies, huh?" His fingers drummed against the table. "And does she know *why* you may have enemies?"

"She does."

"Alright then. You'll owe me big for this, Caleb."

It was my turn to smirk. "You've always known where to find me."

"Have I?" He looked up at me as I stood, his eyes guarded. "You've been alone too long, man. I'll do this for you, but if this is your paranoia because you've lost your marbles, I walk."

"I'm not imagining the threat to her," I growled.

"Yeah? As long as the threat isn't *you*, you mean?"

"We doing this?" I demanded. "Or are you going to shut up and do the job I ask of you?"

"Well, look at that," he said, downing his drink. "There's an alpha in you after all."

Eamon stood, holding out his hand, the silent agreement hanging in the air between us. I took the offered hand and shook it once. Pulling him into me, I lowered my head to speak in the shorter male's ear.

"She gets hurt on your watch, I'm taking it out on your hide."

"Stop flirting with me, man. I told you before, your dick's too small to satisfy me."

I huffed out a laugh as he stepped back. "Good to know you're still an ass," I said grudgingly.

I felt better though. Knowing Eamon was watching Willow's back meant I could focus on what I needed to do.

Now, all that was left was to see who it was that I was baiting.

TWENTY-ONE

Willow

THE NEXT FEW DAYS WERE UNREMARKABLE, WHICH somehow made the tension worse. Caleb had told me to act like everything was normal, but it was hard to relax when I knew I was being watched. Each casual step I took through town felt unnatural and overexaggerated, like I was putting myself on display, walking through a minefield of unknown dangers.

I'd made my way to the gallery, pretending to be as unaware as I could. Stopping to chat with those I knew, just like I would if I didn't have eyes on me from unknown sources. When I finally turned onto Main Street, nerves made me duck into the bakery so I could feel like I could breathe.

I ordered my usual coffee and added a cruller, which I usually avoided, but I needed the sugar rush this morning.

"You suck at acting natural," a guy behind me said under his breath. "May as well paint a sign on you that says 'I know you're watching.'" I went to turn around, but he stopped me, his hand on my arm causing me to flinch. "Don't turn, sweetheart. Don't need the sign to be flashing neon."

"Who are you?" My heart was racing. I desperately wanted to turn around and confront him.

"Caleb's still keeping secrets," he said with a grunt. "Typical." He moved away. I knew he had as I no longer felt the heat from his body. "Do me a favor, sweetheart. Get your breakfast, keep your head down, cross the road, get into the gallery, get a brown paper bag, lock yourself in the bathroom, and breathe."

"I'm not *that* bad," I muttered, pretending to look at my nails.

"You're right," he agreed. "You're worse."

Asshole.

"Hey, Willow, haven't seen you in a while." The server started talking to me, and I moved away from my new *friend.*

With my coffee and breakfast in hand, I looked at the stranger as I left the store, meeting his knowing gaze, seeing the smirk as our eyes met. He dipped his head slightly before I turned away and crossed the road. Balancing my breakfast, I opened the art gallery. After the encounter with Caleb's... "friend," I hated the fact I'd given Lorna the morning off. I wanted someone I knew beside me. But then that meant I was putting Lorna in danger, and I wouldn't do that.

Instead, I hastily drew his profile so I could show it to Caleb later. Then I spent my morning finishing inventory and fielding some calls from past customers who had bought one of my pieces and now had someone reaching out to them, making inquiries to buy them for more than they were worth.

I knew it was Cannon and his pack, but still, in another world, in another lifetime, it would be kind of nice to have a conversation with customers who believed your work was worth more than they paid.

Lorna came in around one. The bag with her held mouthwatering aromas, and I helped her unpack and then ate a hot lunch while she asked me a thousand questions about my relationship with Caleb.

Noel had inadvertently been the alibi Caleb had pounced on to leave town. Noel was short a pair of hands for laboring a big job a couple of hours away. Both Lorna and I were alone while our "men-folk" worked out of town.

I wasn't sure how Caleb was explaining not turning up to Noel. He couldn't be close to me and two hours away at the same time. It just added to my anxiety.

After lunch, I found myself relaxing in Lorna's familiar chatter.

"Noel says Caleb doesn't talk a lot," she said with a sidelong glance at me. "Does he say much to you?"

"Who, Caleb?" I asked her, looking up from my sketchbook. "Yeah, we speak."

"He seems so...stoic."

Putting my pencil down, I gave her my full attention. "He talks when it matters," I told her, fighting the blush in my cheeks as I suddenly remembered exactly how vocal my man could be when he was ordering me around in the bedroom.

Lorna gave me a knowing look. "Uh-huh, just make sure he keeps talking when the honeymoon period is over." She tsked softly. "Young love's all well and good, but if there's no conversation, then what's left when the honeymoon is over?"

"Um..." My mind had snagged on the word *honeymoon*, and I was completely unstuck.

There would be no honeymoon for Caleb and me. He was a shifter, I was not. I didn't think there was a happily ever after in our future.

Lorna changed the topic when she saw how subdued I was.

We said our goodbyes around four, and I refused her offer of a lift. I needed to be seen and lure out my would-be-attackers, so I opted to walk. Like I usually would.

As I walked home, the world felt strange, the hairs on my arms prickling as I walked. It was the tail end of November, Thanksgiving was three days away, and I was bound to be feeling the chill since the snow had started falling.

Only I wasn't cold. In fact, the cool air was pleasant. My steps slowed as I considered the changes in my body since coming off of Blackridge Peak.

My appetite had increased. I wanted more meat in my diet. I felt so much stronger in my body.

I'd only had one ME flare-up since I came out of the bunker, and it was so mild it was barely noticeable.

Fishing in my pocket, I brought out my phone and immediately called Doc. I then hung up as quickly. I couldn't have this conversation in the street. I didn't know who was listening. And then I didn't know if I was *supposed* to have this conversation in the street because I wasn't supposed to *know* people were listening.

God, my head hurt.

I was so caught up in my head that I didn't even realize it was happening until it happened.

The figure moved in my peripheral vision, hovering just long enough for me to register the threat and then recognize the threat. He was closer than I'd expected, and his face was partially hooded, but I would have recognized him anyway.

The man from the bus station.

He walked rapidly towards me with a single-minded intensity that froze me in place. I stumbled slightly in my haste to walk backwards. I knew I needed to move *away*. Recovering myself, I forced myself to turn around, every nerve on high alert as I started to run.

I heard him chasing me, and fear made me run faster. Suddenly, a hand as strong as steel grabbed my shoulder, hauling me backwards as I let out a hoarse scream for help.

A hand was slapped over my mouth as I was lifted off my feet. I got ready to struggle when out of nowhere, the guy was knocked away from me. I fell to the ground, my hands scraping against the sidewalk. When I looked up, the guy from the station was wrestling with the guy from the bakery, and I felt some relief as I watched him wrestle the other shifter.

Then Caleb was there. He crossed the distance between us so fast it was almost unnatural, his shoulders rigid, his eyes as hard as steel. The guy from the station clambered to his feet, took one look at Caleb, his face pale beneath the shadow of his hood, and then he bolted.

The guy who'd tackled him was already on his feet, giving chase. Caleb's arm was around me, pulling me to my feet, crushing me to him. "Are you okay?" His voice was low, and though it was probably meant to sound reassuring, it came out as a growl.

"I'm fine," I whispered, my knees shaking. "I'm okay." I saw the wildness in his eyes. "Go, find out who he is."

"I'm not leaving you," he bit out. His face was dark with fury. I hadn't seen that look of anger on his face since the night on Shadowridge Peak. His fists were twitching, his wolf riding close to the surface, and I saw his eyes change color as he struggled to hold on to his control, as if he were fighting the chance to tear into someone.

I knew what those fists felt like when he lost control. Without thought, I backed away.

Caleb saw my move, saw where my gaze was fixed, and I saw the devastation in his eyes as he realized what had happened. He looked away, masking the pain at seeing my reaction.

I moved towards him, but he held up his hand. "Don't, I don't want to hurt you."

"Caleb…"

His jaw clenched. "It's not over. I need to know who he is and what he's doing. Come, I'll take you home." He walked briskly the short distance to my home, never speaking.

And I didn't know what to say.

At my front door, he backed away. "Lock the doors, open for no one. Not even me."

He was gone before I could say a word.

Inside, I paced the floor of my living room as I bit my thumbnail, waiting for word from Caleb that he was okay. My cell rested on my coffee table, but it never rang.

Eventually, I made a cup of tea, but it lay untouched as time moved on, and when I did lift the cup to my mouth, it was stone cold.

As the night got darker, I did my best to stay away from the windows. Eventually, I called Doc. I needed a distraction. My improved health would serve that purpose.

He answered on the third ring. "Willow? What's wrong?"

"Hi, Doc, nothing's wrong." *Lie lie lie.* "I was wondering if I could ask a few questions?"

"I love questions," he told me, and I heard the warmth in his voice. It was so natural and familiar that I fought back tears. "Shoot."

"I've not been sick," I told him bluntly, forcing my voice to be strong as if nothing was wrong. As if the man I cared so much for hadn't just been devastated by my foolish reaction.

"Since coming home," I clarified. "I've had one flare up. Nothing to really note." I drew in a shaky breath. "What's happening? Am I still human?"

I gave him time to consider it, the silence almost welcome. "You're still human," he finally spoke. "As to what's happening? I need to know more. Can I ask questions?"

"Of course."

"Some may be more personal than we normally share, Willow," he said, his voice lower, clearly uncomfortable, which struck me as odd.

"Shoot," I copied his earlier answer.

"Where's Caleb?" he asked. It sounded almost like an afterthought.

"He's...out." That wasn't a lie. Just not a true reflection of my current reality.

"You two okay?" he asked carefully.

"Couldn't be better," I lied again. "So, your questions?"

Talking to Doc distracted me, but my eyes stayed glued to the door, waiting for Caleb to come home.

We talked about my diet, and he wasn't in approval of some of my food choices, noting more meat in my diet than previously. He didn't ask why I was sleeping so soundly. I guess he didn't need a doctor's degree to know how biology worked.

"Are you using protection?" Doc suddenly asked.

"Condoms?" I squeaked when I finally found my voice.

"Yes."

My face was burning. "Um. No."

"Uh-huh, and are you on birth control?"

He wasn't kidding when he said he was asking uncomfortable questions. "Um, yes."

"Pill?"

"Mm-hmm." This was beyond awkward.

"Yeah, that won't work. Caleb's a shifter," Doc told me, his voice clipped. Professional. "Shifter sperm is tenacious; basic birth control won't do squat against Caleb's little guys, or gals, I should say in this day and age."

"I could be pregnant?" I felt faint.

"Do you feel nauseous in the morning? At night? Do your breasts feel tender? Are you having weird cravings?" He hesitated. "Like meat?"

"I could be pregnant?"

"Willow? Are you going to pass out?" he asked quickly. "If you are, please make sure you're not in a place where you can hurt yourself if you fall. Actually, sit down and put your head between your legs."

I didn't move. My mind was racing, furiously working out period math. "I can't be pregnant," I suddenly blurted. "It's been too soon since my period."

"Shifter pregnancies are quicker, even in humans," Doc said calmly. "Let's discuss your cycle."

He asked me a few more questions, and as he did, my panic lessened. He hadn't outright said it, but I think he was coming around to the idea I wasn't pregnant too.

The panic never fully receded within me though, and as he made me feel like a teenager while he gave me the "safe sex" talk, I listened intently. Caleb was wearing a condom from now on. When I said as much to Doc, he told me they wouldn't be as effective as they were with a human male. Neither would withdrawing before ejaculation—his words, not mine—because shifter sperm was indeed tenacious, and some wanted out before the big finale so they could catch my eggs unawares and knock me up.

It seemed the Goddess Luna was all about fertility.

If they told me at this point it was in their holy texts that she wanted women chained to the kitchen sink, barefoot and pregnant, I wouldn't have been surprised.

"You still with me, Willow?" Doc asked gently.

"I may have passed out," I muttered and heard his chuckle. "I only phoned about my ME..."

"Well, I would have had this talk with you at some point," he conceded, "but you left so quickly I never got the chance. I think you need to accept having Caleb's child is inevitable if you keep having sex with him."

There wasn't much to say to that, so after a few more minutes of chitchat, I said goodbye and then hung up.

I spent the next hour rubbing my belly, repeatedly telling my womb to be unaccommodating to all sperm, and watching the door for signs of Caleb coming back.

I woke up when I was lifted off the couch and carried to the bedroom. Opening my eyes, I saw Caleb's handsome face, noting a few bruises on his cheeks, but otherwise, he seemed unharmed.

"I didn't mean to fall asleep."

"It's late," he told me, placing me with such care on the bed that I almost cried again.

"Did the trap work?"

"It did." His voice was grim, his eyes tight with fury.

"Then it's over?"

"No, it's not over. This is just the beginning." His voice held a hard edge, something dangerous, and I wasn't sure when he looked at me if he wanted to push me away or pull me closer.

"Your information gathering worked though, right?" I was

almost scared to ask the next question. "Which is a good thing... right?"

Caleb looked down at me, his face half-hidden in the shadows of my dimly lit bedroom, his expression one I couldn't quite read. "I won't let anyone hurt you," he said, his voice low, barely controlled. "Not even me."

The intensity of his words and self-loathing made my stomach flip. "I know, Caleb. I trust you, you would never hurt me."

"You mean again?" His voice was heavy with scorn. "We all know I already hurt you, Willow..." He inhaled deeply, and I heard how shaky his control was. "We all know I could do it again."

"No, we don't." Sitting up, I grabbed his arm. "I know you won't. *You* didn't hurt me the first time, it was the darkness that lives on that peak of yours. It wasn't *you*. It would never be you."

For a moment, I thought he'd argue, but he finally looked away, his shoulders deflating. "I wish that one day I have as much confidence in me as you do," he murmured, moving to the door.

"Where are you going?" I asked, fear of losing him clutching at my throat.

"I know who it is that's targeting you. I know what they want."

"Who are they?" I was rooted to the bed. "What do they want?"

"Rogues." He saw my confusion. "Shifters who have left their pack. They roam together, killing, destroying, raiding." His lip curled in a sneer. "Pathetic."

"Oh." That sounded like something that could be handled, didn't it? "What do they want?" I asked again.

Caleb's eyes blazed with fury. "They want my land."

His land?

My stomach dropped like a lead balloon as I understood. "You mean Shadowridge Peak?"

"I mean Shadowridge Peak," he repeated, his voice dangerously low.

"They can't take it though, right?" I desperately tried to remember what they told me about Caleb and his packlands. "You have to give it to them?"

"Or I can be challenged for it," he told me. "Then I would need to fight for it."

I didn't need to ask if he would fight for it; the look in his eyes said it all.

The question wasn't whether he would fight for Shadowridge Peak, the question was what lengths he would go to, to keep it.

TWENTY-TWO

Caleb

SHE WAS ASLEEP, AND I WAS OUTSIDE, SITTING ON HER back step, watching the woods, my wolf prowling beneath my skin, agitated and eager to return to Shadowridge Peak.

I welcomed the cold stone on my ass. It grounded me and kept me from spiraling as the realization solidified in my mind.

This had never been *just* about Willow. They were after my land.

My territory.

In hindsight, it seemed so obvious. I had suspected on the Peak that they wanted my land. I just had the wrong set of shifters. I never thought of those who lived on the cusp of our society. Why would I? I'd had little to do with them. When I was part of a pack, I knew of them, but since I'd been alone, I gave no thought to what they were.

Outcasts.

But that had been all they were. Why did they want my mountain now?

Scowling in the dark, I considered it. Was it because I'd been gone from the mountain for so long? Were they already there?

No...no one had been in those cabins. If the outcasts had taken or tried to take my land, there would've been signs of their intrusion.

So, what had changed? What had prompted them to think they could exploit my weakness, my grief, and take what was mine?

Willow?

She was right. They'd seen her as a way to get to me. Thinking they could use her to break me. A low growl rumbled in my throat so feral it echoed through the trees around me.

But then I thought of Willow's face when I helped her stand earlier. The way she'd looked at me, her eyes wide, almost fearful.

My knuckles cracked in the silence of the night as I flexed my hands. She'd stepped back because I scared her. The shifter that grabbed her may have been a threat, but to her, I'd come off as the real danger. She'd felt it—felt the weight of my anger simmering under my skin, the barely contained fury of my wolf that would have shredded anyone who came near her.

And because of that, she'd looked at me like I was one of *them*.

Little did she know I was barely holding on to the thin threads of my control as it was, and if she knew just how fragile my hold was...I didn't even want to think about it. She was already looking at me differently. I wasn't sure I could take more.

My head turned north, my gaze on the horizon to the peak I couldn't see but that drew me to it.

I could go...

I needed space, a chance to pull myself back, to get a grip on the control I was holding on to so desperately. I could check out the mountain, ensure their sniveling hides hadn't set foot on Shadowridge, and center myself.

My instincts were to protect Willow, but instinct wasn't enough—I needed to shield her from the darker side of me as well. She shouldn't be their target, and she should never feel unsafe in her home. I didn't want that for her, and I didn't want to be the one responsible for her fear.

The thought of her soft body moving under mine filled my head. The husky moans she made when I fucked her willing body...a body that was always ready for me. She felt so right when I was holding her. Caring for her.

Loving her.

Taking a deep breath, I closed my eyes, willing myself to get a grip. I'd have to keep my distance just for now, let her know that I was giving us both space. Healthy relationships survived distance. Right? If anything, it showed her I wasn't one to hover. I would never smother her or push her. She and I, we could survive this. But this was bigger than her and me, and I didn't want her to become collateral damage.

I could go back to Shadowridge Peak, secure the mountain, remind it who its alpha was, and come back. It would be a few days at most. Eamon would stay close by so she wouldn't be alone. Hell, she had her friends around her most of the time. Her own pack. She probably wouldn't even miss me, and she may want some space between us too.

Off of Shadowridge Peak, I was weak. Soft. I'd been away from it for too long. Ten years away from my packlands hadn't done me any favors. The truth was that I couldn't protect her as I was...and without control, I couldn't protect her from myself.

Standing, I went back into the house, locking the door behind me. Moving with a careful step, I entered the kitchen, and with my hip against the counter, I watched the night sky. It was a clear night, very few clouds, and the moon was merely a sliver of silver in the sky. The stars dotted the blanket of night with tiny pinpricks of light.

The view on the ridge would be breathtaking. The view I had from here was muted, tarnished with smog and pollution. I kept my gaze on the moon, hoping for some guidance from Luna.

But all I could sense was Willow. A steady warmth pulling me in, as unshakable as a shaman's faith in his Goddess. I wanted to go to her, but... But I didn't trust myself around her. Not when I knew just how thin the line was between protecting her and hurting her.

I would never forget that night my claws sank into her soft flesh. The look of love in her eyes as I held her broken body. The forgiveness she gave me so freely, which I had no right to claim.

Now look at me, right back there again. What might I do to her if I couldn't keep my instincts in check? Willow was human, living in a world of normalcy. And here I was, throwing her into danger at every turn. She had enough to deal with in life without me adding to the list.

I paused outside her bedroom door, my hand resting on the doorknob. As I pushed the door open gently, my wolf sight could make out her silhouette as she slept, curled on her side. I could hear her deep regular breathing, no doubt exhausted from the events of the day.

My chest tightened at the sight of her.

So innocent.

So vulnerable.

As familiar to me as the scent of pine and soil.

I wanted to be in bed with her, holding her, telling her that nothing could ever come between us. That no force on earth or territory scheme could touch her with me by her side. But deep down, I knew Willow wasn't the type of woman who wanted promises of safety. She wanted something that was slipping out of my hold.

Control.

I knew that I wasn't as steady as I could be right now. As I *should* be.

The worst part was knowing she could feel my pull to Shadowridge Peak. She was seeing it more and more, the strain it was taking to be here, in this life with her, when it was so vastly different from what I was used to. Or needed.

First, I needed to handle the threat to her, one way or another. They needed to know she wasn't bait. They needed to be challenged, but mostly, they needed put down.

Willow sighed in her sleep, her hand reaching out to search for me as she slept. How easily she had adapted to me in her bed. She murmured in her slumber. It was low, even too low for me to hear clearly, but it sounded a lot like my name. Pulling off my shirt, I gently kicked off my boots, getting ready for bed.

One night. One last night.

Tomorrow, I'd tell her I needed to leave for a while, maybe think of a reason that wouldn't make her doubt me or my commitment to her. My wolf snorted his discontent at the idea, fighting me even as I fought it. Leaving Willow felt wrong and unnatural, but dragging her further into this would only make it worse.

I couldn't protect her alone on Shadowridge Peak.

"Caleb?" Her voice was thick with sleep, but she turned towards me as I folded my jeans over the back of a chair. "Why are you up?"

"Getting some water," I lied smoothly. "I'm coming back in now," I promised. When I slid into bed, she moved into me so willingly, so full of trust, it almost erased the memory of her stepping back from me today, fear in her eyes.

Almost.

"I had a strange dream," she murmured, snuggling into my embrace as I lay on my back, staring at the ceiling. "You were alone and needed me." Her yawn was wide, making her voice sound even huskier when she spoke next. "Isn't that silly, that you would need me?" A soft chuckle later, she was back asleep, and I wondered if she would remember her story in the morning or if she had still been deep in sleep's thrall when she'd woke looking for me.

Either way, it wasn't something she would need to think about soon.

Holding her close, like the precious thing she was, I closed my eyes and willed sleep to come.

WALKING INTO THE KITCHEN THE NEXT MORNING, I found her leaning over the counter, her eyes on the woods beyond her home, stirring a cup of coffee, a light frown on her brow. The early morning light painted soft shadows across her face. She heard me approach and looked up, a soft smile on her lips. I could let myself forget there was anything wrong if I just focused on that smile, I thought, as I approached her.

"Do you know, before I met you...met you properly, as in, spends all my time with you, that I rarely drank coffee. I prefer tea. But being with you, twenty-four seven, now I drink coffee in the morning." She looked down at her cup. "Isn't that the weirdest thing?"

"Weird?" Leaning over, I picked up her cup and took a drink of her coffee. "No? But I do like how you drink your coffee exactly like mine." I dodged away from the grab of her hand trying to reclaim her cup. "I'll drink this, you make yourself a pot of tea. You're drinking what I drink for easiness. Get your tea leaves out. Enjoy your morning cup of tea."

I could see her contemplating my words. I could see her considering the argument, and then I saw her simple acceptance I was right. A few minutes later, she was brewing tea leaves in her teapot.

I cleared my throat, feeling the words tighten and twist in my throat, but I couldn't not do this. "Willow, we need to talk."

Her body stilled, her teapot forgotten, looking at me with something shifting in her eyes. "Okay." Pulling out a chair, she sat down, her gaze fixed on mine. "What is it?"

Why had this been so much easier in the shower?

The small distance between us felt like miles. Breaking eye contact, I looked away, immediately chastising myself for showing weakness.

"You saw what happened yesterday," I began, my voice low. "As we thought, they came after you when they thought you were alone. And now we know why they're doing it." I avoided her gaze, focusing on the slight scar she had just above her right eyebrow. "They want Shadowridge Peak and they're willing to go through you to get it. Which means they'll keep coming for you unless I do something about it."

Willow's brows knit together, darkening her response. "So... what does that mean? What happened with the guy from yesterday?" There was a nervous edge to her voice, like she already knew the answer but was asking anyway.

"He won't bother you again."

This time, she was the one who looked away. "And your friend, the guy who helped?"

"Eamon is still here. He's going to be here for a while yet."

"Why?"

I took a deep breath, feeling the weight of what I was about to say settle into my chest. "It means...I need to leave, Willow. At least for a while."

The words hit like a punch, and her face froze. "Leave? Caleb, what are you talking about?" She leaned forward, her voice thick with worry. "How is leaving supposed to fix this?"

"I'll be close," I said quickly, the words tumbling out before I could second-guess them. I didn't want her to think I'd abandon her completely—not yet, not ever. "But if I'm not here, they won't be able to use you against me. And it'll give me space to figure out why they're doing this, why now, and why they're targeting me so intensely."

I raked a hand through my hair, the frustration building, clawing at my control. I hated this—hated the idea of leaving her, of not being able to protect her with my own two hands— but the gnawing, primal instinct inside me was screaming for distance. "You'll be safer if I'm not around, Willow. And right now, that's the only thing that matters to me."

Her jaw tightened, and I could see the spark of fury in her eyes before she even spoke. "They attacked me because they thought you *weren't* here! You leaving means they'll *know* you aren't here!" She walked towards me, her voice rising with every word. "If you want to keep me safe as you claim, then that's the stupidest thing you've ever said to me, Caleb."

Her words were full of disbelief, but I held her gaze, refusing to back down. My flat look seemed to make her flush with anger, but she didn't waver.

"And the fact one of them is now dead means their anger and focus is only on *me*," I said sharply, the growl in my voice barely contained. My wolf prowled beneath the surface, demanding I make her understand, demanding I assert control over this conversation—over her.

Her breath hitched, and for a moment, I thought she might step back, but she didn't. She stood firm, her chin lifted in defiance. "Then why not stay?" she asked, her voice quieter now but no less determined. "If they're coming for you, you're the best defense I have. *We're* the best defense I have."

I shook my head, turning away from her sharp logic. "You don't get it, Willow. If I stay, they'll push harder. They'll use you to get to me, and that'll break me. It's not just about protecting you—it's about making sure I can still fight. If you're in their hands..." My voice cracked, and I swallowed hard, the thought unbearable.

"It won't come to that," she said softly, and I hated how much I wanted to believe her.

But I couldn't.

I exhaled heavily, dragging my hands through my hair again. "This isn't just a fight, Willow. It's a claim. They want to destroy everything...everything I am. And if I can't hold onto my control..." I stopped myself, not wanting to say the rest, not wanting to admit that part of me already felt like it was slipping. "This is the best thing to do."

Her mouth opened, then closed, her gaze hardening. "And you think that's up to you to decide?" she asked, her voice trembling. "Caleb, I...I chose to be where you are. I know what's at risk. Do you really think you can protect me better from a distance?"

My chest ached at her words, but the beast in me refused to yield. The part of me tied to the territory, to my packlands, was louder than ever. It demanded action, separation, dominance.

"I'll be close," I said again, the words hollow now. My feet already felt as though they were moving without my permission, pulling me away from her.

Worry filled her eyes, and as she stepped toward me, her voice was low. "Caleb, are you sure this is right? It doesn't feel right."

"I don't know," I admitted, my voice barely above a whisper. "But I know that every time I'm near you, I feel like I'm one wrong step from losing control." I forced myself to look at her, to let her see the truth in my eyes. "You looked at me yesterday, and you were afraid. And I can't live with that, Willow. Not when I know that stepping back might be the only way to keep you safe."

Her face softened, the anger and worry giving way to something else, something deeper. She reached across the counter, her hand brushing mine, and for a second, I thought maybe I could stay. Maybe I could keep it all together for her sake.

But I knew that wasn't the truth. And maybe, deep down, she did too.

"I know you've made your mind up. I can see it," she said finally, as I moved my hand away, her voice small but steady. "But don't think I accept this." She pushed away from the counter, walked to the sink, and turned the faucet on to rinse her cup. "You're going back to Shadowridge Peak?"

"I have to."

"The place where all your demons dwell?"

"If you want to describe it that way…"

As she looked at me over her shoulder, I saw the fury return in her eyes. "I thought 'the place that turns you batshit crazy' was too harsh." Turning back to me, she grabbed a dishcloth and wiped her hands dry. "But that *is* where you almost lost yourself, where you're at most risk, so I'll ask again…why are you going back to Shadowridge Peak?"

"The mountain calls to me."

My wolf rumbled with unease, but the other part of me, the darker part, was already stretching out, eager for the solitude of the mountains.

She gaped at me and then threw her head back and laughed. "No. Nuh-uh, you're not going there without me. Your darkness will eat you up with a spoon and ask for seconds."

"You're not coming with me. It's too dangerous," I snapped.

"Which is *exactly* why I'm going."

TWENTY-THREE

Willow

"No, you're not." Caleb glowered at me, standing up and moving away from me. "You barely survived the last time."

I stared at him, my hands trembling at my sides as I tried to make sense of his words, put myself in his shoes, and recognize his need to protect me. But I didn't need protection from *him*, and I needed him to understand that, but I also needed to let him see I was willing to listen to him.

And then I could tell the idiot man he was, well...an idiot.

"So your plan is what? Just...leave?" I tried to stay calm, the words felt forced out, and even though I was trying to be reasonable, I could still hear the hurt creeping into my voice. When we'd only been off those mountains for such a short time, the idea of him walking away, it felt like I was being cheated.

Caleb's eyes were on the floor, his jaw clenched. "Willow, can you please understand that this is not a choice I *want* to make? But staying here puts *you* in danger. If I leave now that I know what they want, I can draw them to Shadowridge Peak. Leaving you, it takes you out of the equation."

I closed the space between us, reaching out, though my hand hovered just short of his and he never closed the gap. "Caleb, you keep saying the same thing, like it's your job to protect me. It isn't and if it was, leaving me is not the way to fill the job description." His small huff of amusement encouraged me to keep talking. "You think that leaving is drawing them away and that it will make it easier for me to be safer." I felt my insides swoop as I said the next words. "Have you ever considered that maybe I don't want to be safe if it means being *without* you?"

He lifted his head, and his eyes met mine, their intensity stealing my breath for a second. "It's not about what we want right now, Willow. These shifters...they'll be relentless. And I can't stand seeing them use you against me. If they think you're my weakness, they won't stop until they have what they want. I killed one of them yesterday..." He exhaled sharply, stepping back to break the connection I was desperate to hold on to, despite his admission. "They will want revenge for that, against me. Their blood will be boiling to come after *me*. Let me use their fury to my advantage." He broke eye contact with me, staring out the window to the trees. "I...I don't trust myself to keep you safe if I stay."

A surge of frustration burned in my chest, pushing words out before I could stop them. "Fine. Then as I said, I'll come with you. We'll face it together."

His head jerked back as if I'd slapped him. "No, Willow," he said firmly. "Shadowridge Peak is the last place I want you to be. Do you remember the last time you were on that peak with me? Or were you too busy bleeding in my arms because of what *I* did to you?"

"Will you *please* move past that? I know you didn't mean to hurt me. No—" I held my hand up in a 'stop' sign. "No, *let* me speak. Was it your claws that wanted to churn up my insides? Yes, it was. Was it intentional? *No*, it was not. I'm not a victim, Caleb. You didn't choose to hurt me. You were under the influence of something much darker than you, and if you go onto that mountain with no one at your back, then you may as well hand yourself over to it. You think keeping me here, drawing them away from me to you, is safe. I think the most dangerous thing you can do is walk back onto Shadowridge Peak with no one by your side."

Caleb looked away from me, a muscle twitching in his jaw. "I'll make sure that doesn't happen," he said, but his voice was softer, more distant. And just like that, I knew he'd already made up his mind and he was already slipping away.

"And what do I do, just wait for you to come back?" My voice cracked, and I hated how small I sounded, hated the feeling of him slipping through my fingers when I'd only just begun to know what it was like to have him *with* me in my life.

A partner.

He lifted his hand, brushing his fingers along my cheek, and I stilled under his touch, savoring the warmth that I wasn't ready to let go of. "I'm doing this for you, Willow. If something happens to you, because of me, I won't come back from that, I know that. Let me do this. I don't want to leave you, but I have to."

I reached for him, fingers curling around his arm, feeling the tension there like he was ready to pull away at any second. "Let me help. Don't leave me out of this. We're in this together, Caleb."

He pulled me close, his lips crashing against mine with fierce determination. I parted my lips, and his tongue slid in. It was a powerful, possessive kiss that left no room for doubt about how he felt about me, and I felt hope surge in me that he had listened.

Caleb pulled back, and before I could say anything, he was gone, a flash of movement out the door, and I stood there, heart pounding, frustration building in my chest as I looked at the empty doorway. I thought I'd gotten through to him. I thought he heard me, but he left me anyway.

The silence of my kitchen was louder than I expected.

I glanced around the room, my living room furniture, the kitchen, and the small breakfast bar. This was my life, but as I looked around, I felt how empty it was. This was the life he thought he was keeping intact by walking out?

He was wrong.

He had become as much a part of my life as anything else, and he needed to be reminded of that.

A sudden surge of anger bubbled up, surprising me. *Did he think he could just walk away?* Did he think I would just sit here? Waiting? I took a deep breath, the anger solidifying into something more stubborn, a resolve that steadied my trembling hands.

If Caleb thought he could make this decision for me, he was wrong.

Taking a shaky breath, I forced myself to stay calm. I would never get up that peak without a shifter to help me. I couldn't ask Cannon; he'd probably agree with Caleb that leaving me behind was the safest option. I thought about it again. Was he right in his assumption that the shifters would leave me alone? Those who wanted to get to Caleb by using me would know that Caleb had figured it out, wouldn't they? I mean, they were one less in their group now, weren't they?

So was I really in danger anymore? Maybe not if he was right in the fact he had drawn their attention off of me. But that meant Caleb *was*, and that was not acceptable to me. He thought it was for territory. Now that I knew there were more survivors of the Shadowridge Peak pack than he let on, what if there were more survivors of the Cristone Pack? I already knew I wasn't going to stay behind; I just needed to find someone who would take me up an unclimbable mountain.

In my bedroom, I pulled on jeans, a shirt and a sweater. I grabbed my jacket, and stuffing my phone and wallet into a purse, I headed for the front door. Caleb may think I would be safer here, hidden away, cowering in fear, but he was underestimating how much I was willing to do for him. I was not the delicate human he had to lock away and protect, not anymore.

Checking I wasn't forgetting anything, I shoved my boots on. After checking everything one more time, I was ready to leave. Without any more thought, I closed the door behind me, locked it, and set off at a determined pace straight for the woods that enclosed the town.

He'd mentioned Eamon would still be here, by choice or chance? I knew what he looked like; I just needed to find him. If he was the same kind of *anyone* that Caleb was, then I knew I would find him in the woods.

Anger at Caleb and his bullheaded ways made my steps quick and sure. The threat he was facing was *our* threat. Had he learned *nothing*? This fight was one we'd fight together. He would accept it because I planned on being right there with him.

It shamed me to admit it, but I had never walked any of the hiking trails that ran through the woods up the mountains near Whispering Pines. I wasn't outdoorsy when I was a young teenager, and by the time I moved here, I was a woman who had ME, and that kind of activity was foreign to me. My approach to the first signposted trail was cautious, my pace slowing as I looked at the trees, the path that disappeared where the trees grew thicker and wilder.

Doubt flickered through me. I knew if I had been looking for Caleb, the woods would be where he would be. I guessed Eamon would be the same...but what if the others who were out for Caleb also stuck to the woods?

It was almost their natural habitat, wasn't it?

I would not back down. I hadn't even been gone from my home for fifteen minutes and already I was filled with doubts. No, I wasn't. I could do this. My steps became more confident.

I may not know what I was getting into, but I was still getting into it.

The woods were silent, which freaked me out. The quiet was eerie. My footsteps sounded loud as they crunched over leaves and broken twigs. There was a strange feeling out here, like I was being watched, and I felt an awareness on my skin that I was trying to convince myself was my overactive imagination. If I shouted for this Eamon, would he answer?

Caleb called shifters hunters; was I willingly making myself prey?

I felt the low thrum of our bond, and it tightened my resolve. I had learned a few things in my time with shifters—the weak didn't stand a chance.

I was not weak.

Pushing further, I heard a faint rustling to my right, and while I tried not to look directly at it, I was sure there was something keeping pace with me in the shadows of the trees.

The underbrush rustled louder and suddenly a rabbit

jumped out, stopped suddenly at my loud yelp of fear, and then ran across the trail and disappeared.

"Whoa!" My pulse was racing. "It was just a rabbit."

"Not just a rabbit."

Spinning around, I gaped at the man behind me, his posture relaxed but his eyes sharp and assessing.

"Willow Harper," he greeted me with a slight smirk. His voice was steady, confident, and edged with an unsettling familiarity that I couldn't place. "Imagine my surprise when you wander right into the woods, dressed for a casual stroll as you decide to pick one of the hardest hiking trails around here."

It was? Moving back, I looked him over. He was wearing thick tread boots, worn jeans, a zipped-up hoodie under a padded jacket, a backward baseball cap, and an attitude that just put me on high alert.

"Who are you and why do you know me?"

He leaned forward, still non-threatening. "I think I'm who you're trying to find," he whispered loudly.

Swallowing down my nerves, I tried to keep a hold of my composure. "You're Caleb's friend? Right? You're friends?"

Eamon chuckled, stepping forward. "Friends? Wouldn't call us that exactly." He saw my reaction and he held up a hand in reassurance. "But...I owe him a favor, and that would at least make us acquaintances...right?"

Could I trust him? "What's your name?"

"Eamon," he told me with an almost bored sigh. He cocked his head, the amusement back in his gaze. "I thought it was funny that he'd leave you behind, but then imagine how amusing it was when you followed about twenty minutes later, all hot and bothered and completely oblivious to the fact I've been following you since you left your house."

"You followed me?"

Eamon looked bored again. "Here's my thinking of how this morning has gone for you, Willow Harper. You woke up feeling good. Then Caleb, the joy killer that he is, ruined your good mood by being a self-sacrificing ass and deciding that the best thing for you was to stay put, while he set off to tackle a band of dogs alone." His eyes held a gleam of wicked glee as he watched my face flush. "You, being the strong independent woman you are, thought, 'Nah, fuck that' and decided to follow. You're going the wrong way by the way, but I digress." He covered a smile with a fake cough when he saw me immediately look around in despair at the knowledge I was going the wrong way. "I'm assuming Caleb mentioned me, we've already met after all, and now you think the best person to get you to a shifter as stubborn as that alpha would be...moi." As he held his arms out at his sides, his grin was now a wide smile. "And here I am."

"You're a bit of a dick, right?" I said bluntly, causing him to laugh out loud. "I'm going the wrong way?"

"Completely. North is..." He twisted to point behind us. "That way."

"Shadowridge Peak is north?"

Eamon looked at me as if I were dense. "Yeah, north, and north is that way."

"Will you help me find him?"

"He isn't lost," he quipped, pushing his hands into his jacket pockets. "I know exactly where he's going." Again, that annoying glint of amusement in his eye. "And so do you." He considered me, his eyes narrowing slightly. "He thinks he left you behind and that you're safe. Putting yourself out here isn't going to please him. I could be one of the dicks trying to use you. Plus, Caleb, will not like you disobeying orders."

"Orders?" I scoffed. "No one made him boss. It's not his choice to make."

"The Goddess *Luna* made him boss, so it is most *definitely* his choice to make. You're his woman."

"I'm not a possession!" I snapped with a fierceness that surprised me. "We're a team, whether he likes it or not."

Eamon swept a glance over me, the corner of his mouth curling. "Well, aren't you a little fighter," he murmured. Turning his head slightly, he scanned the tree line, listening to something I couldn't hear. He paused, and then he turned his attention back to me. "You really want to do this?"

"Yes." My answer was so immediate I think I impressed him.

"It's going to be tough. Winter comes early on Shadowridge Peak."

"I've been there, I can handle it."

"Okay, let's go." He turned around and headed back the way I'd just come. "First, we need to get you to change your boots. Those ones aren't taking you anywhere." Eamon turned to look at me over his shoulder. "That Jeep in your driveway? Caleb leave the keys?"

The Jeep. I'd completely forgotten that we could use the Jeep.

"Yes. I think they're—" Eamon's sharp look made me bite my tongue. "Yeah, he did."

"Good. Pick up your pace, Harper. We got a lot of miles to clock today."

Hadn't he just said we were driving?

"Oh, and you may want to tell your friends you're walking out on them," he added with a casualness that didn't detract from the harshness of his rebuke. "It sucks to find out you've been left behind, as you know from the fact that you're out in the woods already lost. You've got a phone, use it."

Shame washed over me. He was right. I had been so focused on following Caleb that I forgot about who *I* was leaving behind.

Shit, I was not looking forward to this next conversation. I called Lily.

TWENTY-FOUR

Willow

I DOUBLE-CHECKED THE BAG I'D THROWN TOGETHER, nerves tightening in my stomach as I pulled it over my shoulder. My phone chimed just as I came out of my bedroom, and walking into the living room, I wasn't surprised to see Lily standing there, her brows knitted in concern.

"A voicemail?" she asked, her arms folded tightly against her chest. "You left me a fricking voicemail?"

"You didn't answer..."

"So you call again. You do *not* leave your best friend a voicemail."

"Understood," I murmured. "I take it you listened to it?"

The flat look was warranted. "No, I picked your message out of the air with my psychic abilities. No, wait, that's your trick, right?"

"I'm guessing you're pissed off?" I asked with a sigh, dropping my bag to the floor. Lily watched the descent of the bag with far too much interest.

"You're leaving whether I listened to the voicemail or not?"

I took a deep breath. It had been such a good voicemail.

Clean, concise, and compact. Boom, boom and boom. Now I had to do the messy in-person stuff. Only one hour ago, I was telling myself I wasn't weak. Staring at Lily right now, I did feel a little bit like a coward.

"I need to meet Caleb," I told her, trying to make it sound like no big deal. "He's, um...gone ahead. I have someone who is helping me catch up."

"Someone?" Her eyebrow quirked in that knowing way, meaning she could smell a rat, and I could see worry threaded into her gaze.

I swallowed hard, debating how much to say. I couldn't share their secret, but I hated lying to her. "An old friend of Caleb's."

"That man has friends?" Lily asked doubtfully. "Mr. Talk-A-Lot?"

"Lily, be nice." I suspected her dad told her he had reservations about Caleb, and Lily valued her father's opinion.

"So...you're being cryptic on purpose?" she guessed. "Which means that it's this thing that you can't tell me more about, but it's why your places were broken into, and it's tied to Caleb, right?"

My eyes closed briefly. I was so tired of being confused. "Yeah," I answered truthfully. "It's tied to Caleb *and* me. We're linked, Lily, and even if we weren't, I would be going."

"Because you love him."

Just flat-out put that out there.

"Um..." My face was burning. I knew Eamon was listening. I knew Lily wasn't expecting to be told otherwise. I...what *was* I waiting for? Squaring my shoulders, I nodded. "Yes. I do."

She watched me her expression softening. "And this friend? Is he crazy? Can he be trusted? What if he's like a serial killer or something? Is he hot?" She seemed to think about the order in how she'd just listed off her questions but then shrugged. When she looked at me, her eyes widened in understanding. "He's in the house, huh?" I bobbed my head slightly. "Of course he is."

"I'm not crazy." Eamon's low voice came from behind her, and she nearly jumped. "Depends on who you're asking me to trust, not a serial killer, but probably not your typical good guy. And I can hold my own in the looks department."

Lily spun to face Eamon, who was leaning against the wall with the faintest hint of a smile.

I moved a little so I could see both of them, and I saw Lily look him up and down, clearly unimpressed with his silent entrance. "And you're...?" Her voice was sharp with suspicion, and I could see her sizing him up.

"Eamon," he replied with a simple dip of his head. "I'm taking Willow to Caleb, depending on how hard she snores. Well, that determines whether she'll be added to the body count."

I saw Lily's mouth drop and I shot Eamon an exasperated look. "That's *not* helping!" I scolded him, but he was already laughing.

She turned back to me, concern marring her beautiful face. "What is going on with you?" she asked quietly, not caring Eamon could hear her. "You meet Caleb and you're not the person you were. The woman I know, the Willow I know, would never *ever* be running after a guy, no matter how good he looked or how well he did in bed."

"Lily!"

She ignored my wide-eyed look.

"Don't Lily me, Willow. What the heck is happening? You told me some of it, and you promised if things got crazy, you'd tell me it all." Lily glanced at Eamon. "Girl, things got crazy a while ago, I'd say. Tell me everything."

"I can't." It was the hardest two words I'd ever said in my life.

Lily's gaze flicked to Eamon once more, before she turned back to me. "Willow?"

Her look of disappointment tore at my heart, but I knew right then that I could never tell her all of it. She must have seen the resolve in my eyes because after a long moment, she nodded her head.

"Alright, listen to me," she said, moving closer to me, but her words were for Eamon. "Willow's my best friend. I don't care who you are to Caleb, friend, or friend of a friend, if you don't bring *my* best friend back in one piece, you'll have me to deal with." Reaching out, she grasped my hand, squeezing tight. "There's some very weird, funky shit going on here, and I don't like it. But Willow..." Her hand was gripping mine tightly. "Willow is loyal, and if she loves Caleb, well...she's too stubborn to listen to reason. So, you bring her back to me in one piece, understand? No more *accidents*."

"Lily," I whispered in protest, but they both ignored me.

Eamon's eyes were brimming with amusement as he watched my fiercely protective best friend lay down the gauntlet. "No more accidents, got it."

Reaching out, I tugged at Lily's coat sleeve. "Hey, come with me." Turning to Eamon, I gave him my best *behave* look and pulled Lily to my room. "I'll be two minutes," I told him.

"Day's wasting," he muttered, scooping my bag off the floor. "I'll be in the Jeep."

With the door closed behind her, Lily turned to me with her hands on her hips. "You're really leaving with *him*?"

"Caleb got a lead on the guys who broke in, he went after them, and I don't want him to be alone." All of this was true, so it felt better than being evasive.

"Why didn't he tell the police?" Lily snapped in frustration. "It's why they're here, to protect us!"

"He's taken it personally," I murmured.

"Men! Idiots." She glared at the door. "This is so unlike you," she grumbled. "It scares me that you won't tell me."

I shook my head slowly. "It's not for me to tell, Lil."

The look I received was warranted. Lily thought it over and then rolled her eyes. "You couldn't tell me that the hunk of the season was standing behind me?"

"You think he's a hunk?"

Lily looked at me as if I were insane. "I know you're all caught up in Caleb, but you're not blind! The guy is ripped."

"He's wearing like three layers of clothing!" I protested, desperately grabbing onto the olive branch she was offering me. "How can you even know?"

"Girl!" Lily rolled her eyes again. One day, they'd roll right out of her head. "You need to imagine taking the clothes *off*."

I burst out laughing. "And you had the cheek to ask me if *he* was insane..."

We shared a look and a smile before she sobered. "You told me you'd tell me if it got dangerous...and I know, I know what you said before, but..." Lily took a deep breath, preparing herself for what she was about to say next. "You were in a bad car accident. Where was Caleb then? Nowhere, that's where. Are you *sure* you want to run after him?" she asked me, doubt heavy in her voice.

"He would do it for me, and yes, even if he wouldn't."

Which I knew he would, but I didn't have time to convert Lily to his cheer squad. "He needs me, Lily. Trust me. Please."

She stared at me, searching for something in my face before nodding. "Fine," she muttered. "Just...text me when you get there?" She saw my frown. "Fine! Text me when you can?"

"Promise." I looked around my room, feeling the tears threaten. "Hey, um...will you water my plants?"

"Ugh, do you even need to ask?"

A sharp rap of knuckles against the door made both of us jump. "Harper, let's move."

With another eye roll, Lily opened the door, leading the way back into the main living room. My keys were already in the door, waiting to lock up. On my front step, I hugged Lily. I knew she'd be worried until she heard from me, and I knew she hated letting me go.

"Stay safe," she instructed.

"Always." I hugged her again. "I love you."

She pulled me in tight. "I love your crazy ass too." Standing back, she looked me up and down. "He better be worth this," she muttered.

"He is."

Once in the Jeep, I rolled the window down so I could speak to her as Eamon got ready to drive. "Love you, thanks for coming to talk."

"Voicemail," she muttered. "It's so two-thousands."

Eamon huffed out a laugh, and I caught Lily checking him out again. He noticed and didn't seem to mind. With the Jeep in drive, I waved as he pulled away.

Once we were a safe distance from the house, I glanced at him. "Thanks for helping with that. She can be protective."

"Yeah, I see that."

I didn't say anything further, merely focusing on the streets as we passed. I was eager to be with Caleb and make sure he was okay.

"You're worried about some mutts taking out your alpha?" Eamon asked, and I could hear the underlying curiosity in his question. "You're sighing a lot and fidgeting," he explained.

Honestly? I wasn't worried about them at all. I worried about Caleb on that mountain without someone by his side adding some reasoning in his ear.

Right now, he was alone with only the darkness to listen to, and I had no way of knowing how bad it was.

***

THE HUM OF THE ENGINE WAS THE ONLY SOUND between us as Eamon drove, his attention fixed on the road ahead. Outside, the last light of day began to fade, casting a deep purple over the sky. I fidgeted, unable to ignore the knot of nerves that had grown since we'd left town.

"Have you done this kind of thing before?" I asked, glancing over at Eamon.

"Depends on what you mean by 'this,'" he replied, his hands steady on the wheel, eyes still trained on the darkening road.

"Finding Caleb?" It felt wrong when I said it, and my body hummed with a low awareness of the link between Caleb and me. "Not finding," I mused. "Watching him...watching over him?"

Eamon's lips twitched with a faint, almost hidden smile. "Caleb's very good at keeping people at arm's length. Watching over him? You'd need to be good."

"But you do," I murmured. Twisting in my seat to face him, I studied him. He was shifter bulky. I'd now come to expect all shifters to have toned physiques. Even the old shaman, while clearly not lifting weights at the gym, was still toned and lithe. Eamon had dirty blond hair, hidden beneath a backward cap, and blue eyes that seemed to hold a hint of amusement. Scruff covered his jaw—not like Caleb's, which was carefully maintained—Eamon's just looked like he couldn't be bothered to shave today. I saw why Lily would call him a hunk. "Does he know?"

Eamon's huff could have been amusement, it could have been irritation, I wasn't sure. "Caleb's who he is. It takes a certain kind of patience to deal with him sometimes."

Even though it was a non-answer, I couldn't help but laugh. "Yeah, I noticed."

Eamon's expression softened as he glanced over, reading something in my face. "You're worried about him, aren't you?" When I nodded, he thought for a moment before speaking. "About the rogues? Or something else?"

I didn't know how honest to be with this man whom I didn't know. But I knew Caleb had trusted him enough to get him to watch me while he went after the shifters threatening me. Threatening him.

"Something else." I hesitated, staring out of the window. "There's a darkness on that mountain, and it calls to him." Turning back, I saw Eamon's frown. "Have you been to Shadowridge Peak?"

His face was carefully smooth as he answered. "Been there? It was my home."

I knew I was gaping at him in surprise. "Your home? You

were Shadowridge Peak Pack?" I asked him incredulously. "How?"

The amusement was back. "How? Mom and Dad lived there, Mom popped out a few kids, I was one of the kids."

"But how did you survive what happened?" My hand flew over my mouth. "Sorry, that was insensitive."

"Nah, it's fine. It's been ten years. Grief never leaves, but it fades." He cleared his throat before he continued. "My mom, dad, and two sisters were home the night it happened. We found them in their beds, so chances are they never even woke." I saw his fingers clench on the steering wheel. "That's what I hope anyway." He glanced at me, his eyes shielded. "I wasn't there. I never knew until I came back."

"I'm so sorry." I hadn't thought about how many there would have been who may not have been on the mountain the night of the massacre, how many people had to return home to find their whole lives ruined. "No one should have to return to that."

Eamon didn't say anything, and we were quiet for a while, both lost to our thoughts.

"What's this darkness you mentioned?" he asked suddenly, making me jump a little. "You said there was a darkness that calls to him. Expand."

"Expand?" I asked him, smiling at the order. "Don't tell me, you did military training too?"

Eamon looked at me curiously. "Why wouldn't I?"

"Oh..." I struggled for something to say. "Well, I thought not all male shifters went to the services."

"They don't. I did."

"You don't strike me as someone who follows orders," I said teasingly, trying to lighten the mood.

He was staring right ahead, his eyes on the road, so I couldn't read his expression well, and in turn, he couldn't see mine, which may have been a good thing because what he said next stunned me. "I went where my alpha went."

And it all made sense.

This was why he still watched him and followed him. "You're his beta." My heart rate picked up. "You were with him when he returned?"

Eamon shook his head. "Not his beta, he wasn't alpha of Shadowridge Peak *then*. I knew, we all knew, he would be when Amos stepped down." He cleared his throat. "But no, I wasn't with him when he returned. He left in the middle of a training day. By the time I found out he'd gone, I was sixteen hours behind him."

"His revenge?"

Eamon's eyes were hard when he looked over at me. "Was *his* revenge. He never let me get mine."

Oh.

He snapped himself out of his dark mood. "Tell me about this darkness?"

"Did Caleb tell you about my...ability?" It sounded so ridiculous when spoken out loud.

"Told me you're human, he cares for you, and some pricks want to use you to draw him out." He checked the rearview. "No mention of anything other than you're human." I watched him think about it. "He said you're tied to something, but he doesn't understand what it is."

"I'm tied to him," I told him quietly. "I started drawing scenes, paintings, sketches, and in them were places I had never seen, a man I had never met. Until one day I did."

"You drew Caleb?"

"I did." My voice was shaky. "And dear Lord, was he pissed about it," I added with a small smile of remembrance.

"So that's what she meant by psychic?" he asked, referencing Lily's jibe at my tie to Caleb.

"Yes." I nodded. "I'm not though. I'm just linked to Caleb."

"Why?"

"I don't know." I wanted to tell him the theories, but I didn't believe them myself to tell someone else them.

Eamon was quiet as he thought about it. "And this darkness? Are you linked to that?"

"No!" Shaking my head, my hands curled into fists. "No, that's his past and the...the spirits of the dead."

He looked at me, his eyebrows raised in surprise. "I knew he'd gone mad," he muttered. "Fucking dick always was wrestling with his demons."

"What do you mean?" I turned again to face him in my seat. "He's done this before?"

"What? No." Eamon shook his head. "He's just, Caleb's a powerful alpha, okay. I dunno how much you know about us, as in *know* about us, but alphas have varying levels of strength. The Goddess likes strong-minded alphas. I don't mean that they're opinionated—though Goddess knows she has a fair few of them too—but inner strength. You've met Alpha Cannon?" When I nodded, he continued. "His father was an absolute bastard, cruel to the bone, but his Will was strong. He believed in what he was doing, so because he did, he had a strong pack. He just beat them down because he was stronger."

"Cannon isn't like that."

"No, absolutely not. I mean, he's overbearing with all his

righteousness sometimes, but he inherited a strong pack because his father made them strong—for the wrong reasons, but the way they mold you is the way they mold you."

"Caleb's father was good?"

"Amos? Yeah, he was the best," he said with a fond smile. "But Caleb is very powerful," he added, the smile fading. "He had a lot of power to control. It was why we went back for the third tour; he felt he just wasn't ready." A flash of bitterness crossed his face. "It cost us everything."

"Do you think you'd have made a difference if you were there that night?" I asked gently.

"The new alpha of the Shadowridge Peak Pack walked into our community hall where the bastards were gathered, *celebrating* their victory, and used his Will to tell them all to not move—that's his Will on shifters *who were not his pack*—and then walked through them, one by one, and cut every one of their throats." Eamon's face was like stone. "He killed them all, and he *never lost his hold on them*. Not *one* of them managed to fight his Will. *That's* how strong he is. How powerful he is."

Jesus Lord.

"It's a lot to get your head around." My voice was barely a whisper. "You resent him for that?"

"I resent him for the third fucking tour I went on, the sand in my ass crack for months that I couldn't get out, the sunburn on my face I couldn't shift to heal, and the fact he was *fucking ready and too weak to admit it*. If we hadn't been fucking about in the desert, we would have been there, and with one word, *one word*, he would have held them *all* in place as they tried to kill us, and my little sisters wouldn't have had to die."

My heart was breaking for his loss, and I could never know

what it was like to face that pain, but still, I needed to speak in Caleb's defense. "But he wasn't there, Eamon," I told him gently, resting my palm on his arm. "Neither of you were." I swallowed past the lump in my throat. "Which is probably why they struck when they did."

"I know," he grumbled. "And then, not only did the prick kill them all before I got back, he tortured that bastard Jonah for days and wouldn't let me near him."

He tortured him? I shuddered at the thought.

"And now." Eamon was still caught up in his anger. "Now you're telling me the spirits of those bastards are fucking pulling him over to losing his shit completely? And he's *letting* them?" He glanced at me in question. "He's doing it to himself," he spat. "Always did have too big a heart, too big a conscience, too much fucking guilt to carry." He thumped his hand off the steering wheel in frustration. "It drove me fucking insane. Gave our rations to beggars every other fucking day." Slamming both his hands off the wheel, he didn't notice he made me jump. "Goddess *damn* him, I will rip him a new asshole if this fucker goes dark because of guilt for those bastards."

I watched the bundle of fury beside me and felt a glimmer of hope. "You should be careful, Eamon, you sound like you care very much for your alpha."

"Fuck you, Harper." He glared at me and saw my small smile. "Fuck you and fuck him."

I was openly grinning, and Eamon saw it. Leaning over, he punched my leg, none too gently. "Ow!"

"I'm going to kick his ass," he warned me. "You have an issue with that?"

Leaning back in my chair, I tipped my head back and

smiled. "Nope. You go right ahead, my friend. You do what you need to, to help me bring him back."

I had an ally I could trust. Someone who cared about Caleb as much as I did. Luna had sent her alpha help, and I wasn't going to let it go to waste.

Caleb

Standing at the foot of Shadowridge Peak, I looked up at the mountain, the ridge too high to see from here. The sun had long since set, and even with wolf sight, the Peak looked ominous in the dark.

I could feel them advancing on me. They knew I was alone, they knew I knew who they were, and like the scavengers they were, they were coming in numbers to take on a sole shifter. To get their *revenge*.

Let them come.

The woods rustled as I stepped onto the ground at the bottom of Shadowridge Peak. I felt the earth below my feet welcome me home. Making my way through the dark woods, I climbed with steadiness and familiarity. I could walk this in my sleep. I *had* walked it in my sleep. My mother had found me many a time as a young pup, curled up at the base of a tree somewhere in the woods, far from the packlands.

I had faint scars on my body from the cuts and falls on this mountain, cuts that I was too young to shift to heal. My father had told me they'd make me stronger. I wasn't sure what he would say if he saw me now.

The outcasts had been following me since I left her. Just as I hoped. They were pissed I'd killed their friend. Well, I was pissed they targeted *her*.

My only focus should have been on them—the shifters who had kept Willow in their sights far too long. Eamon would keep her safe while I put an end to this threat. I knew he would. We had our differences; I knew he blamed me for what happened to our pack, and I knew he resented the fact the blood of our enemies stained my hands only.

But he would keep my girl safe because she was innocent in all this. Like his sisters had been when the Cristone Pack had come to my lands with murder on their minds. Eamon would keep her safe so that I could focus on what needed doing here with no distractions. And when it was over, she'd be free from threat...and maybe, free from me.

I pushed down the ache of leaving her behind. She'd been so willing to stand beside me, but this was not her fight. I snorted at the thought. She couldn't fight even if she wanted to. A shifter would overpower her in seconds, and she'd be dead. The thought chilled me to the bone.

A shifter's world was no place for someone as frail as Willow.

The sound of branches cracking underfoot brought me back to the moment. The subtle rustling of leaves beyond the clearing indicated movement, and I tensed, scenting the air and adjusting to the darker part of the forest, every muscle wound tight. They were close, closer than they should have been.

My mind went back to Willow for a heartbeat. *Eamon would keep her safe*, I reassured myself. I'd left her with a shifter who knew exactly what was at stake. He understood how to keep her hidden, to keep her out of this.

I pushed on ahead, my wolf itching to be free, but I wanted to make sure the fuckers were following me, thinking they were clever enough to herd me to my packlands where they would hope that my rage and grief would rule my emotions. But I'd seen what my inner turmoil did when I let go and lost control.

I'd felt it when Willow bled out in my arms.

The fact that they still followed when I was making a beeline right for the clearing confirmed they were stupid.

Careless.

In human form, Shadowridge Peak was treacherous in the dark, but my mountain seemed to grip a little firmer underfoot as I climbed it, irrespective of the snow. I relied on the strength of my memory and body as I made my way up it. I thought I heard a couple of muffled curses the higher we climbed, and the thought they weren't fairing as well as I was made me smile grimly on the climb.

Stopping, I started to pull off my clothes. I could go no further as a human. I'd been carrying a canvas tote in my jacket pocket. It was one of Willow's. I doubted she'd notice it was missing. Black with gold print, it wasn't exactly inconspicuous, but it served its purpose. Folding my clothes, I packed them into the soft tote, ensuring the handles lay spread out so that when I shifted, my wolf could pick them up. It took a few attempts, but once I had hold of them, my wolf took off running.

I was fast, always had been, and I knew that I was putting distance between me and my pursuers. Which is exactly what I wanted. I wanted time to get to the clearing, shift, and dress before they came at me.

I could stay in wolf form and fight, but before I fought them, I wanted to know why they thought to target me.

And if I were being honest, I was scared to let the wolf out in case he let the darkness *in*.

It took another hour or so. I didn't stop, so when I reached the ridge, I hesitated, looking down through the night, feeling that sense of oneness once again at being back on Shadowridge Peak.

I'd heard a cry on the breeze, and with a snort of amusement, I'd turned and ran the rest of the way to the packlands. The moon appearing from behind the cloud cover illuminated the clearing. The snow wasn't deep, but it was untouched, not even an animal footprint on the blanket of white.

Making my way to Nell's old cabin, I saw the boots at the door, where I'd left them when I was here before. Shifting on the porch, I pulled on my clothes from the tote, grateful that shifter blood ran hotter than humans and the chill of winter wasn't causing me too much discomfort.

I took my time going back to the clearing. The shadows that stretched over the ground seemed to lift and curl around me. Welcoming me back. Already whispering in my ear before I shut them out.

It was longer than I thought before I heard the movement through the trees, just beyond where I stood. I stayed where I was, in the center of the clearing, open and accessible. There was no room for error, and with the strength running through me, I wasn't about to fail.

As they closed in, a part of me took note of the difference in myself. Before meeting Willow, I may have let them track me, just for the thrill of their fear when they realized I was behind them. I wasn't that shifter anymore. I didn't want to take unnecessary risks. It wasn't just my life at stake.

I wanted to end this swiftly, with minimal bloodshed. There was little satisfaction to be gained from this fight.

I caught a faint scent, unfamiliar but distinct, as it filtered through the trees. I narrowed my focus, taking in the pine, the cold frozen earth, the crisp clean scent of snow, and something else—an edge of something sharper and unmistakably hostile. Thoughts of Willow were banished; I couldn't afford to let my concentration be clouded, not right now. Tonight was the end of this threat to her.

The scent had grown, and I'd realized that I had known the stale odor. This was who had come for her. I recognized them from the vision that Luna sent me of Willow's house being broken into.

Now they came for me, in an attempt to make a power move, to exploit my weakness, in a territory that I had abandoned.

They expected resistance. They'd find something far worse.

Catching sight of movement through the trees in the moonlight, I saw more than one of them. They weren't pack. Rogues were never truly a pack, but these shifters moved like it. A blend of stealth and confidence that marked them as threats. I kept my eyes on them as they used the dense trees to their advantage.

This was going to end bloody.

One of them suddenly stepped forward. Heavyset. His muscles were big, but his gut was bigger. A scar ran down his left cheek, which caught my interest. Was he in her house? He scanned the clearing as if expecting me not to be alone.

"You're here for something that doesn't belong to you," I

murmured under my breath, keeping my voice low, willing my wolf to be patient.

The scarred man stilled, his confidence faltering as he took in the way I was standing, completely exposed and unmoving. My shoulders were back, feet planted solidly, as I watched him with an expression as controlled as it was deadly.

"Bold move, standing there on your own," he sneered, though I could hear the note of hesitation in his voice. His men shifted uneasily behind him, casting glances between each other and the woods as if expecting backup to emerge from the shadows.

I held his gaze, letting my silence unnerve him. "Didn't need backup for this conversation." I gave a slow, predatory smile, letting the message settle: it wasn't bravery that had me here, exposed, it was sheer confidence. And I could see the first crack in his composure, a quick flash of doubt crossing his face.

"You think you're the only one who has a claim to this territory?" he asked me, trying to regain his footing. "This isn't some sacred ground. It's just land." He gave a casual shrug. "Just dirt and stone." His boot scuffed the snow on the ground.

"Why the girl?" I asked him.

His mouth twisted into a sneer. "Convenient leverage. Got your attention, didn't it." His voice had an edge to it like he was trying too hard to keep it light.

She meant nothing to them. Good. The threat to her would end tonight.

I nodded my head slowly, not breaking eye contact. "Oh you got my attention alright," I said, letting the words hang heavily between us. "But you don't seem to understand, the only reason you're still here, still standing on your own feet, is because I wanted to *give* you the chance to leave."

His face morphed into a scowl, caught between fury and disbelief. "Leave?" He looked at his buddies, who were being pathetic in their attempt to surround me subtly. "That's rich coming from a wolf who can't even stand to be on this mountain. You're packless. Alone. You're *just* like us, Caleb. Rogue."

I took a step forward, feeling my wolf press against my skin, but my control was still ironclad, even though every fiber of me was charged and ready. "I'm giving you the chance," I told them, my voice a quiet growl, "to leave with your lives intact. *Take* it."

His grin faltered, his gaze shifting to the surroundings. He seemed uncertain. I knew he could feel it—he was cornered by something far more than he'd anticipated. And for the first time, he seemed to realize that standing out here alone wasn't a weakness.

It was a strength.

My strength.

He shifted his weight, visibly unsettled but still playing at bravado. "We'll see about that," he muttered as if to save face to his minions, who were now roughly circling the clearing. I could hear the edge of fear in his voice, and I was sure they could too.

"See about it as you get the fuck off my mountain. This land is Shadowridge Peak packlands. You take one more step towards me, *any* of you"—I directed my glare to the shifter who'd stepped forward to my right—"you're not going back the way you came."

"Meaning?" one of the others spoke up.

I kept my gaze on the scarred spokesperson. "Meaning you're going to die tonight."

I saw him hesitate, I saw him look around at his minions,

and saw his face fill with fury as he took in the sight of some of them who were willing to retreat.

"There's only one of you," he sneered.

"One is all that it will take," I replied with a dark smirk. Taking them all in, I met the eyes of each shifter I would kill tonight to protect Willow and my territory. "This is my final warning." I saw one of the younger shifters flick an uncertain look at the scarred guy. "Go," I urged him. "I've killed more shifters on this peak than you ever will. A few more won't make me lose any sleep."

I wasn't sure that was true, but I was sick of the killing. If he ran, then he would keep running, I was sure.

The young shifter looked back at me and dipped his head. "Alpha," he murmured, and then he turned, shifted, and ran.

Turning back to the scarred shifter, I raised an eyebrow. "Your move."

The scarred man stepped forward, four others close behind. One of them—a wiry figure from Willow's vision, the one with her underwear pressed to his nose—locked eyes with me. He wouldn't make it down this mountain alive. I measured each of them, calculating their intent, feeling my wolf ripple beneath the surface, ready.

"Tonight, you all die," I told them, my voice rough, lethal. I pointed to the fucker from her house, the one who'd touched her underwear. "You will die slowly."

"You don't scare me." His sneer cut through the air. "You're nothing, *Alpha*."

The first shifter spoke. "We challenge you for Shadowridge Pack."

My mouth twisted in a sneer. They thought to make it

formal, knowing I would obey the rules of the challenge. No use of my Will. Just brute strength.

I didn't need my Will to defeat these rogues.

The heavyset shifter lunged forward, and I met his attack, his fist driving into my side. I twisted, barely dodging the force of his blow, when another attacker swung a knife toward my back. I whirled around, blocking his blade with my forearm and grabbing his wrist, twisting sharply until he dropped the weapon with a pained shout. In a flash, I slammed my elbow into his face, sending him sprawling backwards into the snow.

The third attacker moved, striking low at my ribs. Pain flared, but I held ground, keeping my wolf in check.

Keeping the beast of darkness at bay.

As they circled, I squared off against the closest shifter, whose footing slipped in the snow just enough for me to catch his arm and yank him forward. He hit the ground with a stunned gasp, scrambling to rise as I drove a brutal knee to his chest.

I steadied myself, boots crunching over the snow. The wind picked up, whipping around me, stinging my face as I squared off against my attackers closing in, their breaths visible in the cold air.

Another figure leapt at me from behind, and I twisted just in time, planting my feet firmly in the snow for leverage. I flung the assailant off, sending him sprawling back with a thud, snow scattering around him. I could feel the biting chill even as my body pulsed with adrenaline, each breath clouding in front of me. My attackers had taken a step back but were still circling me, the snow coating their boots. The more they circled me, they didn't realize they were trampling down the snow, compacting it, making it easier to fight them. It still slowed them just enough for me to take two down, one after another, until only three remained, watching me with newfound wariness as their friends lay dead at my feet.

These three coordinated their assault.

One slammed his fist into my side, knocking me back a step, while the other struck with a sharp knee to my ribs. The pain flared, but I forced myself to turn the momentum into a savage counterattack. I rammed my shoulder into the scarred shifter's gut, knocking him backward, and then landed a swift, solid punch to his jaw, dropping him.

Breathing heavily, I spun just as the third attacker, the largest of the group, tackled me. We crashed to the ground, his weight nearly forcing the air from my lungs. I drove my elbow into his neck, pushing him off with sheer force, until he staggered back, clutching his throat. Blood smeared my hands, and my vision blurred with fury as I watched the three regroup, my eyes widening in realization.

I knew why they didn't shift, and it was the same reason I didn't. They were rogue, and control was almost lost for them. If they shifted, their wolves would take over, and I knew mine would too.

The longer we could hold on to human form, the longer we had control.

But then, a scent caught my attention—a familiar scent that made my heart lurch with fear.

Willow.

I froze. She stood in the distance, her gaze locked on me, Eamon just a step behind her already ready to fight. The wiry shifter from her house—the one who shouldn't still be standing —broke away, advancing toward her.

A snarl ripped from my throat, deeper and more feral than I'd heard before. "Touch her, and I'll rip you apart."

But he only smirked, ignoring the threat. He moved closer to her, testing my patience, *daring* me. My control frayed, my wolf tearing at the edges, ready to end him.

Willow's eyes widened, but she stood firm, her hand clenching around a broken tree branch she'd picked up along the way. I saw her grip tighten, her gaze flicking to me, refusing to back down. But fear laced her expression, and it drove a knife of rage deeper into me.

The beast ripped free of my control.

I moved forward, intending to put myself between them, but one of the others had shifted too and barreled into my side.

Eamon had shifted, his red-brown wolf circling the other attacker, and I didn't care which one it was. As long as I got to Willow.

The shifter growled low at me and pounced. Spinning, my jaws snapping, I ripped into their side with fangs and claws. With a surge of fury, I tossed their broken body away from me, turning and seeing how close the other shifter was to Willow, his gaze fixed on her like prey.

She swung her branch and my heart stopped when I saw the wiry shifter grab hold of it easily and pull it out of her hands, tossing it to the side as he leapt at her. Too soon, his hand was around her throat, her body pulled into his, as he held her in front of him like a shield.

My paws froze as I took in her wide-eyed, terrified stare.

"So, *Alpha*," he spoke with triumph lacing his words. Behind me, I heard the fight between Eamon and the other rogue stop. "None of us really wanted to challenge you for this land, none of us need an alpha. But if you're dead, the land is ours to claim." He pulled Willow closer to him, his hand tightening around her throat. "One squeeze and she's dead," he told me. "One squeeze, the bitch dies." He smiled savagely. "Or you die...and then she dies anyway."

My wolf took a step back in shock.

"Shifters talk," he said with disgust. "A human, ripped apart by a shifter, then *lives*?" He laughed, the sound hollow. "You did something that tied her to you, didn't you?"

I shifted into human form. "Take your hands off her," I said as I advanced. "And I will kill you quickly, mercifully."

"The only one dying here tonight, *alpha*, is you." His grip tightened and Willow wriggled against him futilely, her lips turning blue as she struggled to breathe. His lips dropped to her ear. "You keep squirming against me like that, bitch, I may have some fun with you before you die."

I saw her eyes widen as her body froze, her fear-filled eyes trained on mine.

I didn't think, I only reacted.

Launching forward with a snarl, I shifted mid-air, knocking Willow aside when the shifter threw her at me as his only means of defense. I heard her cry out as she fell, but my sights were on him.

And he was no match for me.

The beast inside me roared for blood as I tackled the shifter to the ground, and my jaws clamped around his neck. Holding him there. Feeling the pulse of his blood against my fangs as I held his life in my jaws.

I felt his fists pummeling into my body as my Will ordered him to stay in his human form. I felt his body shaking with fear and heard his screams as my teeth sank slowly into his throat. His strikes became harder and fiercer, but my wolf felt nothing.

Stop.

The command of my Will stilled his movements.

You will not fight me.

Blood pooled in my mouth, and the sharp metallic taste made my blood sing. Lifting my paw, I sank my claws into his side, puncturing a lung, ripping his insides like he would have done to her.

A part of me knew he was no longer fighting, no longer screaming, his body held immobile by my Will as his blood stained the snow.

"Caleb!" Willow's voice cut through the haze, her hands in my fur, attempting to pull me back.

The need to protect her had been taken over by the instinct to eliminate the threat to her.

"Caleb..." She was still holding on. Still here. Her hands stroked through my fur, soothing me. "Finish it, this is enough."

My jaw snapped closed, severing his head almost from his body.

I shifted, chest heaving, my body vibrating from the barely controlled rage. I could feel her through our bond, gripping onto me, bringing me back.

Grounding me.

I turned to her, catching her worried gaze, her brows drawn tight. She didn't flinch from the rawness in my eyes, didn't pull away from the predator still stirring beneath my skin.

Instead, she stepped closer, reaching for me.

Only one remained. I met his terrified and broken stare.

Stay.

"Finish him."

Eamon reached up, and in one deft movement, he twisted the rogue's head, snapping his neck.

I met Eamon's gaze as the shifter dropped to the ground. "What the fuck were you thinking bringing her here?"

TWENTY-SIX

Willow

THE SECOND THE ROGUES WERE DEAD, CALEB TURNED on us. His eyes glinted in the dim light, fierce, almost wild as he focused first on Eamon, then me. I'd rarely seen him so close to losing his control. The tension in the air felt thick enough to choke on.

"I asked *what were you thinking?*" His voice was a low, dangerous growl as he stalked toward Eamon, fists clenched.

Eamon held up his hands, but there was a gleam of defiance in his eyes. "She insisted, Caleb. I found her in the woods, *hiking* to come and find me so I could take her to you. I didn't see another option."

Caleb was in his face in seconds. "You didn't see another option?" His voice trembled with anger. "I gave you one job—keep her safe. Does bringing her here, up the mountain in winter, look like 'safe'?" His words were sharp, lethal, and the muscles in his neck stood out as he fought for control. I could almost see his wolf straining to take over.

The silence hung between us like a live wire, ready to snap.

Caleb's gaze was pure heat, simmering with an anger so intense I could feel it radiating through the cold air.

His fists were tight, his breathing heavy. He was angry with Eamon, yes, but that wasn't the worst of it. He was furious with me.

"Caleb—" I started, but he rounded on me, his expression so intense I took a step back.

Caleb took a step closer, and I forced myself to hold my ground. His voice was low, ragged. "What the hell are you doing here, Willow?" Each word felt like a crack in the ice between us, splintering under the weight of his fury. His eyes were bright with anger, his voice low and rough. "I *told* you to stay back. Why did you think following me was a good idea?" He pointed to the five dead shifters in the snow, the ground bloody. "Is this what you wanted to see?" His eyes burned black with the intensity of his rage.

I opened my mouth, ready with a calm answer, but it was like he wasn't even seeing me as he continued, "You think this is a game?" His look was intense, holding me pinned. "This was *exactly* what I told you to stay out of. Exactly."

I swallowed, clasping my hands to keep them from trembling. "I thought you might need me."

"*Need* you?" He closed his eyes, taking in a sharp breath, then opened them, his gaze fixed on me, blazing with the heat of his barely-contained fury. "You don't understand, do you? This isn't some thrill-seeking adventure. These shifters would have killed you, Willow." He carried on, his temper rising, which I hadn't thought possible. "Do you think I needed the distraction of you turning up with a fucking branch?" He scooped it out of the snow, breaking it in half like he was snapping a twig. "This? *This* is what you thought would fight off *shifters*?"

Eamon moved to stand beside me, and I felt his gaze, but I didn't turn. The dude was naked; even with Caleb incensed in front of me, I somehow knew turning to Eamon would be the final straw of Caleb's control. I didn't mind seeing Caleb in all his glory, though he was covered in blood and dirt, so it didn't matter.

So *much* right now didn't matter.

"Maybe *you* don't understand!" I snapped at him. "What would you have done if I wasn't here? Who else would have put their hands in your fur and *pulled you back*? I told you and told you again, we're stronger together. *I* am in this *with* you. That brink you are on the edge of when you're here, *I* am the one holding you back Caleb! Just like I did right here!" He glanced at Eamon and I wasn't having it. "No! Don't look at him like you want to murder him. *I* chose to be here. *Me.* Eamon just got me here quicker than I would get here myself, but you know there was no way in hell I was leaving you on this mountain without me here *to pull you back* from that darkness inside of you."

His gaze softened briefly, almost hurt flashing in his eyes, but he hardened again. "This isn't about that, it's about being able to fight, Willow. You don't know what kind of threat they were. You can't just follow me into danger like an untrained pup." He raked a hand through his hair, then turned to Eamon. "You don't get it. If something happened to her..." His voice broke slightly, but he covered it with another glare as if he could hide the fear with anger.

The silence that followed was thick with tension, the air almost humming with it. Caleb looked away, his fists still tight at his sides, chest heaving as he fought to keep himself under control.

Finally, Eamon's voice broke the silence, calm but firm. "Maybe she does understand, Caleb. You've protected her before. Maybe it was Willow's turn to return the favor this time." I saw him crouch and pull out a pair of sweatpants from the backpack he had carried up the mountain. Pulling them on, he threw a pair at his alpha. "Maybe...maybe she wants to do this *with* you, not watch from the sidelines while you carry it alone."

Caleb's gaze flickered toward him, filled with something dark and raw. "You stay out of this," he said through gritted teeth, his voice cold. He turned back to me, his gaze softer for a second, but his voice was still a low, pained murmur. "You think you're ready for this world, Willow? It isn't like yours. It's brutal, and people don't walk away unscarred."

"I'm already scarred." I met his stare, my pulse racing, a mixture of defiance and fear tightening in my chest, hating the look of pain and guilt in his eyes at the reminder of *who* scarred me. "I'm still here. *Still* beside you. Maybe I'm not ready, Caleb, but it's not *your* choice to make. It's *mine*."

We held each other's gaze, his jaw tight, his eyes burning. For a second, his anger faltered, a hint of something vulnerable slipping through, then hardening again. He took a step back, raking a hand through his hair, breathing heavily.

Finally, his voice came out in a rough whisper. "I need some space." He looked up at the peak. "This is...Goddess, I need to walk away and calm down. Stay here. With Eamon." The look he gave the other man left us in no doubt that "stay" meant *stay*.

Caleb turned without another word, disappearing into the trees, leaving me standing in the cold, watching him disappear into the shadows, his retreating figure barely visible as he took his rage—and his fear—out on the quiet forest around him.

The silence after Caleb left was almost as thick as the tension he'd left in his wake. The air felt heavy, the chill sinking into my bones. Eamon let out a quiet breath and rubbed the back of his neck, glancing sideways at me, clearly unsure what to say.

"Don't you start," I muttered, crossing my arms, trying to keep warm. The anger still buzzed beneath my skin, the sting of Caleb's words twisting in my chest. I hadn't expected a warm welcome, but this...this raw, unrestrained fury at my choice... was more than I expected. More than I'd prepared myself for.

Eamon watched me for a moment, his expression neutral. "You know," he started, his voice casual, but I caught the note of hesitation, "he's not wrong. It was very risky letting them know we were here." He looked down at the broken piece of wood I'd grabbed when I saw that we were too late and the rogues were already here. Surrounding Caleb. "You'd have done nothing with that," he spoke softly, "didn't expect you to run *into* the clearing. You put yourself in danger."

I turned, narrowing my eyes. "I know that, Eamon. I didn't come here blind." The fact I was pointedly ignoring the dead shifters on the ground didn't help my position. I knew that as well.

A faint smile tugged at his mouth, but it didn't reach his eyes. "No, you didn't. But understanding the risks doesn't make them any less real." He paused, glancing in the direction Caleb had gone. "He...he doesn't lose control like that, not often. Not unless he's worried...or scared."

I looked away, biting back the words on the tip of my tongue. I knew Caleb's anger was just another level of fear—fear for me, maybe fear for us? But it didn't make it any easier to swallow. "I just thought...I don't know. I thought he'd understand that I couldn't stay back and wait this out and not know what was happening to him, you know? But when I saw they were already here, I couldn't just...*watch* him fight them alone."

"I know," Eamon said, nodding slowly. "You saw him and thought he was vulnerable. And that's what he doesn't want you to see. Doesn't want you to feel that you need to put yourself at risk, or get hurt, to save him. That's why he's pissed off. He'd rather tear himself apart than let you get a scratch."

There was something tired in his voice, an edge of empathy that made me glance up at him. "I forget you know him so well."

Eamon shrugged, the faintest hint of humor returning to his eyes, this time a little softer. "Well enough to know he's got a thick skull. And he'd risk everything to keep the people he cares about out of harm's way. Doesn't always make sense, but that's Caleb. And even though I brought you here, I would never have let you get this close had I known they were here."

I nodded, taking in a slow breath, feeling the weight of the moment settle between us. Eamon shuffled his feet beside me, hands shoved into his pockets, a slight tension in his posture that mirrored my own.

"Look," he said, his voice dropping slightly, "if it means anything, I think maybe you're right to be here. Not right when we showed up, but I do think you should be where he is," he admitted with a shrug. "Maybe you two aren't exactly on the same page yet, but I can see how much he cares about you. And maybe...just maybe, you being here right now, isn't the worst thing for him."

I looked away, trying to swallow down the jumble of

emotions rising in my throat. "Or...maybe he's right. Maybe I'm just getting in his way."

Eamon chuckled softly, his gaze focused on the darkening woods. "Trust me, Willow, you're more of a help than you know. Even if he's too stubborn to see it." He paused, then glanced back at me. "Give him a bit of time. Seeing you threatened during the fight will have rattled him, and he doesn't always know what to do when he's shaken. But he'll come around. He just needs a chance to realize that having you by his side doesn't mean he's lost control."

A small smile broke through my frustration, and I met Eamon's gaze. "Thanks. For, you know, bringing me here. For not letting him scare you off."

"Someone's gotta look out for him, even if he doesn't know he needs it." Eamon smirked, a spark of mischief in his eyes. "And, well, someone's gotta make sure you don't wander off the side of the mountain."

I bit back my smile, feeling the tension ease, if only slightly. "I *told* you I knew the drop was there." Eamon gave me a look that called bullshit, and pushing my hair off my face, I admitted defeat. "Fine. It maybe would have been too close to the edge to be healthy for me." His eyebrows rose into his hairline at how much I was downplaying the fact I almost fell off the side of the mountain in our climb to get here. "Good thing I had you to keep me right."

Eamon snorted but didn't say anything else about it.

As we stood there in the clearing, surrounded by silence and snow, I felt a surge of gratitude for Eamon—and a renewed determination to stand by Caleb, no matter how hard he tried to push me away.

Eamon turned to me, his tone easy. "Want to help me get

rid of these bodies?" He walked over to the one nearest to us and, bending down, lifted the legs.

Before I could respond, I heard the faint crunch of snow underfoot, drawing our attention to the trees. A moment later, Caleb emerged from the shadows, his expression a storm of conflicting emotions. He was breathing heavily, his dark brows furrowed, and a fierce glint in his eyes sent a shiver down my spine.

"What the hell is going on? Why are you still out here?" he demanded, his gaze flicking between Eamon and me, the tension thickening the air.

"Just talking," Eamon replied easily, though I could see the way his body coiled with readiness. "About to start the tidying up." He gestured to the dead nearby.

Caleb's eyes narrowed. "Talking? About what?"

"The dead shifters and how we dispose of them," I interjected, stepping forward. "Are you okay?" I asked tentatively. "Do you understand why we came?"

"Understand what?" Caleb interrupted, his voice sharp. "How you wanted to get yourself killed? Because that's what you're doing, Willow. You put yourself in danger by coming here. You think the threat is gone because they're dead?"

Did he mean him? That he was a threat? My anger rose swiftly to meet his. "When will *you* understand that *you* will not hurt me? I *trust* you, but I'm not going to sit back and wait for you to handle everything, Caleb! I care about you too much, damn it!"

He took a step toward me, fists clenched at his sides. "And I care about *you*, which is why you shouldn't even be involved in this mess. This whole shit with these bastards targeting you. It was never about you."

"But it was about *you*!" I shot back, desperation clawing at my throat. "Why do you think that doesn't matter? You shut me out every time I try to get through to you, and it's driving me insane!"

Caleb's expression flickered for a moment, the fire in his eyes dimming as he considered my words. But then, just as quickly, his resolve hardened again. "I'm not risking your safety, Willow. Don't you get it? They wanted you to use *you* against me, and I won't let that happen."

"Oh my God, Caleb! I can take care of myself!" I insisted, stepping closer. "You can't just make decisions for me. You think isolating me and leaving me will keep me safe, but it's only going to push me away."

Eamon shifted slightly, sensing the tension was about to explode. "Look, let's just calm down, okay? Emotions are running high. Caleb, we're all on the same side here. Remember?"

"You stay out of this!" Caleb shot back, turning his intense gaze on Eamon. "You brought her here. Why the hell would I listen to you?"

"Because you're a dick," Eamon said calmly, holding Caleb's stare. "I know exactly what I'm doing. I'm helping you keep her safe, and instead of pushing her away, you should be holding on to her with both hands and asking what you did to deserve her."

Caleb's jaw tightened, and I could see the war raging inside him. I took a breath, trying to ground myself, to find the right words that might reach him. "Caleb, please. If you just listened, you'd hear what I'm saying. I'm not scared of what they might have done to me. I'm not scared of what you might do to me. I'm scared of losing you."

The words hung in the air, and for a moment, Caleb's

expression softened, but then I saw his head tilt, so slightly, that I knew he was listening to the shadows that wanted to cling to him.

"Caleb, don't listen to them!" I felt the heat rise in my voice, frustration boiling over. "I don't care what they're whispering. You have *me*. I'm right here and I'm not going anywhere."

He looked at me then, really looked, as if searching for something in my eyes. But instead of breaking through the wall he'd built, he turned away, his hands running through his messy hair in agitation. "I can't do this," he murmured, his voice strained.

"Caleb, wait—" But he was already moving back toward the trees, frustration radiating from him like heat off a flame. I stepped after him, my heart pounding. "You can't just leave!"

He paused, glancing back at me, eyes filled with something I couldn't quite place—pain, maybe. "I have to. You'll be safer if I'm not here."

"Safer?" I echoed incredulously, my voice rising again. "Caleb? No, that's not true, I don't believe that."

His gaze flicked away, jaw set in a stubborn line. "We'll talk later."

He melted into the shadows of the woods, leaving me standing there, wondering when would be the next time he'd come back. I could feel the frustration and fear swirling inside me.

Eamon stepped beside me, the silence stretching thick again, his presence a sudden reminder that I wasn't alone. "Are you alright?" he asked quietly.

"No," I whispered, feeling the weight of everything I was losing.

"Who's *they?*" he asked. "The darkness you mentioned?" he guessed. When I nodded, he bit out a curse.

Despite my outbursts that I was strong and not weak, I wanted to cry. "He doesn't see it, does he? He doesn't see how much he's losing by listening to them."

Eamon shook his head, a hint of sympathy in his eyes. "He's always been a stubborn bastard," he murmured. "Hopefully, he'll think about what you said, and he'll come around."

"Yeah." I sighed, tilting my head backwards to look at the sky. "Or he'll wait us out until we have no choice but to leave." I looked at the dead men in the snow. "I don't really have to help, do I?"

He laughed out loud. "No, princess, you go find a cabin that doesn't reek of death, and I'll find you when I'm done."

"Is..." Oh God, how did you ask that question without reminding him what he'd lost? The atrocity that happened on this mountain happened to Eamon, too, and I'd been so wrapped up in Caleb I'd forgotten he wasn't the only shifter who lost their family. "Is your family's cabin nearby?"

Eamon shook his head, his head lowered so I couldn't see his eyes. "No. I burned our home when I realized the alpha of the pack gave up." He looked up at me, his eyes bright with pain. "There was nothing left here for me."

"I'm so sorry." It didn't feel like enough, and a wave of exhaustion washed over me as the surge of adrenaline that had got me up this mountain drained from my body. "I was in Nell's cabin last time I stayed here. Caleb turned the generator back on. I can go back there?"

Eamon watched me, his expression closed once more. "Okay, you know how to get there?" When I nodded, he bent back down to the dead shifter. "Good. Go get warm. I'll meet you there when I'm done."

I hesitated. "And Caleb?"

Eamon looked between me, the trees, and the dead shifters. "If he's not back by tomorrow, I'll go after him, okay?"

"Thank you." And with that, I turned and headed to Nell's cabin. If Caleb wasn't back by tomorrow, we'd both follow wherever the path led.

I ignored the voice in my head that was asking me if I was tired of chasing down the man who had stolen my heart.

Because what if the answer was yes?

TWENTY-SEVEN

Caleb

THE WIND HOWLED AROUND ME AS I CLIMBED THE ridge, each gust cutting through the trees like a warning. I pushed forward, my breaths coming heavy as the cold air bit at my skin, the snow crunching underfoot.

The peak loomed above, a reminder of everything I'd fought for and everything I was terrified of losing. My fists clenched at my sides, the tension in my muscles a reflection of the turmoil in my mind.

Eamon should have never let Willow come after me.

The moment I'd seen her through the trees, my heart had stopped.

The fact that she was so ready to confront danger with that defiant look in her eyes, a part of me had surged with pride. But that pride had been extinguished as quickly as it came, crushed by the reality of what she had just walked into. She was brave, no doubt about it, but I couldn't shake the image of her bleeding to death in my arms.

The thought of her caught in the crossfire of that

confrontation, or here on Shadowridge again with me, where she'd been hurt before, was more than I could bear.

Images from the fight replayed in my head like a bad dream. I'd seen the shifter's eyes light up at the sight of her, knowing he was going to use her as leverage. I felt sick thinking about what could have happened if I hadn't managed to reach her.

The burden of responsibility weighed heavily on my shoulders, and it felt like it was crushing me.

I reached the top edge of the peak, the point where man or wolf couldn't climb higher. Not without ropes and tools. I'd never had the urge to get the equipment. The fact my wolf could climb this high was enough of an achievement for me. I was standing at the precipice with the world spread out before me. Dawn was breaking and the sight before me was breathtaking. The trees below were dusted with snow, the mountains in the distance wrapped in mist.

But the image in my mind was of light green eyes filled with ire, soft blonde hair that felt like silk as it ran through my fingers, and skin as soft as the finest cotton—that was where I saw beauty. Her frown when she looked at me earlier was a stark reminder of my failures.

I heard the murmuring of many voices around me, reminding me of my failures. My pack was gone because I was too weak to be here to protect them. Willow's blood on my claws as I tore into her flesh, mistaking her for the enemy from my past. Listening to the harsh whispers in my ear as they reminded me of how many I had let down.

Why are you fighting?
There's nothing left for you here.
Let go. Let go of the anger.

Only in death will you find peace.

Aren't you tired, Caleb? Tired of fighting?

I was tired. So tired of living with this guilt. Looking down at the mountain from this high up, everything below me seemed so...small. So, pointless.

I stepped closer to the edge, the drop below beckoning. For a moment, I wondered what it would be like to listen to them, let go, and surrender to the darkness.

For all the pain and doubt to melt away and never bother me again.

Remembering the moments of peace I'd felt these last weeks as I lay in bed, Willow asleep curled up beside me, her faith and trust in me absolute.

Willow.

"Really?" I muttered under my breath, "After all this, you'd kill her too." I shook my head as if to physically dispel the thoughts. "You really are a pathetic coward."

But the demons that shadowed me weren't easily dismissed with a shake of my head.

They clawed at my insides, whispering the same lies I'd fought against for years: that I wasn't strong enough, that I would always let the ones I cared about down, that I didn't deserve love.

With every beat of my heart, the memories flooded back— of running alone through the trees, knowing my pack was dead. Reaching the first cabins, I saw the dead of my pack, fallen in their homes, their bodies of no concern to the ones who took their life.

I remembered losing control. I remembered the cold, hard rage that filled me as I went from cabin to cabin, looking into the faces of my pack in death. Climbing the stairs of my parents' home, I could feel the weight of it all, as the scars of my past pressed down on me. I saw the blood spilled. I saw the mattress still saturated with their blood, even three days later.

I'd skirted the edges of the clearing, seeing the many bonfires as the Cristone Pack celebrated their victory over a pack that was never given the chance to fight back. The doors to the communal hall were open, and I could hear them cheering their victories. I had seen the pile of bodies, human and wolf forms strewn carelessly in a heap, discarded with no respect. I had seen the hand lying at the bottom of the pile. A ring on a finger I would have recognized anywhere.

They put my parents at the bottom of the pile.

Like they were garbage.

I'd taken the ring, so careful not to touch my mother's hand, knowing that it would have broken me too soon. I'd felt the anger of the fallen rise up and surround me that day, and I had carried their thirst for vengeance into the hall where the killers *celebrated* their murderous victory. I'd used my Will and told them all to *hold*. There was no need to rush, I had taken my time, there was no one coming to save them, and I knew none of them would break my Will.

Because I was an alpha, and they were no match for me.

Each shifter had felt the cut of the blade as I drew it slowly along their throat. Each one's body had convulsed as I forced them to stay on their feet, and each one of them had died gasping for breath in a body whose lungs would never fill with air again.

I'd watched each one die before I turned to the next. It took hours.

I left their pack leader to the end, ensuring he had seen how

I brought *his* pack down. Then I made him watch as I killed his wife. His son. His daughter. He died in the same way. He'd wanted his bloodline on this mountain, and I gave him what he wanted. His blood would never leave this mountain because I left none of them alive. The blood of him and his children soaked the floor of the hall, seeping into the dirt to the concrete foundation of the hall, but no further. Cristone blood would not pass that foundation and seep into the heart of the mountain; it would not tarnish this land.

My land.

And when the final breath had left his body, when the blood had dried on his dead skin, only then had I turned to Jonah. His death took longer. It wasn't only his throat I slit that day or the days that followed. First, I had let him scream.

I had let him scream and beg and plead. I had let him do it all, knowing no one was coming for him. No one was left alive to hear him.

He had cried for his Goddess. She hadn't answered him.

The memories stirred the shadows more, making the whispers in my ear sound more like voices I once knew.

Closing my eyes, fighting the feeling of fatigue, I saw the image of another whose blood had spilled on this mountain. Willow bleeding out in my arms was an image I knew I would never forget. The pain and panic at the thought of losing her was still fresh. I had called to my Goddess for mercy, much like Jonah had done, and like Jonah, there was no answer to my call. In desperation, I'd called for the Goddess again, through an old magic.

Forbidden magic.

Blood magic.

Magic that tied the life of one to another. Willow was

already bound to me by the Will of the Goddess. Now, she was bound to me by the rite of blood.

An unbreakable bond.

An unforgivable act.

Hearing that shifter hint at knowing what I had done, I knew I would have to tell Willow. And I knew that in doing so, she would never trust me again.

I didn't blame her. I no longer trusted myself when it came to her. I would go to any lengths to protect her. To keep her safe.

It terrified me. I knew more than anyone what I was capable of. I was afraid that I'd slip back into that darkness that sought to claim me, and in doing so, I'd lose myself again, and there was no one left to pull me back.

The sharp gust of wind pulled me out of my thoughts. Turning from the ridge, I froze mid-step, my eyes wide with disbelief.

As if she were real, I saw my mother in front of me. Her eyes were filled with love and laughter. I shifted to my human form so sure I could reach out and touch her. Dark hair spilled over her shoulders. She wore a simple T-shirt and cotton shorts. Her feet were always bare. She loved to feel Shadowridge Peak beneath her toes.

Reaching forward, I felt nothing but empty air.

I couldn't breathe.

Had I jumped? Was this my welcome to the eternal hunt?

My eyes searched her face, memorizing every detail, seeing the laughter and love twist to sadness as she watched me. Why was she sad? She lifted her arm, her hand reaching for my face, and I would have given anything for one more feel of her hand against my cheek.

You have to let go.

Emotion choked me, my throat was too tight, and I couldn't breathe. Pain crashed through me, crushing me, surrounding me.

I couldn't breathe.

Panic gripped me.

My mother was saying what the shadows whispered to me.

I thought it was my demons, the darkness inside me wanting to be free. But...what if I was wrong?

Gasping for air, I closed my eyes, willing myself to calm down and when I opened them, my mother was gone.

Gulping huge gasps of air, I looked around wildly for her, shifting back into wolf form, I sniffed the air for her scent.

She was just here. I could find her. My paws skimmed across the surface of the peak as I ran recklessly along the ridge, not caring where my paws landed, intent only on finding my mother.

I lost my footing; the fall came too fast for my claws to dig in and halt my momentum as I tumbled down the rock face. Wildly, I jumped, twisting in the air, hoping for better footing upon landing so I could regain control of my descent. The impact jarred me, my paws digging into the ground as I skated along with the landslide racing down the mountain. A flat ledge to my left caught my eye, and I leaped, my body's momentum carrying me too close, but I managed to catch myself at the very last moment. As I stared into the blackness below, I saw her face.

It is enough, my son, let us go.

The despair and the grief almost overwhelmed me. "I can't."

Her frown was so familiar, so missed, that my tears ran freely. "I can't move past it. I can't."

Yes. You can.

My mother's image faded, replaced with one of Willow. Her steady gaze, the fierce determination in her eyes when she stood her ground against the chaos. I remembered how she had refused to back down when I tried to push her away, how she'd insisted that we were stronger together.

Stronger together.

The words echoed in my mind, a whisper of hope in the storm raging inside me.

I took a deep breath, blowing it out slowly, grounding myself in that thought. It was true, wasn't it? With her by my side, I could fight against anything. She had been there, ready to fight, unyielding and brave, reminding me of what I was fighting for.

Who I was fighting for.

The realization hit me like a bolt of lightning, electrifying and terrifying. I was stronger *with* her, not in spite of her.

She didn't make me weak; she made me *whole*.

I closed my eyes, remembering her standing next to me, her eyes sparkling with determination and compassion. I remembered the warmth of her hand in mine, the laughter we shared, and the way she lit up even the darkest corners of my soul.

"Willow," I breathed, the name leaving my lips like a prayer. The thought of losing her was what truly terrified me, not the threat of my own darkness. I needed to protect her, not just from the dangers that lurked in the shadows, but from my own insecurities and fears.

She was bound to me. As strong a tie that any mate bond held.

Because she was *mine*.

Suddenly, I felt a surge of resolve, a fire igniting within me. I wasn't going to let my past dictate my future. I was done letting it *define* me. I was done hiding, done running. I could face the darkness, *my* darkness but I wouldn't have to do it alone. With Willow, I had a chance—a chance to be the man I wanted to be.

The *alpha* I wanted to be.

I wanted to fight for the life we could build...together.

I turned away from the edge, my heart pounding with newfound clarity. I needed to return to her. I had to let her in, and show her that I was willing to fight, not just for myself but for *us*.

As I made my way down the slope, determination surged through me with every step. I wouldn't let my demons win. I would embrace the light she brought into my life and face whatever threats awaited us together.

"Together," I whispered, the word settling deep in my heart as I descended into the woods.

It felt right, like a promise I was finally ready to keep.

I MOVED QUICKLY DOWN THE MOUNTAIN, EACH STEP pulling me closer to Willow. The snow fell softly around me, the cold biting through my fur, but I barely noticed. Everything in me had been sharpened into a single purpose—getting to her. Each step was a reminder of what had happened, of the darkness that was as much a part of Shadowridge Peak as I was, and that each step led to the clear path back.

Her scent reached me first.

Instantly, I settled, like the calm after the storm. As I weaved through the trees, I saw her, wrapped in a blanket on the porch of Nell's cabin, her eyes scanning the shadows. She looked tired and vulnerable, waiting in the pale gray of morning. When her gaze found mine, she stilled but didn't move even as my wolf closed the distance. Willow waited, her look steady and strong as she watched me approach. When I stopped at the foot of the steps to the cabin, she got up and reached out her hand, burying her fingers in my fur.

"Caleb." Her voice was soft, and there was an edge of something else there—something I didn't want to admit that I'd put there. A tremor of worry. "Could have used you for my feet last night," she murmured, stroking her fingers through my fur. "I've got your sweatpants. Eamon found them in the trees."

After walking inside, she came back with them, and I could smell the warmth of the cabin. Shifting, I took them from her, pulling them on hurriedly, eager to talk to her. As I took the first step onto the porch, I hesitated.

No. Enough was enough.

I swallowed hard and climbed the steps with determination. This wasn't like last time, when I hadn't wanted to enter a cabin I knew. This time, my hesitation stemmed from the good memories this place held. Nell shouting at me, calling me a good-for-nothing son-of-an-alpha after catching me stealing her freshly baked apple pie. Or the time Eamon had knocked over her newly planted flowerpots because we were racing each other blindfolded.

Willow stopped me, her hand resting lightly on my bare chest. "You don't need to come in if it's too hard. I can come out."

Goddess, this woman. It was freezing, and even then, she was willing to do what made me comfortable.

I knew then I would give her whatever she wanted for the rest of her life.

Taking her fingers gently, I kissed the fingertips. "Willow." I took a breath, the words on my tongue almost foreign for how raw they felt. "I'm sorry. I was wrong in how I spoke to you. How I've acted." My head dipped down as I glanced at her abdomen. "For what I've done."

When I looked up, a frown was already forming as her eyes searched my face, like she was bracing herself for something she wasn't sure I'd say. Reaching up, I smoothed my thumb over her brow.

"I'm still fucking furious at you for coming up this mountain and putting yourself in danger," I told her, my hands clasping her cheeks as I tilted her head back to look at me. "And you will never *ever* do something so reckless again." I saw her about to fight back and softly kissed her brow. "But I should never have spoken to you and treated you as I did. Fear ruled my tongue. I'm sorry."

I noticed a bruise on her temple, and I softly brushed my thumb over it. "I hate to see you hurt, and I hate when I am the one that hurt you."

Her hand knocked mine away gently. "I fell coming up the mountain. Ask Eamon, I'm sure it will make him laugh for a long time," she grumbled. Willow reached up, her hand cupping my cheek. "You never hurt me, Caleb. I trust you."

And she did. I knew it in my soul.

"I thought keeping you safe meant keeping you out," I admitted, feeling the weight of my words. "But you were right; all I did was make it worse." Her eyebrows shot up in surprise. "I need you to know...I don't want to do this alone anymore. I don't want to keep you out." I couldn't remember the last time

I felt so nervous. "I'm not perfect—Luna knows that better than anyone—but I want to be, for you."

Willow was watching me, her expression unreadable as she held my gaze. For a moment, a flare of panic made me think she was about to turn away, that maybe I had ruined things beyond what I could ever hope to repair. But then she took a breath, letting it out slowly as she reached for me, her fingers resting lightly on my arm.

"You don't have to be perfect, Caleb. I'm not expecting that." Her voice was steady, and it held a note of something firm, unwavering. "But I need you to *trust* me. To be willing to let me in. And that means...you can't just disappear when it gets hard." Her eyes held mine, almost daring me to challenge her.

Even though I had realized it up on the peak, hearing her say it, I knew she was right. I nodded, running a hand over the back of my neck, feeling the weight of her words settle like stones in my chest. My hope that we would be okay was fading, but I had to keep going.

"I know," I managed, my voice low. "And I won't. Being with you...it scares me, I won't lie. Really fucking terrifies me, not because of what's out there—I will handle any threat that comes at you—but because of what I might find inside *myself*." I wanted to close the distance, but I knew I had to finish this. "But I realized one thing tonight. Maybe...maybe with you, I don't have to be afraid."

Willow took a step closer, her fingers finding mine, slipping between them until our hands were intertwined. That small gesture, one that should have felt simple but didn't, made me realize how much I'd been missing.

"Really?" she said softly, her gaze steady and warm. "I don't want you to be scared of being with me. I want you to tell me if you're struggling with anything. I'm human. You're a shifter. We're not supposed to work. But I think we do, and if you really want to, then I think we can make it work together. And if we get shit for it, well, we can face that together too. Every part of it." She looked up at me hopefully. "Deal?"

The corners of my mouth lifted into a real smile, one that felt like a release. "Deal." The word came out as solid as I felt.

Willow's gaze softened, her lips parted, and for a heartbeat, neither of us moved. Her hand tightened in mine, and without a word, she pulled me closer, her warmth drawing me in like always. I reached up, brushing a strand of hair away from her face, my thumb lingering against her cheek, feeling the softness of her skin, the warmth of her breath.

Slowly, I leaned down, our faces so close I could see every shade of green in her eyes and could feel the faint flutter of her heartbeat between us. The bond between us thrummed with a low energy that I could feel wrapping itself around my heart as our lips met.

The kiss started gentle, tentative, but it deepened as I felt her respond, her hand sliding to the back of my neck, pulling me closer. The air around us seemed to still, and I lost myself in the feeling of her mouth on mine, a heady mixture of tenderness and unspoken promise. It wasn't just a kiss—it was an anchor, a pledge, and a release all at once.

When we finally pulled back, my forehead rested against hers, our breaths mingling in the quiet. She smiled up at me, and I felt the last of the tension between us dissolve.

"There," she whispered, her hand still warm in mine. "Now, you're stuck with me."

I couldn't help but smile, a real one, and pull her close

again, wrapping my arm around her and holding her close. "Exactly where I want to be."

As we stood there, I felt a grounding peace settle over me. For the first time, I knew I'd found a place—not in a territory or a duty, but right here, with her—and the unwavering presence of her strength beside me was what I'd been missing for so long.

Home.

TWENTY-EIGHT

Caleb

"Do you want to come inside?" Willow asked, her fingers running over my arm. "There was some stuff left over from the last time I was here. I can make you breakfast?"

She opened the door to Nell's cabin, and I saw a throw from a sofa or somewhere, lying on the floor, poorly covering the crimson stain of Willow's blood. "You slept in here with that reminder of what I did to you on the ground?"

Willow turned to look. "It's just blood. I got more"—she squeezed my hand—"thanks to you."

"Why do you accept me so readily?" I asked her in wonder.

"Everyone has faults, Caleb. Some people's just make you sit up and take notice more than others."

"I gutted you like a hook knife through a fish's belly," I blurted, wincing at my crass wording. "How can you tell me that's a fault?"

"I told you before, I knew it wasn't your choice to do so." Her eyes were clouded as she looked up at me. "That night, I could almost hear the shadows whispering to you too. I know how strong the influence was over you." She smoothed a hand over her belly where her scars lay hidden from my sight. "You may have scarred me, but you also saved me."

"I think we both know you saved me."

Willow rolled her eyes and mock vomited. "If you're going to make it cheesy, you can leave," she said with a light laugh.

"Okay." I stepped back. "We need to get you out of Nell's place. You may be mature enough to be okay with it, but I can't sit and eat breakfast with your blood staining the floor." Looking over my shoulder, I scanned the cabins. "Eamon in one of them?"

"No, he took care of those bodies and then said he would be warmer as his wolf." She peered past me. "I haven't seen him this morning."

My conscience nudged me. "I need to go speak to him," I told her. "See if he's been in another cabin, found one you can move to."

"Okay." Willow headed to the stove and the beat-up old kettle of Nell's. "I'm making a pot of tea. Don't be long you need to sleep."

"Keep the door closed, you need to be warm," I reminded her.

The early morning light filtered through the trees as I made my way to find Eamon. I didn't know where he was, but I suspected, and as I made my way to the edge of the clearing, I saw Eamon sitting, staring at the community hall.

He didn't look up as I approached, probably knowing I'd seek him out when I was ready. I hadn't been ready, not until now. Willow's calm presence this morning and her unflinching strength had eased something in me.

Enough to face my past—and Eamon.

He didn't glance at me as I sat down beside him, ignoring

the wet snow seeping through my pants. Looking over at him, I saw the tension in his jaw, the way his gaze sharpened as he waited for me to speak. I had known I was an alpha from as young as I'd been able to understand what an alpha was. Eamon had been marked to be my beta for as long as I could remember. He'd been beside me every step of the way. Right up to the morning I had left our post and raced back to a pack I was too late to defend.

We'd both suffered, and those losses bound us tighter than I had credited. Grief had created gaps in our relationship that I wasn't sure we could bridge.

"It looks gloomy as fuck," he drawled, his tone light, but his gaze remained fixed on the hall. "Was it always so fucking depressing looking?"

I snorted out a laugh. "Yeah, it was."

"Huh." We sat in silence for a few moments. "So, you finally decided there's something worth living for?" I saw his signature smirk as he spoke.

"Guess you could say that." I leaned back, my hands protesting at the sharp sting of snow, and he turned to face me, and I met his gaze head-on. "You followed me?" I didn't need his nod to know he had. "You've been keeping close watch over the years, haven't you?"

His smirk faltered, and for a brief second, something raw flickered across his face. "Somebody had to." He paused, gaze steady but edged with challenge. "I wasn't about to let you disappear from here. Not again."

Sitting up, I nodded, his words settling heavier than I'd like to admit. "You've never been one to pull punches."

"You've never needed me to hold your hand," he shot back, his eyes narrowing. "I don't think you deserve her," he told me bluntly. "But that woman loves you too much to be dissuaded. Goddess knows I tried."

"I appreciate you failing," I quipped.

He snorted, his eyes back on the hall. "Asshole."

"Why did you keep tabs on me for ten years?"

Eamon gave a half shrug. "Truthfully? Habit?" He stood suddenly, brushing the snow off his pants. "As time went on, I thought you'd find your way back. But you kept drifting farther." He stood back as I got to my feet. "And then, as the years passed, I guess I accepted you died that day too."

The truth in his words made me flinch, and I took a breath, letting the weight of them settle. "After I was done killing Jonah, and knowing what I had done to them all...it was easier to push everyone away than to face it. Face anyone."

Eamon's expression softened, just a hint. "Loss does that to a man. But we all lost something that day. You weren't the only one grieving. Or left with the scars that a loss of that magnitude does to you."

"I know." I met his gaze, the memory of everything we'd been through flashing between us. Eamon hadn't just been a beta; he'd been one of my closest friends, my brother in arms. And in my grief, I'd shut him out, just like I'd shut out everyone else.

He exhaled, finally letting his arms drop to his sides. "And now?"

"Now..." I hesitated, then took a step closer. "Now, I've found something worth holding on to again. And I'm done hiding." My chest felt tight, but I pushed on. "I shouldn't have exacted the justice to them that I did. I should have waited for you. For the others. I should have let you all grieve. I took your revenge from you, from them, and I owe you an apology."

He nodded, sucking his teeth. "And Jonah?"

A rueful laugh left me. "I should have listened to you when you told me he was a backstabbing bastard."

"Cunt." Eamon didn't flinch. "I told you he was a backstabbing cunt. I told you when we were sixteen, I reminded you when we were eighteen, and I told you the night you found him balls deep in Kelly after you asked her to the Luna Ball. Friends don't do that to friends. I hope whatever you did to him was drawn out and painful."

"It was," I confirmed, my mind racing. "I forgot all about Kelly," I mused.

"She's in a pack in northern Canada. Got three kids and a husband that strays too far from home if you're interested."

"I'm not," I said with a tight smile. "Her family was never settled here. It was better when they left."

"So...what's the point of this? You purging your soul or some shit?" Eamon folded his arms across his chest. He jerked his head towards the cabins in the trees. "She's human."

I mirrored his pose. "You have a problem with that?" I knew some shifters would. I would deal with them just like I would any other hater. Swiftly and painfully.

"No." He snorted. "Not when I see you together. There's more than just attraction. Have you seen what she draws?" When I nodded, he turned serious. "She's Luna-touched," he said, his voice low. "Right? Has to be."

"I did something," I blurted. Seeing his eyebrows shoot to his hairline, I hurried on before he could speak. "I hurt her, gouged out her insides when I was deep in the darkness." Eamon was glaring at me as I spoke. "I used blood magic to bring her back."

His jaw dropped. "Blood... Are you fucking *insane*?" he

hissed, stepping closer. "That old mumbo jumbo your gran used to spout?" He was seething with rage.

When I nodded, his punch landed me flat on my ass in the snow.

"You reckless, selfish bastard!" He stood over me, his fists clenched at his sides. "She could have died? Have you not got enough blood on your hands?"

"Fuck you," I growled, pushing myself to my feet. "She *was* dying!"

"So you bound her to you with blood magic?" he asked me incredulously. "Did you even know if it was going to work?"

"We're already bound by Luna!" I defended myself, but I think Eamon knew I was riddled with guilt.

"Goddess, Caleb, she isn't your mate. She can *never* be your mate!" he growled at me.

"Then tell me why I can feel her inside me? Tell me why I know what she's thinking, feeling. I can *feel* her through the bond."

"Or you can feel what you want to feel because you are a fucked-up, crazy dick."

I was going to argue. Instead, I sighed. "Or I'm a fucked-up, crazy dick." I rubbed the back of my neck. "Or...Luna found my mate?"

"A human mate?" He gave me a flat look. "Insanity."

"You just reminded me I'm crazy..."

Eamon's lips twitched. "Does she know?"

"Not all of it."

His look was one of exasperation. "You are in so much shit." He turned away from me, his attention back on the hall. "Here was me thinking you'd turned a corner."

"I have." I came and stood beside him, and we stayed like

that, both staring at the hall as I thought about all of the things that had led me here. "I'm having a crazy thought," I said, breaking the silence quietly.

"That you need to tell her what you've done? I agree," he snapped. When he saw that wasn't what I meant, his head tilted to the side. "Do I need to run for cover?" he asked me with a slight touch of familiar lightness.

"No." Turning towards him, I waited until he looked at me. "Let's burn it."

Eamon's eyes widened. "The community hall?" He looked between me and it. "Your father's father's something-or-other father built this."

"My great-great-grandfather, you mean?" I asked him dryly. "So? Let's burn it."

"Why?"

"I want to purge my packlands of the death here," I told him honestly. "This..." I shook my head. "I thought it was a memorial to the dead." Licking my lips, I chose my words carefully. "It is, but it's not a memorial to *our* dead." I considered the imposing structure. "It's always been gloomy. Now, looking at it reminds me of what I did, and I don't need a cabin to remind me of that. I carry that with me, I always will." I looked back at Eamon. "You in?"

He considered me for a long moment, and then a wide grin spread across his face. "Hell yeah."

Willow found us a few hours later, sitting in the middle of the clearing, the snow melted from the burning blaze that lit the afternoon sky.

"Oh my God, what have you done?" she exclaimed, eyes wide.

"We're saying goodbye to the past," I told her, pulling her

into my side and planting a kiss on the top of her head. "You're cold," I murmured. "We'll move closer to keep you warm."

"Won't you get into trouble?"

Eamon laughed, taking a pull from a bottle of whiskey he found in a cabin. "He's the alpha, this is his packland, and no one can stop him."

She looked up at me, and I nodded. "This is still my territory. If I want to burn it all to the ground, I can." Eamon handed me the bottle, and I took a drink. I held it out to Willow, who looked between me, the bottle, and Eamon.

"Are you both drunk?"

"Nah."

"Maybe."

Eamon rolled his eyes at my *maybe*. "Never could hold your booze," he muttered.

"I'm making you both food," Willow scolded us. "Burning buildings is not how we move on with our grief." When we both just looked at each other and swapped the bottle between us, she stormed off, muttering about men being idiots.

"I like her." Eamon didn't look at me as he spoke. "She's got spunk for someone so skinny."

"I love her," I told him smugly, laughing when he snatched the bottle from my hand. I watched the flames climb higher into the sky.

"Now, if you can keep that woman of yours from knocking sense into you before I do, maybe we'll all finally find some peace."

His tone was flippant, but I heard the seriousness underneath. I felt it too. It had been ten years since we last felt at peace.

The crackling wood drew my attention back to the hall. It

felt good seeing it burn. It felt right. I could feel the chains of the past burning from me, no longer tying me down.

A flare of fire whooshed up and Eamon and I both jumped back. "Maybe we should have made sure it was contained," Eamon murmured.

I shook my head. "No, this is a cleansing fire. Luna is watching over it."

"No more whiskey for you," he said under his breath, but I still saw him lift his eyes to the sky and dip his head.

"Eamon?"

"Mm-hmm?"

Emotion once more had me in its clutches. "Will you help me clear out the cabins?" I reached blindly for the bottle. "I haven't been... I can't go inside them. Not again. Not alone."

His hand clasped my shoulder. "I'm here." His hand dropped away. "We'll do it together."

"Thank you." With a deep inhale, my nose filled with the smell of burning wood. "Today, we cleanse the packlands."

"And tomorrow?"

"We rebuild." Looking over at him, I raised an eyebrow. "You with me? Or do you want to go? Your choice, I won't force you."

"Force me? Try asking me," he said, taking a drink and realizing we'd finished the bottle. He stepped back and threw it into the flames.

"Will you stay?" I asked, unsure of his answer.

"Willow's right, you *are* an idiot." He walked past me, turning away from the hall and heading to the cabins. "You never needed to ask, Alpha. I've been here all along. You're just finally ready to see it."

I stood there for a moment, my heart too full to move. The

flames danced in front of me, as they burned the tomb of my sins away. I felt a tug on the bond, knowing it was Willow and she was still irked at our behavior. It made me smile. She wasn't really pissed. I could feel her sense of relief that I was okay too.

Then I felt another tug. Fainter. Slighter. I hadn't felt that kind of pull in a long time.

Pack.

Eamon disappeared into the tree line, but I knew exactly where he was. Tears filled my eyes as my knees went weak, and emotion threatened to overwhelm me. "Holy shit," I breathed out, dashing tears away before they had a chance to fall. "Luna... thank you for this gift," I told her solemnly.

"You better not be standing still back there," Eamon shouted through the trees. "I'm not doing all the work alone!"

"I'm coming!" I yelled back, sending another prayer of thanks to the sky as I hurried to catch up to him.

"What are we doing?" Willow's voice sounded from across the way.

"Cleansing the cabins," Eamon shouted back.

"I can help!" She sounded closer. "I heated up some stew I found in the freezer. Should I bring it?"

"Obviously!" Eamon called back. "I'm starving."

My smile turned to a grin as I jogged across the clearing towards something I never thought I'd get.

A second chance.

TWENTY-NINE

Willow

In the quiet aftermath, the air felt sharper, fresher—like the storm had finally passed. I looked over at Caleb, standing there beside me, tired but unbowed, his strength radiating in the stillness of the forest around us. We'd spent almost two weeks emptying the cabins, laughing at the stories he and Eamon had of the ones who had lived here, and feeling the weight of their passing.

The final confrontation was behind us, yet the path forward was somehow clearer than it had ever been.

I caught him watching me, and he gave me a small smile. It was that same smile that had always stirred something in me, had always pulled me in, even when I'd tried to keep my distance.

"I guess that's the last of them," he said, his voice both relieved and steady, and it anchored me in a way I hadn't realized I'd needed.

I took a breath, stepping closer, the weight of all that we'd been through settling in a way that felt whole, complete. "It is," I replied softly.

Caleb looked at the last cabin as it burned, tugging me into his arms. We'd cleared out some cabins, others we'd burned. "It's because of you, both of you; I couldn't have done this alone."

Slipping my hand into his, I squeezed his fingers. "You don't have to be alone anymore, Caleb. You have us..." I looked around for Eamon, but he had wandered off a few minutes ago. "Does it feel good to have this done?"

Caleb nodded, his eyes bright with emotion. He looked around, taking in the changes. When we first started, I hadn't been privy to the reason certain ones were saved, but as the day went on, I learned that when there were too many memories associated with the former occupants, the cabin was burned.

The cabins were replaceable, the owners were not.

"I could sleep for a week," I told him, relishing the warmth of his arms around me.

"Your ME has been very well-behaved," Caleb noted, pulling away and looking down at me. "You sure you're okay?"

"Yeah, I feel good." I beamed up at him. "I can show you if you like?"

His eyes gleamed with wicked intent, but Eamon's very loud, deliberate approach had me hiding my smile as Caleb glared towards his friend.

"You can bang each other all night long as soon as my cabin's built," Eamon growled, walking past with charred wood. "Until then, *Alpha*, why don't you do something useful, like help clear the dead wood?"

"He never used to be so...bossy," Caleb grumbled, kissing my lips and hurrying after Eamon.

We'd done so much work that I wondered why I wasn't lying passed out in the snow. But apart from a few days where

I'd been sluggish and needed to rest, I was fine. I might actually be able to say I'd been healthy...well, maybe that was a push, but I'd definitely been able to do more than I thought possible. But I'd also had time to consider what would happen when I wasn't able to do anything. Shifters didn't get sick; what would happen if I needed a doctor? Would Doc be on call? He was hours away. It was a thought I hadn't been able to push to the side.

The morning sun slipped through the gaps in the trees, casting a gentle warmth over the cabins that still stood. It had been days of hard work, and while Caleb, Eamon, and I had fallen into a routine of clearing the cabins, each day was a mix of clearing and quiet conversation, finding our way back to the peace we were all so clearly craving.

I was also craving some fresh food.

One of us needed to leave Shadowridge Peak and get us something other than rabbit. And I knew I needed to go home and see my friends and decide what to do next. Caleb and I had been so honest with each other since he opened up to me, it felt wrong to keep these thoughts to myself.

Caleb was chopping wood when I found him, his steady movements a comforting sight. I looked around for Eamon, but he was out of my line of sight. I took a breath and called to Caleb, watching as he paused, turning to look at me with a raised eyebrow.

"Hey," I started, a little uncertain but determined. "I wanted to talk to you about something."

He set the axe down, giving me his full attention. "What's on your mind?"

I took a breath, choosing my words carefully. "I was thinking about going back home for a little while. Just to check in, see Lily and the others, and...clear my head."

His jaw tightened slightly, his gaze unreadable. But after a second, he nodded. "Makes sense. I know it's been a lot, all of this. You don't have to explain."

"No, I want to explain," I said, my voice quiet but firm as I stepped closer. "This isn't me running away. I just need some time to...figure out how everything fits together. There's a lot to work through, and it's not about needing space from you or this place—it's about needing clarity."

He looked down, exhaling slowly as his hand gripped the handle of the axe. "You're wondering if this life fits, aren't you?" he asked, the words careful, almost resigned. "If you and I even belong together in this world I've dragged you into."

I closed the distance between us, my hand resting on his arm. "That's just it," I said, gently squeezing his arm. "You didn't drag me into anything, Caleb. I chose to be here. But... there's a lot about myself I still need to figure out. I need to know for sure that this is what I want, not just because of everything we've been through, but because I'm certain it's right."

"I need to tell you something."

Warily, I stepped back. I recognized that look in his eyes too well. "What have you done?" I asked in trepidation.

"Take a walk with me?"

"Or you can tell me what you did?" I suggested.

"Let's walk. I have something to show you." He started to move away. Looking back over his shoulder, he gestured for me to follow. "Come on, it isn't far."

We walked in silence, questions burning on my tongue and as quickly dying out when I opened my mouth to ask them. Was I scared of what he was going to say?

The trees grew thicker, denser, and more than once, Caleb had to lift me over a fallen log, and if I hadn't known better, I would have been sure this was the place where my body would be buried.

All sinister thoughts were swept aside when we broke through the trees and the most beautiful waterfall tumbled into a small pond. The sound had been in my ears for a while, but I hadn't put it together.

"Oh my God, it's real," I whispered as I looked around the scene I had painted a long time ago. It looked different in the snow, but it was still breathtaking. I saw the two flat rocks that I had painted but left the wolf out of the scene. "It's beautiful."

Turning, I looked up at Caleb and saw he was watching me closely. "This was my mother's favorite place," he told me simply. His gaze swept the scenery once, a glimmer of pain in his eyes as he stepped back in his memories. "She would like that you are here."

"It's gorgeous. Thank you for showing me."

Caleb nodded once, his gaze averted, and then he turned his head to look at me. "The night you almost died"—he cleared his throat—"I gave you my blood."

"I know." I stepped closer. "You saved me." I reached for him, but he stepped back.

"My grandmother was an old one," he told me gruffly. "Not a shaman, though Luna may have welcomed her, my grandmother was..." He struggled for the words. "Eccentric?" he offered. "Some may say odd, some may say delusional."

"She sounds interesting."

"She was." He nodded and it seemed to help him come to terms with what he had to say.

"She used to tell me high tales of nonsense when I was young. Father would scold her for filling my head with gibberish. Mother would scold her for scaring me."

The thought of Caleb scared of fairy tales made me smile.

"She would tell me stories of times before, when we were more animal than shifter. There was a time when we preferred to stay in wolf form. Rogues that we worry about today, the worries they had about me..." He hesitated. "They are founded on our knowledge. Our history."

"I don't understand."

Caleb didn't meet my eyes. "In times before, we weren't pack. It was more one wolf for themselves, rather than one wolf looking after a pack. Luna allowed us to run free and wild. Wildness causes its own problems." His gaze shifted to my belly where my scars were hidden. "You've seen what wildness can do."

"But you're not wild," I reminded him gently.

"No," he agreed. "But I could be. I have been." Caleb licked his lips. "I accept now that the darkness of the beast will always be within me and, that to move on, to *live*, I need to accept that."

"That's good..." Anxiety was dancing all over my body, and I felt nauseous as I waited nervously for the bomb to drop. I knew one was coming, I just didn't know why.

"You've saved me, Willow." His lips curled into a soft smile. "I owe you my life."

Shaking my head in denial, I moved closer to him. "No, you saved me, remember?"

"My grandmother told me tales of shifters who lusted after human women, who wanted to keep them *with* them. Shifters live longer, did you know that?"

Did I? "Um...I know you don't age the same as I do." My thoughts were racing. "And the shaman is *really* old, so when I think about it, then yes, I guess I did."

Caleb nodded. "The shifters of old wanted to keep their human women with them for as long as possible. Not always for a good reason and not always successful." His frown deepened and his voice grew harder. "Dangerous to do so. Exposure of our kind is the most guarded secret. But men aren't always wise." Caleb's hard gaze kept mine transfixed. "Blood magic is a dangerous thing. An unholy thing."

"Blood magic?"

"Tying a life to yours by blood is not the Will of the Goddess." He swallowed. "It's unpredictable. A life for a life, a life bound to a life...it's not the Will of Luna."

I was confused, my head was spinning with this weird conversation. "Okay?"

Caleb saw I was struggling. "You were dying." The sound of the words was like a hammer in the silence. "I killed you, Willow. You would have died." He swallowed hard. "I did the only thing I knew to save you."

"I know, you gave me your blood."

"I gave you more than blood," he murmured. "Ask me now and I wouldn't remember the spell..."

Spell?

"Ask me now, and I wouldn't be able to perform the rite."

"What rite?"

"But with you in my arms, dying, bleeding all over me... *Losing* you? I couldn't do it. I *wouldn't* do it."

Apprehension made me step back. "Caleb? What did you do?"

He looked at me, really looked at me, I felt him in my soul. I felt the bond strumming between us. Tying us together. *Binding* us.

"My life for yours, Willow. My blood for your blood."

"What?" It was no more than a whisper. It sounded as loud as a scream.

"I bound you to me through blood magic. My blood healed you. Strengthened you."

"Your life for mine?" I mumbled. "But you're not dead. I don't understand."

"No. I could've been," he admitted. Caleb's eyes shifted up to the sky. "She is not finished with me yet," he murmured. Looking back at me, he shook his head. "The way you think you feel about me...it could be because of the blood magic."

"No." The answer was so sudden, so clear, he looked as surprised as I did. "The way I feel about you is the way *I* feel about you. Nothing else."

"You should take the time when you are away to think about it."

That was it? It was that simple?

"That's it? You tell me you performed some creepy blood spell on me, that your ancestors used to *bind* women to them, and then tell me to think about it?"

Caleb let out a breath. "I don't know what else to tell you," he said honestly. "I did what I did to keep you alive. I will *always* keep you alive."

"You made a choice for me." I sounded as bitter as I felt. "You had no right."

"I know." He bowed his head. "It won't help me any by admitting this, but I'd do it again."

I knew I was gaping at him. "You know it's wrong?"

"I will *always* choose you, Willow."

"And if I don't choose you?" My voice sounded harsh, the thumping of my heart against my ribcage sounding loud.

"Then it's your choice."

Moving away from him, I turned my back as I struggled to think about what he had told me. "Why has it taken you so long to tell me?" I looked back at him. "The others know?"

"They do." He stood still against the backdrop of white. "I waited to tell you..." He sighed heavily. "Because I knew I could lose you when you knew what I had done."

"Nothing I feel is real?"

He looked pained at the question. "I can't answer that," he spoke slowly. "I know for me, it's all real, but...you have to decide."

He moved closer, until he was in front of me, and his hand came to rest over mine, his fingers warm and steady. "I think you're right. You need to go, figure it out, away from me, and see how you feel now you know it all, Willow," he said, his tone softer now. "I won't stand in your way. I only want you here if you want to be here."

"You're impossible, this...this isn't normal." Looking up at him, I felt like crying. "That you kept this from me... You should have told me sooner."

"I don't want to lose you."

I felt the first tear slip over. "What if you already have?"

"Is that how you feel?"

"I don't *know*, Caleb!" I shouted in the quiet of my surroundings. "You just blindsided me, and I *don't* know how I feel about *anything*!"

"Then take as long as you need."

"And if I go and decide I don't want to be with you?"

He looked at me, sadness in his eyes. "Then it's your choice. I will understand."

The confusion I felt ebbed even as relief settled in. "I hope so." I hesitated, adding, "I don't think I am handling this well,"

I confessed. "I was so sure of *us*, of this bond... I just..." I needed to pull myself together. "I just want to make sure I'm sure before I make any big decisions."

"Can I touch you?"

It was such an odd request. He'd never asked permission before, and he'd never needed to. I gave a sharp nod of my head.

He pulled me into his arms, and I melted into his warmth, feeling his hand cradling the back of my neck. I could sense the protective hold he had over me, a hold that felt more like home than anything I'd known. "Take all the time you need," he murmured, his voice low and close to my ear. "When you're ready, if this is where you want to be...I'll be waiting."

I nodded, swallowing the lump forming in my throat. I wasn't sure what to think, what to feel. This was such a mess.

He pulled back slightly, his gaze searching mine. "And if you realize that being here isn't right for you, Willow..." The words lingered between us, raw and real. "Then you never need to come back."

"You'd accept that?" I asked. "You'd accept me wanting nothing to do with you?"

Caleb grunted as if in pain. "It would hurt like hell," he admitted. "But that was the last thing I held from you, no more secrets. If you choose to never see me again, then I will accept your decision."

"My choice." My eyes narrowed as I watched him. "You'll accept it?"

"Of course."

Wrapping my arms around myself, I took in the beauty of the pond and the waterfall. "You know, before this, I wasn't leaving because I was unsure of *us*, Caleb. I was leaving because

I want to make sure we're building something real, something lasting and that I *can* live here. Safely."

He watched me carefully.

"And then you tell me that, and now I'm questioning *everything*."

"I know."

Turning, I looked at him. "And you told me anyway."

"I don't want to hide anymore."

God, this man.

"Will you be okay without me? You and Eamon?"

"We'll survive," he said with a faint smile, though his gaze held a hint of longing. "And when you're ready, or wherever you decide you belong, I want that choice to be yours."

I took a breath, nodding. "It will." My chest felt too tight. "Just...don't kill Eamon, okay?"

He chuckled softly, his eyes softening. "I'll try my best."

THIRTY

Willow

THE BUS RATTLED ALONG THE FAMILIAR HIGHWAY, and I settled into my seat, watching the landscape outside morph from rugged countryside to the edges of towns and back to countryside before I was finally on the edge of Whispering Pines.

I hadn't realized how much I would miss this place—the way the trees hugged the road, the winding streets I knew like the back of my hand. It felt comforting and strange all at once.

I pulled out my phone, hesitating for a moment before typing a message to Lily. But before I could get very far, it buzzed in my hand with an incoming call. Lily's name lit up the screen.

"Willow!" Her voice burst through as soon as I answered, bubbling with excitement. "Are you almost here? I'm about to explode with questions!"

I couldn't help but laugh, the sound feeling bright and free-ing. "I'm on the bus, almost there," I said, glancing out the window at the quaint houses starting to line the road. "But save your questions for when I'm not on speaker with every other passenger."

"Fine, fine!" she said, but I could hear the eagerness laced in her tone. "But seriously, I was so worried! You leave with that guy, I don't hear from you, and it's like you vanished, and then you call saying you're coming back, and sounding...different. What's going on?"

I took a deep breath, my heart fluttering. "There's a lot to explain," I said, carefully choosing my words. "And I will do that when I am *off* the bus."

"Ugh, *fine*." I could practically hear the eye roll as she hung up.

Grinning, I enjoyed a few more moments of peace on the bus before I got overrun with questions from my best friend. I knew Lily was still at work, so I walked home, with a light backpack that had hardly anything in it, and because of that, I took my time. Savored the feel of the town as I walked at a leisurely pace.

The air wasn't as fresh here. It was still good, but I already missed the clean, crisp air of Shadowridge Peak. There was a thin covering of snow, but nothing like on the mountain.

My mind was still struggling to accept everything he had told me. Blood magic. Bound together, not through the Will of his Goddess but a creepy old spell I expected to read about in horror books. The shaman had told me when I was on Blackridge Peak, he had said that Caleb's blood would have bound us, but I didn't think he meant *actually* bind us, where I had no sense of...what? *Self*?

I'd tried to puzzle it all out on the bus journey, but some things had no easy answer.

I could go back. My pulse raced when I thought about it,

and then I worried about being able to return. Eamon and I had gone a different way when we were racing to catch Caleb. It wasn't as steep as the way Caleb approached the climb. Plus, Eamon had a route that actually liked vehicles.

You couldn't drive very far, but I would take *some* help before no help any day of the week. When I asked Eamon why Caleb took me the hard way, he had a one-word answer: masochist.

And here I was, already worrying about the return when I hadn't even decided if I was ever going back. Was it even my decision to go back if I *did* go back? Or was it the bond?

I mean...ugh. It was too much.

I forced myself to think of other things. I had already called and spoken to Lorna. The shop was doing great, and she was loving working there. It was such a relief not to worry about work, and maybe the fact I was taking more care of myself was helping my ME. I'd only had a few spells, and they were merely blips on the radar of my health; I hadn't lost days, and I didn't feel as exhausted.

Arriving home, I unlocked the door, and once inside, I took a moment to savor the quiet. The last time I had been here, I recognized it as empty. Lifeless. Now...it still looked empty and lifeless, but *I* wasn't. Not anymore.

Or was I?

Tipping my head back, I looked at the ceiling, wishing I could see beyond it. "*Is* it real, this bond?" I asked. "Would you answer a human, Luna?"

I took the silence to be my answer.

I'd barely had a bathroom break and started to unpack when my front door banged off the wall as it opened.

"Willow!"

"I'm here!" I yelled back, leaving my room and seeing her in the living room. I braced myself as she flung her arms around me.

"I missed you so much!"

Squeezing her, I smiled widely. "I missed you too," I told Lily as I stepped back. "You look amazing," I complimented her. Her brown bob was sleek and shiny as always, but her dark skin was glowing and her eyes were shining with excitement, and while I knew she would be happy to see me...I also suspected my bestie had a man in her life.

"You met a guy?" I guessed.

"I did!" She laughed loudly. "I was at a wedding and he's amazing, but we can talk about me all day tomorrow. *Tonight*, I want to hear all about *you*." Her eyes narrowed as she looked me over. "Are you okay?"

"Lily, I'm fine. Really. I think I've finally figured out a few things about myself." Or thought I had.

"Does this have anything to do with Caleb?" she asked cautiously, sinking down onto my sofa as she watched me warily, and I could feel the weight of that question hanging in the air.

I hesitated, the mention of him stirring something deep within me. "Yeah, it does. And...everything, really. Life outside of here. It's been different but good. It's hard to explain. I just need a little time to process it."

"You've got time," she said quietly. "Right?"

I had about two weeks. Caleb hadn't mentioned it, but Eamon had. Apparently, Shadowridge Peak wasn't hospitable for climbers in winter. Was it ever hospitable to climb?

"Yeah." I nodded, trying not to think of the ever present question in my head. "I've got time."

I told her about my most recent adventure, while not actually telling her anything. However, I was able to talk about the regeneration of the cabins and Caleb's work at an exclusive work site. I didn't mention shifters, attacks, burning of shrines to dead people...I kept it all light and fluffy.

"Willow, are you happy?" she asked, her voice suddenly soft and serious. "Because you don't look happy."

I was going to cry. "I thought I was, and then I found something out, something that made me question everything."

"Tell me?"

How do you explain blood magic?

"Have you ever been so caught up in the moment, you thought it was perfect, and you're ignorant of everything, and then the bubble bursts and the outside world comes in, and you start to question everything?"

"I think so?" She thought about it. "My first boyfriend was a bad boy." She saw my look and grinned. "I know, no surprise. He was a *bad*, bad boy though. Dad hated him. It made me only want him more. He did crazy shit. Dangerous. I thought it was sexy. And then one night he took it too far, people got hurt. It's not so sexy when the police come and ask you where you were the night of a robbery."

"Oh shit."

Lily sniffed. "So yeah, when I woke up out of my lust-filled haze, I saw he wasn't fun, he wasn't sexy, he was just a thug." She gave me a thin smile. "Is that what you mean?"

No. Never. Maybe?

"Kind of. I thought I was happy. Until I learned something about Caleb, about something he did, and now I don't know what to think."

"Did he hurt someone?"

Depends who you asked...

"No. Not really." I shook my head. "Not like that."

"Did he refuse to help someone?"

"Caleb? Never."

Lily bit her lip as she watched me. "Cheat?"

"No." I saw her about to speak. "He did lie though."

She frowned. "Who told you he lied?"

"He did."

We held each other's stare. "Is it forgivable?" She leaned forward and patted my hand.

Her question struck me like a bolt of lightning, and I took a moment to gather my thoughts. "I don't know yet," I replied, the truth of it filling me with relief and a sense of revelation. "But it's complicated. There's so much I still need to figure out."

Lily let out a thoughtful hum. "When you get to that point, I'm here to listen. But only you can know the answer." Lily moved in her chair. "Doc was looking for you. He's worried. It's been a long time since he saw you, he said." She flicked imaginary hair from her pant leg. "There a story there?" she asked not so innocently.

Hearing Doc's name made my heart twist. I felt a pang of guilt for how easily I had let my old life fade into the background. "No, nothing like that. He's a good friend. I haven't needed to see him," I said. "But I'll give him a call. I've missed his unique style of doctoring."

There was a pause as Lily watched me. "Well, make sure you give him enough of your time. It's not everyone who has such a committed doctor."

That was true, but I didn't think it mattered to Doc.

"I'm planning to stay a little longer this time," I assured her, though a tug in my heart reminded me of the mountains and Caleb. "I just...need to see everyone and catch up."

"Good. You better be ready for all the hugs," she said, and I couldn't help but smile.

I looked out the window, letting the familiar view blur as my mind drifted to Caleb. His quiet strength, his protectiveness, the way he'd become this steady presence in my life, even if he'd tried to keep his distance at first. I hadn't planned on feeling this way, on finding someone who felt like...home.

I hadn't planned on questioning the truth of how I felt. Were the feelings mine, or were they the result of shifter magic?

I thought about the fact I'd been drawing him, pulled to him, long before I almost died. The attraction had always been there. The need to help had always been inside me.

The need to be with him...it was *mine* and mine alone.

Blood magic never took me up the mountain that night. My love for Caleb had.

"You're not staying," Lily spoke softly, carefully watching me. "You're leaving."

"I just got here," I tried to joke with her.

"I can see it in your eyes," she told me. "You're not even fully here right now, and I can tell you already want to leave."

Hearing her say it made me realize it was true, but I hesitated, wondering if I should tell her, but I didn't want to lie. "I thought I finally knew where I was supposed to be, Lil. Where I needed to be, and it's... I don't think it's here anymore."

I heard her intake of breath, and for a second, I worried she'd judge me or tell me I was rushing into something reckless. "Oh, wow," she said, voice soft. "So it really is serious, huh? With him? You've already forgiven him?"

A small, tentative smile curved my lips. "I'm not sure about that." I took a deep breath. "But it's more than that, Lily. When I'm with him...I feel this strength I didn't know I had. It's not just about Caleb—it's about who I'm becoming because of him. Because of everything I've learned."

Lily was silent for a long moment. "I guess I always knew you'd find something, someone who'd pull you out of here. You were never really settled here. I think I just didn't expect you to find it this way. Or for it to be, you know, a mountain-hiker silent type who'd sweep you off your feet."

We both laughed, and I felt a little tension leave me. But as the laughter faded, I felt the ache again, the bond I knew tugging at me.

"Lily...I don't know how long I'll be here," I admitted, letting the honesty settle between us. "I need to say goodbye to some things here, to make sure everyone's okay with it—including you. But I think..." I wrestled with the words. The truth. "I think my heart's already made up."

She sighed, but there was warmth in it, even pride. "I can tell. I've never seen you so sure of something in all the years I've known you. Even with the doubts you just shared." She made a sad face. "But, Willow, if this is what makes you happy, if *he* makes you happy, then that's all I care about. Just promise you won't disappear completely, okay? And that Caleb Foster knows how lucky he is."

I felt a pang of emotion at her words, a little sadness mixed with a lot of gratitude. "I promise, Lily. You'll always be a part of me. But thank you...thank you for listening. And understanding."

"Always," she replied, her voice strong, and I could see the worry giving way to excitement.

I laughed, my heart feeling lighter. "Can I ask about *your* guy now?"

As she launched into how she met her new man, I knew I was being honest with myself and that—deep down—I had always known this was just a visit.

A farewell to a life I'd loved and a place I'd always belong to but one I was ready to leave behind.

Because in my heart of hearts, I was already up that mountain where Caleb was waiting for me.

THIRTY-ONE

Willow

THE GOOD THING ABOUT BEING A HUMAN AND knowing about shifters and part shifters was that you could call in a favor.

Ned and Doc drove to Whispering Pines, I sat through *numerous* tests by Doc, and then after many tears, hugging, and more tears, I packed my stuff into Ned's truck and left Whispering Pines, but not my friends, behind me. My friends would not be able to visit me on the Peak, but I wasn't stuck to it. I knew I would be able to come and go as I pleased.

I just needed to learn how to drive first. And hike. My ME wouldn't thank me, but I was no longer going to be held back by it either.

We were in my house, and I was making sure it was locked up and ready to be left over the winter. Ned asked me why I didn't just sell it, but I wanted a place for Caleb and me to come to when we left Shadowridge Peak.

"How much is the animosity about shifters and humans?" I asked Ned suddenly, causing him to jerk in surprise at the question.

"Some get a bit heated about it, most accept it as one of those things."

"How many are *some*?"

He looked at me and sighed. "You have to understand, you're taking an *alpha* out of circulation. Some won't like it, and they'll be loud about it."

"Do you? Like it?"

His eyebrows shot into his hairline. "You seriously asking me that?"

I felt myself blush with shame. "No. Sorry. It messes with my head."

"Doesn't mean you need to be stupid."

"Sorry."

Ned grunted and started to lift a box of my art supplies. "You paint anything worth sharing?" he asked, trying to lighten the mood.

Taking my sketch pad out of my tote, I flipped to the latest sketch. It was of a wooden cabin, two stories, nice wraparound porch. "You like?"

Ned grunted as he nodded. "I do."

"But?"

"He's an alpha, not an architect."

I grinned as I swiped at him for his nerve, but he just sauntered out the door, whistling casually.

Doc came in, his head turning to follow Ned. When he looked at me, his eyebrow rose curiously. "Why's he so happy?"

"Because he's cheeky," I told him with a grin.

"I already hate this drive, and you two are like siblings. It's going to be hell, I'm just telling you now."

"We'll behave." I hesitated. "Do you think I'm crazy?"

I'd told them both what Caleb had told me and hadn't been

in the least surprised when they both knew. Just pissed off they kept it to themselves.

But neither of them felt that the bond influenced my decision, and that had made me feel better. Ned had reminded me, as I had reminded myself, that I was already in love with Caleb before the night on the mountain. The blood magic hadn't changed that. It just strengthened our connection.

He watched me. "No. I think this was always your choice."

"I do too."

"You have concerns?" he asked me carefully.

"Fresh food?" I admitted. "Hospitals?" I sighed. "So much to figure out..." I looked away as I muttered one of my more pressing concerns. "Babies?"

"Crops will be planted," he told me easily. "It's shifters' way of life. There are fields and greenhouses you haven't seen, lower down Shadowridge Peak. Now that he's back, it's likely some of his old pack will come home. Or new ones will want to join. Shifters work their land. You'll have food soon. Until then, I suggest you bulk buy lots of frozen vegetables."

"I didn't know that. About crops and things."

"You have a lot to learn." He wasn't being condescending, he was being himself. And then he looked unsure. "I will speak with Caleb. I've already addressed it with Cannon. If your alpha allows, I will split my time between both packs." He gave me a rueful smile. "You're actually someone who needs a doctor, your children too."

Hope surged within me. "Really? You'd do that?"

"Willow, you're human, with an illness that needs managing. If you are agreeable to it, I would very much like to continue being your physician."

"He'll say yes." I was grinning like an idiot. "I'll make him say yes."

"Let's wait and ask him," he told me wryly. He grunted when I launched myself at him, giving him a hug.

"Thank you, Doc. I mean it, this makes me so happy."

He hugged me back. "Yeah, well, remember this when you know I'm only a door or two away to make sure you're looking after yourself."

"And then you ruined it," I mocked playfully.

"I'm ready," Ned announced. "Let's go."

And just as quick as that, I was once more locking up my house not knowing when I'd be back.

We broke the journey up by staying at a motel for one night. Doc really was a worrier. I think I loved that about him, and I felt safe for whatever the future held in store for me, or anyone else who came along.

The next day, when I tried to tell Ned the way Eamon had taken me, he gave me a look, and we ended up parking where he believed was best. He started hauling some of the important stuff out of the truck, and then the three of us began the hike.

Shadowridge Peak was not a nice mountain to climb. In fact, it's a bit of a dick. But at the top of it was the love of my life, so I was climbing this godforsaken mountain if it killed me. And I'd keep on climbing it, until I could travel up it as easily as the others.

Eamon met us halfway down, wary of my two friends, but he looked pleased to see me. He took stuff off Ned, and Ned went back down to collect more.

Eamon ended up putting all that he carried down and carried me the rest of the way. Doc was adamant he didn't need help. Eamon looked at me, took me to the edge of the packlands, and then promptly went back to rescue Doc....possibly from his own stubbornness.

Caleb was hammering nails into a frame that looked like the side of a house. He tensed as I approached, lifting his head, and his expression shifted from wary to something softer.

"You're back," he said, a touch of wonder in his voice, as though he'd still doubted I would return. "I felt it, but I wasn't sure I believed it."

I was smiling and nodding, and I knew I was getting too emotional. "I am. For good, if you'll have me." Stepping closer, I reached for his hand. "I needed to be sure of where I belonged."

Caleb's eyes searched mine, and there was a depth of emotion there that he'd always kept locked away, a tenderness he was no longer holding back when he looked at me. "You belong with me, Willow. Do you see that now? I don't want you anywhere else." He paused, the faintest hesitation lingering in his gaze. "I love you."

It was such a simple statement, but it held the weight of everything he'd fought through, the sacrifices, and the fears he'd harbored about letting someone in. That he was being so honest and open was a testament to how far he'd come.

Warmth and a sense of purpose filled me, knowing I was exactly where I was meant to be. I was going to start blubbering like a fool, so I did what I did best. I changed the subject.

"What are you building?" I asked him, trying to think of something to say rather than just drowning in his chocolate-colored eyes.

Caleb blushed and I knew my mouth dropped at the sight. "I was thinking we'd need a home..." He didn't look at me as he spoke.

"We do," I agreed, my fingers itching to take out my sketch pad and show him our house. "How many bedrooms?"

"I was planning two?"

"Three. We might have visitors," I told him and then added confidently, "or children." His eyes widened, his gaze dropping to my stomach. "No, not yet," I corrected him. "But...Doc says it's inevitable. Apparently, shifter sperm is stubborn"—I gave him a look—"like their alpha."

He beamed back at me, not in the slightest fazed at the accusation. "I'm afraid that's probably true."

I nodded, apprehension filling me. "You would be okay, with us...having children? Not shifter children?"

"My children will be *our* children."

I felt my eyes fill with tears. "Some shifters will hate me. For being human."

"Some shifters need to go fuck themselves."

"Is it that easy? To ignore them?"

Caleb grunted. "It will be for me. You?"

He smiled when I nodded. "Haters gonna hate," I murmured.

A noise made him look behind me. "Who's with you?"

"Ned and Doc."

"Let's go meet them," he said, holding his hand out to me, which I took eagerly, and we began to walk. "Actually, wait." Caleb pulled me to a stop. "I need this first."

He kissed me softly, his mouth moving over mine gently, his tongue tasting my bottom lip. "Welcome home," he said before kissing me again.

A silent promise pulsed between us, unspoken yet powerful, as though all the broken pieces had fallen into place without either of us needing to say a word.

We walked through the trees side by side to the clearing where Eamon and Ned were already bonding. Doc was panting and looking a little wild-eyed.

"Eamon's scared the crap out of Doc," Caleb said with a groan. "I bet he took him too close to the ridge."

I hid my smile as he mumbled; it was so refreshing to see him like this. Unburdened.

"They always told me that your beta's supposed to be the diplomatic one," he grumbled at me, walking faster to meet them, with me hurrying beside him.

As the sun began to dip, our breaths were visible in the cool mountain air. Each step felt like it carried a weight—not a burden—but the kind of weight that reminded me of how far we'd come.

As Caleb greeted the others and scolded Eamon, who quite clearly didn't care what his alpha said to him, I wrapped my arms around my midriff as I watched them all. Watched Caleb be the leader I always knew he could be as he explained his vision for the future to Ned, who was looking at the decimated hall with interest and was already asking him questions about rebuilding.

I was so proud of Caleb.

He must have felt my stare on him, because he turned his head towards me as Ned asked questions, and I saw the smile that Caleb had for me. Holding out his hand, he wordlessly beckoned me to his side, and I joined them.

Our journey to get here hadn't erased the challenges, hadn't wiped away the memories that haunted both of us. It hadn't given us the illusion that everything would be simple or easy. But it had shown me, shown both of us, that we could face those things together.

We were stronger together.

Caleb stood beside me, tall and steady, with a calmness in his gaze that I hadn't seen there before. There was no more wrestling with himself, no more push-and-pull between who he was and who he wanted to be. I could feel that certainty from him, a strength I knew wasn't just his own but something we'd built together.

Eamon pulled Ned and Doc away from us as he explained the rebuilding, and I wasn't surprised at all when I heard Ned and Doc volunteer to help.

Without a word, Caleb slipped an arm around my shoulders, pulling me close. I leaned into him, fitting perfectly against his side, and let out a sigh of contentment. For the first time in so long, I felt fully home.

"This is our life," he said softly, speaking low, his voice carrying a warmth that matched the setting sun. He looked down at me, his eyes steady and sure. "Whatever it brings, we'll face it together."

I turned to meet his gaze, a smile tugging at my lips as I felt that promise settle, firm and deep. "Together," I whispered back. "I love you so much."

His breath caught, and he stared at me wide-eyed for a moment, before the most beautiful smile spread across his face, highlighting the dimple in his left cheek.

"Well now you're never getting off this mountain," he teased as he leaned down to kiss me.

That kiss—it was everything. It held our fears, our hopes, all the brokenness and beauty that had brought us here. It sealed the future we both wanted, the life we'd carved out that didn't force us to choose one world over another. A life that held the wild freedom of his world and the quiet intimacy of mine.

A life that was, finally, ours.

As the last rays of sunlight disappeared, wrapping us in the cool twilight, the world felt utterly peaceful, a silence filled with possibility. We stood together, watching the stars begin to pierce the darkening sky, knowing that whatever came next, we would face it as one.

Epilogue

THE EARLY MORNING SUN SPILLED ACROSS THE PEAKS, painting the rugged landscape in hues of green and gold. From where I stood, I could see the whole valley below—our valley. The wind carried the faint scent of pine and earth, the familiar grounding scent of home.

I could hear some of the pack already up and about. Doc had been right. When word spread that Caleb had presented himself to the Pack Council as alpha of Shadowridge Peak, the few who remained from before had returned.

Together they rebuilt their community, and not one of them had rejected me. They embraced me as the wife of their alpha.

Behind me, the cabin Caleb had built with his own hands stood tall, a blend of practicality and beauty, much like him. I smiled, feeling his presence before he even spoke.

"Lost in thought?" His voice was warm, and I turned to see him leaning against the doorframe, his hair tousled and his eyes soft in the light of dawn.

"Just thinking about how far we've come," I said.

He stepped closer, his hand slipping around my waist. "Do you regret it?"

"Not for a second," I said, my voice steady.

The bond between us wasn't what it had been in the beginning, fraught with uncertainty and the weight of expectations. It had deepened, matured, becoming something more profound than either of us had imagined. We weren't mates—our connection didn't feel like destiny's decree. It felt like a choice, one we made every day, to stand by each other, to fight for each other, to love each other.

And through that choice, something unexpected had grown.

"It's strange," I said, my fingers brushing against the skin of his arm. "Your blood...it's like it's woven into me, even now. I can feel you in ways I never could before."

Caleb nodded, his gaze distant for a moment. "It's not just the bond," he said. "It's you. The way you've healed, the way you've...adapted. Maybe Doc was right. Maybe the pack isn't just a thing for shifters."

I remembered all those months ago, feeling better and healthier when Lorna had looked after me after my break-in. I had been better then too.

Since coming here, since being part of his world, my body had become stronger. At first, I thought it was just the environment—the clean air, the physical demands of life on the peak. But now, I wasn't so sure. "Oh my God, I'm a pack animal?" I said with laughter in my voice.

"*My* pack animal," Caleb growled, nuzzling my neck.

"It's like your blood and being part of this pack has rewired something in me," I told him thoughtfully. I wasn't cured of ME—I knew I never would be—but I was definitely healthier.

"I don't have a wolf, but I feel the strength of yours. And yours..." I hesitated, looking up at him. "It feels stronger too."

His smile was small but full of meaning. "You keep me grounded, Willow. That's not just a feeling—that's a fact. The darkness inside me isn't clawing for control anymore. You gave me back the balance."

We stood in silence for a moment, letting the truth of those words settle between us.

"We've got something no one else has," he said finally, his voice low. "A bond we've built, not one that was handed to us." His hand caressed my swollen stomach. "And if that means our children might have the chance to live in both worlds...then maybe that's why we found each other."

Children. The thought filled me with a quiet awe, not fear. Because Caleb wasn't just talking about carrying on a legacy— he was talking about building a future together.

"Do you think they'll be shifters?" I asked, curious, glancing down at my pregnant belly. "The shaman seems convinced they will be...but...I don't see how."

"Maybe they will," he said, his lips quirking into a smile. "Maybe not. But whatever they are, they'll be ours. And that's enough for me."

I rested my head against his chest, listening to the steady beat of his heart. This was our life—a bridge between two worlds, one we'd fought for, one we'd chosen. Our pack didn't shun humans; we didn't welcome them recklessly, but for those who wanted to raise their part-shifter children here, they were welcome.

The sound of footsteps pulled us from our moment. Eamon appeared at the edge of the clearing, his expression torn between exasperation and amusement. "You two planning to stand there all day, or are you coming down to breakfast with the rest of us? There's a list of shit that needs doing this morning," he reminded Caleb.

Caleb snorted, his arm tightening around me. "You've got it handled, Beta."

Eamon grumbled something unintelligible under his breath, but the fondness in his eyes was unmistakable as he turned and headed back down the trail.

Caleb pressed a kiss to my temple, lingering. "Ready?"

I smiled, looking out at the horizon. The future was still uncertain, still filled with challenges we couldn't yet see. But we'd face them together.

"Always," I said, and we started down the mountain, side by side.

As the cabin faded into the distance, I glanced back one last time, feeling a deep sense of peace. Our story wasn't over—it was only just beginning.

Acknowledgments

To Mr. M, thank you for your unwavering support, endless patience, and love. I couldn't have done this without you.

To every reader who has picked up this book, thank you for stepping into this world, for turning the pages, and for sharing this journey with me.

I hope you've enjoyed reading this series as much as I've loved writing it—it's been an incredible adventure, and I'm so grateful you've been a part of it.

Until next time.

About the Author

Eve L. Mitchell is a USA Today Bestselling author of Contemporary Romance, New Adult Romance, and Paranormal Romance. If you love morally gray alpha-holes, there's a good chance Eve has your next book boyfriend ready and waiting to be claimed.

A lifelong book lover, Eve still considers herself a reader first. She believes there's nothing quite like the thrill of getting a new book, whether on her e-reader or in her hands. Sharing that sense of excitement with fellow readers is one of her greatest joys. Writing under a pen name helps preserve her "Secret Agent" status (because who doesn't love a little mystery?).

Eve lives in the North East of Scotland with her three coffee machines (one is never enough) and her significant other, Mr. M. When she's not writing, she can usually be found watching NFL football (or complaining that it's not football season yet), playing music loudly, or having long conversations with the voices in her head—conversations that often turn into her next story.

The Watcher Series is a paranormal romance trilogy that will take you on a journey where you will get lost in a world that will hold you in its depths. With a blend of steam, humour and angst, be ready to buckle up for the ride.

With demons, devils and one sassy, clueless witch, what more could you ask for? Join Star as she gets a crash course in what not to do when you get involved with the Watchers.

An enemies-to-lovers story that has all the emotions packed between the pages as the heroine deals with love, betrayal, loss and so much more.

This series is a trilogy and must be read in order. If you love cliffhangers, this series is for you. If you hate cliffhangers, don't worry, the next book's already written.

The series includes **A Glow of Stars & Dust**, **A Flame of Stars & Midnight** and **A Blaze of Stars & Dawn**.

GET THE SERIES
WWW.EVELMITCHELL.COM

The Denver Series is a three-book mafia romance shared world series. Each book is a standalone, featuring cameos from the other books. Although it is recommended that the books be read in order, it is not necessary to do so.

The series covers tropes of opposites attract, enemies-to-lovers, and forbidden romance (stepcousins).

The Denver Series is a steamy contemporary romance series that dabbles in the mafia romance genre, with book one hinting at it and the other two exploring the darker side of this much-loved genre.

A complete three-book series where sassy heroines meet and fall for their dark alphahole heroes.

The series includes **Her Greatest Mistake, Beautifully Broken** and **Keeping Harmony**.

THE RUTHLESS DEVILS SERIES

A college sports romance series following twin brothers and their cousin. Three football stars who have it all: looks, money, talent and the world at their feet. No one messes with the Devils. Each book deals with a different Devil and their love interest who will either make them or break them.

The series covers tropes of enemies-to-lovers, second-chance romance and forced proximity.

This is interconnected three-book series with an underlying story arc that carries through from book one to book three, and therefore the series must be read in order. The series deals with some elements that sensitive readers may find triggering.

This series includes **Ruthless Heart, Ruthless Desire** and **Ruthless Charm**.

TORN & BROKEN DUET

The Torn & Broken duet is a duet with a twist. You can read either book as a standalone. *Torn by Grace* was written first and one of the female side characters in that book is the main character in *Broken by Faith*, however, you don't need to know what happened in *Torn by Grace* to enjoy *Broken by Faith*. There is a little bit of crossover, but no spoilers.

Torn by Grace is a second chance, enemies-to-lovers, brothers-best-friend romance.
Broken by Faith is an enemies-to-lovers, forced proximity, fake relationship romance.
The series includes **Torn by Grace and Broken by Faith.**